THE

Wild
Princess

THE

Wild Princess

MARY HART PERRY

WILLIAM MORROW
An Imprint of HarperCollins*Publishers*

THE WILD PRINCESS. Copyright © 2012 by Kathryn Kimball Johnson. All rights reserved. Printed in the United States of America. No part of this book may be used or
reproduced in any manner whatsoever without written permission except in the case
of brief quotations embodied in critical articles and reviews. For information address
HarperCollins Publishers, 10 East 53rd Street, New York, NY 10022.

HarperCollins books may be purchased for educational, business, or sales promo-
tional use. For information please write: Special Markets Department, HarperCollins
Publishers, 10 East 53rd Street, New York, NY 10022.

FIRST EDITION

Designed by Diahann Sturge

Library of Congress Cataloging-in-Publication Data has been applied for.

ISBN 978-0-06-212346-6

12 13 14 15 16   OV/RRD   10 9 8 7 6 5 4 3 2 1

This book is dedicated to Mallory—not a royal princess but, in her own way, no less amazing than Louise. Her talents and dedication to all living things will make a joyful difference in the world. I can't imagine a more wonderful granddaughter.

This is a novel. That means it is fiction, fantasy, make-believe—not a true historical account. Did any of the people in this story live and any of these events happen? Yes, quite a few. But the joy of fiction comes from its ability to borrow facts and details from the real world and then encourage the author to embellish them and produce a unique entertainment. The wise reader will consider this story nearly entirely the result of the author's imagination.

Queen Victoria and Prince Albert's Children and Grandchildren

Victoria (1819–1901) = Albert (1819–1861)

Princes/Princesses		Spouses
Victoria (Vicky) Princess Royal (1840–1901)	=	Frederick III (Fritz) (became German Emperor) (1831–1888)
Edward VII (Bertie) King of England (1841–1920)	=	Alexandra Princess of Denmark (1844–1925)
Alice (1843–1878)	=	Louis IV Grand Duke of Hesse-Darmstadt (1837–1892)

The Grandchildren

William II (became German emperor)
Charlotte
Henry
Sigismund
Victoria (became Queen of Greece)
Waldemar
Sophie
Margaret

Albert Victor
George V = Mary (King & Queen of England)
Louise
Victoria
Maud
John

Victoria
Elizabeth
Irene = Henry, Prince of Prussia
Ernst Louis, Grand Duke of Hesse
Frederick William
Alexandra = Nicholas II, Tsar of Russia
Mary Victoria

Princes/Princesses		Spouses
Alfred Duke of Edinburg (1844–1900)	=	Marie (1853–1920) (Grand Duchess of Russia)
Helena (Lenchen) (1846–1923)	=	Christian (1831–1917)
Louise (1848–1939)	=	John (Lorne) 9th Duke of Argyll (1845–1914)
Arthur (1850–1942)	=	Louise Margaret (Princess of Prussia) (1860–1917)
Leopold (1853–1884)	=	Helena (1861–1922)
Beatrice (1857–1944)	=	Henry (Liko) Prince of Battenberg (1858–1896)

The Grandchildren

Alfred
Marie (later, Queen of Romania)
Victoria Melita
Alexandra
Beatrice

Christian Victor
Albert
Helena Victoria
Marie Louise
Frederick Harald

None

Margaret
Arthur
Patricia

Alice
Charles Edward

Alexander
Victoria Eugenie (Ena) = Alfonso XIII
    (King and Queen of Spain)
Leopold
Maurice

Osborne House, Isle of Wight
Wednesday, 23 January 1901
My dearest Edward,

I write to you with a grieving heart. My emotions are so a-jumble at this moment I can barely stop my hand from trembling long enough to put pen to paper. As all of London wakes to the sad news, you too must by now be aware that Victoria, Queen by the Grace of God of the United Kingdom of Great Britain and Northern Ireland, Defender of the Faith, Empress of India—my mother—has passed from this life. Last night I stood at her bedside along with my surviving sisters and brothers, the many grand-children, and those most favored among her court. We bid our final good-byes, and she drifted away. Among us was the devoted Colonel the Lord Edward Pelham-Clinton, who delivers this letter and accompanying documents, by hand, into your possession.

The doctors say it was a cerebral hemorrhage, not un-common for a woman in her eighties, but I believe she was just tired and ready to rest after reigning these tumultuous sixty-three years, many of them without her beloved Prince Consort, Albert, my father, who died before you were born.

She was not a physically affectionate mother, demanded far more than she ever gave, often drove me to anger and tears, and very nearly destroyed my life . . . more than once. Yet I did, in my own way, love her.

The enclosed manuscript is my means for setting straight in my own mind the alarming events of several critical years in my life. But more than that, it will bring to you, although belatedly—and for that I apologize—the truth. Your mother, my dearest friend, wished to tell you of these matters long ago. Indeed, it was she who compiled most of the information herein, using her rare skills as an observer of human nature and, later in life, as a gifted investigative journalist. I have filled in the few facts she was unable to uncover on her own. For selfish reasons I begged her to keep our secrets a while longer . . . and a while longer. Then she too departed from this world for a better one, leaving no one to press me to reveal these most shameful deeds. Indeed, Edward dear, I would not even now strip bare the deceptions played out in my lifetime, had they not so intimately involved you.

Do these words shock you? If so, then you had best burn these pages and live the rest of your life in ignorance. But as I remember, you were a curious lad, and so I expect you will read on. However, before you go further, I must ask of you a solemn favor. What I am about to reveal is for your knowledge alone, that you might better understand both the gifts and the sins passed along to you. To share this account with others would cause scandal so damaging that our government would surely topple. Therefore, I implore you to choose—either destroy the enclosed manuscript this

*instant without reading it, or do the same after reading in
private.*

*Regardless of your decision, I pray you will ever think
of me as your devoted godmother and friend, and not hate
me for the things I have done to protect you or, on my own
behalf, simply to survive.*

Be assured of my love,
Princess Louise, Duchess of Argyll

One

Under siege, that's what we are, Louise thought as she observed the mayhem beyond the church's massive oak doors. Indeed the week-long crush of boisterous visitors had become truly dangerous.

"There must be thousands of them," she murmured, more to herself than to any of her bridesmaids clustered around her.

Her brother Bertie gently closed the door, shutting out the cheers of the crowd. "It's all right. The guardsmen have things well in hand."

Scores of well-wishers from London and the surrounding countryside had arrived on foot and horseback, along with souvenir vendors, draymen with cartloads of sightseers, and hawkers of ale, roasted potatoes, and meat pies. They clogged Berkshire's country roads, converging on Windsor, making virtual prisoners of the royal family and their guests within the great castle's walls.

Many travelers hadn't been content with a tourist's hasty view of Windsor in the days before the wedding. They'd set up crude campsites outside the walls, lit bonfires that blazed through the night. Toasts to the bride and groom turned into drunken revelry. Hundreds pressed against groaning castle gates, hoping for a chance glimpse of the royal couple. Crowd control, never before an issue at a royal wedding, became a necessity. A nervous Queen Victoria called up her Hussars and a fleet of local constables to reinforce the castle's guardsmen.

Louise stepped away from the chapel's doors, fingering the delicate Honiton lace of her gown. Strangely, she wasn't worried about being hurt by the mob of well-wishers. What concerned her was what her mother's subjects might expect of her.

To do her duty as a princess, she supposed, whatever that might mean to them. Or simply to "be a good girl and don't make trouble," as her mother had so often scolded her since her earliest years.

Standing at the very foot of the church's long nave, Louise tried to reassure herself that all the pomp and fuss over her marriage was of no consequence. It would pass with the end of this day. The mob would disperse. The groundsmen clear away the mountains of trash. The important thing was—she had agreed to wed the Marquess of Lorne as her mother wished. She was doing the responsible thing for her family. Surely, all would be well.

Louise rested her fingertips lightly on Bertie's arm. The Prince of Wales stood ready to escort her down the aisle. She desperately wished her father were still alive to give her away. On the other hand, Papa might have talked her mother into letting her wait a little longer to marry. But, of the six girls in their family, it was her turn. In the queen's mind, Louise at twenty-three was already teetering on the slippery verge of spinsterhood. An unwed, childless daughter knocking about the palace was a waste of good breeding stock.

Louise felt Bertie step forward, cued by the exultant chords of organ music swelling to the intricate harp obbligato strains of the "Wedding March." She matched his stride, moving slowly down the long rose petal–strewn quire toward her bridegroom.

Another trembling step closer to the altar, then another. Wedding night jitters? Was that the source of her edginess?

Definitely not. The panic swelling in her breast could have little to do with a bride's fragile insecurity regarding her wifely duties in bed. Louise felt anything but fragile and more than a little eager for her husband's touch. Nevertheless, she sensed that something about the day was disturbingly wrong. Sooner or later, she feared it would snap its head around and bite her.

She closed her eyes for a few seconds and drew three deep breaths while letting her feet keep their own pace with the music.

"Are you all right?" Her brother's voice.

She forced a smile for his benefit. "Yes, Bertie."

"He's a good man." The prince had trimmed his dark mustache and looked elegantly regal, dressed in the uniform of their mother's Hussars. He had initially stood against the marriage, believing his sister should hold out for a royal match. But now he seemed resigned and loath to spoil her day.

"I know. Of course he's good."

"You like him, don't you?" Not *love* him. They both knew love didn't enter into the equation for princesses. The daughters of British royals were bred to marry the heads of state, forge international alliances, produce the next generation to sit upon the thrones of Europe.

"I do like him."

"Then you'll be fine."

"Yes," she said firmly. "I will." Somehow.

Three of her five bridesmaids—all in white, bedecked with garlands of hothouse lilies, rosebuds, and camellias—led the way down the long aisle, leaving the two youngest girls in Louise's wake to control the heavy satin train behind her. The diamond coronet Lorne had given her as a wedding present held in place the lace veil she herself had designed.

She felt the swish of stiff petticoats against her limbs. The coolness of the air, captured within the church's magnificent soaring

Gothic arches, chilled her bare shoulders. Yards upon yards of precious handworked lace seemed to weigh her down, as though holding her back from the altar. An icy clutch of jewels at her throat felt suddenly too tight, making it hard to breathe.

Her nose tingled at the sweet waxy scent of thousands of burning candles mixed with perfume as her guests rose to view the procession. The pulse of the organ's bass notes vibrated in her clenched stomach. Ladies of the Court, splendid in silks and brocades and jewels, the gentlemen in dignified black or charcoal gray frock coats, turned heads her way in anticipation—a dizzy blur of smiling, staring faces as she passed them by.

But a few stood out in sharp relief against the dazzling splendor: her dear friend, Amanda Locock beside her handsome doctor-husband, their little boy wriggling in Amanda's arms. The always dour Prime Minister Gladstone. A grim-faced Napoleon III, badly reduced in health after his recent defeat by the Prussians. Her brothers and sisters: Affie, then Alice and Vicky with their noble spouses. A predictably bored-looking Arthur, always solemn Lenchen, and young, fidgety Leo. Bertie's lovely Danish wife, Alix, clasped a hand over each of their two little boys to keep them quiet.

Louise lifted her gaze to the raised box to her left where she knew her mother would be seated. Beatrice, youngest of Louise's eight siblings, sat close by the queen, gazing down wide-eyed at the ceremony. Victoria herself, a plump figure in black mourning muslin ten years after her husband's death, her grim costume relieved only by the rubies and blues of the Order of the Garter star clipped over her left breast, looked down on the wedding party as though a goddess from Mount Olympus.

They'd all come to witness Louise's union with the striking young man waiting for her at the chapel's altar. The Marquess of Lorne. John Douglas Sutherland Campbell. A stranger to her in many ways, yet soon to be her wedded mate. Beside him stood his kinsmen in striking Campbell-green kilts, sword scabbards strapped to hips, hats cocked forward.

Louise felt an almost equal urge to rush into her intended's arms . . . and to turn around and run back out through the chapel doors. Into the fresh spring air, breaking through the crowd to escape down Windsor's famous Long Walk and into the country-side. To freedom.

But was that even a possibility now?

All of the country had lapped up news of her betrothal as ea-gerly as a cat does cream. Hadn't the newspapers been chock full of personal details for months? The chaperoned carriage rides through Hyde Park. The elaborate French menu for the wedding feast. Everything—from the details of her gown to advertisements placed by a London perfume manufacturer announcing their newest fragrance, Love-Lorne—had been gossiped about in and outside of the court.

And then all of that fled her mind as Bertie deposited her before the archbishop and beside Lorne. Her husband-to-be stood breath-takingly handsome in his dark blue dress uniform of the Royal Ar-gyllshire Artillery with its bits of gold braid, burnished buttons, and shining black leather boots that shaped his long legs to above the knees. A silver-hilted sword hung from the wide black patent belt that encircled his narrow waist. His hair, a glorious pale blond mane brushed back from his face, long enough to feather over his collar, looked slightly risqué and tempted her fingertips.

He took her hand in his. At his touch, she finally settled inside herself.

During the ceremony Louise was aware of her bridegroom's eyes turning frequently to her. She did her best to meet his gaze, to bring a little smile to her lips and hope that some of it slipped into her eyes for him. Like her, he had blue eyes. But while hers were a soft shade, the mesmerizing sapphire brilliance of the young marquess's eyes never failed to startle people on meeting him for the first time. He was a Scot, one of her mother's northern subjects. When his father passed, he would become the Duke of Argyll. A minor title, but better than none at all in her mother's view. For Louise's part, titles were of no consequence. They marked a man as neither good nor bad, kind nor cruel, rich nor poor.

She had every reason to believe they'd get along well, even though they'd not once been left alone together. Still, their escorts had been discreet, allowing them to speak freely. Lorne had even shyly kissed her on the cheek, last night. In time, they might fall in love. She'd like that. And even if they didn't, he would give her the children she so longed for. Life was full of compromises.

The archbishop was speaking in that singsong voice of his that was at once soft yet somehow carried to the very back of the grandest church. Louise let the words wash over her, a warm and calming stream. She daydreamed of her honeymoon—Lorne making tender love to her, his soft hands opening her gown to touch the places on her body that most longed for his caresses. And she would discover ways to please him.

The images in her mind brought a rush of heat to her cheeks. She raised her eyelashes shyly to glance up at him in anticipation.

Their gazes met.

He grinned and winked. Did he know what she was thinking?

It was at that moment something odd caught her eye. A motion off to her left and above. Startled, she turned her head just far enough to take in her mother's box.

John Brown, once a lowly gillie in the queen's stables at Balmoral in Scotland, and now her personal attendant and self-appointed bodyguard, stood behind Victoria, physically blocking a man who seemed to be trying to force his way into the queen's box. A frisson of alarm shot through Louise.

"Steady," Lorne whispered in her ear, grasping her hand. "Brown's handling it."

The archbishop, too, seemed to have noticed the disturbance, but he droned on, the ultimate performer under pressure.

Louise glimpsed Victoria waving off Brown. The stranger bent down, as though to whisper something in the queen's ear. He wore rough riding clothes, a long, dung brown overcoat of a less than fashionable cut, in what appeared to be scuffed leather. He looked unshaven. As if he hadn't bothered to even run a comb through his spiky black hair. In one hand he held not a stovepipe top hat, which was the only acceptable headwear for a gentleman in London, but a strange wide-brimmed style of black felt hat she'd never seen on any head in all of England.

Louise turned back to face the bishop, fearful of missing the rest of her own wedding. The next time she glanced back, the stranger had gone.

Lorne squeezed her hand, as if to say, *All is well.*

Was it? She shivered but forced a smile in return.

Then all at once, the archbishop was giving them his blessing. A joyous "Hurrah!" rang out in the chapel. Her new husband kissed her sweetly on the lips, and every concern fled her mind at this excruciatingly joyful moment.

All she could think of was the night that lay before them—her first night as a married woman.

Two

Amanda Locock stood beside the dressing table in the bridal suite at Claremont House while Lady Caroline Barrington unpinned Louise's hair and brushed it into soft golden brown waves down her back. "I'm so sorry about bringing Eddie with me to your wedding dinner and concert," Amanda said.

The music that followed the lavish meal at Windsor had been one formal event too many for a restless four-year-old. Amanda walked him up and down the great echo-y hallway outside the grand salon until he'd fallen asleep on her shoulder. She'd been able to bring him back inside in time for her to hear the lovely Bach violin solo, played so beautifully by Herr Joachim.

"You know how unpredictable my husband is. He promised to watch Eddie while I stayed for the reception and concert, but one of his patients was in urgent need of him."

Louise waved off her concern, reached up and ruffled the little boy's hair. No longer a toddler, Eddie still loved to be propped on his mother's hip. He buried his face shyly against her breast now, looking pink-eyed and exhausted by the day's activities.

"You know I love to see Eddie any chance I get." Louise opened the drawer in her dressing table and pulled out a tin of saltwater taffies. "What you need, my darling, is a little more energy to get you through the rest of the day."

"More sugar?" Amanda rolled her eyes. "Henry has this notion that my indulging the child with sweets keeps him up late at night." But she laughed as he selected with great concentration a single candy from the tin. "Here, love, let me unwrap that for you. Then you go sit on your favorite chair over there and suck on it while I talk to your godmother."

"He's growing so fast," Louise said, her eyes misting with affection as she watched the child stride away from them. "Soon he'll be all grown up."

"I know. That's why I'm particularly happy with the news I have to tell you." Amanda bounced on her toes and felt she might burst like an iridescent soap bubble with happiness.

"News?"

"I'm with child." She giggled at Louise's shriek of joy. "Henry says the baby will be here in August." They had tried for a brother or sister for Eddie for years, but after miscarrying two babies she'd nearly given up hope. "I didn't say anything to you sooner because of the other times, you know." The thought of her lost babes nearly undid her.

Louise shot to her feet, tears in her eyes, nearly knocking over Lady Car in her haste to reach Amanda and clasp her in her arms. "Oh, my dear, I'm so happy for you. Maybe a little girl then?"

"We'll see. Why so weepy? Are they tears of happiness for me?"

"Of course."

Amanda knew better. "You and Lorne will have your own brood in no time. You'll be tripping over little ones."

Louise laughed and wiped away her teardrops. "I'd love that. Truly."

"Your Royal Highness," Lady Car interrupted with a meaningful glance toward the door.

Louise smiled. "Yes, of course." She turned back to Amanda. "Speaking of Lorne."

Amanda gasped. "What a ninny I am, standing here gossiping with you while your new husband is waiting to take you off to bed." She laughed, thrilled for her friend. No matter what Louise might think, Amanda was sure that marriage would agree with her friend. Children meant so very much to her, and Lorne seemed such a stable counterpart to Louise's sometimes impulsive nature. "Come, Eddie. Let's run along and let your Auntie Loosy be alone with her new husband." She cast Louise a knowing look and teased, "Don't need no pointers from an old married woman, do you now?"

Louise lifted her gaze to the ceiling but watched Lady Car out the door before she responded. "It's not as though it's the first time; we both know that."

Amanda smiled. "'deed I do." She had started toward the doorway when Louise reached out to clasp her arm and hold her back.

"What do I *tell* him?" Louise's face was tight with anxiety, her voice tremulous.

Before she answered, Amanda pushed her son a few steps in front of her and out the door. "You wait for me right there," she instructed him then ducked back inside the bedchamber. "The truth," she whispered. "What else?"

"I was wondering, maybe I could just say . . . *nothing*?"

"And you think the man won't realize you're not a virgin?" Amanda laughed. "That's wishful, girl." She winced. "Sorry I'm reverting to my old ways, Your Highness."

Louise cuffed her gently on the arm. "Stop that. We stand on no formalities, you and I." She sighed. "I had guessed, from things my mother said in recent days, that Lorne might already know. So, why bring it up? I mean, it's quite possible she's told him about my wild years."

"About Donovan, you mean?"

Louise shut her eyes and nodded. "I truly did love him, you know. To think he so suddenly took off. Not a word. . . ."

"Most of them do, dear."

"Well, I suppose I was naïve."

"Very."

"And I didn't know that—"

"Now isn't the time to blame yourself." Amanda touched Louise on the shoulder and gave her a comforting smile. "You were so very young. We both were. Anyway Donovan is in the past. I can't imagine Lorne will reject you when he finds out you've had someone before him. Someone who really didn't matter. Or at least . . . he doesn't now. Lorne's such a sensible, modern man."

Louise bit down on her bottom lip and gave her an anguished look. "I don't know what to think." She groaned. "But it would make sense that Mama would have told him I'd had . . . experience. Why else would she champion a marriage with someone who wasn't a royal? A man with such a minor title."

"I don't understand all the fuss." Shaking her head, Amanda peered out the door to check on Eddie. Lady Car was entertaining him, coaxing the little boy to march up and down the hallway like a Beefeater. "You make it sound as if it's never been done before, marrying a commoner."

Louise let out a bitter laugh. "Not for over three hundred years has a daughter of an English monarch married outside of the royal families of Europe."

Amanda winced. She hadn't realized that. "Then your mother must have discussed this with him, don't you think?"

Louise shook her head. "I just don't know." She looked down at her hands, clenched in front of her. "I do need to tell him. I know that, Amanda. It's only fair. And if he is upset . . . well, I must then deal with the consequences."

"I'm sure he'll come around. Men's egos, they're fragile things, tough as they pretend to be in front of their friends." Amanda kissed her on the cheek, pried Louise's locked hands apart, and gave them a squeeze for courage. "After you return from Scotland, come to the shop and tell me how it went. Better yet, write to me. Soon."

"I will," Louise promised.

Three

Louise watched the door slowly close, shutting her, alone, inside the Lavender Suite at Claremont House.

Hushed voices came to her from the hallway outside. Lady Car taking her leave for the night. Amanda passing by Lorne with little Eddie in hand, perhaps teasing a blushing bridegroom with a saucy remark about his wedding night.

Louise sat down on the edge of the bed, its embroidered coverlets already turned back to reveal an expanse of pure white linen. She held her breath, waiting for Lorne to step through the door.

Feeling light-headed with anticipation, she at last remembered to breathe. She straightened the delicate peach silk nightgown, trimmed with baby pearls and ecru lace, and pulled the hem down to demurely cover her ankles.

The door remained shut.

She rested folded hands in her lap. Her stomach clenched. Her head spun. She closed her eyes on a wave of nausea.

More than anything, Louise wanted to start her marriage by establishing a relationship of trust and mutual respect. If she said or did anything this very first night to make her young husband angry or turn him against her, they'd never develop the lovely intimacy her mother and father had shared.

She drew another breath and settled herself a few inches farther back on the mattress. Rearranged her gown to reveal, through the side slit, the curve of her calf and a slim ankle. Tugged the neckline down just a wee bit.

Never had showing a modest hint of décolletage hurt a woman's negotiations with a man. Louise stared at the door.

It did not open.

The voices had stopped; Lorne must be alone now. And he'd know she was ready. Wouldn't he?

Perhaps she should call out to him. Invite him to enter. He couldn't possibly be waiting for a formal invitation when it was his right to come in and take her, whether or not she was prepared physically or emotionally. But, she reminded herself, Lorne was a gentle soul. Always so thoughtful and concerned for others' feelings whenever she'd been around him.

Louise slid back all the way onto the bed, drew her legs up under her, turned and plumped up three lavender-scented pillows at the head of the bed, then lounged back against them in a seductive pose. Encouragement, that's what the poor man needed. Until this moment, she hadn't considered that he might be as nervous as she about their first night as a married couple. Though, of course, not for the same reason.

She had a confession to make. And by now it had wedged itself like a lump of stale bread in her throat.

Her head began to ache. She looked down at her hands, unclenched them and blotted her damp palms on the sheets.

What on earth was he *doing* out there?

She was just about to call out to her husband when a soft knock sounded on the door.

"Yes?" More of a croak than a word. She cleared her throat and tried again. "Yes, Lorne, please come in."

The door swung open slowly, and he stepped through.

She had been prepared to see him in his nightshirt. Or perhaps wrapped in a silk robe. Or even, if he were in an uncharacteristically aggressive mood, entirely naked. She was surprised—no, shocked!—to see he was fully dressed, just as she'd left him nearly two hours earlier, all but for the sword. He still wore the high-collared blue military jacket with braiding, medals, polished black boots and belt. He looked trim and vigorous and glorious, but not at all ready for bed.

Lorne took two steps into the room, his brilliant blue eyes roaming the spacious chamber, as if it were a foreign territory he'd been sent to conquer. He fixed first on the dressing table where Car had arranged her crystal atomizers, gold brush and comb, and velvet jewel case in which rested her wedding diamonds. Then his gaze swept the rest of the room. He seemed almost startled when he found her already on the bed.

Wrong, she thought in desperation, realizing her mistake in trying to play the seductress. He was evidently terribly shy. And now she'd made it all worse by her sultry posing. She tucked her bare ankles up under the bottom flounce of her gown. Poor boy. He'd been out in the other room, building up his courage, and here she was playing the vamp.

She patted the bed beside her. "I was just trying to relax," she said giving him an encouraging smile. "It's been such an exhausting day, hasn't it?"

He dipped his squared-off chin in acknowledgment, but his eyes didn't entirely meet hers.

She frowned. "Do you like the gown?" *What an asinine thing to say, Louise.* But it was all she could think of at the moment with her heart racing so.

At last, he gave her an overall scan, and blushed. "Very much. You've never looked lovelier, my dear."

My dear. That was progress.

She patted the bed again. "Come sit with me. Let's just talk." She drew a deep breath. "There's something I need to tell you,

Lorne." And suddenly the conversation she'd rehearsed a hundred times seemed tenfold more difficult. Nevertheless she steeled herself and held out her hand to him.

He straightened his long, lean form and strode quickly toward her, his eyes bright and wide, their celebrated blue more dazzling than the delicious cobalt hue she often chose for her palette when painting a landscape sky. As he came closer she could see the perspiration dampening his collar.

No matter. She'd get the hard part out of the way quickly. Reassure him that Donovan—*no, don't say his name!*—reassure him that she had been but a child, innocent, foolish, uneducated as to the ways of men when she'd let herself be led astray just once. She'd swear to him that this stranger from her past meant absolutely nothing to her and, indeed, she hadn't seen him in years. He'd disappeared from her life.

Well, at least that last part was true. Donovan Heath had well and good vanished, just as certainly as if God's hand had reached down from heaven and plucked him up to heaven. But, ah, how she'd adored that boy. What might have come of them if they'd stayed together? Both struggling young artists, though he was from a different social class entirely and never would have been accepted by Victoria.

She jumped, startled when the mattress dipped, bringing her back to her wedding night and Lorne. Louise shook her head, chasing away memories of the young man who had so charmed her when she was but eighteen years old.

She looked up at her husband as he crooked a knee to balance one hip on the edge of the mattress. He leaned toward her, kissed her ever so gently on the forehead, then took her hands in his. "You may well be the most beautiful woman in all of London," he murmured, his voice a touch hoarse with emotion. "I swear I've never seen lovelier."

"Lorne." She was moved nearly to tears by his sincerity. And this from a man who, if men could be called beautiful, truly was. His smooth almost boyish face was unravaged by the sun, despite his love of the outdoors. His eyes shone with the innocence of youth yet his mouth was full lipped and sensual. Suddenly she wanted more than anything to *really* kiss him, to feel his lips and hands on her body.

This can work. This has to work.

She'd wait to tell him she was no longer a virgin until after they had made love. He'd of course by then have discovered the truth for himself, but having already pleased him between the sheets, she might find it easier to explain and ask for his understanding. After all, new brides assumed their husbands had bedded other women before them. Although she thought the double standard ridiculous, society adhered to the old ways. A man might be forgiven his mistresses and affairs so long as he provided for his wife and children and treated them fairly.

She closed her eyes, hoping the gesture, faintly submissive, would further encourage him. She lifted her face to him. He squeezed her hands again. But no kiss came.

When Louise opened her eyes, tears were coursing down her young husband's face.

"Oh, Lorne! My darling, what is it?" She pulled her fingertips out from his suddenly cold hands and framed his stricken face with her palms. "Tell me, what have I done to—"

But he shook his head, murmuring, "No, no, nothing. Not you."

She assumed in that horror-stricken moment that he was weeping because someone—not Amanda, surely not her—had told him about her affair. But now it occurred to her that something else was wrong. Incredibly wrong.

"I-I have a confession to make, my dear." He took a deep, shuddering breath and seemed to hold it forever before letting it out.

Possibilities raced through her mind.

He's had affairs—not a shocker.

He's been with a prostitute and feels unclean for me. To confide such now was merely being considerate.

He's in love with another woman. Much more difficult to accept.

He's having second thoughts about our marriage and wishes to back out of it. But why? He benefitted hugely by their union. Simply by taking his wedding vows today, he'd stepped up from the expected inheritance of a minor Scottish duchy to becoming the consort of a royal princess, daughter of the Queen of England. That was an immense leap, socially and financially. Lorne would receive a royal stipend for life, an estate (or, at the very least, luxurious apartments in one of the family's castles), and additional prestigious titles. And he'd never need to lift a finger to support himself, his wife, and their children.

At last he seemed to catch his breath. She captured his eyes with her own, without words demanding of him an explanation.

"Dear Louise," he said, "I have used you. I have used you abysmally. I fear I will never be able to make it up to you."

She stared at him, her breath coming in hysterical gulps. She couldn't imagine where in God's name this was going. "Lorne, please. What is it? You're frightening me. If you mean that our social stations are so very diff—"

He flushed bright red. "Society and stations be damned! That has nothing to do with this." He seemed almost restored by his sudden anger. His voice gained strength. "You deserve a full accounting. Please, be patient. In the end, I hope you will forgive me for what I've done to—Actually, I don't know *what* I've done." He choked on a nervous laugh, looking close to tears. "Probably nothing short of mucking up your entire life."

She opened her arms and drew him to her, cradling his head against her breast as if he were a child, stroking the back of his sweat-damp neck. He let her hold him for a few moments before pulling away again to face her. This time he held her hands firmly in his, resting them on his thigh just above the top of his boot.

She had the strangest feeling that he'd intentionally pinned her in self-defense. As if he feared she might strike him if she were free to do so.

"Your mother," he began, looking directly into her eyes, "I believe she is very fond of Mr. Oscar Wilde?"

"Ye-e-s," she said. Although what the new playwright might have to do with their marriage she had no idea. "She believes Mr. Wilde is a gifted and promising writer. He's already had more than one success on the stage."

"He is"—Lorne's voice hitched, hesitated—"quite brilliant. And—"

"And?" she prompted.

"And he is a dear and close personal friend of mine."

So? Then it struck her—what he was getting at, and why the subject of the playwright had come up at all.

She closed her eyes and forced herself to suck down air to stop her head from spinning. But Lorne said nothing more, as if waiting for her to process the information he'd merely hinted at. He let her make the mental leap alone. A trapeze artist without a net.

"Mr. Wilde," she began again, "has been rumored to prefer the company of other men."

"So they say."

"Which, by law, is considered lewd and unnatural behavior, and is punishable by imprisonment."

"Exactly." Lorne watched her expression.

Her heart felt as if it were cracking down its middle. She was spiraling down into the dark space between its broken halves. "And you are an . . . an *intimate* friend of his?"

He blinked his beautiful china blue eyes and touched her cheek tenderly. "Yes, my dear. I am."

Oh Lord.

"Lorne, just to be clear, are you telling me . . . That is, do you also prefer the physical closeness of other men to the touch of a woman?" She'd never asked a more difficult question in her life.

He gave her his sweetest smile. "I do, my dear. I really do."

What was left of her heart exploded into a thousand jagged, opalescent shards . . . which fell at her feet. For a long moment, she felt sure the shock had killed her. She felt nothing.

"Then why—why this marriage?" she demanded, anger driving blood back into her ice-cold hands.

"But isn't it obvious?" He had the temerity to shrug his shoulders in casual surprise. "I admit I've been abominable, putting you in this position. But I was terrified, you see. Titled men of good families, men far more famous than Oscar are being packed off to prison for their so-called sins." His voice became clipped, indignant. He peered deeply into her eyes, as if through them he could reach her better than with words alone. "I believed it was only a matter of time before the law made the connection between us— Oscar and I—and others in our circle. Who knows how dedicated Scotland Yard will be in rounding us all up and shoving us into some dank cell like common criminals."

His weeping had stopped. For that she was thankful. And he was right; the danger was real for a man like him. "Oh, Lorne. What will we do?"

"Yes, well, *we* . . . that's the question isn't it?"

"Are you saying you wish to annul our marriage?" The prospect of the scandal left her feeling woozy.

"Heavens no!" He stared at her. "You still don't understand, do you?"

"I'm afraid not."

"I said that I've used you because I knowingly agreed to this marriage to protect myself. If I'm married to a woman of such obvious charms as Her Royal Highness, Princess Louise, how can anyone doubt my sexual inclination? I'm safe."

"I see." And now she really did understand. Resentment muted her compassion, though she tried not to show how confused and desperate she was beginning to feel. "But how are we to be . . . to be together, to have children, if you don't have relations with women?"

"That's the crux of the problem, as I see it." He nodded his head. White-blond waves fell over his forehead, shadowing the azure glow of his eyes. "Louise, I swear to you, I would never have agreed to marry you if I'd thought I couldn't find a way to give you children. I supposed I would be able to make love to you, now and again, for the purpose of procreation, you see. And perhaps a bit more often, if you required it of me."

"Required it?" She suddenly felt her entire body a-flush with anger. Every muscle tensed. Her head pounded a ragged tattoo. *Required!*

"For your pleasure. To satisfy your needs. Yes, of course. I believed I would be capable of making a go of it, although I never have done it with a woman."

"Lorne."

"You're looking frightfully pale, my dear." He gently took her by the shoulders and laid her back against the pillows. "I'll get you a drink of water, shall I?"

Louise didn't answer. Couldn't answer. She closed her eyes, felt him leave the bed then return to rest the cool lip of a glass against her lower lip. Was she delirious? This couldn't possibly be happening to her.

She sipped the water. Closed her eyes tighter. Imagined her life spooling out before her over the years, a desolate, childless, loveless landscape. A farce of a marriage.

Members of the royal family never divorced. *Never.* Well, there was her ancestor Henry VIII. But ridding himself of his wives had caused the restructure of religion in England and persecution of thousands. To do so now, to divorce Lorne, would result in unbelievable scandal.

Moreover she'd need to give a reason for separating from him.

Telling the truth was tantamount to throwing him to the wolves. And into prison. She must try harder. Surely she could entice him to want her—or, if not that, at least to do his duty.

Louise reached up and slipped one shoulder strap of her gown slowly down and off of her arm. The pearl-studded bodice fell open. Lorne's gaze dropped to her naked right breast. She felt the heat coming off his body escalate.

Drawing a breath for courage, she reached out for the silver buckle at his waist. He didn't move, seemed not to breathe as he allowed her to unclasp his belt. Her fingers trembled as she slipped her hand beneath his jacket and unbuttoned the fly of his trousers.

His face went white. "Louise."

"Hush. It will be all right," she whispered. "I don't care about your other life. I really don't. Do this for me, for us. Please. I know you can." She pressed her hand over his groin, but the rigid manhood she'd hoped to find there, wasn't. Tears filled her eyes. In desperation, she grasped his hand and drew it between her warm thighs. "I'll teach you to love me, my darling."

Lorne looked at her and seemed to make a decision. He stood and took off his jacket, then his shirt, and sat to remove his boots. She lay back and watched as he rose again, mechanically finished unbuttoning his trousers and stepped out of them, leaving only his linen undergarments snugly covering his hips. Her gaze roamed his hairless, beautifully muscled chest, his firm abdomen. He approached her with an expression of determination, although she could see no sign of an erection, yet.

Then, suddenly, just as Lorne reached out with one hand, as if to caress her displayed breast, something in his demeanor changed. His eyes flared with a new set of emotions. Embarrassment. Disappointment. Revulsion. He pulled back his hand with a sharp curse.

"Damn it to hell—you don't understand, Louise. I *want* to give you children. I told the queen I would be able to do so, but now that the time has come . . ." He took an unsteady step away from her and the bed. "I simply can't do it."

She propped herself up on her elbows and glared at him. "You discussed this with my *mother*? This plot of yours?"

"Not in so many words." He shrugged again, wearily, and sat down on the far end of the bed to pull on his trousers even as she looked on in disbelief. "But I believe she knew of my habits, and I expect she only bothered to consider me as a potential husband for you because of your . . . well, earlier indiscretions."

So he'd known all along she wasn't a virgin. She'd been sick with fear at the thought of telling him, and she needn't have been. *Because he had his own secrets.* The room began to spin.

Never in her life had she fainted, and she damned well was *not . . . going . . . to . . . now.*

Louise sat up so quickly that Lorne leaned away too fast, nearly falling off the mattress.

"What are we going to *do*, Lorne?" she shouted at him. Only one other time in her life had she been this furious with another person. "What do you imagine our life together will be like?"

He sighed. "I imagine, my dear, very little of it will be *together*, as you put it. If I were a man like so many others, I'd be supremely blessed to have you in my bed. But I'm not and won't apologize for my taste in lovers." He looked surer of himself now as he continued dressing. "My concern is what I've done to hurt you. I know now I cannot make love to you any more than I can to any other woman. It's simply not in me. I'm sorry that there will be no children, at least not from these loins."

"Then you tell me what the hell I'm supposed to do. Am I then expected to seek a lover?" she shouted at him, having recovered enough to shift from crushed to furious. How could he put her in this position? Worse yet, how could her mother have contrived such a union?

A shadow crossed Lorne's delicate features. "I don't know, my dear. I can't tell you what to do." He smoothed his shirtfront, took a shuddering breath. "If it becomes known that you enjoy the company of other men, and I do nothing to interfere, surely questions will be asked. Suspicion will fall on me."

"Then I shall be forced to remain celibate? Be denied children? Denied pleasure in a man's arms?"

He shook his head, as if acknowledging the unfairness of the situation but helpless to suggest a solution.

Suddenly, his face brightened. "I have something to offer you that other husbands don't."

"And that is?"

"*Freedom.*" He quirked one eyebrow and smiled, looking pleased with himself.

She scowled at him, confused.

"Freedom," he explained, "to be Louise." He stepped back toward the bed, took her hands again, moved his face close to hers and spoke with something that sounded like admiration. "You've never wanted to be like other female royals. That's what I've always admired about you, my dear. You've lived a Bohemian life among artists and friends you've chosen from among commoners as often as from nobility. Amanda and her family being a case in point. You've aligned yourself with reformists for the rights and protection of women. You've built for yourself a truly independent lifestyle. All of this would be taken from you if you married any other man in our day."

She stared at him, momentarily speechless. *He was right.* He was so very right. Hadn't all of these reasons been behind her wishing to delay marriage?

"You will allow me to make my own life," she said, feeling a little calmer now.

"Yes. And in return, you will protect me by being my wife in all ways but in bed. We will help each other as we can. It is the best I can offer, my darling Louise."

He stood then, looking down on her with those beautiful eyes of his, as guiltless as a child's, as winsome as a puppy's. She had to look away. Her heart could take no more.

"My word," he murmured, "you *are* lovely. It's a miracle no man has yet captured your beauty in a painting."

But one has, she thought. *He* did. Donovan.

"Please," she said, her voice barely above a hoarse whisper. *Please don't reject me.* "Try again, Lorne. For me."

But when she reached out to him, he pushed her away with a look of utter disgust. "No. Not now, Louise. Not ever." He shook his head in violent denial. "I'm sorry. So . . . so very sorry."

And then he was gone.

Louise stared up at the ceiling over her marriage bed. Her eyes misted over, blurring the gilded cupids at each corner of the painted ceiling. It occurred to her that this was to be the first in a long series of lonely nights for her. And her appearances in public, as half of a happily wed royal couple, would be a sham. She lay back down, pressed her face into the silk pillow, and wept.

Four

Stephen Byrne rode his mount at a gallop, leather duster flapping against his road-muddied boots, up to the Queen's Guard stationed outside the iron fence at Buckingham Palace. He presented his credentials and, when waved through the gate by the captain of the guard, rode into the yard.

Byrne adjusted the stiff-brimmed black felt hat John Batterson Stetson himself had fashioned for him when they'd met up in San Angelo, Texas—Byrne's birthplace. But that's not where his thoughts were today. He was relieved to see the queen's party hadn't yet left for Scotland. Some of the tension released from his road-weary back.

Three days after the grand celebration surrounding Princess Louise's wedding to the marquess, carriages lined the raked gravel drive, looking like a parade of trained circus elephants—tail to nose. This was to be the couple's honeymoon, though not a traditional one, because it included not only the queen herself but also part of her court. Starting with the largest and most ostentatious coach reserved for the queen and newlyweds to share, the carriages diminished in size and luxury to the humblest flatbed cart piled high with overflow luggage. The line of conveyances stretched around the drive, nearly to the Indian chestnut trees in the winter-ravished gardens.

Each carriage was accompanied by a driver and footman. Most appeared already to contain their passengers, but for a few gentlemen of the court who had become impatient and stood off to the side, idling about and smoking. He'd say from their irritated expressions they must have been cooling their aristocratic heels for a good while already.

He, for one, was glad the procession was running late. Catching up with the royal party on the road north would have made his task far more difficult. As it was, he thought the fuss and spectacle of the excursion to Balmoral, in the north of Scotland, ridiculous and foolhardy. He might have been amused had the situation been less serious. But things were far more grave than anyone in the queen's entourage could possibly guess.

The journey required days of hard travel and necessitated overnight stops at the estates of the queen's wealthiest subjects, who would then be obliged to provide lavish food, suites of rooms, and entertainment for Her Royal Majesty and her court. At least a portion of the passage might have been made easier if Victoria had agreed to use the new northern train line that she and Albert had enjoyed riding together. But she claimed now to hate the noisy, smoke-belching locomotives. So the trip up and back would be by plodding coach, through village after village after factory town, making the work of her security detail a veritable nightmare.

Aside from his feelings about the idiocy and unnecessary risk of such a trip, he had other opinions of the royal goings-on. If *he* were marrying—which he wasn't, and never would—he'd damn well *not* take his mother-in-law and her friends along on his honeymoon. But then, the more he'd seen of the young marquess, the more he wondered if Lorne might not care one way or the other about protecting his private time with his new wife.

Nearly a year earlier, Byrne had first come to England as a

member of Her Royal Majesty's elite Secret Service, on loan from President Ulysses S. Grant's detecting force, based in New York City. Now, as before, he did as he was commanded to do. He reported directly to the queen and never asked questions. Almost never.

To his frustration, his first assignment in England had less to do with the Crown's security than with good old-fashioned matchmaking. "I require tactfully acquired personal information on several gentlemen I am considering as potential husbands for my fourth daughter," the queen had told him.

"But, ma'am," Byrne protested, "I'm sure there are other sources for such—"

"This is my preference," Victoria said firmly, her gaze fixed on him like a leech. "You will say nothing to others of this assignment and report directly to me."

There seemed no point in arguing.

Slowly he warmed to his task as he came to learn more about Princess Louise from a discreet distance. She was a blue-eyed beauty with a flawless oval face and long, soft brown hair. Her figure was much more agreeable to his taste than those of her sisters or mother. Somewhat taller than any of them, she lacked their classic Hanoverian bosom, which seemed perfect for the prow of a ship but less so for a lady in real life. And she was by far the best dresser of the bunch. To his mind, Louise would have no trouble at all finding a husband on her own.

He doubted she even realized he was watching, and investigating, her as closely as he was her prospective mates. He collected a detailed personal history for each gentleman as well as an inventory of assets, debts, assignations, and religious inclination. To this he added any gambling, drinking, or other addictions or obsessions Victoria might find distasteful in a son-in-law.

At first, the Marquess of Lorne was one of five men on the queen's list and, to Byrne's mind, by no means the most promising. He'd felt sure, once he informed Victoria of the marquess's habitual attendance at certain disreputable gentlemen's clubs in London—including the infamous Cleveland Street Club—as well as the gentleman-only private parties and weekend hunts in the country (no ladies allowed), she would immediately eliminate the minor lord as a contender for her daughter's hand. Byrne had been shocked when the marquess rapidly vaulted to the top of her list.

This had awakened his curiosity.

Why would the Queen of England allow such a common—no, not even that—a *questionable* union? One that had the potential to result in scandal. Her three eldest daughters had married extremely well. Vicky, the Princess Royal, wed Prince Frederick William of Prussia. There was every reason to believe that "Fritz" would someday become emperor. Alice married Louis IV of Hesse and already had produced an heir and spares. Bashful Helena (known as Lenchen in the family) was only twenty-five but had presented her royal husband, Prince Christian of Schleswig-Holstein, with three babies.

Whereas, and this was what puzzled him and he noted in his journal: *The marquess of Lorne offers little more than a minor hereditary title and a modest Scotch duchy. As far as I can see, he has little money of his own and no skills other than a love of the hunt.*

To Byrne's surprise, the newspapers barely blinked at the announcement of the engagement. Instead they gossiped that this must be a rare but true love match. All of London gushed at the romance of the pairing and dismissed the unsavory rumors involving Lorne.

But Stephen Byrne was a military man accustomed to ferreting out secrets. And he smelled a whopper.

He didn't have to wonder for long why a Scottish subject of the queen, with a less than gleaming reputation, might hold out hope of winning this particular English princess as his wife. While on an unconnected mission to the Isle of Wight, Byrne ran into two gruff old pub sitters. They were only too willing—for the price of a couple of pints—to gossip for his benefit on the subject of the royal family.

"Years back, when the princess was not much more'n a girl, she showed up on the island with only a tutor for company. Polite folks said her mama sent her here to study, away from London's distractions."

"At Osborne House," the other local man supplied, "the royal family's estate."

"And what did folks who weren't so polite say?" Byrne asked, after offering another round of liquid lubrication.

The more talkative of the two leaned closer to the queen's agent. "Was a rumor, sayin' the queen was pure frantic to get her daughter away from boys at her school. Chaps that might lead her astray." He winked.

In fact Byrne had already learned that Louise, who was perhaps seventeen or eighteen at the time, had been studying at the National Art Training School in South Kensington. Some of the students were a bit wild and experimented with strong drink, laudanum, and other drugs. He wouldn't have been shocked if sex had been part of the mix.

If Louise had gotten herself deflowered or, worse yet, knocked up, Byrne speculated the queen would have had more than enough reason to remove her daughter from her unsavory friends and shield her from court gossip. Aside from Louise's reputation as the wild child of Victoria's family (which might mean anything or nothing, given the shaky validity of London's rumor mill), if she was no longer a virgin her choice of husbands would be severely limited.

But Lorne—what if Lorne had his own secrets to hide? Even if he were innocent of what British law termed "debauchery," a man with his eye on gaining status in society would make no complaint against a wife who came to him experienced, ruined, tarnished, compromised, or whatever label society cared to brand her with, particularly if she provided an entrée into the royal family.

Now, back at Buckingham, Byrne caught the eye of an equerry of the royal mews and handed over the reins of his horse. He strode toward the diplomatic entrance to the palace to report a different sort of news to the queen, but his mind lingered on Louise. What did a spirited young princess think of the match her mother had made for her? At the very least, it would seem, the queen had set her daughter up for a celibate life.

To his mind, this was an unthinkably cruel act and an utter waste of womanhood. The few times he'd been in a position to observe the princess, his body had responded with healthy approval. And, he'd noticed, he was not alone in his lust. The woman was a looker.

Louise's passing figure turned men's heads everywhere she went. Moreover he suspected she rather enjoyed the attention. Her eyes sparkled with sensual playfulness. The fact that she always behaved in the most proper way, at least whenever he'd observed her, made her all the more intriguing to men.

Distracted by these troubling thoughts, Byrne watched the gray, frost-covered paving stones pass beneath his feet without really seeing them. He crossed the courtyard, took the stone steps, approaching the door that would take him into the great hall and from there to the queen's private offices.

The heavy chestnut wood door, studded with fist-size iron bolts, swung open ahead of him. He paid no attention to whoever had conveniently opened it for him until it struck him that something solid blocked his way, entirely filling the doorway.

Forced to stop and wait until the object moved out of his path, Byrne looked up to find a towering, kilted John Brown, fists braced on his tree-trunk hips.

"And where do you think you're goin', laddie?" the Scot's voice rumbled.

Laddie? Byrne glared up at the man. Even bareheaded, Brown gave the appearance of standing nearly to the height of the tallest of the queen's fur-helmeted Hussars.

"I'm on Her Majesty's business," Byrne said. "She expects me."

"She does, does she? You'll have to come back after she returns from the north."

Byrne refused to be intimidated. Brown might have charmed the queen, but the American agent knew the man for what he was—an iron-nosed, hard-drinking bully.

"I need to see Her Majesty before she leaves for Balmoral."

"She's with the prime minister."

"Gladstone?"

"And Mr. Disraeli."

"In the same room?" Benjamin Disraeli was the former PM and a fierce rival of Gladstone's. "She's a brave woman."

"I'll not argue that," Brown said. "Soon as I get those two rascals away from her, we're off. As it is, we're behind schedule. I don't intend to have her out on the road after dark tonight."

"Then I'd better go straight in and give her an excuse to dismiss them."

Brown folded his arms over his chest and stood firm. "Turn around, Raven, and fly away."

Byrne narrowed his eyes at the other man. No one but Victoria called him Raven these days. The name *Byrne* was Irish for *blackbird.* Raven had been his code name during the American War between the States. The queen fancied pet names for those around her, and she seemed delighted to have discovered this one for him. "It sounds deliciously sinister," she'd once told him. At the time he'd thought she must have been reading that queer American author, Mr. Poe.

He was trying to gauge how far to push Brown when a shriek of terror echoed through the castle and continued reverberating off the stone walls even as both men spun toward the cry.

"The kitchen?" Byrne said, thinking perhaps one of the maids had burnt herself or dropped a tray of china, although he'd heard no crash from the basement where the servants labored.

"The bairn's wing!" Brown shouted, as though to orient himself. The Scot drew a dirk of impressive length from his belt and took off at a loping run.

As Brown seemed to have forgotten him in the frenzy of the moment, Byrne took it upon himself to follow rather than find his own way to the trouble. He was far from familiar with the twisting halls of the palace, a veritable maze of hundreds of rooms.

High-pitched screeches to rival the performance of an operatic soprano echoed through the hallways, growing ever louder as they ran.

Definitely female, he thought. *Definitely hysterical.* Two of them, he guessed, from the varying octaves.

Suddenly Byrne feared the intelligence he'd come to report to the queen might have arrived too late.

Only that morning, he'd paid an informant for shocking news. The Fenians, Irish radicals, apparently had succeeded in doing what Scotland Yard and the Secret Service most feared. They'd brought in two explosives experts from outside of the country, intending to employ them in carrying out a dramatic attack. Their aim was to impress upon the world the importance of the Irish cause. His man couldn't say where or when they would strike, or even what the plot might entail. Only that it somehow involved the royal family.

Byrne's heart hammered within his ribcage. As fast as he was running, the Scot was pulling ahead of him, even though the man must have outweighed him by eighty or more pounds and didn't appear built for speed. Byrne caromed off a stone wall as he rounded a corner; pain shot through his elbow. His breath came in shallow, urgent puffs.

Why the hell did they make these places so damn *big*?

He pressed on as they shot up a flight of steps to the third floor. The screams had turned to sobs and weakening wails. He expected nothing short of a bloodbath.

At last he saw *them*.

Two weeping females clung to each other just outside a closed door to one of the rooms in the children's wing. Brown descended on them in a powerful stride—a vengeful giant to be reckoned with. The pair fell back, looking more frightened than comforted by his appearance.

Byrne recognized the youngest of the princesses, Beatrice. A honey-haired, sweet-faced angel of a child. The older woman, in cap and dark-colored day gown, he didn't recognize but guessed from her garb she might be the girl's governess or nurse.

No blood visible yet. Praise be.

"What is it then?" Brown bellowed. "Stop yer catterwallin' and tell me what's wrong, woman!"

The governess waved a limp hand toward the closed door. Byrne drew his Bowie knife from his boot by its carved bone grip and let himself into the room without waiting for Brown. He closed the door softly behind him, lowering himself into a half crouch. A fighter's stance. The muscles of his legs tensed, ready to spring, should he need to move fast.

Pulse racing, eyes hot with anticipation of an attack, he surveyed the room, prepared for the worst. A dead body. An armed intruder. But then why would the women retreat only as far as the other side of a door? Wouldn't that leave their assailant free to pursue them?

Had a bomb been lobbed through the window and failed to detonate? Surely he would have heard the explosion if there had been one. But there was no shattered glass, no smoke, no blaze, no biting metallic scent of black powder. And no Fenian soldier pounced on him with knife or pistol, or tried to escape out one of the windows or through any of the three doors leading out of the expansive bedchamber.

Whoever had frightened the princess and her companion must already have escaped. The question was, escaped to where? If one or more intruders were loose in the castle, the queen was in danger. Brown needed to alert the captain of the guard and—

Byrne's whirling mind clicked into focus at the sight of two dark shapes, followed by a third, scurrying from beneath the princess's bed. They sped across the lovely crimson-and-leaf-green tapestry carpet. All three hairy, squat vermin leaped up onto a small table that had been set for tea with cakes and fruit and delicate china. A long ropelike tail whipped around, sending a teacup and saucer crashing to the floor.

"Rats," he groaned, relieved but still wary of worse. How the hell had they made their way up to the third floor with hundreds of staff constantly cleaning, polishing, and on the lookout for intruders or the least unpleasantness? Impossible. Unless . . .

Unless someone who wasn't considered an intruder intentionally made a delivery.

His eyes swept the room, nerves sparking like flint on steel. Ignoring the beasts while he searched from floor to ceiling, from armoire to canopied bed. He stopped at a small square of paper—a note?—pinned to the heavy damask draperies surrounding the princess's bed as protection from drafts. He snatched up the paper, stuffed it into his coat pocket, not daring to take the time to read it until he was satisfied that no one lurked in the room to cause further threat.

The door to the hallway flew wide. One of the rats dashed toward the light.

"Shut it!" he shouted at Brown.

The Scot stepped inside and slammed the door behind him.

Byrne didn't need to point out the mangy creature racing toward him. Before the thing recognized its mistake, Brown's immense boot came down on its head with a dull crunch.

It lay still.

"The women said there was three of 'em," Brown snarled. "Nothin' more. Just bloody rats."

"Right. Two there on the tabletop, having their tea." They seemed undisturbed by the men's presence, so delighted were they to discover the feast.

"How did they get in?"

Byrne shrugged. "How the hell do I know? Isn't palace security your job?" Not officially, of course. But since the Highlander seemed determined to claim for himself the roll of bodyguard to the queen, to Byrne's mind he might as well take responsibility for this invasion of the private quarters.

Brown glared at him, his face going beet red with anger. "Did you know about this? Was this why you insisted on seeing her?"

"No, not this. Listen, can you deal with things here? I honestly need to speak with Victoria. She'll be in that much more of a hurry to leave as soon as she hears about the rats."

The Scot gave a snort and a nod of his bearish head. "I'll be done with these filthy demons in two shakes. You talk fast, Raven. I'm gettin' her out of here quick as I can."

Byrne flew out through the door, slamming it behind him. A bevy of tittering servants, along with a half dozen ladies and gentlemen of the court, had gathered in the hallway. They fell silent, their eyes fixed on the eight-inch blade in his right hand. He sheathed the knife. Behind him, a stream of oaths and the sounds of furniture and fragile things crashing to the floor came through the door to the bedchamber. He smiled. Maybe the rats were more of a challenge than Brown had expected.

"Everything's under control now," Byrne said to his wide-eyed audience. "Feel free to return to whatever you were doing. No need for concern." As most started to move away, he pulled the piece of paper he'd found out of his pocket and read it for the first time.

His blood ran cold as a December night.

Cursing under his breath, he tucked it away again. He cut a path through the lingering crowd toward the woman who had set off the alarm with Princess Beatrice. The governess looked calmer now, though still pale and red-eyed with fright.

"Excuse me, miss. Was anyone other than the two of you in the room?"

She stared at him, pressing a handkerchief over her mouth. "I . . . well, no. Why would there be?"

"Can't you see she's upset? Leave her alone."

He spun toward the scolding voice. Princess Louise.

Beatrice had stepped into the arms of her older sister while he'd been in the room. Louise must have arrived at Buckingham earlier that morning from the private estate where she'd stayed with her husband after the wedding.

Louise glared at him, her eyes flashing reproof.

It struck him that this was the first time he'd seen her up close, less than an arm's reach away. Everything he'd heard and thought about her was true. She *was* beautiful, stunningly so. The woman gave off a light—no, more like a brilliant energy that played havoc with his senses. If other females glowed as candles that brightened a room, Louise was one of those newfangled electric lightbulbs, outshining a score of flames.

Her charm was unconventional though. He could see that now. Not every man would appreciate her. She wore a simple day dress of pale yellow, without a bustle, thereby showing off her natural figure. The color was a bold contrast to the dark fabrics of the day's somber, far more formal styles. And she'd left her hair brushed loose and shining down her back, as if she were still a young girl. Or at least young at heart.

He shook sense back into his head and finally managed to form words. "I beg your pardon, Your Royal Highness. I need to know if an intruder or anyone at all—staff, maids, a messenger—was admitted to your sister's room."

"No, sir!" Beatrice burst out. "There were just those disgusting, horrid rats." She blinked up at him, eyes bright with tears, face splotchy as a toddler's after a weepy tantrum. "I saw them first. Glowing eyes beneath my bed when I bent down to retrieve a pencil I'd dropped."

"And a letter? Did you see a note of any kind?"

"No."

"You're sure?" The words came out more harshly than he'd intended.

"I-I'm pretty sure." The girl's voice broke. She stared at him, her lower lip trembling as if he had scolded her.

Louise rocked her sister in her arms. "Please, can't this wait? What purpose is served by reminding her of the filthy beasts? And how can knowing whether there were two or twenty people in the room, or letters were left about . . . how can that matter?" She stroked Beatrice's long blond hair with heartbreaking tenderness. "The creatures must have come in through the air vent. Awful things. Now please, do leave us."

There was extraordinary determination and power in her voice, and in those lovely sky blue eyes, although they looked everywhere but directly at him. She seemed frustrated that he was ignoring her attempts to dismiss him, as if she wasn't accustomed to the help ignoring her commands. *A little bit of her mother in her,* he thought. But he suspected she more upset than angry, only trying to protect her little sister from further distress.

And she was right about one thing.

Whether or not the governess and young princess saw the note was of little importance. It must have arrived at the same time as the rats. And now that he knew that neither the little princess nor the woman with her had seen anyone in the room, he also knew that both rodents and letter must have been delivered while they were away from the room. Because he was certain that the rats' appearance was not by way of their wandering randomly through vents in the walls. They were meant to cause hysteria, to strike fear in royal breasts. And where better to accomplish that than in the intimacy of the youngest family member's privy chamber?

"I'm sorry," Byrne said. "I'll go immediately and inform the queen of the situation."

He was halfway down the hallway when he heard light steps running after him.

"Wait! Wait there. Don't you go a step farther, sir."

He slowed down, smiling at Louise's challenge even before he turned to face her. But he kept walking backward, wanting to get to Victoria before Brown finished with his rat extermination.

"Yes, Your Royal Highness?"

Louise marched toward him, looking a force to be reckoned with. Shoulders back, head high, eyes aflame—absolutely breath-taking. "Who *are* you, sir, and what exactly are you doing in the family quarters?"

He laughed, amused. She was challenging *him*? He stopped his backward march and planted his feet, forcing her to come to an abrupt halt in front of him.

"My name is Stephen Byrne. I'm here under the authority of Her Royal Majesty's Secret Service, on a mission of dire impor-tance. And you are delaying me, Princess." He gave her a stony look . . . which seemed to have no effect whatsoever.

"And exactly what mission is that, sir?" Her eyes dropped from his face, down the length of his outfit.

At first he thought her gaze critical of his choice of clothing.

Many people in London were. But his garments satisfied more practical requirements than the fashion of the day. The leather duster and vest were a kind of armor, offering far more protection from a knife attack or even a fall from a horse than any cloth top-coat. Plus it hid the Colt strapped to his hip. And he favored for durability the sturdy dark blue canvas material and riveted seams of his pants over anything available in England.

Too late, he realized his garments weren't what interested her. He followed her gaze to the paper corner peeking from his pocket. Before he could stop her, Louise had reached out and plucked the note away.

"Is this it? Is this the letter you were asking my sister about?"

"Give that to me."

Louise lifted a brow at his tone, ignored his outstretched hand, and muttered something about manners and Americans.

She uncrumpled the scrap of paper. Her eyes flicked over the words before he snapped it out from her fingertips.

The lovely heat in her cheeks drained away to white ash. She looked away from him and anchored her bottom lip between her teeth, as though trying to process what she'd just read.

"Now that you've seen," he said, "you'll know why I need to speak with your mother. Immediately."

"Yes, yes of course." A hand fluttered to her throat. She wavered on her feet.

Instinctively, he clasped his hand around her arm to steady her. Within the delicate goldenrod fabric, she felt fragile to his touch. He released his grip almost at once for fear of bruising her.

"Are you all right, Princess?"

"Yes. I think so." She closed her eyes for a moment, as if to rally herself.

When she opened them again, their gazes connected. He thought he saw a brilliant little spark behind her eyes. But in the next second it was snuffed out. She hastily looked away from him.

"I'm so sorry," she said. "You must think me terribly rude. I didn't mean to shout at you or accuse. It's just that this is all so disturbing. Rats and threats and"—she hesitated—"and *everything*."

"Of course, Your Highness."

"Do you know your way from here to my mother's office? No, of course you don't. It's a rat's maze. Oh dear, that was an unfortunate choice. Here then, follow me, Mr. Byrne."

Five

Brash. Coarse. Unnervingly powerful.

What a horrid, ill-mannered man, Louise thought as she raced through Buckingham's maze of corridors with her mother's agent close behind her. But recalling that vile note set her thoughts spinning off in a different direction.

How often, she wondered, *do we fail to recognize a critical moment in our lives while it's actually happening?*

This, she couldn't help believing, was one of those special moments. And not just because of a few silly rats. She had the oddest sense that time itself was waiting for her to open her eyes and take notice of the importance of this particular day, this singular moment, because nothing—*nothing*—ever would be the same for her. Maybe not for any of them.

Her skin prickled with apprehension as she lengthened her stride, aware of Byrne close behind her—keeping up easily. He moved more like a predator, an animal, than a man. Silent, serious, instinctively tuned into his surroundings. Her nerves tingled with an uneasy awareness of his presence. And then, at last, they were at their destination.

From inside her mother's private office, the same the queen had shared with her beloved Prince Albert when he was alive, Louise could hear familiar male voices. On no other day, under no less urgent circumstances, would she have dared interrupt a meeting between Victoria and her prime minister. But no one stood at the ready to stop them or give permission, and circumstances dictated action not protocol.

She rapped twice on the heavy oak door. Stephen Byrne didn't even wait for a response. He pushed past her, shoved wide the door, and she followed his bold entrance into the room to face the five astonished faces of PM Gladstone, Gladstone's secretary, Mr. Benjamin Disraeli, her mother's secretary, and the queen herself.

"Mama"—Louise belatedly thought to curtsy—"I apologize for the intrusion, but this gentleman has urgent business with you."

Victoria turned cold eyes from her daughter to Byrne. "I instructed your superiors to allow you to report directly to me, to insure this new so-called Secret Service does not keep vital information from me. I also realize how impulsive Americans tend to be." Her eyes narrowed and targeted him, as if he were a grouse she was about to dispatch. "But your report certainly can wait ten minutes, Mr. Byrne."

Louise shook her head when Byrne let out a little grunt of frustration and seemed about to take a step back. "No. You must give that to her *now*!"

She waved her hand at the scrap of paper dangling from his fingertips. A sudden image leaped into her head of one of the no-doubt-by-now-dead rats hanging limply by its tail from Brown's big fist. The difference being, this little piece of paper was far more dangerous than any rodent.

"Mama, this can't wait. Please."

Victoria scowled at her disapprovingly. "If this message is so very important, perhaps Mr. Gladstone should also know of its contents?"

Byrne cleared his throat. "Ma'am, I don't think it's a good—"

The queen silenced him with a look of bleak displeasure. "Mr.

Rhodes," she said, turning to the PM's secretary, "please do the honor of reading to all present this message that is so critical it stops our government from working."

The gaunt-featured man stepped forward, head bowed meekly. He smoothed his thin mustache with two fingers then gingerly plucked the square of paper from Byrne's hand. He cleared his throat as he silently scanned the words that would remain forever implanted in Louise's mind.

The man's eyes widened in shock. "Oh dear," he whispered.

"Mr. Rhodes," Gladstone's stentorious voice rumbled in warning. He nodded his head, enveloped in a cloud of white hair, toward the paper. "Proceed, sir."

Rhodes ran a finger under his collar. "Beg pardon, but I'd rather not. Not, that is, in front of the ladies."

"Read, Rhodes!"

The secretary's eyes snapped obediently back to the note. He moistened his lips, swallowed audibly, then let the words tumble out all in one breath. "'Where three got in on four legs another might on two. Does it take a dead princess to win freedom for our Irish brothers?'"

The room fell silent.

Louise looked at her mother, sitting absolutely still behind her desk in her widow's black bombazine and crape, her plump fingers wearing only funereal jet rings, hands pressed flat against a gold-embossed blotter. But Victoria's moon face did not lose its color as Louise had imagined it would. Rather, it blossomed into hot rage.

"Where did this foolish riddle come from? What does this mean, Mr. Byrne?"

"It means, ma'am, that we've just come from Princess Beatrice's bedchamber, where she and her governess confronted three very large and hungry rats."

"In the palace? Impossible."

"No, ma'am, they were most definitely rats."

Louise shot a glance at Byrne's dark eyes and felt an unexpected emotional tug she couldn't define. Although his gaze revealed nothing, and despite the seriousness of the threat to her sister, she had a feeling he was holding back a smile. She would have kicked him in the shin good and hard for seeing any humor in this most grave situation, if he'd been within reach. Shouldn't they be discovering how this intruder had got in? Where he, or they, might be even now? And what if there was another visitation with far more dire consequences than a warning?

"It was terrifying, truly," Louise said. "Bea is in such a state, and Miss Witherstone near apoplexy. Brown remains back there even now"—she shuddered at the thought—"eradicating the beasts."

Victoria drew a deep breath, filling her ponderous bosom and letting it deflate again. "I see. Are we to assume this is the work of those Fenian madmen who have been setting off bombs in our city on behalf of the Irish rebels?" She looked pointedly at Byrne but didn't wait for an answer. "Have you alerted our guardsmen?"

Gladstone had taken the note from his secretary. After reading it for himself he passed it to Disraeli, who barely let his eyes drift with disdain over its surface before hastily placing it on the corner of the queen's desk.

"Brown will handle that, ma'am. Anyone leaving the palace will be stopped and questioned. It's my suggestion that the wedding party, and all accompanying them, move to the carriages at once. Vacating the palace will allow Brown's men to search for any other surprises from the Fenians or whoever may be to blame."

Gladstone coughed into his lavender gloved hand. "My apologies, Your Majesty, for this unpleasantness. The Irish problem is a tangled one, but it is unconscionable that your family be exposed to—"

"Nevertheless, we are exposed, as you put it," Victoria cut him off. "We will continue our discussion, Mr. Prime Minister, on our return from Balmoral, whenever my men tell me it's safe. Louise, inform any of our Ladies of the Court who aren't already in their carriages to move to them with the utmost haste."

"Yes, Mama." She turned to leave and was halfway to the door, only vaguely aware of Gladstone and Disraeli bidding her mother a safe journey, when Byrne's deep voice made her prick up her ears.

"If I may have a word with you in private, ma'am?"

"Of course," the queen said.

Louise kept on walking, intent on her mission. But she couldn't help wondering what it was Byrne felt compelled to say that he didn't want anyone but Victoria to hear.

Brown didn't like him; that much was obvious. She had heard the Scot call the American "Raven" in a clearly mocking tone. Normally Brown's craggy, bearded face screened his emotions. Anyone he didn't like was simply denied access to her mother. He had that much power these days. Victoria took his advice on almost everything, much to the annoyance of her sons and ministers, both of whom viewed the Scot as opportunistic and crude.

Yet the queen seemed to trust this foreigner despite Brown's disapproval.

How odd.

Nearly as odd as her reaction had been to Stephen Byrne back at the nursery. Ordering him about as if she were the queen or her older sister Vicky, who sometimes behaved even more pompously with the royal staff than their mother. Why had she become so defensive when she was around the man? She, who enjoyed the relaxed friendship of commoners from all stations in life. She who prided herself on treating everyone with equal cordiality.

It seemed that the roguish American brought out the worst in her. Or, at least, brought out something she wasn't sure she could control.

Six

Rupert Clark scooped black powder into a paper cylinder. He pinched then twisted the end tight between calloused fingers. Every now and then he stopped what he was doing to check on the work of the younger man beside him. Details were what mattered in this game. Details made you famous, or blew off your hand. Or worse.

Rupert had joined up with Major General Richard Taylor in the 28th Louisiana Infantry back in '63. He had learned from his sergeant the technique of rigging an artillery shell with a primer sensitive enough to detonate the shell if a man or horse stepped on a pressure plate. Rupert quickly discovered he had talent for the work.

Soon he was designing his own, even more sophisticated, explosive devices. General Robert E. Lee heard about his successes and ordered Rupert transferred to the general's own Army of Northern Virginia, not long after the Confederate victory at Fredericksburg. Will McMahon came on board at Chancellorsville, and he'd taught the boy enough to make of him a good assistant, even if he was a little slow and, sometimes, too impatient for such sensitive work.

After that they'd marched together, mining roads and blowing up bridges for the South wherever they were most needed.

Rupert gloried in constructing more and more sophisticated mines and bombs, and he felt proud of his successes. He'd only made one mistake; it had cost him three fingers from his right hand. But he could kill more Yanks in one short minute than any man he knew. And without wasting a single bullet or jeopardizing his comrades' lives. Never had he felt so empowered, so important as during those grand and glorious campaigns.

As it turned out, it was all for naught.

Rupert had believed in their cause, breaking away from the tyranny of the North, saving his family's land and their way of life for the children he would someday have with his sweet Annemarie. Now there was nothing left back home. Nothing worth returning to anyway. His parents were dead—of natural causes, or so he'd been told. His brother had taken off for somewhere out west. Annemarie perished in the blaze that burned down their house by the ferry landing in Irish Bend, Louisiana.

Had his wife stayed to try to protect their home? Had those damn Yanks sullied her before setting the house afire? The bitterness of not knowing burned in his gut like a white-hot sulfur flame. Tortured him. Devoured him.

"We might could head on up to West Virginia, work in the mines," he told Will.

"Guess we could."

But blasting out shafts was dirty and particularly dangerous work. Blowing a path through granite and shale mountains for the railways out west was more to his liking.

"Okay by me," an always agreeable Will said.

"Trouble is, those damn Chinese work cheap and know their way around dynamite." In the end, they gave up on that too. Mines or railways—there was nothing else for a man with such a singular talent when there wasn't a war going on. "Maybe we should just work our way up north. Might be jobs, one sort or another in Chicago."

He and Will had left the sickening devastation of their homeland. But they found nothing other than the stinking-of-death, bloody stockyards for work. Nothing, that is, until they stumbled on an Irish-American rally to raise money for militants bent on winning freedom for Ireland. If one brave endeavor couldn't be won, Rupert reasoned, perhaps another might be. His missing fingers itched at the thought of being back in the fight.

He and Will dropped a few words here and there in Chicago about their experiences in the military, taking care not to mention on which side they'd served.

Two days later a Fenian recruiter scouted them out in McGinty's on the South Side. The three moved to a dark booth at the back of the bar.

"Our army o' freedom fighters," the man with muttonchop whiskers and a musical Irish lilt to his words explained, "is half Irish boys and half Americans and Canadians who sympathize with our struggle. All brave lads, I'll tell you. But what we most need these days, boys, are dynamiteers. I hear you know a bit about the subject?"

"We do," Rupert said, feeling the old excitement rise through his veins like a thread of mercury in the thermometer. He gave the recruiter an accounting of his and Will's successes, each mission bringing with it a surge of remembered pride.

This was what he missed as sorely as a man who'd lost a limb to battle—this feeling of wholeness, of comradeship, of being respected for his trade and expertise.

"Good black-powder men are hard to find. Joining our war against England is your chance to do some good," the recruiter said after ordering up fresh pints of Guinness, molasses dark and fragrant with hops. "Dust off the feeling o' shame at your loss, boys. Turn your gifts into victory. Can you not see how grand it will be?" The man raised his glass to them.

Rupert could see it. Most assuredly, he could. The aching sting of his own losses—land and wife—seemed less painful when he considered returning to his old art after months of doing nothing but working in the yards under bosses who snickered at his "Loo-si-ana" accent.

Of course they'd accepted. How could they not?

Now, all the way on the other side of the ocean, on a deserted road north of London, Rupert brushed his red hair out of his eyes and waved Will over beside him. The two of them squatted down and wired their primers and fuses, just so. They didn't need to speak. They knew what they were about, having done it hundreds of times before.

"You think it's too much?" Will asked then smiled that sweet boyish smile of his. Rupert had seen his partner shove a bayonet through a man's liver while wearing that same innocent grin. "I mean, the Lieutenant said 'disable the horses.' Not blow the whole caravan to kingdom come."

"The Lieutenant" was the only name they knew for their handler. Most of the men in this outfit went by code names or rank. Very cautious the Fenians were. In fact they'd only met the man who gave them their orders once. A well-dressed fellow he was. But it had been at night, his face obscured by his top hat brim, features distorted by the gaslight bouncing off the soupy mustard-yellow London fog. After that, the Lieutenant always sent runners with coded messages or with cash to keep them fed and in a decent rooming house.

The good pay aside, Rupert would rather have known the man for who he was. Seeing a man's eyes—that's how he judged his character. Lee's eyes were what had made Rupert willing to follow the general into blazing hell. They reflected truth, intelligence, *honor.* But Rupert couldn't have said whether the Fenian lieutenant's eyes were black, brown, or polka-dotted purple.

Their first assignment in London had been a beauty of a job. A single spectacular explosion knocked out a wall of Parliament, damaging two meeting rooms. The assault on the government horrified the public and did exactly what it was supposed to do—make the English think twice about holding on to a belligerent island. London hadn't stopped talking about it for weeks.

"You s'pose we'll get a bonus for this job?" Will asked.

"No tellin', my boy. No tellin'." Rupert felt positively cheerful at the thought. He looked around the rolling countryside. They were well beyond the city limits but still close enough for them to escape back into the dank thieves' dens of Whitechapel. "These lads seem to have deep pockets, they do."

Will sat back on his heels and plucked a slim green shoot of grass to tuck between his teeth. "When will the others arrive?"

"Soon as the charges blow under the horses of the queen's carriage." The rest of the crew—now waiting in a safe house nearby so as not to attract too much attention from locals who might send out an alarm—would descend quickly on the disabled coach.

What puzzled Rupert was how the Lieutenant knew exactly when the wedding party was to leave London and which route they'd take. One of the lesser Fenian officers had hinted that an informant was in place, maybe even inside Buckingham Palace. And it was rumored among the men that the spy was someone high up, with access to Victoria's court.

Rupert pulled out his pocket watch. By his calculations, the royal party should reach them in about one hour. A Fenian rider was clandestinely pacing the entourage on horseback. He'd warn the dynamiteers minutes before the royal carriages arrived. Rupert insisted upon detonating the road mine himself, not risking a pressure plate for this job. He needed to make sure the charge didn't go off directly under the queen's carriage, or they'd have nothing but body parts and gore everywhere.

"We done?" Will asked, spitting out the grass, brushing hair out of eyes that glittered with excitement.

"Just about." Rupert had a feeling Will rather enjoyed seeing blown-apart bodies. He had caught him on the battlefield, pulling watches and rings off of severed hands; coins out of gaping, gory torsos. He suspected something had snapped in the lad at Vicksburg, if not before. Rupert patted him on the back. "Feels good, bein' appreciated again, don't it?"

"Sure does."

"Just remember, once she blows, we're up and over that hill back of us. No dawdlin' to admire our handiwork. Let the foot soldiers grab her royalness."

Because that was the plan—as daring as it might seem.

Kidnap the Queen of England.

Seven

Louise settled herself on the velvet cushion inside the coach beside Beatrice. Lorne sat on her sister's other side, next to the far door. She was glad Bea hadn't relinquished her customary position in the middle seat. As tender as Louise had felt toward Lorne during the days before their wedding, all of her hopes and every one of her dreams had been extinguished the moment he'd told her the facts of his life and what he saw as the ground rules of their marriage.

Although her anger had waned, she still felt wounded, callously betrayed. By him and by her mother.

Victoria sat directly across from Louise, preferring a window seat that faced forward. Her youngest sons, Leo and Arthur, filled in the rest of the seat, making a party of six in the grand coach. Lenchen was staying behind at Buckingham Palace, nursing a sniffly cold, which Brown deemed a safer place for her now that the others had left. Vicky and Fritz were already on their way back across the Continent to his beloved Germany. Others in the family were busy in their own ways, and the queen hadn't objected to their not going along to Balmoral.

"I'm sure I shall be enough company for my darling newlyweds," she'd cooed.

More than enough, Louise thought grimly.

Through the window on her left, Louise looked out on the rolling green countryside. Eventually the air completely cleared of the horrid mustard yellow smog and coal dust that drifted over and out from the city. Louise removed her handkerchief, covered in black specks from the sooty air, from over her nose and mouth. At last, she could breathe.

She heard John Brown barking out an order to the coachman. The Scot was sitting above them with the driver—where he preferred to be, in the open air. She suspected the arrangement suited him all the better for enabling him to take sips from his flask without her mother's knowledge.

Louise turned to her sister. Bea still looked shaken by the rat ordeal. Louise whispered to her, "It's a long drive, Baby. Might as well catch a nap." She scooped an arm around her golden-haired younger sister. "I'll wake you when we arrive."

It wasn't long before Bea dropped off to sleep, her head resting on Louise's shoulder as they jolted and jostled down the rutted highway.

Louise glanced across the carriage at her mother, whose lap was piled with letters she'd planned to read as they drove. Her stationery box with pens and ink and sealing wax lay at her feet, although Louise couldn't imagine trying to write while the carriage bumped over country roads. Victoria folded her hands on top of her correspondence, to keep the letters from sliding off her knees. Louise wished her mother had been willing to transport them all on *Fairy*, the royal yacht. Traveling up the coast by water to Scotland was the much pleasanter way to go, faster too.

Victoria had closed her eyes to nap, or else as a ploy to cut off conversation with her newlywed daughter. Louise didn't care at the moment. They had spoken but a few words since the ceremony; no real opportunity for intimate conversation between mother and daughter having presented itself, with servants, staff, and relations always hovering around the queen. Louise longed to ask her mother if she'd knowingly arranged her marriage to a man who was incapable of pleasing her in bed or giving her children. It was unthinkably mean.

But then, hadn't her mother already proven herself capable of unforgivable deeds?

They had never seen eye to eye. Her mother had once complained to Vicky in a letter, which Louise had snuck a peak at, that her fourth daughter was "*difficile*." The one thing they'd ever shared, when Louise was a girl, was a love of drawing. Their mutual devotion to art was the reason the queen finally gave in to Louise's pleas to be allowed to attend art school, even though this put her daughter in touch with commoners, a dreaded situation assiduously avoided by her family.

Unfortunately—Louise had to admit—her mother's fears proved warranted. Although that one year in Kensington had been the most exciting, enlightening, and challenging of her young life, disaster ensued. Painful images flashed across her mind, even now, in the rumbling coach, so many years later. She brought a gloved fist to her mouth and pressed hard, holding back a sob of grief . . . and guilt.

With effort Louise pushed those memories out of her mind and fixed on the budding trees and early blossoming, white-petaled snowdrops speckling the grass alongside the road. And the pain slowly faded. In a few days they'd settle in at dear Balmoral, the castle built on an ancient site by her father. It sat close to where her husband had been born into the powerful Campbell clan, and where his family still lived. As always, the castle would offer shelter from the politics and intrigue of London.

Occasionally she caught a glimpse of her mother's agent, Stephen Byrne, riding up and down the line of carriages, his black-brown duster flapping in the wind, that strange American plainsman's hat with the high crown and wide brim tugged low over his brow, his piercing gaze flicking toward buildings, trees, people they passed. Watching for God-only-knew-what threat.

She had to give the man credit. He, and Brown, had acted swiftly and efficiently to get them on their way north. It was no small task, herding their entourage into the waiting carriages. She'd expected outraged arguments from courtiers. But something unpredictable and dangerous shadowed Byrne's dark eyes, discouraging argument from even the highest ranking in her mother's court.

She looked along the seat and over her sister's sleeping head at Lorne. His gaze was fixed on a distant point outside the far window. His blond hair feathered in the chill spring breeze. They hadn't said more than two words to each other this day. Or the one before it. In the presence of her mother, he'd kissed her on the cheek and wished her a cheerful good morning at family breakfast. But since then he'd touched her no more than was necessary to put on a show of affection and, later, to hand her up into the carriage.

She felt more alone than ever, shut inside this rattling ebony box with her nonhusband and her incomprehensible mother. How could she look forward to a life of celibacy, in the company of a man who could only love other men? What was she to *do*? If this had been a conscious plan on her mother's part, had it been intended as punishment for her daughter's past failings?

Louise's head began to pound in rhythm with the horses' hoofbeats. Her throat felt raw and tightened with the effort to fight back tears. She wouldn't succumb to self-pity. Certainly not here in front of everyone.

The queen's carriage set a rapid pace between towns, at Brown's direction. Eventually they slowed down as they approached the industrial town of Leicester, more densely populated than others before it along the route. Smokestacks spewed gritty steam from the factories along the canal and the River Soar, but the air remained far less foul than the choking effluvium that hovered over London.

And then they stopped.

Victoria roused herself, opening her eyes. "What is it? Why are we not moving?"

Louise leaned a little out the window to see beyond the horses that drew the carriage. "It appears to be market day. The streets are clogged with farm wagons and stalls." Every few feet along the street a different display of winter crops lay in a cart, arranged on planks or on the ground: piles of new potatoes, purple turnips, plump rutabagas, green and red leafy chard, brilliant orange and emerald winter squashes. The air smelled of the earth, rich manure, and, more pleasantly, of pasties baking.

Farther ahead of the coach and the mounted guard, a flatbed lorry loaded with sacks of flour straddled the road, unmoving, apparently blocked by something that kept it from negotiating the tight turn.

Lorne roused himself to lean out the opposite window.

"Bother," her mother fumed. "Brown promised we wouldn't be caught on the road at night. This will put us off schedule for our first overnight with the baron and baroness."

"It's all right," Lorne said, his voice soothing as he settled back into his seat and drew out a cigar. After a pointed glare from Victoria, he tucked his smoke away without lighting up. "They're working to move the thing out of the way. Once we're through the town, we'll have open country again. Nothing to worry about, ladies."

But with the caravan at a halt, townspeople began to crush forward in a human wave, peering into the carriages, eager for a glimpse of the royal family. As word spread, more people burst from doorways, pressing still closer. Two little girls ran up to the queen's carriage and tossed a nosegay through the window.

"Oh!" Bea cried, waking up when the posies landed in her lap. She smiled sleepily. "Pretty."

Another woman lofted a hand-worked doily through the window. "We love you. God save the queen!" she cried.

Victoria looked down at the little scrap of ecru tatting on the floor of her carriage. "I suppose they mean well," she murmured. "But these people make me so nervous."

"It's all right, Mama," Louise comforted her. Her mother sometimes behaved as if commoners belonged to another species. One that frightened her but she felt compelled, on occasion, to appear before.

Brown climbed down from the top of the carriage to curse the lorry driver and order him out of their way. Stephen Byrne leaned down from his horse to instruct their two footmen and closest guardsmen to ease the queen's admirers back a few paces.

Preoccupied with her own thoughts, Louise took in only a hazy view of all that was going on outside their carriage. There seemed little reason to be concerned as, sooner or later, they'd move on.

She didn't, at first, take notice of the young man who broke through the line of horse guards and rushed toward their carriage with something in his hand. *No doubt*, her subconscious whispered, *another token of respect*.

But when his arm thrust through the window nearest her mother, Louise could see that neither flowers nor anything else equally harmless rested in his hand. The object was solid, metallic, dark in color—with a short, mean muzzle.

A pistol!

Louise felt a physical jolt, first of disbelief then shock as she stared at the narrow, beardless face. Now only inches away from hers.

The man's eyes, wild with intent, searched the passengers' faces for only a moment before fixing on the eldest female in the carriage in black mourning garb. Momentarily frozen in time, Louise watched in horror as the young man's arm swung to the left, pistol with it, to stop and point at her mother's face.

Instinct took over, setting Louise's body in motion. She thrust her sister aside and into Lorne's chest. It wasn't, then, so much a voluntary act as imagining herself transported to the space between the evil weapon and Victoria. Leaning across the gap between the two bench seats, Louise swung her arm as hard as she could at the rough wool coat sleeve stretched out in front of her, hoping to knock the gun from his grip.

Unfortunately, before Louise could connect with either arm or weapon, or even before she could push her mother out of harm's way, she felt herself pitching forward. A brilliant, bluish white flash issued from the gun's muzzle. She smelled a metallic tang in the air. Heard the explosion. And at the same awful moment realized she'd put her chest directly between the gun and Victoria. A blaze of heat from the ignition of powder struck the base of her throat and flew up the left side of her face.

It was as if time sped up a thousandfold—everything happening at once: men shouted from outside the carriage. Screams echoed from inside—her sister's, her mother's. Lorne yelled, "Assassin! Assassin!" Her two brothers threw themselves out the far door and into the street.

"She's shot! My daughter," Victoria screamed. "Lord, help us."

Louise realized she was actually grasping the man's gun, though it remained still in his grip. The hot metal seared through her glove into her tender palm. The astringent smell of burnt powder stung her nostrils. Her chest cramped with fear. Knowing she must be hit, but not daring to look down at her body, she assumed shock was probably blocking the pain but that it would soon be overcome by the severity of her wound.

Outside, someone snatched the man. She lost her grip on his sleeve and tumbled down onto the carriage floor—dazed, confused, unable to breathe.

Behind her, she heard Brown ordering the others out of the carriage. Sobbing and wailing, the queen and Beatrice fled through the far door, their skirts dragging across Louise's face as she gasped for air, instinctively searching with her gloved fingers for the flow-

ing wound. She must compress her hands over it, slow the bleeding until help arrived.

Why, she wondered, was time moving so damn slowly now
when it had been like lightning moments before?

Then the door at her feet flew open. Byrne crawled in on hands
and knees between the two seats and, quite literally, on top of
her. He stayed low, holding his weight off of her but hovering
inches above—as if to shield her while he examined her, head to
foot.

His bright, black eyes fixed on her bodice. She followed them,
taking a quick breath for courage. Her cashmere cloak had come
open, and the lace ruffles over the bodice of her saffron traveling
gown were blackened with powder burns. Byrne didn't hesitate.
His fingers tore into the delicate scorched fabric, opening layers all
at once, straight through to her skin.

"Sir!" she cried.

"Hush," he ordered. She did as told but closed her eyes against
the indignity of his inspection. "Are you hurt?"

"Of course I'm hurt. I've been shot, and you're kneeling on top
of me, you bloody ox!"

From outside the carriage she heard a terrible commotion.
Someone, her assailant most likely, blathering incoherently about
the injustice of the monarchy and the queen's Imperial hold over
India.

Brown appeared at the carriage door beyond her feet. "Blanks,"
he growled at the American. "That's all. Just blanks in his gun.
Bloody student protestor was—Good God, man!—what are ye
doin' to Her Royal Highness?"

Louise caught an irritated look from Byrne and a roll of his eyes.
"How else am I to see through all these infernal layers of clothing
and under things and—" He snatched a carriage robe that had laid
across Lorne's lap as they rode and covered her. Easing himself up

off of Louise, he helped her to sit up then rise onto the carriage seat.

"Then I'm not shot?" she asked, only then reality sinking in.

"Apparently not, Princess," Byrne said. "Your attacker was trying to make a point but not with bullets. Still, the powder burns have ruined your dress."

"Even if they hadn't, you've certainly finished the job," she said ruefully, peeking beneath the shielding blanket at shredded layers of lace and fine muslin.

Brown looked relieved. "No one hurt then. All right." He wiped the back of his hand across his barn door of a brow, dripping with sweat. "What say, Mr. Byrne, we take precautions? Change our route, just in case another loony has a wee surprise in mind."

"Agreed. Local roads all the way, the more circuitous the better." Byrne's eyes hadn't left Louise's. They were darker than dark, solemn as Judgment Day, brimming with closed thoughts. They made her shiver. "Give me a moment to tidy up here, Mr. Brown, before the party re-boards. Have one of the princess's ladies bring her a fresh gown and shawl."

"Will do, lad." And the Scot was off again, bawling out orders for a change of horses in the next town, an altered route, and a faster pace with fewer stops along the way.

Louise sat very still, trying to catch her breath. Her knees burned where they'd struck the hard coach floor. Other than that she felt no pain. Stephen Byrne sat down on the bench across from her, his long legs eating up the space between them. He stared at her in a way that reduced the panic and terror of minutes earlier to a gray shadow, but made her uneasy and mindful of her disastrous appearance.

"You're being rude," she said, "looking at me that way. Leave me to rearrange myself."

He didn't move. "Why?" he said.

"Why? Isn't it obvious? So that I may restore my appearance in privacy." She smoothed her skirts, happily in much better shape than her bodice.

But the dress as a whole had well and good been ruined, if not by powder burns then—as she'd already accused him—by his big hands. His big, strong hands that had touched her flesh and left it feeling pleasantly, if disturbingly, warm. She dared not meet his eyes. Dared not let a hint of cordiality into her voice or he'd know that she was feeling things she shouldn't be feeling.

"No," he said. "It's not that. I want to know why you intentionally sacrificed yourself. You put your body between a gunman's weapon and the queen."

"You think I was being patriotic?" She laughed. Did she sound a little hysterical? "She's *my mother.*"

"Of course. But you didn't know there were blanks in his pistol."

"No, I didn't. And I wasn't trying to make a martyr of myself. Or take a bullet for her. I was attempting to smack his arm out of the way, dislodge the gun. But I lost my balance and fell into his gun's path as a result of my haste. It was quite clumsy of me."

She felt more embarrassed than anything, what with the lingering sensations of his fingers plying open her bodice. And why was he staring at her so critically? The nerve of the man.

"That was one of the bravest acts I've ever witnessed," he said, his stone-cold-sober gaze holding her eyes, making it impossible for her to look away.

She didn't know what to say, but he gave her no time to say it. In the next second he was up and out of the carriage, making way for Lady Car who, with frightened eyes and tear-stained face, rushed in, carrying an armful of clothing.

Eight

"Off on her honeymoon, she is. Lucky gal," Amanda said. "Oh, Henry, I wish you'd been there."

"Been where?" Her husband's attention remained on his black medical bag. He carefully wrapped two more vials of amber liquid in gauze and packed them, with several white paper envelopes of powders, into it..

As a physician Henry Locock diagnosed illnesses and diseases and dispensed medications but left broken bones and other injuries to the lowly surgeons. Because surgery required work with the hands, its practitioners were afforded less prestige. The theory being that manual labor of any sort was ungentlemanly—a notion that she thought laughable.

As the wife of a physician, if Amanda wished she could be presented in court, whereas the spouse of a surgeon or pharmacist could not. But the intrigues and formalities of Victoria's court held little interest for Amanda. She only cared for their effects, good or ill, on her dearest friend, the Princess Louise . . . and for the chances she sometimes got, as Louise's guest, to hear the exquisite music of great composers and musicians of the day.

"Been where? Why, at the wedding concert, my love. Weren't

you listening to me? The music, it was like nothing I've ever heard." She came up behind Henry and hugged him around the waist, lying her cheek against his shoulder blade. "It was so very beautiful, the Great Hall all hung with garlands of flowers, and more violins, harps, and trumpets than Eddie could count on his little fingers."

"I always say, more musicians than you can count on your fingers is far too many."

She laughed at him. "You never said such a thing."

Henry Locock turned to face her, his eyes twinkling with mischief, and captured his wife in his long arms. He towered over her petite figure by two heads and was a good deal thinner around than she, even when she wasn't pregnant, but she felt there could be no more perfect match for her.

"How do you know what I say when I'm away from you?" he teased. "Do you know me that well?" He kissed her on the mouth, and she let her lips linger on his. This was more happiness than she believed she deserved.

"You are an ongoing mystery to me, sir. But I am learning a little more each day. I doubt that caring for your patients has given you time to even think about royal orchestras and such."

He smiled down at her. "So true." He gently freed himself from her embrace. "And now, I must be off. I have more calls to make than will fit in one day. Yet I must make every one or we lose patients."

"If you had fewer, you'd have more time to spend at home with your wife. We might have succeeded all the sooner at making a brother or sister for Eddie."

"It's hardly work, with you, my dear." He bussed her affectionately on the cheek. "I promise, we'll send the little bugger off to bed early tonight and spend some time together, alone. Shall we?"

Amanda let out a little squeal of delight, which attracted the attention of her son, sitting on the floor amid an assortment of pots and spoons, whacking out discordant music and singing gleefully as though to drown out his parents' chatter.

"It's all right, darling," she reassured her son as she patted her husband's backside on his way out the door. "Mummy's just happy."

Eddie shrugged and banged away.

"Oh, that's a good merry tune it is," she told him. "Just a few more minutes, though. Then we need to be off to the shop."

Amanda had been working at the Women's Work Society since Louise opened it a few years earlier. The consignment shop was already a grand success. Its purpose was to provide women without means of support a place to sell their crafts and handwork. Amanda would have gladly worked there for nothing—just to help those who were now in the same desperate situation she'd once found herself.

Thankfully, she had a husband to provide for her, but she still enjoyed the satisfaction of earning a small income to benefit her little family. Despite Louise's generosity, which had helped Henry set up his practice, and the money he earned from his patients, they would be eating less well without the salary Louise pressed upon her.

While Eddie finished his concert, Amanda sat down at her kitchen table with a cup of hot Darjeeling tea and recalled times past, just to remind herself of the blessings she'd been given. She recalled, with crystal clarity, that first day when she met Louise at the art school . . .

Amanda had been down on her knees, scrubbing the stone steps that led up from the street to the door of the National Art Training School in Kensington. She slopped soapy water from her wooden bucket onto the sooty slabs. Her chapped fingers clamped down on the boar bristle brush, and she scrubbed until her arms and shoulders ached.

The carriage must have come and gone without her noticing. When she looked up at the sound of a soft cough, Louise was standing there, watching her with those too-perceptive hydrangea blue eyes of hers and that proud tilt of chin. There had been no doubt in Amanda's mind who this young woman was. Hadn't everyone in London seen scores of pictures of the royal family in London newspapers, on postcards, and in souvenir shops?

But if a person was already down on the ground, a curtsy seemed pointless and not a little awkward. And so, Amanda sat back on her heels and looked up at the princess, waiting for her to pass so she could get on with her work.

Louise didn't move. She stood at the foot of the steps, observing Amanda. Stood in her pretty, pearl gray walking dress, matching gloves, fringed silk shawl, doeskin slippers, and mandarin-style rose-topped hat with its long white satin ribbon streamers falling down her back.

Irritation blossomed in Amanda's breast. The nerve of the girl. Watching her labor, in her lye-soaked skirts, with her raw hands and throbbing knees. Watching her as if she were an ox plowing a field.

Before she could stop them, words spurted from her lips, "Never seen steps washed down afore, missy?" Not *Your Royal Highness* as was proper but *missy*, of all things.

But Louise didn't seem offended. Only a slightly elevated brow indicated she'd even noticed the impropriety. "I was unsure whether I can climb the wet steps without making the job worse for you," she said. "I'm sure to drag in more dirt from the street."

Amanda was touched and more than a little surprised by her consideration. "I expect they'll be more behind you traipsin' up to that door. Don't matter to me. I'll be scrubbin' 'em again tomorrow."

"Yes, I suppose you will be," the princess said, sounding thoughtful. She placed a delicate foot on the first step then stopped and looked down at Amanda again. "By the way, I know how hard that is. I've done it myself."

Now Amanda knew she was having fun at her expense. "Ha! Likely I'll believe that, Princess. The day I see one of your family down on their hands and knees with a bucket of dirty water is the day I know I've passed on to the next life."

Louise propped her hands on her hips and scowled down at her. "You think I'd lie about a thing like that? I'm serious." She tapped her toe impatiently. "The baron, who was put in charge of our education—he thought it a fine educational experience for us to spend a summer learning how a house is kept. We each received tasks. Scrubbing the floors, washing the windows, baking bread, sweeping the porch, doing laundry, and—"

"You did this for a whole summer?" Amanda interrupted. She still wasn't sure she should believe the princess.

"For *five* whole weeks. Then we were obliged to return to our studies."

Amanda nodded her head. "Five weeks for some, a lifetime for others."

Louise gazed down at her as if she were fast becoming bored with the conversation. "The baron told us, 'It is your lot in life to prepare to rule nations. Others' lots are to keep nations clean.'"

Amanda laughed wickedly. "I'll bet he never in his life got down on *his* knees for anythin' . . . but to please a lady."

Louise frowned at her, as if she didn't understand. Amanda thought it best to just let it go. She'd hoped to shock the princess, but if the girl was so innocent the ribald joke went over her head, well, why bother . . .

"Anyway," Louise continued, stepping over the tread where Amanda's brush had returned to work, "those weeks made me understand how doing something with one's hands could bring satisfaction. That was when I first tried to sculpt. Since then, art is all I've cared about."

Savin' my skin from Roger Darvey is all I care about, Amanda thought. Only a month had passed since, in her desperation, she'd eluded the bawd and begged a job as a maid of all work at the school. Since then, she at least had a bed in the attic she didn't have to share with the men Darvey sent. And regular meals, without squirming maggots.

Amanda felt Louise's gaze again and looked up to see she'd climbed to the top step and was about to let herself in through the front door of the school.

"Your Highness?"

"Yes?"

"How is it the queen lets you come here on your own when she don't even let any of her court mix with commoners?"

Louise flashed her a radiant smile. "I tell her I speak to no one."

"Go on!"

"I do. And I bribe my driver to leave me here and go off for the day to his daughter's house."

Amanda giggled. "They say you's the wild one of the family. I guess it's true."

Louise looked pleased with her reputation, but she still hesitated before going inside. "Would you be offended if I asked to sketch you someday?"

"Me? An artist's model?" Amanda swiped at her cheek, where she'd just splashed sludgy water. The thought pleased her. "You goin' to dress me up in a fine lady's gown?"

"No. I'd like to sketch you as you are now, at your work."

Amanda frowned and went back to her scrubbing with a fury. The princess was making fun of her. It would be an ugly painting, made for posh friends of the queen to laugh at.

But Louise seemed to read her mind. "Please, don't be hurt. I want to show how women struggle to support themselves and their families. Women in the real world. I hope to have a special place one day where only women may display their art and things they make with their hands. Drawings of women at work would be perfect for the walls. Please?"

Amanda shrugged. Even when the princess said it like that, so important like, it still sounded silly to her. "If you like, Your Highness."

"What's your name?"

"Amanda."

"Thank you, Amanda. I hope to chat with you again sometime soon."

Then Princess Louise breezed through the door to the school, and Amanda went back to digging every little bit of grit out of the granite with the bristles of her brush, her hands burning with the lye, her eyes running from the fumes. And it didn't for one minute occur to her that this conversation might be the beginning of a friendship with the power to alter her life.

Nine

The Balmoral of Louise's childhood had been neither more nor less beautiful than it was now. The early spring had teased life out of the budding hawthorns, chased away the snow, called back the larks—and yet the air still chilled her to the bone. She breathed out, and a frosty cloud puffed in front of her face before drifting away. Her fingers felt numb. Her toes, though encased in good Scottish wool stockings, stung with the cold, and her face stiffened until either smiling or frowning required a concerted effort.

Louise trudged on through the prickly gorse, up the hill smelling of sweet heather, and away from the castle her parents had built the year she turned three. It was the fairy-tale castle of her youth, complete with clock tower, turrets, woodlands, gardens, baronial outer buildings, and unlimited, deliciously clean air to breathe.

But even here, Louise could not escape her despair. Her chest felt as tight as a clenched fist, and the tears she'd fought off for days finally came, freezing on her cheeks before they could drop off. Ever since they'd arrived in Scotland, her head had hurt, her eyes burned. Now that she'd let herself start crying, she couldn't seem to stop. Less than two weeks had passed since her wedding day, but the long hours had been the loneliest of her life. This could not go on. It simply couldn't. She must somehow clear her head enough to think about her future.

If only Amanda were here. She longed to confide in her, to ask her advice. After walking on a good deal farther, she decided that she must write to her. Immediately. And hope she would have some wisdom to share.

Louise found a fallen tree, warmed by the sun, sat on the smooth trunk, and took out the sketch pad and pencil she always carried with her on her hikes about the countryside. As stationery, the plain white paper lacked the prestige of her usual creamy vellum with its royal crest, but she knew Amanda wouldn't care. She began:

Amanda dear,

You asked that I write, probably believing I'd find little time, so preoccupied would I be with my new husband. I fear this is far from the reality of my situation. I shall make short work of describing what transpired on my wedding night, as even now it is painful to think of.

Lorne is not the man I believed him to be. To be blunt: his passions are directed in every way toward his own sex. He has no interest in me, in any woman, or in performing his duty as a husband. I am trying not to be bitter, but this is a terribly difficult pill to swallow. At the moment, I am trying to determine the wisest course of action. It is my hope that you will be able to help me puzzle through this dilemma. Here are my choices, as I see them now:

First, I might divorce Lorne and hope to find a mate better suited to my own passions and character. But I would need to offer specific reasons for wishing to dissolve the marriage. To state the truth would destroy the marquess. He might well be sent to prison—which is his worst fear, and I would not wish it on him. I've confided in Bertie, and he told me they put men of Lorne's persuasion to hard labor, force them to sleep in damp, crowded cells with no heat, no mattress or blanket for warmth, and give them too little food to restore their strength. I imagine the harassment of the guards is most dreadful. Under such conditions, even a short term of a few years might ruin a man's health. It is just a matter of time before a prisoner succumbs to consumption. A delicate soul like Lorne would likely wither all the more rapidly.

My second option is to maintain our charade, stay married to Lorne and pretend happiness. In time, I may convince myself that I am content with my lot. That would please Mama and silence London gossips. If I bury myself in my work for the poor and in my art, I may yet build for myself a fulfilling life. Do you remember my speaking of someday carving a life-size statue of Father to honor his memory? I still have so much to learn before attempting such a challenging project. But, married to Lorne, with no obligations or restraints made upon my time by pregnancy and children, I will be free to follow my muse, and dedicate myself to service to the poor. Shouldn't that make me happy?

Children, though. That is what I shall miss, perhaps even more than a man's affections. How I'd wanted a bevy of them. A squealing, kissing, hugging, drooling flock of little ones. Oh, Amanda my dear, what will I do about that? Lorne will never give them to me. Do you think I'm capable of sleeping with another man simply to induce pregnancy? I might keep my children's fatherhood a secret. Demand that Lorne claim my babies as his, thereby cloaking them in legitimacy.

Well, I guess I've miscounted, because that's actually

a third option—keeping a lover on the side for pleasure and baby making. A stud as it were, no different than the stallions in Windsor's stables. But the risk of being found out is appalling. The scandal would destroy the family. And Mama—well, she would be frantic about the royal lineage. Even bastard children may lay claim to the crown under the right circumstances.

I just feel so very confused, and hurt, and desperately in need of your advice. The idea of taking a companion lover, for the sake of assuaging my loneliness and satisfying the lust I feel when a strong man looks my way—well, that seems utterly distasteful and unappealing. I would feel as though I were giving in to the basest of animal instincts if I didn't love the man I took to my bed. And what if he didn't love me—even a little? How sad that would be.

Anyway, I know few men with whom I'd even want to be intimate.

Louise hesitated, her sketching pencil poised above the page. Dare she continue? She'd never been able to reveal such intimate feelings to her own sisters. But then, hadn't she and Amanda already shared the bond of a secret even more shocking than Lorne's?

Drawing a breath for strength, Louise set to completing her letter . . .

I can imagine you chiding me now, reminding me that, some time ago, one man was quite capable of winning my heart, soul, and body—and therefore it stands to reason there will be others. But I would argue this isn't necessarily how life works. Sweet, blithe-spirited Donovan of my innocent youth was quite unique. I don't know that another man could make my heart, or body, sing as he did. If we two ever were reunited by chance or design, I might again fly into his arms and be his—ignoring my mother's, and possibly your, warnings.

Who can say why he left me and where he went? I've struggled these many years to answer those questions. Perhaps he loved me so deeply he left to save me worse heartache—knowing we could never marry. I suppose any number of other explanations are possible. He might have been attacked in an alley and terribly injured, or even killed. Then again, he might still be alive, wishing we could be together. If there were any way of discovering the truth . . .

But more to the point, I must look to my own future. Have you any thoughts at all on this most troubling marriage of mine? Give them to me, Amanda, please do. I need your clever mind and down-to-earth views on life to help me through this most painful predicament of mine.

Write soon, dear friend. Ever faithfully yours,
Louise

Louise closed her sketch pad. She'd post the letter tomorrow and pray that Amanda would have a solution to her problem . . . though she had little real hope.

She walked faster, drying her tears, using her riding crop to whack away at brush that had started closing over her favorite path leading away from the castle and toward the town. The farther she walked, the more determined she became to seize control of her life, to make something of it and not wallow in self-pity. Her mother, her husband, the court—she refused to let them determine her happiness, or lack of it.

"Where do you think you're going?"

Louise gasped and spun around, crop raised in front of her as a weapon against the intruder with the deep voice. Stephen Byrne stood not twenty feet behind her on the path. Yet she hadn't heard as much as a single snap of a branch to announce his approach.

"I require no one's permission to take exercise," she said, sounding far too defensive to her own ears.

"Don't be stupid."

"I beg your pardon!" She glared at the man, standing there in judgment of her. Here was a common hired hand—when it came right down to it, that's what he was—not even a subject of the queen. A foreigner. And he was insulting her and attempting to order her about?

After delivering the royal party to Balmoral, Byrne had disappeared for a full forty-eight hours. She knew because she'd watched for him. Well, didn't she need to discuss something important with him? So she'd asked several of the staff if they knew where she could find him, since the maids would have had to make up a room for him. They said they didn't believe he'd stayed even one night at the castle. She expected he'd gone off on another mission for her mother, or returned to London to report to his superiors. But here he was now, hunting her down as if she were a hound that had wandered from the kennel.

"Did you just call me stupid, sir?"

He winced. "You're an intelligent woman," he said, as if this were a rare thing in his experience. "What happened the other day on your way north is not an isolated incident. You're putting yourself at risk walking out alone like this."

She laughed. "He was a *college boy*, drunk and politically confused. Acting on impulse and his own fantasies, John Brown says. Not part of any nefarious plot."

Byrne stepped closer. She eyed him warily, took a step back. Only three men had ever touched her in an intimate manner. Donovan, her mother's physician, and . . . *him*. After all, if being pinned to the floor of a coach by a man's hard body as he manhandled her wasn't intimate, what was? At that shocking moment she'd barely been aware of the existence of clothing between them.

"As it happens, that's all true," Byrne said. "The boy had no intent to murder. But had he not interrupted the journey and prompted us to change our route, I fear a great deal worse might have occurred."

She raised her eyes to the pink-gray dawn sky, seeking patience, then turned away to continue her walk. The man obviously loved the drama of his job. Or else he was insane. She simply couldn't communicate with him.

Byrne strode up beside her, nearly nudging her off the narrow path with his wide shoulders. "Listen to me, please, Your Highness."

"You have a vivid imagination, Mr. Byrne. I fear listening to you would make me scared of my own shadow."

He drew something from his coat pocket. "This isn't imaginary."

She looked down. The thing resting in his bare hand looked like a dirty little piece of twine, nearly invisible against the deep grooves on his calloused palm. She said, "I have no idea what you're going on about or what that object might be."

"It's a fuse," he said.

Something colder than the frost clinging to the dead twigs underfoot closed around her heart. She stopped walking. "As in part of a bomb?"

"Precisely."

"And you found this here on the castle grounds?"

"No. It was on the Edinburgh road. Just north of Leicester, where we were stopped by the young idiot with the pistol."

It took her a moment, but she suddenly understood. "That was the way Brown originally had intended to bring us?"

"Yes." His eyes, she realized now, were not dark brown at all, as she had earlier supposed. They were as black as any she'd ever seen. As black as the night sky over Osborne House, where she'd spent long weeks searching the heavens and her soul.

"And you've reported this to Brown and the queen?"

"To Brown, yes. Whether he chooses to inform Her Majesty, I can't say."

She thought for a moment. "And it's your belief that this was part of an ambush, a bomb meant to blow up the entire party?" Because she couldn't imagine the Fenians being able to target just one person in an entourage as large as theirs.

Until recently, the explosions the radicals had set off were unpredictably destructive—taking out a wall here, the house of a minister there, or going off in an omnibus and killing dozens of innocent people. Only recently had the dynamiteers seemed to become terrifyingly efficient, blowing up an exterior wall of Parliament, as if to reveal the men inside as . . . what? As fools for arguing against freedom for Ireland?

"No," Byrne said, snapping her attention back to him, "not the whole wedding caravan." He was studying the bit of fuse, less than two inches long, rolling it between his fingers. "No, I think this was a trap meant to disrupt the journey, create panic, stop the carriages, and throw the guard into disarray."

"Stop us? From coming here to Balmoral? Why on earth—"

His eyes darkened with such suddenness and intensity that, when they lifted to meet hers, she felt compelled to close her lips and look away. Instead she fought the urge and held his gaze.

"This," he said, "was a trap set by experts, not by the usual Fenian volunteers."

"How do you know?" She shook her head, laughing. "You can't just toss about outrageous theories like this, Mr. Byrne."

"They aren't theories."

"No?" She crossed her arms over her chest in a then-prove-it stance.

"I've found other evidence. They knew exactly how much charge to lay and how to time it to cause the most confusion. It's my guess they weren't planning on murdering any of the royal family. If some of her guard was killed in the attack that would be fine. But deaths in the family would result in public outrage and possibly turn opinion more firmly against their cause. What they need is leverage with Parliament."

It dawned on her then, where he was going with this. "They intended to kidnap my mother?"

"Or you, Arthur, Leo, or Beatrice. I don't suppose it will matter so much who they snatch, as the purpose is likely to have in their possession any royal they can ransom in exchange for Irish separation."

Louise narrowed her eyes at him. How dare he speak of her family with such familiarity? Yet he seemed unaware of having breached court etiquette. She gave a sniff. "You don't know my mother. She would never agree to blackmail. She'd stand the firmer in her resolve to retain her hold on the Irish."

"You actually believe she'd sacrifice the life of one of her children for the good of the Empire?"

"I believe," Louise said, unable to block past ugliness from her mind, "my mother would do anything in her power to get her own way. I sometimes think she imagines her personal desires as identical to 'the good of the Empire.'" She swiveled on her heel and started walking again, this time back toward the castle. Suddenly, the bracing morning air and solitude of the wild hills held less appeal. Who knew what or who might lurk in these woods? Maybe the American was right to urge caution.

Byrne fell into step beside her again.

They hiked the path side by side for several minutes in silence. She was about to tell him he needn't accompany her all the way back to the garden gate when it occurred to her that maybe she *did* want him here. If the Fenians had become so bold as to plan an attack in broad daylight on the queen's caravan, why should they not lurk outside the walls of one of the family estates to pick off an unsuspecting prince or princess?

"Where are you from, Mr. Byrne?" she asked, not so much curious as disliking his silence and wary of what he might be thinking.
She hoped to God it had nothing to do with what she'd looked like
with her dress bodice torn half off her.

"Texas. San Angelo, a little cattle town in the western part of
the state."

"Therefore your intriguing garb?" She raised an eyebrow.

He smiled and touched the brim of his hat. "It's practical,
ma'am."

They walked on, and she thought about him and all she didn't
know about the man. "You don't sound like an uneducated man,
Mr. Byrne."

"They do have schools in Texas."

She ignored his making fun of her. "Is that where you studied?"

"No. My mother was from out east. I attended college back
where she grew up, in Connecticut. I'd be in New Haven or there-
abouts still if it hadn't been for the war."

"America's War between the States?"

"Yes."

"You fought for the North?"

"In a manner of speaking."

She waited for him to say more. When he didn't she couldn't
help prodding. "I assume that means you weren't a traditional soldier?"

"I was under assignment directly to Mr. Lincoln." The shadow
of a smile disappeared from his lips. His chipped-granite expression warned her to tread carefully. Something about the conversation had rubbed him the wrong way.

"Your president's assassination was most terrible," she said. "My
mother was so shocked and troubled by it, she wrote a long letter
of condolence to Mrs. Lincoln . . . then doubled the guardsmen
kept at the royal residence."

"Booth was a coward and a snake," Byrne said. "To shoot a man, any unarmed man, from the back and without a single word of warning, with his wife sitting right there beside—"

Louise jerked to a stop and turned to stare at her mother's agent, aghast. "You make it sound as if you were *there* that night."

For a long while he didn't answer. His gaze slipped away from hers and flitted about the gorse, never staying long on one spot.

"Yes." The word seemed to rise from the depths of his soul and poison the air around them with his bitterness. "Had I been in the gallery behind the president, I'd have stopped Booth. Instead, I heard the shot from the hallway below."

"Oh dear," she murmured and touched his sleeve in sympathy.

He didn't seem to feel it, and she quickly withdrew her hand. "I wasn't technically on duty that night. But I should have . . . should have—" He shook his head. His eyes clouded with sadness.

There was nothing she could say. Her hand moved toward his arm again, but she pulled it back with the same caution as when approaching a hot stove. "You were Mr. Lincoln's bodyguard?"

"Not officially. I worked undercover for the Union during the war, a spy if you will. The information I gathered always went directly to Mr. Lincoln. After the war, as a civilian, I asked to be put on assignment in Washington, to continue on the president's security detail, but I was told he needed no one else."

"And your knowledge of bombs?"

"Part of my job was to track Confederate soldiers intent on blowing up bridges, ammunition dumps, supply lines, and other things critical to the North's winning the war. Sometimes when I found a bomb, there wasn't time to summon the men trained to disarm them. I had no choice but to do it myself, or else trigger the thing to save lives but sacrifice a vital road or bridge."

"So you learned by trial and error." It seemed to her a dangerous way to train.

"Most of the devices were pretty simple." He shrugged and started walking again, watching the ground as his boots crunched over the frost heaves and dead leaves. She followed along, matching his strides. "They were either meant to be set off by hand and thrown, or planted and triggered by pressure. Sometimes a mechanical trip wire was used to strike a flint and light the fuse after the dynamiteers were well clear. During that time, I discovered a few soldiers from the South who were particularly creative. Their work was nearly undetectable, and the materials they used were always the same."

He held up the twine then produced—as if he were a magician performing a sleight-of-hand trick—a sliver of gray stone.

"Flint?" she guessed.

"Good Louisiana flint. So far as I know, there's none like it in all of England." He looked at her, his meaning clear. She felt incapable of speech her throat had tightened so. He continued. "I believe the Fenians have recently recruited two of the best black powder men in America. I doubt that dodging their trap just once will put them off their game."

Ten

Having done all he could by the end of the day to make certain the royals in residence at Balmoral were safe, Stephen Byrne took himself off for a strenuous ponder. The locations best suited to problem solving were, in his estimation, working men's pubs. Having obtained a stool at the end of the centuries-old oak bar in The Wooden Ox, not far down the road from the castle, he asked for a good dark stout and set to work on both it and his thoughts.

If he'd thought it necessary to station himself outside Louise's door and watch over her the night long to keep her safe, he would have. But Brown had the place locked up tighter than the Tower of London, his own men stationed at every entrance plus reinforcements ordered up from Aberdeen to patrol and post as sentries. So there seemed little need for him to lose sleep in a drafty hallway. How the princess had slipped past the guards that morning was beyond him. He imagined she'd spent a good part of her youth at Balmoral, and like as not, she and her siblings had discovered secret passageways they'd used in their play. He'd have to alert Brown to that possibility.

Aside from his confidence in the Scot's security measures, Byrne had another excuse for staying away from the castle. He expected the marquess would be paying a visit to his wife's bedroom, if only as a matter of form and to calm any untoward gossip among the court. But perhaps Lorne would attempt to perform his husbandly duty.

Byrne didn't like to think of the dandy, or any other man, touching Louise. Lurid images flashed through his mind, leaving him feeling raw.

Who could really say what went on between the couple? If anything at all. He'd seen them in the carriage during the trip north, sitting apart, never reaching out for each other, never holding hands or touching surreptitiously when others weren't watching as newlyweds always do. The younger princess wedged between them seemed to serve as a mutually agreed upon barrier.

Maybe Louise was just angry with her husband over a disagreement they'd had, and she was making her point by temporarily withdrawing her affection. Despite Lorne's attraction to partners of his own sex, he might still have relations with his wife. It wasn't unheard of for a man who favored other men's company to be capable of servicing a woman. The warmth they'd displayed at the wedding seemed real enough. It was only after their wedding night that a chill seemed to descend over them.

To Byrne's thinking, this was the very opposite of what should have been. Affection for a mate naturally grew with time.

A thought struck him then, and he chuckled. Might it be the marquess had attempted to fulfill his obligations in bed but failed to perform satisfactorily for the lady? If *he*, Byrne, entertained the princess in *his* bed, he'd be damned if she left it without rosy blooms in her cheeks and stars in her eyes.

Then another possibility came to him. Perhaps the man had demanded acts from her that had shocked her. Offended her. Hurt her.

The bastard.

Byrne's hand tightened on his glass. He had to make an effort to loosen his grip before it shattered under the pressure. *No use speculating*, he told himself. Whether or not Louise was married, whether or not she was happy or miserable—the woman was beyond his reach in every imaginable way. He might as well have designs on the famous Lillie Langtry or the queen herself—though that last thought was a singularly unappealing one. Whatever life held for Louise was none of his concern and beyond his control. There was little sense in working himself into a lather over it.

Byrne looked around the pub he'd chosen. When he'd first entered The Ox he sensed a ripple of nervousness, stifled conversation. He was a stranger in these parts. The farm boys and town's merchants took their time checking him out. But he hadn't come here to make friends and didn't want to encourage anyone to approach him. He cast a steely glare around the room before dropping his gaze into his foamy ale, signaling his lack of interest in friendly banter. He couldn't think while he was talking or listening to tall tales and local gossip. What he most needed to do tonight was try and figure out Rupert Clark's next move.

He had no doubt that it was Clark the Fenians had brought over from America. Clark with his brilliant red hair and missing fingers. He'd never met the man in person but had seen a photograph of him, standing in the front row in his uniform with his Confederate unit.

The black powder man's face was unremarkable—square jawed, clean shaven, pockmarked from childhood illness like many, his eyes dulled with sadness. In the photograph his hair color was impossible to tell, but he'd heard a description of the man from a prostitute who'd slept with him, a Union sympathizer. In the picture, Clark held the barrel of a rifle in his injured hand, showing only the thumb and index finger, the other three having been blown away. He could have hidden the maimed hand behind his back, but it appeared to Byrne that he was intentionally displaying his loss. As if the hand was his badge of courage.

Byrne knew the man's work only too well. He'd seen the deadly results. There was nothing more horrifying than what dynamite could do to a human body—the damage far more grisly than bayonet, gunshot, or even cannon wounds.

On the Edinburgh road, where he'd found the telltales of Clark's presence, he'd learned the master dynamiteer had an assistant. That was probably the only reason he'd found any evidence at all. It had been the other man's job to clean up before they retreated. Evidently, whoever he was, he wasn't as careful or as experienced as Clark.

There was another reason, one he hadn't mentioned to Louise, for his being sure that a trap had been laid to enable the Fenians to snatch, rather than murder, a member of the royal family. He'd discovered broken brush on the hillside above the road, signs of horses and riders. Twenty or more, he guessed. A small army of men had been lying in wait for the caravan. With the distraction of the explosions, and orders to grab just one member of the royal family they'd already selected, their odds for success were fairly high.

So now, Byrne wondered, *would they try again?*

Absolutely.

Right away, or later? And where? Those were the more difficult questions.

His head hurt from trying to puzzle it out. If he guessed wrong, missed a vital clue, the results might be catastrophic. The only advantage he had was that the Fenians didn't yet know that he knew their intentions. They would assume they still held the trump card—the element of surprise.

He called for another pint from the bartender, drank it down a little more slowly than the first. But before he could come to any theory worth trusting, he became aware of another stall in the conversation throughout the dim, smoke-filled pub. Another stranger had arrived.

Byrne kept his head down at the same angle, eyes fixed on his brew. He sensed motion coming toward him, tensed. But the newcomer passed on. Byrne kept his body and head still but shifted the angle of his gaze to follow the retreating figure.

Blond waves curled down the back of the man's neck. The fine fabric of his evening frock coat, light-colored waistcoat, and noble posture left no doubt in his mind who it was. The Marquess of Lorne had come alone, probably without Brown's or anyone else's knowledge except for the guard he must have bribed to let him pass. He'd bet the best horse in the queen's stable that Louise hadn't shared her secret means of escape with her husband. After all, here it was their honeymoon, and he was sneaking off for a sociable drink with his mates? More likely, come to prowl, Byrne speculated.

There were no women here. Only farm boys, townsmen and tradesmen, maybe a traveler or two. Lorne seemed familiar with the place. Byrne remembered that Balmoral, and therefore The Ox, wasn't far from the Campbell family's estate. Perhaps this pub was already a favorite haunt?

Lorne didn't take long to strike up a conversation with a young man at a table in the dark corner. The local boy finished his drink then left. Lorne stayed, waving off the barkeep's offer of another ale, drumming his fingertips on the tabletop. Biding his time. Then the marquess paid up and, with a casual air, walked out the door into the night.

Byrne sucked down a deep breath, argued with himself, stalled for another minute, then tossed his tab on the bar and followed out the door.

A full moon shone down on the village square and the few buildings surrounding it. The air smelled of clover, farmland dung, pine, and an oncoming frost. Byrne spotted Lorne standing a short ways off, hands in his pockets, looking at ease, as if he was simply enjoying the night air. At last he straightened, looked around, as if to get his bearings. The castle was off to the right. Lorne turned left.

Byrne gave him a head start then tailed him down the road, staying far enough back to remain cloaked by the darkness. After less than a quarter mile, Lorne stepped off the road and into a field of maize. He seemed to be heading toward a line of woods. Soon a light pricked out from among the trees, and the marquess adjusted his course toward it. Byrne stopped at the edge of the road and watched the lone figure continue across the moonlit field until he'd nearly reached the first trees. The light went out.

Byrne swore.

So the rumors and his guesses were true. He had no feelings one way or the other about another man's choice of bed partners. Let him poke where he pleased. Hell, what was the joke about lonely shepherds?

What set him to burning was the dishonor the man was doing his lovely wife. Had the marquess even consummated their marriage? What did he expect Louise to do for affection or even for simple sexual satisfaction? He didn't for a minute believe the commonly held belief that females of good family lacked sexual yearnings. In his experience, women of any and all ranks in society were equally passionate when with the right man.

A woman without a title might divorce her husband or, more likely, accept a series of lovers. But a princess didn't have the luxury of anonymity. Kings, princes, male nobility of lesser stature, were more or less expected to take mistresses. In some marriages contracted purely for the purpose of political alliance, the woman might even encourage her less-than-appealing husband to take to another woman's bed, rather than suffer his unwelcome attentions. But a queen or princess could not have a lover, or at least not admit to having one, without suffering dire consequences. In the not-so-distant past, queens had died for their indiscretions.

Byrne cast one final bleak look toward the shadowed line of woods then whipped around and marched back toward the public house. "None of your bloody concern," he reminded himself. "Leave him to it."

But after another two stouts on top of the ale, he still couldn't forget what he'd seen or dismiss what he knew. Anger swelled in him like a gouty foot.

Did Louise know? Of course she must. The woman was neither blind nor a fool. But the fact that her husband hadn't been able to control his sexual appetite for even one month after their wedding—Byrne just didn't understand that.

He hurt for her. He felt the insult as a dull, throbbing pain at the back of his skull.

But what could he do about it?

On loan to the Queen's Secret Service, he was expected to protect members of the royal family. Technically, that included Lorne, who hadn't yet reappeared at the pub or passed by on the road outside the window, where Byrne had stationed himself at a table, keeping an eye out. What if the marquess stayed away from the castle all night? What if this sneaking about became routine? If Lorne wasn't discreet, he'd cause both Louise and the queen great embarrassment. What with all this Irish trouble, perhaps he'd even get himself killed.

Byrne conversed with the dregs of his third stout, which had begun nagging him toward action. *No! I'll damn well not hike off into those woods to drag the fellow home by the scruff of his neck like a truant schoolboy.* On the other hand, sooner or later, he'd have to deal with this mess.

Despite all attempts to calm himself with yet another pint, he was still seething when the door to the pub swung open and the doorway blossomed into a tartan kilt wrapped around a powerful package of muscle. John Brown made his way to the bar in two strides the length of an omnibus, and held up a pair of thick fingers. The barkeep brought him his drinks and quickly retreated, as if taking cover at the first sign of a gale.

The man must have seen Brown drunk before.

Sensing it was the wrong thing to do, but unable to stop himself—emboldened as he was by his beverages—Byrne left his table. He wove his way over to the bar and slung a hip over the stool next to Brown's. The Scot seemed not at all surprised to see him. He nodded at the barkeep, who brought Byrne yet another foamy glass. Byrne's head was already swimming, but it was poor manners to turn down a man's gift.

"All quiet up on the hill?" Byrne asked.

"Quiet as can be." Brown drank deeply. "'Bout done in myself, what with these crazies pestering HRM. Any idea what they have in mind next?"

He didn't need to say who *they* was. The Fenians. "Not a clue. You?"

"Naw, laddie. Wish that I did." He ordered up another drink for himself.

Byrne declined a fifth . . . or was it a sixth? When he shook his head, it felt like it was sloshing with a brew of beer and worries. He knew he should keep his mouth shut. It had a habit of getting him into trouble. But he couldn't ignore what he'd just witnessed.

"I've been here drinking close to two hours," he murmured.

Brown released a soft humph of amusement. "Alone?"

Byrne nodded. "One of our friends from up the castle dropped by for a short while. Don't think he saw me."

The Scot scratched his beard and nodded his head. "Someone I should know 'bout?"

"Maybe you already do."

"Wouldn't be our bonnie bridegroom would it?" Brown offered him a quick glimpse of bearish yellow teeth, almost a snarl.

Byrne didn't bother to answer. "Does she know?" The words stuck in his throat. He felt the muscles of his neck and shoulders go rock hard. His jaw locked.

"The princess?" Brown drained his current pint, at the same time signaling the barkeep for another. "Expect she does. Victoria said she was sure Louise was aware of the company the man kept in the past. But I don't know. The princess discounts court gossip more often than believes it. This is one rumor she should have listened to."

"Such a beautiful woman," Byrne mumbled. "Ah, Louise, Louise . . ." He was feeling dizzier by the moment. The bottles arranged along the bar back blurred and swam before his burning eyes. Pretty shades of amber, ruby, crystalline clear and jade, they looked to him rather like a pretty image through a child's kaleidoscope.

Byrne heard himself talking, as if his voice came from another person across the room. As if he was just sitting there on his stool, listening to a stranger ramble on about whatever rattled through his brain, as blokes do when in their cups. It wasn't until he felt a shadow fall across him, blocking the light from the lamp over the bar, that he looked up to see Brown standing there, fists digging into hips, glowering down at him.

"Watch what you say, laddie," he growled, threat crowding his words.

"I'll say what I pleash," Byrne slurred, not entirely sure what he had said but feeling boozily determined to defend his opinions, whatever they might be.

All of a sudden, the anger and bitterness and frustration that had been building inside of him rose as an unbearable pressure in his chest. The thought that this very special woman had signed on for a lifetime of deception and unhappiness was too much for him to handle while in his sodden state. The indignity of her situation burned like a hot poker.

"All I said," he blurted, "was Louise is bea-oo-ti-ful." Or something along those lines. More or less.

Brown appeared to swell in size, his head moving toward the ceiling as he drew himself fully erect. "You said more'n that, you villain. It's blasphemous it is. Even thinkin' of putting yourself in that man's place in her bed—"

"I said that?" Byrne smiled. It was the first pleasing thought of the evening. "Well then, who's to say it's such a bad idea. Me and the princess—"

He never got to finish his sentence.

Brown's fist connected with Byrne's jaw, sending him flying off his stool, sprawling on the rough oak floorboards. Although he was nowhere near as large a man as John Brown, and that massive clot of knuckles had the power to shatter bones, Byrne's jaw survived intact. It happened to be one part of his anatomy, he'd learned from experience, that was as hard as Connecticut granite.

He glared up from the floor at the Scot. The room's spinning slowed then snapped into focus as the giant's blow produced a rapid sobering effect.

"I meant no offense to Her Royal Highness," Byrne said, pushing himself to his feet. "But, Mr. Brown, you and I both know it was bloody wrong, that match. I won't pretend otherwise."

The Scot's chest expanded as he pulled in a mighty breath that sounded like the wind foreshadowing a violent storm. "I'll not have you so much as lookin' at the lady. Hear me well, Raven. You mind your investigatin' and stay away from Victoria's family."

Byrne nearly laughed at the man's preposterous bullying but thought better of it. He also should have thought better of his next move. He poked a finger at the center button of the giant's shirtfront, emphasizing his words. "*It's—not—your—place* to give orders to a man in the queen's Secret Service."

Brown's fists kneaded at his sides. His eyes glowed, dangerous coals. "I says it is."

This time when the Scot lunged for him, Byrne was ready. He ducked then went in low and fast with a right fist to Brown's gut. Followed with a lightning fast left hook to the ridge of bone just under one eye.

Brown swung back at him, powerful as a steam locomotive. If the punch had connected with the intended side of his opponent's head, there was a good chance Byrne might not have stood up again. Ever.

Byrne dodged and ducked again. Fist and arm sizzled over his head.

The rest of the fight happened fast, as bar fights do, eating up no more than five minutes before it was over. But to Byrne's bleary memory, it was a beautiful battle: stools cracking over backs and shoulders, bottles exploding, knuckles smashing and oozing blood . . . until neither man was capable of lifting a hand through his exhaustion.

Only then did the barman climb out from behind his counter, club in hand, and chase them out the door into the night with a warning they'd be paying for the damages.

Eleven

Louise woke to a blinding streak of ochre sunlight slashing through her window that forced her to close her eyes again. She smelled the early blooming lilacs Lady Car had arranged in a vase beside her bed the day before, and the sundried linen beneath her cheek. Urgent-sounding footsteps raced lightly across her room. A cupboard door clicked open then snapped shut.

It occurred to Louise that a terrible emergency must have arisen during the night. But when she sat upright in bed and looked around, she saw that a silver tray had been set on her bedside table, and Car was pulling Louise's blue day dress from the wardrobe.

Louise lifted the domed lid on the sterling salver to find a generous serving of bacon rashers and thick slices of toasted oat bread. Pots of honey and dairy-fresh butter accompanied, making enough breakfast for three.

"What's happened to make you feel the need to fortify me so?"

Lady Car turned to her, concern mirrored in her gentle eyes as she flew back across the room with Louise's clothing. "Your Highness, I fear this morning may prove a bit more taxing than others."

"Oh, dear." Louise blinked, preparing herself for the worst. Another intruder? One of her siblings ill? Her mother . . . well, it could be anything if it had to do with her. "Details then. No sugarcoating."

"Yes, well . . ." Car set royal blue satin slippers to match Louise's dress on the floor beside the bed. "Her Majesty has sent word that you are to rise immediately and come to her as soon as you are dressed. It appears that a serious issue has presented itself. Her secretary would only say that the queen refuses to deal with it on her own." She shrugged her shoulders in apology. "I'm sorry, that's all I know."

Something her mother felt incapable of handling without her? Now she was just as curious as worried.

Louise tossed off the bedclothes, struggled out of her night shift, and made a hasty job of her toilet. While her lady laced her up Louise thrust a piece of bacon into her mouth, bit into the toast, and chewed. She sipped her tea, well sweetened with honey. She'd eaten spartanly since the attack on the coach, having lost her appetite for days after. The thought that, had there been a live bullet in the young protester's gun, she might not now be alive, had quite unsettled her.

Louise dusted the toast crumbs from her fingertips then waved off all attempts by Car to dress her hair. "No, no. Leave it loose. It will take too much time." Anyway, she much preferred to let her long brown tresses fall down her back. Though her mother wouldn't like it.

"I will go with you," Lady Car offered.

"No. It might be nothing." But if it was serious, she didn't want to expose the poor woman to unnecessary trauma. Best she face her mother alone.

When Louise arrived, breathless, at her mother's suite, she knocked once then opened the door and stepped inside.

Victoria was sitting primly behind her desk in a black mourning gown whose only noticeable difference from her others was a high starched white collar held together at the throat by a simple cameo pin. The queen's expression was stern, her eyes sparking anger, but it was not Louise's little dragon of a mother who captured her attention. Her gaze immediately shifted across the room to stop on the two men standing at attention in the middle of the crimson-and-gold Persian carpet under Victoria's steely gaze.

Louise clapped a hand over her mouth and gasped. John Brown and Stephen Byrne appeared to have freshly arrived from the front lines of a war.

The Scot and the Raven were a bruised, bloody, scraped, and scabby mess. Their shirts and trousers might have been torn from their bodies, run over by market carts in a filthy road, and restored to their use as garments without any attempt at laundering. And they smelled. Of various forms of alcohol, if she wasn't mistaken.

"What happened to you two?" Louise said. "Were you attacked? Are others hurt?"

Her mother lifted a small, plump hand. "My dear child, calm yourself. The injuries are of their own foolish doing. A common bar brawl, the two of them drinking themselves to irrationality. They deserve no sympathy."

"Oh, dear." Louise felt a bubble of relieved laughter working its way up and pressed her lips firmly together.

"It is my understanding, having already received a bill for the cost of damages, that this display was witnessed by at least a dozen men of the town." Victoria's face resembled a hot, red sun just before it sinks below the horizon. Her body seemed in such agitation it visibly vibrated. "By now the entire countryside will be discussing whatever personal business their drunken lips may have revealed during their scuffle. And by personal business, I mean *our family's* business." She narrowed her eyes at her daughter.

Louise no longer saw humor in the situation. Did this really have anything to do with her? Or, more likely, with Lorne. "Do you mean—"

"Neither of them admits to the exact conversation." The queen glared at one then the other of her men. "They claim to have no memory of the argument that started them fighting. But it is clear to *us* they were acting inappropriately and without concern for *our* subjects' respect." When her mother reverted to the "royal we," Louise knew she was indeed angry.

Louise let out the breath she'd been holding. Perhaps her mother was overreacting, simply projecting her own worst fears onto the situation. This might be nothing more than two men, who had drunk more than they should have, disagreeing on some inconsequential matter. Like politics. Or the weather?

At least now she understood why her mother had summoned her. Although Victoria counted Brown as a trusted friend (and perhaps more), his size and brusque manner could be intimidating even for the queen. Pair Brown's powerful personality and figure with the dark masculine presence of Stephen Byrne, and the two of them filled the room with a male essence that was nearly over-powering. Victoria had sent for Louise as reinforcement—to provide hormonal balance, as it were.

Louise stepped to her mother's side and laid a hand on her shoulder. She kept her tone solemn. "Gentlemen, your behavior is most reprehensible and cannot be tolerated. At the very least, you have set a poor example for the men beneath you."

She thought she heard a smothered snicker from one of them at her last words.

The two combatants exchanged quick glances, as if considering saying something more than they'd mutually agreed upon. But in the end, they remained silent, hats clasped in swollen and bruised hands in front of them, eyes cast meekly down at the carpet beneath scuffed boots.

Louise singled out the American to study. She wondered if Byrne ever removed that leather topcoat of his, even for sleep. She'd never seen him in anything but the long duster and close-fitting dark blue canvas riding pants.

She felt a disturbing warmth travel down through her body at the vision that came to her of Stephen Byrne peeling himself out of his "uniform." She'd experienced the strength of his taut arms and torso muscles when he had crawled on top of her in the carriage. More than once since then she'd wondered—had such proximity been absolutely necessary?

"I have made my decision," Victoria said, jolting Louise out of an all-too-pleasant reverie. "Mr. Brown, you shall attend to my personal security, and to that of the grounds at whichever estate we happen to be dwelling—Balmoral, Buckingham, Windsor, or Osborne House." She turned to Stephen Byrne. "And you, sir, shall be solely in charge of the security of my children and our traveling arrangements. I will inform your superiors and ask that you be given whatever support you require. But you are not to trouble yourself with my welfare, or with the property itself, unless Mr. Brown asks for your assistance." She looked sternly to one man then the other. "Is all of this clearly understood, gentlemen?"

Brown cleared his throat. "But, ma'am—"

"That is the way it shall be, Mr. Brown. I believe Mr. Byrne has shown himself capable in ways I cannot expect of you. His wartime experience with men such as those who have designs upon our safety has already proved invaluable. Even if his only duty were to keep us informed of the Fenians' intentions, I would want him to stay on with us." She looked at Louise, as if for support.

Louise nodded her agreement. "I don't see that it can hurt to have another pair of eyes inside the castle or close by the family as we travel, in case of another emergency." Louise stifled a grin as she added, "I am sure the two of you will find ways to cooperate and not be at each other's throats."

Her mother allowed a whisper of a smile, as if satisfied with a task fully accomplished. But Louise wasn't convinced of her own words as she observed the two men. The Scot stood, huge feet planted like the roots of an elm tree, eyes focused straight ahead, his expression blank. He reminded her of a naughty schoolboy who hadn't a shred of remorse for what he'd done. When she turned to the Raven again, she thought how apt his nickname was—his black hair falling like wing feathers over his forehead, those peculiarly piercing black eyes no less intent or dangerous than those of the young man who'd wildly flung himself through the coach window, pistol in hand.

But the American, she was beginning to believe, posed a different sort of threat.

He seemed to her the emotional opposite of her beautiful, gentle husband. The black to Lorne's white. The blazing summer to Lorne's chill winter. And a tougher more mature version of her artist-lover Donovan. While her husband had lied to her about who he was, Donovan had deceived her by telling her he loved her then leaving without a word of explanation. But Byrne seemed as if he'd never waste the energy to devise a lie. Anyone who disagreed with him, didn't care for him, or got in his way . . . well, that was too bad. He'd tell them what was what.

Stephen Byrne was hidebound, powerful, unnerving—and she felt drawn to him in ways she found deeply, viscerally troubling.

"Louise?"

"Hmm?" She startled, then turned to her mother, wondering what she'd missed while her mind wandered.

"The men have their instructions. Leave me now, all of you. I have much work to do."

Louise realized Brown and Byrne had moved to the door but were standing aside, waiting for her to leave the room ahead of them, as was proper. She inclined her head to them in passing; they bowed briefly. They smelled of sweat, the lingering sweetness of liquor, and the slightly ferric aroma of dried blood. She hoped they'd bathe very soon.

Louise listened to the regular rhythm of their heavy steps, echoing behind her as she started up the stairs back to her own room. Not a word passed between them or to her. Then their foot-falls began to fade as they moved farther away.

Before she passed out of hearing, she heard Brown's guttural threat from a distance, hushed as if he intended no one but Byrne to hear. "I'll be watchin' ye, laddie."

Sighing, Louise climbed the stairs to her privy chamber, paying little attention to servants as they rushed past her, preparing for that evening's formal dinner and concert. Her comparisons of Lorne and Byrne, and even with dear Donovan, grew increasingly more disturbing.

What if the nascent love of two young people never had the good fortune to mature into what it was intended to be? It was this last scenario that pained her most deeply when she thought of Donovan. What might have become of them had they a little more time together? Their affair—or, as her mother put it, *Louise's fall from grace*—was the most thoroughly poignant, thrilling, consuming relationship she'd experienced with any human being. And the only one that involved sex.

Yet their love had evaporated into the ethers without resolution. Because Donovan. Dear. Beautiful. Exquisitely tender and intoxicating Donovan abandoned her.

Why? Why did you leave me?

Louise rushed through chilly stone corridors draped in price-less tapestries depicting classical themes in rich crimson, sapphire, and jade hues. Intended to defeat the eternal Scottish drafts and dampness, they did nothing to warm her now. Back in her room, a painful lump in her throat, tears threatening, she shooed away Car and collapsed into the velvet-curtained window seat that over-looked Balmoral's early spring gardens.

Louise hadn't seen Lorne since they'd arrived, except at family meals. They'd barely spoken a word even then. Her body, so ready for a man's touch just days ago, ached with need. Her womb would forever remain barren. Her heart never cry out in ecstasy.

Passion! How she yearned for it again in her life.

She let the tears she'd held back for so long come, releasing the pain, soothing her with memories of a happier time when she believed with the innocence of youth that no one could take her dreams from her. That was the year she recalled being allowed to venture into the world of commoners . . .

Twelve

London, 1866

"It's so unfair! Why won't you let me go to art school? I shall never be a true artist without proper training." Every afternoon at tea, and sometimes even at family breakfast, Louise fought with her mother, using every weapon in a princess's arsenal.

"Stop it, Louise," Victoria scolded. "You are becoming an embarrassment. Royal children do not mix with their mother's subjects."

"I shall stop eating entirely," she proclaimed, pushing aside the tempting plate of biscuits and sandwiches. "Not a bite will pass my lips until I'm allowed to attend art school. If I am to become a professional artist, I must have a proper education."

Her mother looked toward one of her elder daughters, Lenchen, for support. "Tell your sister how ridiculous she's being."

"How can you even think of walking out among ordinary people, mixing with men and women off the street, uneducated, working-class commoners?" Her sister actually shuddered, or pretended to for their mother's benefit.

"It's dangerous, Loosie," her brother Arthur said, more intent upon his newspaper and choosing a delicate pastry from the tray than on the conversation. "You must be reasonable and confine your socializing to the appropriate class of people."

Louise lifted her eyes to the ceiling. "Don't you see that talent doesn't depend upon who an artist's parents might be and whether or not they have a title? And I hardly think people wander in off the street to register for art classes." She huffed. "This is utterly ridiculous. The National Art Training School is a highly respected institution of learning and within walking distance of Buckingham. Yet you deny me a proper education, Mama."

"For your own protection, yes." Victoria observed her, lips pinched. "Experiment all you like with your paintings and sculpture here in the palace. Listen to your tutors. They are more than sufficient for teaching you all you need to know. When you marry, your husband will want a wife, a mistress over his household, and mother for his children, not a vagabond *artiste*."

"Oh!" Louise screeched in protest, pushing herself up and out of her chair. She let her cup and saucer clatter carelessly onto the silver tray. "You are all impossible."

She ran in tears from the room but didn't give up pleading her case. When hunger strikes didn't work, she tried formal letters of petition to her mother. When that didn't work, she enlisted Mr. Brown's influence and, finally, threats of running away to Paris. In the end, exhausted by her daughter's hysterical pleading, Victoria gave in.

Louise arrived victorious by carriage on her first day at the school, positively thrilled with her new and hard-won freedom. But when she stood before the registrar's desk that most perfect of all mornings, she was shocked by her reception.

"We are most honored to have you join us at NATS, Your Royal Highness." The registrar gave her a fatherly smile. "Let me show you to where our young ladies take their lessons."

Louise turned with confusion to her chaperone. On entering the building they'd passed a room where she'd seen several young men in smocks setting up their easels. "Are you saying I won't be with those students across the hallway? The girls have separate classes?"

"Of course, Princess." He gave her an impatient scowl and moved toward the door, as if wanting her to follow him and stop asking questions.

She stood her ground, suspicious of the separation of the sexes. Was this another way to control her, to take away from her what by rights should be hers? "Why? Why should we be separated if we are to learn the same skills?"

He let out a breath of exasperation. "Because young men and young women study and learn in different ways. It's not healthy for girls to be exposed to the same rigorous demands as boys." She crossed her arms and narrowed her eyes at him. He shook his head, as if amused by her reaction. "You'll be with the other young ladies in a very nice building all your own. I'm certain you will enjoy yourself, Your Highness."

This did not sound good at all. "Which building?"

"The Female School of Art, just across the way there." He pointed toward the door she'd just come in.

And so Louise, accompanied by the elderly Lady Vail, who had been appointed by her mother to watch over Louise whenever she left the palace for school, turned around and followed the registrar back into South Kensington's streets, overlooking Hyde Park, and walked the few hundred feet down the brick walkway to classrooms kept solely for students of the "fragile" sex. At the end of that day, and each one after, Louise and Vail were retrieved like loaned pieces of furniture by the same carriage, driver, and footman that had brought them.

Louise felt robbed. The lessons at the Female School were little more than the same tedious instruction she'd received at home. Her one pleasure was carrying back to the palace tales to amuse and shock Lenchen and their baby sister, Beatrice.

"Do not men paint too?" Bea asked when Louise told them of

the all-girl classes. The littlest princess sat at Louise's feet in the nursery, gazing up at her with huge, worshipful eyes.

"Of course, they do," Lenchen said before Louise could answer. The eldest unmarried daughter at that time, Lenchen was only two years ahead of Louise but beat Beatrice into the world by more than ten. "You have seen their portraits and landscapes right here in the castle."

"But *they* take no classes at the academy?"

"Oh, Bea, they certainly do." Louise shot to her feet to pace off her frustration over the nursery floor. "The boys have their own much more professional curriculum."

"Why?" Lenchen asked.

"Because our parents and teachers think they are protecting us delicate, too easily influenced females. They believe we'll be damaged emotionally or turn to evil ways if we so much as glimpse a nude figure." Louise threw up her hands in disgust. "Women are encouraged to paint flowers, woodland creatures, studies of ripe fruit, stinky dead fish, and glass goblets. Absolutely no *naked* people for us girls. Especially not ones with hairy bottoms or dangly thingies between their legs."

Lenchen giggled, her eyes dancing at the danger of speaking such words. Happily, their governess had nodded off in her chair in front of the fireplace.

Little Beatrice tilted her head and observed Louise with a solemn expression. "I wouldn't mind so awfully just painting pretty flowers. I don't think I ever want to see a naked person."

"I do!" Louise felt her skin glow with a heady warmth. "Well, a naked man anyway. I've seen my own body and know what we women look like."

Beatrice wrinkled her nose. "That's so dirty. Looking at a bare man."

"Someday you will see your husband's body," Lenchen reminded her gently, "when he comes to your bed."

"I will make him wear a nightshirt clear down to his toes. Or not come beneath the linens with me."

"Then how will he make babies in you?" Louise asked.

Beatrice stared at her. "Babies come whenever God pleases."

Louise and Lenchen exchanged knowing looks. Young women of good families didn't learn the truth of such things until their wedding night. But the two older girls had caught their eldest sister, Vicky, alone one night after her marriage to Fritz, when she'd had a bit too much wine. The Crown Princess had described *in great and delicious detail* the event of a man and woman joining their sexes. Her sisters had been horrified . . . and delighted.

Later, when Louise combined this secret knowledge with her private studies of nudes painted or sculpted by the masters—Michelangelo, Rubens, Caravaggio, Donatello, and even Jan van Eyck—she was able to understand how a man's organ cleverly fit into a woman's secret hollow between her limbs. Best of all, Vicky (blushing furiously when she'd said it) claimed the act was not unpleasant, and sometimes a child came as a result.

"Well, I for one look forward to seeing a man in his altogether," Louise repeated. "I wish to be a sculptress, not a painter of plucked blooms and boring lifeless objects. How else, other than by observing real human bodies, may I make my art honest and realistic?"

Beatrice crossed her chubby arms and pouted. "Sculpt for me a little cat or one of our hunting dogs. I'd like that a whole lot better than a dirty old boy without clothes."

Louise laughed and hugged her little sister. "I'll make you a kitty then," she promised. But she vowed that very day to find a way to get into the advanced sculpting classes that were offered only to young men.

Thirteen

It took Louise longer than she'd hoped. During those months she often saw Amanda and stopped to chat with her. She was curious why a young woman as attractive and clever as Amanda spent her life as a scullery maid.

"You think it's what I choose?" the girl demanded, looking astonished. "Do you know how many there are like me—women out on the streets through no fault of our own? My da made a good livin' in the print shop at the *Times*, he did. We had us a nice little house, and I kept it right smart for the two of us."

"What happened?" They were sitting on the front stoop, and Louise offered the girl a slice of her apple.

Amanda winced then shook her head. "After my da died, the house went to my uncle as the only male heir. My mum (bless her soul) was already dead, her brother saw the profit in sellin' the place to the railway as they were buyin' up a path for the new track into the city. But when I asked what part of the money was my share he said, by the law it was all his."

"He just put you out on the street?"

"Might as well have. I had nothin' to live on." She eyed what was left of the apple. "Would you mind my havin' another slice; that was awful good."

"Here," Louise said, handing her the rest she hadn't yet cut with her palette knife. "I wasn't hungry anyway."

"Can't remember the last time I could say that." Amanda laughed and took a hearty bite, smiling at her.

"So what did you do?"

"What most women on their own do for a safe and warm place to sleep."

Louise stared at her, horrified.

"Don't give me those eyes of yours, all saucer-y and shocked. What would you do, Princess, the old queen turned you out?" She shrugged. "As if that's even likely."

"Sell apples, matches . . . maybe flowers like I see girls doing at street corners."

"And if you've no money to buy what you're sellin'? Would you be stealin' someone else's flowers to make a few shillings? Or sell your pretty hair? When that's gone and all you have is your body"—Amanda's voice dropped to a dark place—"you'd have no choice if you didn't want to starve."

Louise shivered at the thought. She wasn't even sure what selling one's body meant. If a man paid her money to be with him, what would he expect from her? When it came right down to it, she'd never considered what people who didn't live in a castle did with their days. She'd never needed to worry about where her meals came from or whether she'd have a warm bed and walls to protect her from the weather or the wickedness of the world.

Meeting Amanda opened a whole new world to her. One that troubled Louise even as it made her thankful for all her family had . . . and more than a little guilty for her wardrobe's collection of exquisite gowns, shoes, and fur-trimmed cloaks.

But, for the time being, there seemed little she could do for Amanda or other women in her new friend's pitiable situation. She had all she could manage winning herself the freedom she needed to follow her dream of becoming an independent woman and artist. And the next step was convincing her mother that a chaperone's time was sadly wasted during class hours.

After a while, Louise found an ally in Lady Vail, her watcher. The woman clearly was bored—having nothing to do all day long except her needlework—and she missed the gossip of court. With encouragement from Louise, Vail requested release from her duties, claiming the princess was perfectly safe under Maestro's watchful eye. The queen decided an escort of a driver and footman was sufficient to get her daughter to and from the girls' art school. Without anyone watching her every move and reporting to the queen, Louise was free more often to talk to Amanda, or any of the students whenever she wished, without being chastised for "mixing with the lower classes."

She turned to the other girls for advice on how to get into the boys' classes, but they just shook their heads.

"They'll never let a girl into the live model sessions," Amanda told her one day. "Never."

"I'll get in. One way or another."

"Well, good luck to you." Amanda dragged her mop across the floor.

"Amanda," Louise said, putting her hand out to stop the girl from leaving. "If you could do anything, be anyone. What would it be?"

"Oh, we're into daydreamin' now, are we?" The girl laughed and winked at her.

Louise gave her a smile and a gentle nod of encouragement.

"Well then, I'd work for the *Times*, like my da. Only not in the print shop."

"Where then?"

Amanda flushed with embarrassment. "We're just dreamin', right? You won't laugh at me?"

"I'd never laugh at you," Louise assured her.

Amanda hesitated, but her eyes lit with anticipation. "I'd write articles like I seen in the newspapers my da brought home from work."

"You can read?" Louise gaped at her, then realized how awful that sounded, assuming her friend's ignorance. "I'm sorry. It's just that I—"

"It's all right. Just look at me, all covered in grime most of the time, talkin' like a street crosser." She sighed. "Da taught me. It's just, you live on the streets awhile, you lose a lot of your shine. Like that brass knob on that door over there, if I don't polish it. You sink to the level of the gutters where you live."

"Never you mind." Louise reached out and patted Amanda's hand. "What you've lost you can get back. Right?"

"Mebbe." Amanda shrugged and kicked her mop head with the toe of her boot. "Mebbe someday."

Despite all the other girls' doubts, Louise never stopped believing that Maestro would eventually give in to her. After all, princesses are denied precious little in life, except the independence of a commoner. After weeks of pleading, promises, and veiled threats, Maestro allowed her to cross over into the main building and take a few basic sculpting lessons with the boys.

At first she was disappointed with the tediousness. They studied various techniques for molding and shaving away at lumps of clay, as they weren't allowed to take a chisel to stone until mastering the ugly gray globs. Then, on the tenth week, a young man with tawny complexion, lustrous straw-colored hair, and cool gray eyes stepped into the room wearing, it appeared to her, only a robe.

Maestro announced, "You will first draw the model's figure. After I have approved your sketch, you may create a clay model. If you are able to do that much satisfactorily, in a week or two you will render the pose in soapstone. It is the softest and easiest stone to carve." He turned to Louise, whose worktable he'd placed at the very back of the room, to attract the least attention from his boys. "Your Royal Highness, follow me."

For a panicky moment, she feared he was going to make her leave the room. Tears of frustration sprang to her eyes.

"Come, come," he repeated, walking as he continued to speak. "As a condition to your inclusion in live modeling sessions, I must insist upon the highest discretion. You see here a curtain. Behind this you will find your work station for today."

She frowned. This was as remote as possible from the model's platform while still inside the long, narrow atelier. "Why must I work here? I can see much better up close."

"That is the point, Princess," Maestro said, in an annoyed growl. "You will see as much as is absolutely necessary to do your work and no more. And the other students and model will not be distracted by your presence."

She was aware of the boys in the class watching as she stepped behind the curtain. There she found all of her supplies laid out neatly on the table and an easel set up for drawing. She glared at the ridiculous curtain. "I can't see through it. Am I allowed to part the fabric to view the model?"

"Of course. Briefly." Maestro coughed, looking not entirely pleased with the arrangement even then. "I warn you. Should you swoon even once, or show the least sign of weakness or shock, you will never again be allowed in this room. It is for your own good, I assure you."

Louise looked him in the eye. "I do not *swoon*. And I believe you seriously underestimate my sex, sir."

He coughed into his hand. "We shall see." He stepped outside of her privacy screen and signaled the model with a backward wave of his hand.

The young man stepped up onto a raised pedestal. He dropped his robe at his feet.

Louise blinked and sucked in a breath. Her heart stopped—she was certain it actually did—for the space of three full beats. She swallowed. Swallowed again, blinking to clear her vision.

His body appeared as smooth as alabaster, utterly hairless but for the lowest, most intriguing regions of his torso. He was beautiful. More appealing than Michelangelo's *David*. His flesh gave off subtle warmth impossible from the finest marble, serpentine, or onyx. Even from her distant vantage point, she sensed his skin's velvety texture and vibrancy. Maestro signaled the young man to make a quarter turn, putting his back to her.

Louise sat on her stool and tucked her hands inside her smock to hide their agitation, as if her teacher could see her through the curtain. She bit down on her bottom lip, fighting the oddest urge that had just come over her. She longed to walk straight to the front of the room, reach out, and touch the boy's body. Before she drew him, or even thought of sculpting him, she wanted to feel the contours of his flesh, muscle, bone, sinew. She'd slide her fingers through his hair and down his shoulder blades, back, and buttocks. Only then did she believe she'd be able to shape with her inexperienced hands an honest likeness of him.

Maestro was speaking, though he seemed miles away, his voice a distant chime and easy to ignore. After a while the young man turned again, and she dared to let her eyes drop again to the part of him that held the most interest for her. She felt a blaze of heat race up from her chest to her throat and cheeks.

It was just then that it happened.

As if the boy knew she was there, hidden behind her curtain, he turned his head toward her, smiled . . . and his manhood stiffened.

"Stand still!" barked Maestro. "You are posing for these artists, not dancing. And calm yourself, young man."

Louise covered her mouth to stifle a laugh.

"Prin-cessss," Maestro hissed from nearby, having slipped behind her curtain while she was distracted. His impatience came at her as a tangible wave of displeasure. She wobbled on her stool. "You must sketch before we begin with the clay. Why do you hesitate?" His eyes glittered with what she imagined was anticipation of her failure. "I can see this experience shocks you. As I tried to warn you, this is not an activity for delicate young females. If you wish to withdraw—"

"No!" Louse shook her head violently. "I am not at all shocked, sir. I simply wished to consider the best way to begin." She picked up a powdery charcoal willow stick and held its tip an inch above the surface of the paper clipped to her easel.

"Your hand is unsteady." Maestro's eyes narrowed. He shifted his gaze to her face.

Louise pulled in a breath, steadied herself. This was a test. The critical one. If she failed at this simple drawing exercise, became unglued and visibly shaken by the model's nakedness, her reaction would give the teacher all the excuse he needed to ban her from the class. He would claim it was for her protection, and her mother would no doubt agree with his decision.

She could not . . . *would* not . . . give him a reason for taking away the opportunity she'd fought for so very long.

Louise drew another long, slow breath, let it out, then placed the tip of the charcoal against the clean white sheet. Following the curves of the model's shoulders, the wings of his shoulder blades, inward curve of lower back, swell of his buttocks, and down muscular legs, she let her hand respond instinctively, mimicking the path of her eyes. A narrow black line appeared, firmly drawn with an unswerving hand.

An immutable statement of sensuality appeared against virgin background.

Louise felt Maestro's eyes shift from drawing to model and back again to the paper as she held her breath, awaiting his approval.

"Well enough done. Continue," he pronounced curtly, then spun around, parted her curtain, and walked away to check his other students' work.

She let out a breath of relief, giddy at her small but decisive victory.

Now that she had begun the work, she let instinct guide the charcoal twig in her hand as she rapidly sketched the rest of the young man's body. She used his natural contours, the pale golden light from the expanse of windows high above the atelier, the deeper shadows created by body parts turned away from the sun's light—defining, perfecting her study of the male body.

Maestro again ordered the model to remain turned so that his back faced her, protecting his male organs from her fascinated gaze. She smiled. Did her teacher actually think women so weak they might be traumatized by the mere sight of genitalia that didn't belong to their husbands? *Preposterous.* This was the most exciting day of her life.

Louise couldn't wait to get home to tell Bea and Lenchen.

Fourteen

Days later, Louise watched as Donovan, the model, left with the other students for lunch. As the only adult male she'd ever seen fully disrobed, he intrigued her. The experience of studying his body in minute detail (although at an annoying distance) made her feel bound to him in a way she couldn't explain. Even more intriguing, each time he posed for the class, he slid his sultry, heavy-lidded gaze toward the curtain hung to separate her from indecency. She imagined his eyes meeting hers through the fabric, beckoning her to step out from behind. Sometimes she did, to fetch another stick of charcoal or clean sheet of paper. But she hadn't found an opportunity to exchange even a single word with him.

Although Maestro's cook always prepared her lunch and let her sit in an empty classroom to eat, it seemed infinitely more appealing to rush off with the gaggle of laughing students into the streets when they went out for their meals. With the addition of Donovan to their group, their company became all the more irresistible. But she wasn't supposed to leave the school until her driver returned to fetch her.

Louise glared at the disgusting plate of boiled mutton, dry dark bread, and stewed cabbage Cook had placed in front of her. She waited for the woman to leave her alone in the room. She heaved a sigh and poked at the gray mass. On impulse, she stood up, wiped the food off her plate and into the metal waste can already half full of paint-spattered cloths, broken ends of charcoal and pastel sticks, and discarded paper. She set the plate back on the table and peered out into the empty hallway.

Cook was humming busily in the kitchen. The fat old thing never checked on her, probably considering her a bother and an extra chore she had little time for in her day. Maestro, she knew, had left the building on an errand. The director's door was closed. Even Amanda was nowhere in sight.

Without another thought, Louise flew down the warped floorboards, slipped out the front door and into the street.

Her schoolmates hadn't gone far. She could still see them wending their boisterous way down the avenue. She ran to catch them up, falling into step behind the last few girls. Her mind whirred with her daring. She felt deliciously light-headed at the adventure of venturing into the streets without a keeper.

She'd become one of them now. She imagined making true and ever-lasting friends among the girls, encouraging them to do as she'd done—insist upon as complete an education as any boy received. She'd flirt outrageously with the boys, but of course be very proper about turning away advances of the wrong sort.

And if Cook missed her while she was gone?

She'd simply explain she'd not felt well and went off to lie down in one of the back rooms until the afternoon session. Maestro would never know. More importantly, her mother would never find out.

Fortunately she'd already made the acquaintance of several of the girls in the group. Mary, Sarah, and Florence were giggling and rustling their skirts as they walked arm in arm in long strides to keep up with the boys.

Mary turned and glanced over her shoulder, as if to see whose footsteps she heard behind her. Her eyes widened when she saw Louise. "Your Royal Highness, what are you doing here?"

The other girls turned and stopped walking, looking almost frightened.

"I get hungry, just like you." Louise bit down on her lip. She sounded so stiff and defensive. She softened her tone, not wanting to appear arrogant. "I hope you don't object to my eating with you. Please, I'd very much enjoy your company."

"This isn't right, Princess," Sarah whispered under her breath, glancing around her as if worried they'd be seen. "We know the rules. You are to eat at the school. You can't leave until your carriage comes."

"We don't want to get in trouble," Florence added in apology. She looked at the other girls. "Maybe we should walk her back now."

"No, please!" Louise cried, making people on the street turn and stare at them.

"If we do, we won't have time to eat." Sarah flashed Louise an irritated look. "You're making trouble for us, don't you see?"

Louise had never been spoken to in such an impertinent tone before. Yes, her tutors had ordered her about, and more than once Victoria had given Nurse or one of the governesses permission to slap her for her naughtiness. But commoners simply did not tell a royal person what to do.

"You won't get into trouble, I promise," Louise said. "It's my decision where I eat and with whom." She put on a cheery face. "So . . . where are we going and what's on the menu?"

"Menu? Listen to her." Sarah snorted.

Florence, the nicest of the three, with a sunny round face and plump figure that marked her as a lover of sweets, slipped her arm through Louise's and started walking again. "I'm sure street food is not as fine as what you're accustomed to, Your Highness. But come along." The other girls had no choice but to move forward with them.

Louise shrugged. "I don't care whether it's fine, just as long as it's filling. I'm starving." Why did her stomach rumble now, when she hadn't felt in the least interested in the food prepared by Cook?

She noticed then that a group of the boy students, jostling and play-boxing one another, had stopped just ahead of them. Donovan was watching her over his shoulder from the middle of the pack. They stood in front of a vendor's stall near the edge of the park. It was only at that moment—while the others were buying their lardy meat pies wrapped in greasy paper to keep the warm juices from spilling out, paying with coins they pulled from pockets and little change purses—that she realized she had a problem.

Never had there been a need for her to carry coins on her person. She'd always been accompanied by an older family member or servant, who paid for whatever she wished to purchase. She had no money.

When her turn came to order she stepped back out of line and away. Not knowing what else to do she started walking along with those who had already purchased their meal and were moving into the park to eat in the shade beneath the trees.

A hand touched her shoulder. She turned.

"Aren't you going to buy something to eat?" It was Donovan.

"I'm not very hungry," she lied and gave him a sunny smile. He was actually speaking to her. She felt light-headed with the thrill of it.

He squinted. "That so?"

Louise shrugged.

He laughed. "I see. The little princess is out in the world on her own for her first time." Her cheeks blushed feverishly. He scooped a few more coins out of his pocket, took her hand, and led her back to the vendor's stall. "What will you have, Princess?"

"Oh no, I can't let you—" He always came in the same clothes, was thinner than a lamppost. He must be very poor.

"What are you doing there, Donovan?" Sarah asked, suspicion mirrored in her bright eyes. "You don't buy any of *us* pies."

"Now there's a thing you don't see every day." One of the boys poked another in the ribs. "Donovan parting with a coin."

Two other boys slapped Donovan on the back, as if congratulating him on what Louise knew not. He pushed them roughly away and turned back to her. "It's not a gift, Your Highness. I expect you to repay me."

Then it would be all right, she thought. He was loaning her the money. "Of course. Yes, I will pay you back tomorrow, with a little more for your trouble. Thank you. Oh, thank you."

The whole group ate together in Hyde Park, and she thought it so much nicer than any of the elaborate Buckingham garden picnics her mother arranged for the children of her ministers, nobility, and favored upper-class subjects. So friendly was this little group, all of them young and talking so brilliantly about their art. The sun shone down between the branches. Sparrows twittered above them. Horse-drawn omnibuses and hansom cabs clip-clopped past. Vendors sang out their wares from the streets beyond. She'd never realized the noises of the city could be so lovely.

As she ate, Louise noticed her classmates seemed to cluster around her before sitting down, almost as if trying to screen her from the prying eyes of those strolling past. She couldn't decide if this was because they felt obligated to protect her, or they feared someone recognizing her and accusing them of doing something wrong.

After a while, though, everyone seemed to relax, and the storytelling and jokes began. By the time the midday meal was over and they'd returned to the school, they were all laughing and including her in their conversations. Louise had never been happier.

The next day Louise arrived in class, her reticule plump with coins. From the time she'd been very young, she'd received money for birthdays and holidays, and she kept a china bank into which she deposited her precious coins—money she'd never needed until now. If she liked, she could buy everyone's meat pie all week long.

As before, she waited alone in the classroom and listened until she heard the girls taking off for their noon meal. They would join up with the boys along the way. She dumped Cook's lunch and caught up with her new friends.

Because she wanted to remain one of them, not hold herself above her classmates by displaying her wealth, she very quietly slipped into Donovan's hand payment for the previous day, adding another shilling for his being so kind to her. Walking alongside her, he looked down at the coins before pocketing them. *Counting*, she thought. For a moment, it seemed to her he was considering refusing the extra money, or maybe even all of it. But then something changed in his eyes, and a bit of his pride fell away.

"Thank you," he said, his voice barely a whisper. Then she knew how desperately he must need money, and her heart went out to him. His gift to her the previous day became all the more precious to her.

After that she went with the others every day to lunch. When questioned by Cook, who at last missed her, she pretended haughtiness and told the woman she'd prefer to fast until returning to the palace, where the food was more to her liking. It was what the Crown Princess, her sister Vicky, would have said.

Somehow Maestro must have soothed Cook's feelings because nothing more was said of the matter. Even Maestro seemed weary of keeping an eye on her. He assumed an attitude of indifference to her socializing, only chiding her if she was late in returning. Instead it was Amanda who warned her away from the other students.

"Playin' with fire, you are, Princess. You best stay away from that lot or they'll bring you trouble."

"And who are you to be telling me what to do?" She wrinkled

her nose at the maid of all work, down on her knees, waxing the school's hallway floor with wide swirls of her rag. "I like them. They're fun and ever so clever."

Amanda didn't look up. "The girls mebbe. But a lady like you ought to beware of those boys, 'specially that Donovan. He's mischief and more, that one."

Louise huffed at her. "You sound like my governess. All sour pickles when it comes to enjoying oneself. Anyway, I'm learning so much more about life than I ever could cooped up in the palace."

"About life," Amanda muttered, putting muscle into her task. "Right."

Fifteen

One day Donovan failed to appear at the school. A different model stood in his place, and they started all over with fresh sketches. By the end of the week, it was clear to Louise the young man had been permanently replaced.

"Where has Donovan gone?" she asked Mary when they walked out at noon.

"I've no idea, Your Highness. They come and go, you know. There are a lot of hungry boys. Girls too. All willing to pose for a little money."

"He will never come back then?" When Donovan had been among them, he'd seemed just one of their lively group, although a bit special to her for his generosity that first day she'd eaten with them. Now that he was gone she missed him.

"He may, if he gets hungry enough," Sarah said, elbowing her way between her and Mary, her eyes twinkling impishly. "But I doubt it. He's a pretty boy. A fellow like that won't be out on the streets for long." The other girls giggled.

Louise frowned. "I don't understand."

Mary pulled her aside. "Princess, ignore them. They're being crude. Sarah means that some wealthy woman will take a liking to Don, provide him with a room, nice clothes, and food. Then he won't need to pose anymore."

Louise's eyes shot wide, despite her attempt to contain her shock. "You mean, in return for . . . favors?" She'd heard that word used when describing such arrangements between a wealthy man and, usually, a younger woman who weren't married.

Mary shrugged and blushed. "What else?"

Louise sighed. She supposed this was another element of the adult world she'd only guessed at until now. She knew that men bought their mistresses gowns, a carriage and four, even town houses in the city if they were rich enough. But she'd never thought of women buying men luxuries.

It was then that Louise decided she must find Donovan and discover for herself what had happened to him. Wasn't it her duty, as a friend, to at least make sure he was safe?

The next day, before everyone left for lunch, Louise approached two of the boys who had spent the most time with Donovan and asked if they had any idea where she might find him.

"He has a job with two artists," Jacob, the taller of the two, said. "Gabriel Rossetti and William Morris."

"Where do they live?"

"Rossetti's garret is at Chatham Place, just north of Blackfriar's Bridge."

"I don't know where that is," she said, disappointed. "Is it far?"

Jacob and Felix glanced at each other, maybe for the first time realizing why she was asking.

Felix said, "You can see St. Paul's Cathedral from there. But it's not the nicest part of the city, Princess. I wouldn't go there, if I were you."

Louise cocked her head at him. "I can go where I please."

"Listen." Jacob bent toward her confidentially. "I suspect the queen thinks us a wild bunch. But Rossetti? She'd call the man immoral. Have you ever seen his paintings?"

She shook her head.

"Or read his poetry?" Felix chimed in with a grin. "Quite racy, I'd say."

Jacob nodded in enthusiastic agreement, and Louise immediately made a mental note to find a copy of Mr. Rossetti's poems. "I only want to see Donovan, not his employers. To repay him money I borrowed. That's all."

Jacob shrugged, and she wondered if he saw through her lie. "Do you want us to go with you?" he asked. "You know, for protection."

She smiled, stopping just short of laughing. These two skinny young men from titled families, just as sheltered as she was, were offering to put themselves between her and potential danger.

"Thank you for the offer, gentlemen. I'll have two able-bodied men from the palace to attend me." But if she had any say in the matter, her footman and driver would go no farther than the artists' front door.

From high in the sky, the sun shot brilliant beams down between tightly packed buildings and succeeded in burning off as much of the yellow-green smog as ever it could. Visible specks of coal dust filtered through the air like fine black snow. Louise sat in the barouche and waved a delicate pierced-ivory fan in front of her face, but it helped little.

Her heart picked up the rhythm of the horses' hooves over the uneven paving stones. The metal-rimmed wheels of her carriage rumbled and scraped along the road. The sheer excitement of a new adventure made her feel all the more alive.

Louise amused herself by memorizing the route her driver took through unfamiliar streets, creating a map of sorts in her head. Luckily, he chose main thoroughfares, cutting as straight a line across the city as possible from Kensington High Street along the southern edge of lush green Hyde Park to Knightsbridge, through

Piccadilly and then again south to the Strand, lined with its stately Jacobean mansions. She recognized the Duke of Northumberland's house, having been there to a ball that spring, and then elegant Durham House and Salisbury House before coming to the eyesore of Westminster, the Savoy Hospital for the poor, with its sad clusters of cripples and indigents haunting the alleys around it. Fleet Street took them to a left onto Farringdon, which dumped them into a nicer neighborhood that fronted on a tiny but pleasant-looking park. Should she ever need to come back here on her own, she decided it would be wise not to get lost.

The neighborhood wasn't as bad as she'd expected after her conversation with Jacob and Felix. In fact it wasn't at all frightening. Rather it exuded romance and adventure with its colorful mix of artisans, street artists, and, she imagined, even poets—all set against the vibrant backdrop of shops crammed with supplies to support their talents. The lodgings seemed modest—older houses divided into multiple tenancies—but the stoops were swept and clear of garbage, the cafés charming and jammed with smiling, laughing people.

When at last the carriage stopped and the brawny footman hopped down from his perch to open her door, Louise rechecked the address she'd written down to make sure they'd found the right place. The building wasn't marked with a number; few were in this part of the city. But one house across the street sported a placard with a promisingly close number, so this seemed about right.

"Shall I accompany you, Your Highness?" her footman asked.

"No. It's better if I go in alone. My friend . . . she's shy. I won't be long. We'll be going straight back to the school," she informed him cheerfully. By using her lunchtime break she would be back before Maestro realized she had gone farther than the two streets to where her crowd usually lunched.

"You're certain?" He looked worried. Should *she* be?

"I am." She wasn't.

The tremors that had started as trills of anticipation in her heart now traveled through the rest of her body. She drew a breath and told herself she had nothing to worry about. She and Donovan were friends. He was sweet, gentle, amusing to be around. Nothing he'd ever said or done in her presence could in the slightest way be construed as threatening. She had no reason to feel vulnerable.

After all, she had seen the fellow at his most exposed state—totally naked. If either of them held an advantage—it was she.

Yet, she mused as she gathered her skirts and stepped down from the carriage, he hadn't seemed at a disadvantage while posing in the altogether on his platform. His attitude was always proud, removed. As if he owned the school, as if the students and staff were his guests, whom he chose to ignore until he dressed again and struck out with them in a companionable manner for a bite to eat.

His ability to remove himself emotionally from a situation was a trick Louise envied. There were times she would have liked to mentally absent herself from a royal reception or formal dinner. And she longed to show those around her that *she* was in charge. That *she* was not a woman whose future was to be negotiated for the purpose of others' power, wealth, or property. *She* was the one who would control her own life.

"I won't be long," she repeated firmly to her footman.

Of course, she had no proof that Donovan would be here at all. And even if he were here, he might be asleep after spending the night out with friends or working tedious hours for Rossetti. On the other hand, for all she knew, he might have moved on to yet another job by now.

But she felt compelled to at least try to find him. She had so few real friends it seemed tragic to lose one.

Louise checked the names scrawled on little paper cards in

metal slots beside the door. ROSSETTI/MORRIS: THIRD FLOOR. Three flights of creaking, splintery wooden steps later, she was facing a warped, water-stained door with functioning but rusty hinges and latch. She raised a gloved hand to knock, but the door swung open before her knuckles touched wood.

Donovan stood in long, loose muslin pants, gathered by a drawstring at the waist, riding low on his narrow hips. He wore nothing else.

She swallowed, smiled nervously. A tickling sensation traveled up from her knees and settled cozily in her stomach. "How did you know I'd come?" she asked.

He laughed and jerked his thumb toward the windows. "Do you suppose one of HRM's carriages pulls up outside a place like this every day?"

She felt her cheeks go hot as she remembered the royal crest embossed on the barouche's door. "I suppose not."

He studied her, still standing in the doorway. Beyond his bare shoulder, she could see two men, each painting at an easel. A woman wrapped in a paisley shawl sat in a ladder-back chair, the illumination from a skylight above her brightening her features.

"Why are you here, Princess?"

She jumped at Donovan's voice; he sounded more irritated than happy to see her.

"I was worried about you and wanted to see that you were well."

"And do I look well to you?"

She blushed hotter, brought her fan up to cool her cheeks and tried to focus on his face rather than his naked chest . . . or bare feet . . . or smoothly muscled arms. "You appear in good health."

He reached out his hand, taking hers, drawing her a little closer. "As do you," he whispered.

She shot a worried look at the painters, but they seemed involved in their work. The noise of pots banging together in one of the other apartments mixed with the shouts of vendors down in the street. Everything seemed so normal, so unremarkably ordinary. Why should she feel uneasy?

"I am well," she said. She didn't know what else to say.

He still held her hand. She looked down at their touching fingers. Hers gloved. His naked and pale, long and graceful. She would sculpt a model of his hand one day, if he let her.

"Can you come back, Louise?"

She wasn't sure she'd heard him right. "Come back?"

"Another day when I'm not working. If you like. Say, on Thursday after school?" He lowered his voice still more. "Rossetti and Morris will be gone then, to the exhibition hall, setting up their paintings for display."

She peeked over his shoulder again at the two men, so intent on their work. They probably hadn't even noticed the carriage outside. Or her standing like a peddler at their door. She looked back at Donovan. "We'd be alone then?"

He nodded, his eyes fixed on hers. She wondered that she hadn't already melted under his gaze, as if she were pinned beneath a magnifying lens like the one Leo, when he was little, had used for roasting flies and moths in the sun's burning rays.

"So we could talk more," he said. "Would you like that?"

"I would . . . yes, of course." Then the words she'd been holding back rushed out of her. "I would so very much like for us to be friends, Donovan. We could talk about all the things that are important to us."

He smiled. "Good. Come after class. Bring food if you like. There's nothing here, and we might get hungry."

"Yes, of course. Yes, I will." A picnic in an artist's garret—how scrumptiously romantic.

But part of her felt the tiniest bit unsure of the circumstances. Could she really do this? Come here, alone, to this common man's part of the city, late in the day when it might soon become dark?

Come here to be alone with a man in the place where he lived? As Vicky would have said: "This simply isn't done." Louise didn't dare think what her mother would say.

Louise had already started backing away toward the top step when Donovan leaned out through the open doorway and brushed his lips across her cheek. An appalling breach of etiquette. She should slap him and leave. Refusing his invitation would certainly be appropriate.

"I'll be waiting," he whispered, his bashful gaze lingering, encouraging.

Her heart fluttered. "I'll be here."

Sixteen

be appropriate.

To have friends, *real friends*—not a brother or sister or cousin required to include her in their games or make polite conversation—this was thrilling to Louise. She and her eight siblings had been isolated from the world and under Nanny's care until the age of five, when they could be handed over to governesses for strict tutoring.

Prince Albert's personal adviser, Baron Stockmar, took charge of their education and allowed few breaks from their books. Of course, they must all learn to ride, hunt, dance, and behave properly in court. But as young children they were not allowed at court functions and were never, ever exposed to commoners.

Louise recalled her parents describing the middle and lower classes as dirty, immoral, simple-minded folk who were incapable of anything more mentally demanding than manual labor. It was fine to pity or act charitably toward the poor souls, but that was the limit of contact. Even the sons and daughters of lesser nobility were considered inappropriate playmates for the royal offspring.

However, the crowd she'd fallen in with at the art school brimmed with brilliant young people, many from decent (though by no means noble) families. Her friends had new and exciting ideas to share with her about politics, art, and the sciences. She loved her days at the school. There she learned so much more about life than she possibly could have, shut up in one of the family's castles. In prison, as it were—waiting to be married off to a man she barely knew. During their midday meals clever Donovan, all on his own, had been teaching her so much about the way real people lived in the world. She desperately wanted to keep him as a friend. Just a friend. She dared not think of him as more than that.

The week crept along. Louise could hardly contain her elation when Thursday came at last. As soon as her final class of the day was over, she gathered her shawl, the basket of food she'd purchased during their break, and swept down the steps, hardly noticing Amanda resting on the curb, a broom across her knees.

"I will join my lady friends for a supper in Chatham Park," she loudly told her driver as the footman lifted the basket from her arm and set it inside the carriage on the floor. "Please hurry. I don't want to keep them waiting."

She hoped the lie had worked but could tell nothing from the expressions of either of the men. She had a sense of Amanda's eyes fixed in a less than approving way on her as they drove off.

This time the neighborhoods through which they passed were not new to her. But she drank them in as she hadn't before. Each minute detail appealed to her artist's eye. The edges of objects felt so crisp and perfectly defined she could almost reach out and touch them. Colors shone as vividly as if they were undiluted pigments, hand ground and swathed across the London streetscape. Despite the coal dust–gray air and the filth of even the finest streets, every brick mansion or stucco tenement, every statue or signpost, ragman's horse, leather seller, drayman, smudgy-faced crossing sweeper boy, tarted-up fancy girl, greasy sausage vendor, omnibus and cab—each stood out in sharp relief before her eyes. She longed to paint them all. And although the sun was starting to dip behind the wall of buildings, and the lamplighter would soon be making his rounds of the gasoliers, the world seemed to her a brighter place than ever before.

When the carriage neared Chatham Place, Louise rapped on the ceiling for the driver to stop diagonally across the street from Rossetti's garret. "Park alongside those other carriages and hansoms," she said. This seemed more discreet than pulling up directly in front of the house.

She beat her footman Grady out the carriage door in her eagerness and peeked from beneath lowered eyelashes at the buildings across the street. Of course she would need to take a roundabout route to reach the door without her mother's men seeing her. But at least with the carriage parked at a distance from the building, alongside those belonging to people who were strolling the gravel paths of the park, fewer of the curious would be aware of her destination.

She took the picnic basket from Grady, who seemed reluctant to give it up. "You don't need to accompany me," she said, coloring her voice with a little of her mother's imperious tone. "I shall be at least two hours. Feel free to get yourself and Berryman a meal while I'm gone."

Grady nodded, his expression as unreadable as ever. "As you wish, Your Highness. But might I not suggest an escort to your friends?"

"No, thank you. I am certain they wait for me just beyond that small rise." She waved a hand in the general direction of the path. "I prefer not to stand out, as none of them will be accompanied by servants."

"Understood, Your Highness."

Louise walked into the edge of the park, just far enough to pass behind a screen of dense laurel bushes, then cut to the left until she was moving along a path parallel to Rossetti's street. Sheltered by the curve of the woods, she crossed the road and hurried up the stone steps, then inside the dark hallway.

At the top of the third flight she stood breathless on the landing and turned toward the door she'd stood before earlier that week. It was closed all the way this time. The apartment behind it felt silent, unoccupied. Her heart rose into her throat. Had Donovan forgotten their special day?

She knocked.

No answer.

Louise rapped harder this time, cringing at the startling echo she'd sent down the stairwell. She felt as if all the world might hear, and thus know *what she was doing*. Coming at dusk to a man's private rooms, alone. How scandalous! She snickered, pleased by her boldness.

Suddenly the door swung wide, and Donovan gave her a cheerful smile. "Sorry, tidying up. Wondered all week if you'd lose your nerve, Louise."

It was the first time he'd said her name, she realized. Lou-ise. It sounded lovely, almost musical spilling from his lips, and sent a delicious tingle through her.

She looked him over. He was fully dressed this time. Nicely dressed actually, with a striped cravat, soft gray waistcoat, white shirtsleeves and turned-up collar. Even leather shoes.

"Class finished late," she said by way of apology, "otherwise I would have been here sooner. And I had a little walk over from the park."

He nodded, as if ladies left their carriages blocks away every day of the week to hike up to his room for a picnic. Somehow that thought excited rather than upset her.

Mama had once—just once, for she rarely discussed such things—spoken of "dangerous men." That was when she'd been trying to argue Louise out of enrolling at Kensington. She wondered if Victoria would include Donovan among those perilous males. But that seemed silly. Such a nice fellow. Before she could change her mind, she ducked past him and into the room.

The artist's studio looked very different without the sun beaming down through its skylight. True, she'd only glimpsed a slice of the room that other day, most of it blocked by Donovan standing in the doorway. Now she walked around, exploring it as if it were an uncharted continent.

Enormous windows stretched floor to ceiling and spanned the street-side wall. Along with the overhead panes they'd let in glorious golden light to paint by during the day. But now the room was cast into gloom by the overhang of the mansard roof and taller houses across the street. It almost felt as though night had fallen, although at least another hour of daylight remained.

Louise turned to face the dim room. The furnishings were few. A horsehair divan, its nubby upholstery faded to an unpleasant dun color. Candles, the cheap sort, stank of rancid tallow and burned low from saucers puddled with waxy liquid. A small wooden table, too cluttered to be usable for meals, held a mountain of tubes and jars of pigments, vials of linseed oil, pungent chemical thinners, brushes stuck bristles-up in mason jars to dry, paint-smeared rags and palette knives, and far more paraphernalia than she could take in with a quick glance. An easel, to one side of the room, supported a canvas stretcher. The pungent odor of drying paint clung in the air, making the place smell just like the classrooms at the art school.

The familiar tools and their odors quieted her nerves. "This is wonderful," she breathed.

"It's not bad, as garrets go," Donovan said. "The light's good. No rats."

She stepped farther into the room, aware he was watching her as if she were a timid deer that might bolt at any moment. Maybe he didn't yet know how much she really wanted to be here.

Artists' supplies aside, she thought, *this is how ordinary people live.* Sparingly. Without the new electric power to bring dazzling white light into rooms, without money to afford to turn on the gas and flame the wall sconces, or provide heat in winter to drive the damp chill from the room. There was no sign of an icebox or even a simple cupboard in which to store food. Only the single, lumpy divan might serve as a bed. That or the floor.

Just being in this place, Louise felt adventurous, daring . . . adult. Such wonderfully heady stuff this was—this scrumptious freedom.

"I hope you're not cold," Donovan said, startling her because she'd nearly forgotten he was there. "Rossetti can't afford gas this month. After the exhibition maybe, if he sells something. So it's candles or nothing." He paused, looking her over. "We should save some of them, don't you think?" Not waiting for an answer, he pinched out the flames from two wicks, leaving just a single smoking candle lit.

Louise blinked, hoping her eyes would soon adjust to the dark. She lifted the basket to remind him of their feast. "How will we see to eat?"

"Not a problem." He moved the candle from its shelf down to a crate set beside the divan. A silk robe lay across the upholstered back and one arm, making her think it might recently have been used as a prop in a painting. She walked around to the other side of the easel and studied the canvas, an unfinished painting of a woman reclining on the divan. But the furniture's dull color had been altered to a rich crimson hue to contrast with the woman's porcelain flesh. Her body was veiled in diaphanous white gauze that seemed to float about her skin.

Louise felt her cheeks warm as she studied the woman's nearly nude figure. The model's eyes seemed to seek out hers, declaring "I am not ashamed of my body—it is beautiful."

"Come along now, I'm hungry. Aren't you?" Donovan took the basket from her and set it on the middle cushion of the divan. He sat down beside it and flipped open its lid. "We could use the table, but the chair is wobbly and there's only one. It's much more comfortable here, don't you think?"

"I do." She beamed at him and perched demurely on the other side of the basket, still feeling nervous but liking the lovely strangeness of the place, so exotic and jumbled.

When she turned again to look at Donovan he was pulling the parcels of meat and cheese, wrapped by the shopkeeper, from beneath the pretty gingham napkins she'd also bought. His gaze traveled down from her face to her hands resting in her lap. "You might want to take off your gloves, Princess. Don't want to get them greasy."

She smiled, a little embarrassed that he'd noticed how new all of this was to her. She'd have to snap out of her daze and start acting like a woman of the world—the kind Donovan no doubt socialized with. "Of course, I wasn't going to wear them while I ate." She laughed, pulling them off by tugging on each doeskin fingertip before setting them aside.

He laid the little parcels in a line between them and set the basket on the floor. "What do we have here? Smells marvelous, it does."

"Cold roast chicken." She pointed to one. "And this one is rye bread, and this one a wedge of good Stilton cheese, and there are two apples and two pears at the bottom of the basket."

He peered back inside the hamper. "No beer or wine?"

She blinked at him, ashamed for not having thought of it. "No, I'm afraid not."

"Not to worry. My contribution." Donovan marched across the room, fished behind the shelves, and came back with an unlabeled jug. He pulled the cork and took a long drink. "We're lucky the boys left some. One of their customers paid for a portrait with wine and some medicines for Rossetti's lady friend."

"Oh, is she very ill?"

He shrugged. "She's a delicate thing. Never easy to tell with a girl like that." He leaned forward and held the jug out to her. "Have a little? It's not half bad."

Louise sipped gingerly at the jug's mouth, swallowed, and shook her head, laughing and coughing as the thick, ruby red liquid burned down her throat and made her eyes water. "It's much stronger than the wines I'm used to, and not very sweet."

He laughed. "Not fit for the palace table, is it?" There was a bitter undercurrent to his tone that hadn't been there before.

Louise slanted a look at him then hurried to make certain she hadn't hurt his feelings. "But it's good. Truly. I do like it. Here, have some chicken." She tore open each of the packages and laid out the food.

Donovan ate hungrily and drank more of the wine. She drank along with him, wanting to show she was as good company as any other girl, and not so particular she wouldn't drink common wine. Before long, her head began to spin and the garret took on a warm, buzzing glow that wasn't entirely due to the lone candle's flickering flame.

Louise leaned back into the divan's cushions and asked Donovan about his modeling and latest painting projects. He shared with her his goal of traveling to France, Germany, and especially to Italy. "Rossetti is teaching me to paint in his style. I want to study in Rome, to see the Sistine Chapel then visit Florence with its magnificent art."

"I would love to go to Rome too," she said. "But my mother says Europe is too unstable, too dangerous for us to travel now. Although my sister Vicky lives in Germany." And might soon become empress, she thought but didn't say to him.

Donovan reached out and played with a tendril of her hair that had come loose and fallen across her cheek. He wound it around and around his finger while watching her eyes. "We will run off together, you and I. To Rome. Yes, Princess? And make love in all the most romantic places."

"Oh, yes." She nodded her head in enthusiastic agreement, not sure whether they were playing a game or serious, but wanting to do nothing to discourage such a delicious fantasy.

She lifted the jug to her lips again. The wine had begun to taste smoother. Her eyelids grew heavy with the pleasure of it. Such a lovely, lovely way to spend an hour, or two.

When she moved the rough edge of the jug's rim away from her mouth, Donovan's lips pressed over hers. She held very still, liking the moist, warm sensation of his mouth on hers. The flesh around her lips and down her throat sang. She closed her eyes and savored the feeling. The jug levitated out of her hand. She heard it softly clank on the floor at their feet.

When she raised drowsy eyelids, Donovan was reaching for the silk robe. He swung it around and over his shoulders, like a magician's cape, then leaned toward her, easing her down onto the seat cushions.

"What are you doing?" She laughed, shaking her head at him, confused but delighted that he wanted to be so close to her. The robe sheltered them from the rest of the room, from the world.

"What do you think I'm doing, Princess?" he said, his words throaty and rich to her ears.

She laughed again and shook her head. "Making me feel dizzier still, lying down like this. I think I might've"—she hiccupped—"drunk too much wine." For some reason, she couldn't stop laughing.

He lowered his body still farther until she felt the entire length of him, fiery warm and lovely, his weight pressing down on her belly, flattening her breasts, snuggling against her hips.

"Just close your eyes and let the wine take you away. You're probably not used to drinking so much. It will wear off."

"But it is a lovely kind of dizz-dizz—dizziness." She breathed in and out softly, humming to herself, aware of his hands moving here and there, over the fabric of her dress. His gentle touch soothed her. She imagined herself a contented kitten, lovingly petted by her master. She lay very still. Just breathing. Her eyes closed. Smiling. Sensing his hands playing with the ruffles of her skirt then tangled somewhere between the layers of her petticoats.

"Where are you?" he whispered in her ear.

"Right here," she murmured drowsily.

Then his fingertips found her skin. And it all felt so natural, as it should be. Skin on skin. His on hers. One flesh indiscernible from the other. Together.

She floated, unwilling to move, unwilling even to crack open her eyes for fear the spell would be broken. His fingers drew little patterns on her stomach, the coils widening, tracing lightly from waist to hips.

Her flesh felt alive, vibrating, *molten*.

"Together," she whispered. She didn't like being alone. Never had. This was the nicest kind of togetherness she'd ever known. He *liked* her! He accepted her—her body as well as her art.

Louise drew a deep breath and sighed it out again. She curled into his arms. He stroked the length of her arm, the swell of her hip, the roundness of her small breast. She felt she could be happy here, like this, forever.

He kissed her again, deeper, and his hand wandered farther then slipped between her thighs. Ever so gently he cupped the place no one but she had ever touched. Yet it felt right that he knew it would please her.

Why had she never guessed she could *feel* this way?

The room spun as the wine's effect intensified, but his body anchored her, made her feel safe. She reached up and lapped her arms around his slender, boyish shoulders as he moved again. Then some part of him, not his hand, pressed against her resisting flesh. Her eyes flew open at a sharp sting. After that, it was as if no force on earth could ever separate them.

Louise wrapped her legs around her lover's slim hips and held him there as the sound of his pleasured groan turned her world golden. She lay in a shimmering haze, enthralled and amazed at what they had done.

Seventeen

She wouldn't have known that someone had entered the room but for the sudden draft that breathed across her bare skin a moment after Donovan rolled off of her. Only then did she hear the voices.

Still half asleep, woozy from the wine, Louise left her lovely, dreamy lethargy with reluctance. She instinctively reached for the silk robe to pull it back up over her. She'd leave it to her lover— *Her lover! She had a lover*—to chase off whoever had intruded upon their intimacy. But when the voices rose, filling the room with bursts of angry words, her eyelids fluttered open.

Donovan stood naked, his manly bottom turned to her as he shouted and waved his arms at someone she couldn't yet see. "Least you could do is bloody well knock. What are you doing here? You were supposed to be at the—"

"Which one of your tarts you got in here now?" an unfamiliar voice asked.

"Don't be talking like that in front of her," Donovan scolded. "She's special she is."

This generated a great deal of amusement from not one person but, it sounded to her, like two. *Two men*, from the raucous bass boom of their laughter. Inside the room now. And she was . . . well, rather indecent at the moment.

It occurred rather fuzzily to Louise that she should probably make herself more presentable and help Donovan chase off these two jokers, whoever they might be. But her head felt as capable of thinking as a bushel of turnips. She reached down and pulled the silk robe up to her chin.

As her fingers moved up her body she realized how embarrassingly few articles of her clothing remained where they should have been. Her eyes shot wide open at the suspicion that events might have transpired she couldn't quite recall. Not in detail anyway. And that made her wonder how much time had passed since she'd climbed the stairs to an unexpected taste of heaven in Donovan's arms.

The fogginess in her brain altered in an instant to a throbbing sensation, which was far less pleasant. Louise pressed her palms over her face, feeling as if she needed to hold it in place. The room swam. Her stomach soured. At last she forced herself to drop her hands and locate Donovan again.

He was stepping into his trousers, tugging them up to his waist while the heated conversation among the men continued. But now he no longer blocked her view of the two intruders. Older men. Both much broader in the shoulders, fuller in the belly than her young lover. The dark-haired, taller of the two tried to get a look at her even as a half-clothed Donovan dodged back in front of him to keep him from seeing her.

"I doubt she's any different than the others," the other man said in an offhand way. "Yes, let's do have a peek at her, Gabe. Weren't you saying you were short a model for tomorrow?"

"Ah, yes." His friend laughed. "I need a Mary for my stable scene. Think she'd suit, Donovan old boy?"

Louise roused herself enough to pull up her blouse, which had fallen beneath her breasts. She was beginning to recall details now. Donovan's hands soothing her. His kisses. His . . . forbidden caresses. She'd let him do things to her that she'd admittedly enjoyed, though now that the wine's effects were retreating, she suspected her mother might object rather strongly. Her governesses had often emphasized that princesses ought never to allow themselves to be caught alone in a room with a grown man who wasn't family. No reason was ever given for the rule.

Now, she believed she knew.

Her face flushed with heat at the thought of their recent intimacy. But she wouldn't have wished away her night with Donovan for anything.

It seemed laughable to fear something so beautiful and natural. This was how lovemaking happened. This secret way of showing tenderness and passion was what being a woman was all about. And after all, she was eighteen years old . . . and a woman.

A surge of excitement and pride nearly chased away the worry that she'd unwittingly crossed a forbidden line. But sorting out these tangled feelings, and the arbitrary rules of society, would just have to wait. She had rather more pressing wardrobe issues to deal with.

Her skirt and petticoats and chemise, in extreme disarray, had become bunched up around her waist. She tugged them down under cover of the robe. Where her drawers had gone, she'd no idea.

Meanwhile, Donovan was having little luck trying to physically force the two men out of the room. Decently covered now, Louise sat up straight, tossed off the robe, and swung her legs off the side of the divan. She planted her bare feet firmly on the floor and stood up, hands on hips, aiming her haughtiest glare at the two strangers.

"These are not public rooms, gentlemen," she announced quite loudly. "How dare you barge in here like this. I demand you leave at once and give us our privacy."

Her little speech had an unexpectedly powerful effect. Eyes wide, jaws dropped, the pair appeared stunned to the point of speechlessness. Louise combed her long, brown hair away from her face with her fingers, patting the waves into place, feeling sure the pair would now tactfully depart.

However, the strangers appeared to have frozen into biblical pillars of salt. They stared at her, shifted horrified gazes to each other then back to Donovan.

The one called Gabe was the first to move, and it now occurred to her that this was probably the artist Dante Gabriel Rossetti. So perhaps he had a right to be here, as this was his studio. Still, she thought his manners quite abominable.

Having recovered his mobility, Rossetti stepped forward with a vicious snarl, grasped Donovan by the shoulders, and gave him a rough shake. "Tell me this isn't who I think it is. Tell me, you fool."

Donovan turned to look at her, and for the first time, his eyes looked worried and his bravado visibly leaked away. He lifted his lips in a tremulous smile. "Mr. Rossetti. Mr. Morris. Really, it's all right. She *wanted* to be with me. She did. She came of her own free—"

"*Tell* me her name. *This instant!*" Rossetti's eyes blazed, dark fired and fearsome as a hellhound's.

"I am," Louise said, taking an only slightly tipsy step forward while thrusting her chin high, "Princess Louise Caroline Alberta of England—Your Royal Highness to you gentlemen. And now I demand you leave us."

Rossetti's companion let out an audible whimper and fell back two steps, a hand over his heart, gasping for air. "Gads! What have you done, boy?"

In the awkward silence that followed, Donovan regained his composure. "You have no right to criticize me, Morris. The way you and Rossetti use this studio, your women coming and going, day and night. Why can I not have a little fun as well?"

Fun? she thought.

Her head was hurting worse after the exertion of standing up and defending herself and her lover. Louise plopped back down on the divan, exhausted, and dropped her face into her palms. But not before she saw Rossetti lunge forward and cuff Donovan on the side of his head. The violence of the blow sent the young man staggering. He fell to the floor with a look of shock and wounded pride.

"Stupid boy! Have you no sense at all? Do you have any idea of the trouble you've made for yourself? For all of us? What do you think our good queen will say when she learns her daughter has been fornicating with a guttersnipe?"

Louise winced, her eyes still covered. The artist made their love sound wicked, dirty . . . and it wasn't. It was a wonderful, sweet miracle. Couldn't he see that? Their bodies had fitted together so perfectly. It was as if they'd been fashioned to become one. Adam and Eve. Tristan and Isolde. Paris and Helena. They were meant to be together.

She loved Donovan. And he clearly loved her if he wished to be so tender and close to her. How could true love shared between a man and a woman be wrong?

But in the weeks that followed, she remembered bitterly, the dangers of a princess falling in love with the wrong man became all too clear.

Eighteen

Balmoral, 1871

Within hours after the royal family's arrival at Balmoral, Byrne had been certain he would go mad with restlessness. Something about that day when they'd left London for the north haunted him. Something far worse than rats. The instincts of a military man warned him he'd best find out what was setting his nerves on edge before the unknown took them all by disastrous surprise. And that was why he'd left the Scottish royal estate to trace the wedding party's original intended route.

As Byrne had already explained to Louise, and soon after to her mother, he'd discovered what he suspected and most feared—evidence that the rat incident had been a ruse, part of a larger, more deadly plot by the Fenians to kidnap a member of the royal family.

But, unlike her daughter, the queen refused to believe him. "The vermin were obviously just a cruel prank, meant to frighten poor Baby, nothing more. We shall rise above the incident and ignore it."

Byrne shook his head in frustration. "Let me return to London. I'll find out who among the radicals is calling the shots. If our

Secret Service boys capture the Fenian officer in charge," he said, "we may disrupt their chain of command, get other names from him, and capture key figures in the Irish Republican movement." To his mind, a preemptive strike was critical to the safety of the queen and her family.

"Your duty is to remain with us here, my Raven," she insisted. "Headquarters in London will look into your theories and search for this Fenian officer."

He had to satisfy himself with sending a courier with a message to his superiors, requesting they assign men to the hunt. After seeing off the rider, he walked back inside the castle, sat in one of the dark, empty salons, and brooded. He didn't hold out much hope of results. His experience thus far in the queen's Secret Service had shown him how green and untried this infant branch of the government was.

His hands tied, Byrne tried to concentrate on the task of keeping tabs on Victoria's four youngest children, traveling with her to Scotland. Arthur, at twenty-one years old, and Leopold, just eighteen, seemed far younger and less worldly than most young men he'd met. They liked to ride and hunt with companions in the court who had accompanied the queen. Mostly they seemed content to occupy themselves in ways easy for him to monitor. Beatrice, "Baby" to the queen and sometimes to her brothers, was nearly always with her mother. Again, easy to know where she was and keep her safe. But her older sister, Louise, was a challenge.

If Victoria had given him the sole task of looking after the fourth princess, that alone would have kept him busy. The woman never sat still. She often rode out from the granite Aberdeenshire castle on her own, on a mount of her choosing from her mother's stable. With nearly fifty thousand acres of estate to explore she sometimes disappeared for half a day before he located her again. Other times she dashed off letters in support of one of her pet causes. Then she'd walk—walk *alone*, mind you—into the village to post them. Or she spirited Beatrice away from their demanding mother to call on neighbors. How to keep up with the princess without neglecting her siblings was beyond him.

What made his job even more difficult was her damned stubbornness. She repeatedly ignored his warnings, refused to wait for an escort before venturing out, and seemed in general to resent his presence, even though he was there for her protection.

It was almost as if she didn't care for her own safety. As if she were daring the radicals to target her, intentionally presenting herself as a target. To save others in the family from attack? He had no idea how the woman's mind worked.

His attempts to rein her in had become increasingly exhausting. But once again he went in search of her as he made his usual rounds through the castle, checking on each family member, passing by scores of guardsmen, stationed at close intervals along the corridors.

Byrne found Arthur and Leo playing a game of chess in the castle's billiard room, looking very dapper and gentlemanly, dressed formally for dinner in kilts, as their mother preferred when they were in residence at Balmoral. Like nearly every other room in the castle, this one had been treated to the ultimate in Highland decorative touches, transforming it into a traditional shooting lodge. Tartan draperies and upholstery, framed clan crests, mounted stag heads, wall pennants, collections of Claddagh quaiches, pewter candlesticks, cushions with needlepoint hunting scenes. And everywhere the symbol of the thistle carved into woodwork, furniture, and worked into tapestries.

The two young princes ignored his appearance in the room, as they would any servant.

Good, he thought. *At least they're safe for the time being.* He preferred they take as little notice of him as possible. That meant less chance of their remarking on his absence if he decided to ignore Victoria's orders and slip away for a day or more.

He continued in search of Louise. Down a flight of stairs, through a long gallery lined with shields, armor, and priceless art, then into the orangerie—smelling of loam and earthy molds, warm and humid to benefit the tropical plants collected there under glass. He'd learned it was one of Louise's favorite places, but she wasn't there now.

Where had the woman got to?

His thoughts circled back to his darkest concerns as he continued his search.

He should just get on the train to London. Go do the job he was meant to do. Find the bastard who was hatching plots against England's monarch. And yet . . . he had a feeling that if he blatantly disobeyed Victoria, she'd send him packing. Her dismissal would force headquarters to take him off royal protection entirely. Send him back to America. To his shattered country still reeling from civil war, scarred, mourning her lost sons, unable to heal. He didn't want to be there, not now.

To be relieved of his responsibility for the survival of the British monarch and her brood should please him. But he felt a strange compulsion to watch over this odd little family. He felt tenderness toward them he couldn't explain, despite their eccentricities.

Of all of them, Louise seemed the most vulnerable of the pack. As stubborn and bossy as she could be, something about the woman pulled at the threads of his soul, unraveled him inside, drew him bodily toward her. He was unable to define her hold over him. He'd fought it. But that insistent tug held strong, making him wonder all the more urgently now—where the hell was she?

Sometimes he wondered if these feelings about the princess explained his animosity toward the young marquess. Was he jealous of the man? Certainly not. Jealousy required a man to believe he had a claim on a woman. And he had no right at all to Louise. None whatsoever. And never would have.

He stopped in front of the drawing room Louise favored most often. He pushed on the door with one finger. It glided open on silent hinges. And there, at last, she was. Louise reclined on a settee by the window, a book open in her lap, her lemon yellow skirts pooling around her on the seat cushion, her rich golden brown hair spread across a needlepoint pillow.

His heart stopped.

She seemed to know he was there even before she turned her head to coolly observe him with her pretty eyes. He opened his mouth to excuse himself for interrupting her rest but she spoke first. "You are discreet, are you not, Mr. Byrne?"

"Princess?" He stepped into the room, shut the door behind him.

"I mean to say"—her eyes slipped away from his as he moved toward her—"your attitude, manners, and dress are unconventional, to say the least. But since my mother seems to trust you, and she demands loyalty, honesty and discretion, may I expect you to treat me with the same regard?"

What the hell was the woman talking about? Could this have anything to do with her faithless husband? For a terrifying moment he feared she might have discovered that he'd followed Lorne and was going to request detailed information about the marquess's nocturnal adventures.

"Are you asking," he began carefully, "if I am keeping secrets *for* you . . . or *from* you?"

She winced, as if stung by an invisible insect. "Not exactly. I'd simply like to discuss your ability to keep sensitive information to yourself."

He'd never liked court word games or the witty social banter so loved by the aristocracy. Its aim was to inflate the ego of the cleverer player and poke fun at the person who couldn't keep up with the riddles and plays on words. He was tired, desperate to make progress toward stopping the Fenians, and fast losing patience with whatever sport this woman was proposing.

"Why don't you come right out and say what's on your mind, Your Highness?"

She glanced at him sideways, her eyes flashing. "Americans. So abrupt."

"We get to the point quickly. It has its advantages."

"Yes, well, I suppose that's true. And perhaps this is one of those times when plain talk is most appropriate." She let long dark eyelashes drift closed over her blue eyes and folded the book shut in her lap. When she opened her eyes again and pushed herself up to sitting on the settee, she again let her gaze slide past him and out the window at the end of the room. "I have a favor to ask of you, Raven."

He narrowed his eyes at her use of the queen's code name. He thought he knew what was coming. She was going to ask him to turn a blind eye to her husband's dalliances. Or, even worse, as he'd first suspected, she wanted him to spy on Lorne. He said nothing.

She drew a deep breath and let it out slowly, as if reaching inside herself for the courage to continue.

"Some years ago," she began in the softly distant voice that might have signaled the beginning of a child's fairy tale, "when I was attending art school in Kensington, I made many friends. They were good people and great fun to be around. I felt a delicious sense of freedom while there. No castle walls to contain me. No tutors, parents, or staff to constantly control my life. No court gossips to report my every move. I became my own person, a little canary sprung from her cage."

"The queen allowed you to attend a public school with commoners, unchaperoned?" Knowing Victoria, he couldn't believe that was possible.

She flashed him a mischievous smile. "Not precisely. I gradually convinced my mother that, while I was in my classes, it would be a waste of one of her ladies' time to sit with me. Eventually a footman became unnecessary as well. All I had to do was bribe my driver to spend the day with his daughter on the other side of the city. Then I could come and go as I pleased during the day."

"Naughty girl." He kept a straight face, giving away nothing of the little he already knew of those years in her life.

"Yes, well, I suppose I was. As well as naïve, and foolish." She brushed a hand through the air, as if waving away the years as well as her innocence. "At any rate, there was one particular friend, a young man not much older than I at the time—eighteen. His name was Donovan Heath. A special companionship developed between us." Color rose beneath the ivory surface of her cheeks. She immediately stood up, tenderly clutching her book to her bosom as if it were a child. She walked with a brisk step away from him toward the window and stared out into the distance. "He became very dear to me, Mr. Byrne."

From her protective tone, he understood she would reveal no more about the relationship. But he was fairly sure from her wistfulness and sudden high coloring that this encounter, however far it had gone, had been her first romantic experience. He'd been told by more than one lady that a woman never forgot her first lover.

Byrne held back the questions that immediately sprang to his mind. More than anything, he wanted her to continue talking. Her voice came to him as a kind of melancholy melody. Her words, lyrics heavy with emotion. He sensed this conversation was not only difficult for her; this might also be the very first time she'd spoken about this matter for a long time.

"One day, Donovan just went missing," Louise said, keeping her back to him, her gaze reaching far and away, as if she could see out the window and past the distant hills purple with spring heather. "He gave no indication that he would be leaving London or that our friendship should end. I looked for him, of course, concerned for his welfare. London can be a dangerous place. But none of his friends knew where he'd gone."

"He broke your heart." The words came out before he could bite them back.

"No!" She spun to face him, her eyes bright with denial.

He watched her take a breath in an attempt to compose herself, but it didn't seem to work. She put her book down on a table and paced in agitation in front of the window, hands clasped over her skirt, gaze fixed in fierce concentration on the carpet.

"That's *not* how it was, Mr. Byrne. I was just worried about him. You see, he had no money. He depended upon others for a little work and food. He mostly slept in artists' studios. The poor boy might have fallen sick, or been injured. Don't you see? He had no one to go to for help, except to me." She stopped and turned to Byrne, looking directly into his eyes, as if to force him to understand. "And *he would have come to me.* I am certain he would have . . . if he could."

He now saw where this was going. "You want me to find out what happened to Donovan Heath."

"Yes, if you can. Yes, please." The words rushed out of her, as if she were both ashamed and excited by the possibility. "And if he is still alive, I'd like to know where he is now."

Bad idea, he thought. *Very bad.* "Is that wise, Princess?"

Her eyes widened at his questioning her. "I don't care whether it's wise or not. It's not your job, Mr. Byrne, to doubt my wisdom or argue my decisions. I am asking this as a favor. No, *not* as a favor," she hastily amended with a dismissive flutter of her hand. A nervous gesture she shared with her mother. "I understand your mercenary nature. I will pay you well for your services. Consider it a job."

He stiffened at her implication. "I already have a job. And money isn't the reason I joined the queen's Secret Service."

She sniffed and turned her back to him. "Very well then. I shall find someone else."

He lifted his eyes to the vaulted ceiling and shook his head. Bother. Now he'd made things worse, hadn't he? He'd angered her. If he didn't accommodate her, or at least pretend to, she would stop listening to him, no longer heed any warning or advice he gave. No matter how serious the issue or how dangerous the situation into which she was prepared to thrust herself.

Byrne wasn't accustomed to apologizing for his actions, but there was no other way. "I'm sorry, Your Royal Highness. I didn't mean to offend. It's just that, in my experience, the past is often best left . . . in the past." He watched her lovely shoulders rise and fall as she took a deep breath.

Slowly, as if the slightest movement required deliberate effort, she pivoted to face him. She blinked several times—flecks of darker blue within paler irises. And he realized, to his dismay, she was trying to hold back tears. For the first time it struck him that she might still be in love with this Donovan bloke.

He let out a breath of resignation. "All right. Listen, I'll do what I can. And I suspect your little speech about discretion at the beginning of this conversation means you don't want me to mention this investigation to anyone, including your mother."

She gave a tiny nod of her head and started to raise a sleeve toward her face, as if to blot away the tears brimming over her lashes. But she thought better of revealing too much and stopped herself. "Thank you. Yes. That's my wish."

"There is one problem," he said.

"And that is?"

"I'm supposed to remain here at Balmoral, watching after you, your sister, and brothers. Leaving will be interpreted as a neglect of my duty."

"I see." She looked so utterly bereft and disappointed he wanted to wrap his arms around her in consolation, but he planted his boots and stayed where he was. For a moment her eyes flitted about the room, as if searching dim recesses for an answer to her problem. "So you're afraid of my mother too?"

He tightened his lips to keep from smiling. "In a manner of speaking, isn't everyone?"

"Not always." She grimaced, as if remembering something painful from another time. Then suddenly her face lit up. "This is what you'll do. You will go to John Brown. Ask him to detail two of his men to watch over us in your place, just for a few days. Three men, if he wishes. Surely that will suffice."

"May I remind you, Mr. Brown and I are not on the best of terms."

"But if you tell him there is an urgent reason for your brief return to London. Perhaps a family emergency? No, you've no family in this country. Is that right?"

"Exactly."

She tapped her chin with one finger. "I know. Your commander has ordered your return for some reason. I'm sure you can create an excuse that will sound logical to Brown. And to my mother."

She was asking him to lie to the queen. That was tiptoeing dangerously close to treason, even if he wasn't one of her subjects.

But the cause was a good one. London, he thought. Exactly where he wanted to be. The temptation was almost too great. Kill two birds with one stone: do a fast search for the missing artists' model while spending most of his time tracking down the Fenian commander.

Louise must have seen acquiescence in his expression. She smiled. A tear trickled from her lashes, but this time she swiped it away quickly with her sleeve, as if it was no longer of consequence. "How much will you charge me?"

"Nothing, Princess—for the time being. I don't mind waiting for suitable compensation."

Her eyes latched on to his, and he felt a rush of heat through his body. What had possessed him to say that? To flirt with a princess. He hadn't meant to step over the line of propriety. Hadn't intended to say anything that might be construed as provocative. But he was secretly gratified by the sparkle in her eyes and upward turn of her lips.

"Yes, well, when you have arrived at a reasonable return for your time and services," she said solemnly, "please do let me know."

"I most surely will." He hesitated. There was another matter. But he was unsure how much harder he dare press for information. He stepped away toward a low table and picked up a graceful figurine carved from wood—a hunting dog. Perhaps one of her early art projects? "I have the young man's name. Donovan Heath?"

"Correct."

He ran a finger over the smooth head of the hound, trying to appear casual as he admired the detail of the dog's furry ruff. "And he would now be in his early twenties?"

"Perhaps twenty-three or -four, if he still lives," she said softly.

"Can you give me addresses he once frequented?"

"Of course."

He was hesitant, circling around the one critical question. Hoping it would seem of no more importance than the others. "And you said he had no other close friends or family in London, or elsewhere. So far as you know."

She frowned at him, as if unable to understand why this should be of concern to him. "It's been five or more years. Many of our friends from the school have moved on in their lives, as have I. I'm afraid you must work with the little I've supplied."

"Nevertheless, giving me as much information as possible, about your relationship with your friend and others who knew him, will help."

"Of course." She gave him a sideways look.

"Was your mother aware of the relationship?" There it was—the one question he needed answered before this went any further.

Louise's eyes narrowed, as if she were a wild creature that sniffed a trap. "Aware of our . . . friendship?"

"Yes."

Her gaze drifted away from him. When she at last spoke her voice was barely a whisper, but it sliced like a saber through the silence between them. "No. I should think not."

"You never mentioned his name to the queen?"

"Why should that matter, Mr. Byrne? I'm losing patience with you, I must say."

"Because if the friendship seemed to Victoria a serious one, she might have disapproved. Don't you think, Princess?"

"If you're implying that the queen would have done anything to keep me from seeing my friend again, I suppose you're right," she snapped back at him. "Oh all right, yes, I *did* mention him to her. She knew we were friends."

A shadow seemed to fall over the room, chilling it. He knew Victoria would have been furious with her daughter if she even guessed Louise was encouraging a personal, possibly intimate relationship with a commoner. And a destitute artist at that. There was no way she would have tolerated the notion of their becoming a couple.

He was aware of Louise's wide-eyed gaze, studying him with something like fear. As if she were trying to decide whether he was friend or foe. Calculating the risk of honesty.

"You're saying," she began, "that you believe my mother might have had something to do with Donovan's going missing?" There seemed barely enough air behind her words to propel them into the room. He swore he could hear her pulse from ten feet away. "That's simply outrageous."

"Maybe," he said. "But she might have sent someone to persuade him to leave London. Out of concern for you. A mother protecting her innocent young daughter."

Louise let her gaze drop to her hands, clutched again in front of her skirt. All the spit and fire seemed to drain from her body as he watched. Her shoulders lowered and shrank. Her color fled. "Yes. All right. Yes, I suppose she might have done something to—" She shook her head and sighed. "I actually thought as much at one time. But my friend would have got word to me, don't you think? He would have sent a letter, a message through mutual acquaintances, something to let me know she'd frightened him off."

"If he could have." Byrne looked at her with meaning, wishing he didn't have to say such things to her. Words that might or might not be the truth, but that would be guaranteed to hurt.

She blinked at him, shaking her head in unconcealed revulsion. "You don't believe she could have done anything . . . *drastic*, do you?"

There was no doubt in his mind the lengths to which Victoria would go to protect her family. The only question in his mind was this: how far had her daughter's relationship with the fellow already gone before Donovan disappeared? If Louise had taken him as a lover, and Victoria confronted Louise, who then refused to be parted from him, would the queen have been desperate enough to . . .

To do what?

She would have done whatever was necessary to scare off the young man. Threats, beatings . . . or worse. And if it was this last option, if an assassin had been dispatched to resolve the problem of her daughter's indiscretion, then Byrne knew he'd never find Donovan Heath alive.

Nineteen

Louise waited patiently, then not so patiently for word from Stephen Byrne after he left for London. She neither saw nor heard from the man for thirteen days. Gossip among the staff and reduced court at Balmoral had it that the handsome American was recalled to London by his superiors. Probably for disciplinary measures. And yet several of the queen's ladies expressed, within Louise's hearing, a wistful longing for his return. The man seemed to have a powerful effect on females, her mother included. Maybe that was why John Brown appeared happy to see him gone. The Scot would have the queen's full attention for as long as Byrne stayed away.

Louise admitted to herself, although to no one else, that she was not entirely immune to Byrne's brooding, dark good looks and demonstrable physical prowess. The man was positively magnificent astride a horse. And his entrance into a room seemed to suck all of the air out of it. Nevertheless, she intended to limit their relationship to conversations of a purely business nature. Anything more *friendly* was, after all, impossible. She was a married woman and would remain so until either she or Lorne passed from this life.

Even the vaguest romantic imaginings that included the Raven, she chased from her mind.

When Byrne finally returned to Balmoral, he sent Louise a maddeningly curt note by way of Lady Car:

Nothing of value to report on the matter of your inquiry.

Louise didn't trust the man. Despite his refusal to accept payment for his time, she had given him a very generous stipend to cover his travel expenses, meant to last for as long as it took him to find Donovan. For all she knew, he'd already spent it on gambling, drink, and the sorts of women who plied their trade in the artists' districts where she'd indicated he'd most likely find Donovan.

Before Louise could corner the annoying man and demand to know—*in detail, sir, with a list of interviews you've accomplished on my behalf!*—what the hell he'd been doing all of that time. Victoria decided the family must return to London. Parliament was soon to be called into session, and the PM was adamant that the queen make an appearance on opening day.

And so barely two months after their arrival in Scotland, all of the queen's ladies and gentlemen, family members in residence, and staff, again packed up their finery and necessities to head for London. But this time Brown, with the support of the American agent and the captain of the royal guard, insisted that the journey south be accomplished by railway, a more secure and faster means of travel.

Victoria allowed that this made sense, considering the level of alarm raised by recent articles in the London press with regard to the "Irish problem." But she informed Louise and Baby, "I will be in agony and tears the entire trip, thinking of my dear husband who last traveled this way with me."

Louise had come to believe her mother relished mourning more than most any other activity in the world, and said nothing.

Once they were on their way, in the far more comfortable accommodations offered by the private train cars provided for the royal family, Louise spent hours seated beside her silent husband, dwelling upon her future—such as it was. She made several important decisions, which she shared with no one. Nevertheless they provided her with a modicum of comfort.

First, she would join Amanda in attending a demonstration in support of women's suffrage, despite her mother's admonitions that she should not become "involved." Her friend had become more active than she in the movement and often wrote broadsides to be posted about the city.

Louise was so very proud of Amanda, who had come such a long way since her days as a lowly maid of all work. To Louise's joy, Amanda's marriage to young Dr. Henry Locock had transformed her friend. While little Edward was but a baby, and Amanda tied to home and hearth, Louise had sent one of her old tutors to her, so that she might learn to write better and improve her speaking skills, a desire Amanda often had confided to her. Amanda's success was proof of what women, when properly educated, were capable of.

What truly perplexed Louise was her mother's attitude toward suffrage. For some unfathomable reason, the Queen of England, the most independent-minded woman she knew, refused to acknowledge her sisters' basic rights. Louise knew her mother would be furious if she found out one of her daughters had attended a public rally or, worse yet, a protest march. But she felt compelled to lend her voice and proclaim the injustice of male rule.

Louise's second decision, made during the journey back to London, involved the Raven. At the first opportunity after they settled back into Buckingham Palace for the Season, she would confront Byrne and demand a full report. Exactly where had he inquired and what had he learned about Donovan Heath's fate? No matter how slight the information might seem to him, *she wanted it*!

Louise was convinced the American knew something and was

holding back from her. Why else would he avoid her like this, communicating only through a terse note? There were days when she had sensed his presence at Balmoral, yet when she went looking for him he disappeared, as if he were no more than a puff of smoke on the wind.

Thirdly, she vowed to devote more of her time to the Women's Work Society—reorganizing the crafts and handwork they'd acquired, updating the displays, and working with Amanda to create new brochures to pass out or post around the city and let people know about the shop. She also wanted to develop a training program to broaden the skills of the women who came to her, giving them more options for earning a living wage.

And lastly, there was her art, which she dearly missed. Preparing for the wedding, she'd neglected it. She hadn't begrudged the time she'd taken from her sculpting and painting, because she truly believed she was investing in a sound and satisfying marriage. Now that time seemed squandered. As soon as possible, she would set up a studio in the house she and Lorne would share. While their new home was being prepared for them, they would occupy a suite at Buckingham and she'd paint in the garden or set up her easel in the music room where the light was best. Her sculpting would need to wait for more space and privacy.

All in all, Louise kept telling herself, she was lucky to have a full, meaningful, and challenging life. She was young, in excellent health, and moderately attractive, if she did say so herself. As the daughter of the queen, she would never have to worry about money. The idea that her future entirely lacked sexual gratification, that she would never again enjoy the physical companionship of a man she cared deeply for, or bear children—well, she would simply have to put these losses firmly out of her mind and move on. The many excellent avocations and people already part of her world would have to suffice.

* * *

The morning of the suffrage rally, Amanda was in exceptionally high spirits. As Louise watched in dismay, her friend literally bounced off cabinets and walls in her enthusiasm, twice knocking over displays, shattering a pottery bowl, and spilling loose tea leaves all over a set of embroidered antimacassars.

Amanda barely took a breath between words as she chattered away at Louise. "And do you realize who will be there?"

"The prime minister?" Louise teased, knowing full well Mr. Gladstone would rather shoot himself in the foot than attend a women's suffrage rally.

"Of course not." Amanda laughed, her eyes sparkling with anticipation. "Although there are members of Parliament who support our cause in theory, I doubt they'll dare show their faces at a major public demonstration like *this* one."

"What's so special about today's?" Louise handed Amanda three hand-worked lace collars to add to the display in the consignment shop's window, along with a charming painted tea set and selection of crocheted sweaters.

"Representatives of the NSWS have said they'll come. Do you believe it? Oh, this will be a great and historic event, I can just feel it."

Louise knew the National Society for Women's Suffrage lobbied all the MPs, regardless of their party affiliation, encouraging them to support women's suffrage. Perhaps soon they would have a little success. If they managed to get even a handful of these powerful men to step up and announce their commitment to the cause, it would be an amazing coup for women's rights.

"Our la-dies are a-comin' from all o'er the town," Amanda sang to a bawdy tune then reverted to less melodious speech. "And from well into the countryside, I do hear. Rumor has it Laura McLaren is traveling all the way from Edinburgh, and the famous Millicent Fawcett will attend as well." She patted an ecru lace collar into place on a throat-and-shoulders plaster mannequin that Louise had designed to show off their wares. "This is so very thrilling. I feel as if we are on the verge of a revolution of sorts. Don't you taste it in the air, Louise? This modern age will be so wonderful for all of us."

"Don't get your hopes up too high, my girl." After all, as daughter to the queen, she was in the privileged position of overhearing the queen's ministers' opinions, which weren't often encouraging. The MPs clung to the old ways, foolishly arguing that women could depend upon the generosity of their men for everything good in their lives. But she only had to remember desperate stories of women like Amanda to know that leaving the protection of women, and children, to the males of the species guaranteed nothing. Hadn't the *Times* only recently revealed in an editorial that tens of thousands of homeless women wandered the streets, begging or selling their bodies simply to survive? And what about all of the orphaned children? What men had stood up to save *them*?

It was an outrageous situation that had to end.

"Do you know how many will be at the rally?" Louise asked.

"Oh, hundreds . . . perhaps thousands!" Amanda climbed down from the shop window, grabbed Louise around the waist, and danced her around the room, narrowly avoiding the refurbished picture frames stacked in one corner.

Louise laughed and firmly brought her friend to a stop. "Where's little Eddie today?"

"Henry offered to stay with him. Eddie will probably sleep through much of the afternoon. The child was so tired this morning after a late night with his mum and da. Once he's asleep nothing will wake him. Henry will be able to see afternoon patients without distraction." She threw her shawl around her shoulders and twirled one last time in the middle of the shop. "Oh, it will be absolutely glorious—we sisters, rich and poor alike, linked by a common cause."

Louise hugged her. "Yes, dear heart, I'm sure it will be. And we'll all do what we can to make the day come sooner when we can determine our own fates." It occurred to her that, ironically, her friend, a commoner, would likely have more freedom than *she*, a princess, ever would. Louise fought off a wave of remorse and placed a sign in the shop window, saying they would return in two hours. She locked the door behind them.

The day was warm, the sun brilliant. After a recent rain the air now smelled cleaner than on most London days. The ever-present smog seemed to have temporarily washed away. They strolled, arm in arm, up the street and back through the market district, toward Hyde Park, where the rally would take place. From blocks away, Louise could hear drums thumping, horns blaring. The buzz of hundreds of voices came to them, louder and louder as they approached.

Louise felt her heart rise on a wave of hope. She wanted, like Amanda, to believe they were on the precipice of a historic moment. Someday, very soon, women would hold the same rights as men in English society—and, who knew, perhaps around the world. What a triumph that would be. Women would be free to enter into any profession, to travel as far as they wished, on their own if they liked. They would own property, perhaps even businesses—and wasn't their little shop a modest beginning in that direction?

With each step Louise's anticipation grew. She matched her stride to Amanda's, felt her body take up the intoxicating rhythm of the drumbeat. Soon they were marching alongside dozens of other women, all descending upon the park. Some were attired in the height of fashion, in full afternoon toilette or chic Dolly Varden walking suits, others in the smocks of shopgirls. A few broke into a run in their enthusiasm to greet their sisters. Others moved with stately seriousness. Then there were those who ventured only small, timid steps, parasols half hiding their faces, as if fearful they were doing something wrong but still wished to be part of the brave effort.

The rally began with a prayer for solidarity, everyone holding hands in long human chains. Some men stood alongside their wives, sisters, or mothers, but they were few. Then a woman in a black coatdress and wide-brimmed hat that dwarfed her tiny face stepped onto a makeshift stage. She spoke to the gathering in a voice that carried surprisingly far. No one had introduced her, but her name was whispered throughout the crowd.

This is the famous Millicent Fawcett. The woman who had been an inspirational force in the struggle since its very inception.

She spoke of dedication. Of the need to reassure members of Parliament, husbands, brothers, and even other women that their goals were nonpartisan and nonthreatening. She encouraged her audience to seek the support of any man or woman who agreed that all people, regardless of sex, should possess the same rights. It was a stirring and brilliant speech. At its conclusion a great shout of joy and dedication swept through the crowd.

"Oh no, look there!" Amanda reached out and grasped Louise's hand.

Louise turned and saw a line of police officers file into the park. She frowned. "This is a peaceful rally. I'm sure the police haven't been instructed to interfere." At least, not today, or so she hoped.

There had been a backlash against the police after they'd stormed a recent women's rally. Each side had accused the other of brutal physical assaults. Only a few journalists claimed the women had provoked the attack by hurling stones at the police. Many more newspapers carried sketches and cartoons, showing women being knocked to the pavement and clubbed by bobbies the artists depicted as monstrous ogres. The public had been outraged. It seemed unlikely, so soon after such a large dose of bad press, the police would dare repeat their error.

"No, not the police." Amanda's voice shook and her grip on Louise's hand tightened painfully. "On the far side of the stage. Oh, God, it's *him*!"

"Who?" Louise scanned the crowd, unable to pick out a familiar face.

"Darvey. The pimp who . . . Don't you remember? I hope he doesn't see me."

It took Louise a moment to recall why that name should be important. But the sheer terror in Amanda's eyes soon brought it back to her. Roger Darvey—the bawd under whose fist Amanda had labored before she'd escaped to a better life.

"Surely he won't recognize you now. Dressed as you are and all these years later."

"I pray not. Oh please no, he's coming this way." Amanda danced in place, wild with agitation, hemmed in by the packed crowd but ready to bolt.

Louise held her firm, hoping to calm her. Running through this mob of women, standing shoulder to shoulder as they cheered Mrs. Fawcett, would be impossible. And the disturbance created by Amanda's frantic dash would only draw the pimp's attention to her, if he hadn't already seen her.

"He can't have noticed you from this far away, among all these other women. Anyway, why would he still be looking for you? Or even care where you've gone."

Amanda's pretty face contorted, her eyes fever bright with frenzy. "He punishes those who cross him," she hissed. "I seen him kick a woman to death."

"Amanda, please listen—"

"His pride, don't you see?" her friend whispered urgently, lips an inch from Louise's ear. "I was the girl who got away. Makes him look bad." When Louise pulled away to look in Amanda's eyes, tears had filled them.

"Quiet now," Louise soothed. "Be brave. Keep your head down. He'll pass by and be gone soon." She watched the man move slowly through the crowd, shoulders hunched, head lowered, as if intent on private thoughts. He wasn't even looking their way.

Some of the tension in Amanda's face smoothed away. But her gaze never left the man in the patched jacket and battered top hat. She let out a breath, relaxed her death grip on Louise. "Thank you," she whispered. "How many girls on the street find a princess to befriend them? To dig them out of the gutters. That's why we're here. So girls like me won't have to—"

"Hush!" Louise warned.

At first it seemed to her that Darvey was rudely cutting through the middle of the crowd, solely to display his annoyance with the women's presence. She'd seen similar behavior from men who ordinarily had better manners. Darvey's downturned eyes were hard and angry and spiteful, as if he resented every single female standing there and demanding what, by right, ought to be hers. Moving faster now, he shoved one woman after another out of his way, making no attempt to excuse himself.

Louise felt her lips begin to turn up in a relieved smile, believing he'd missed them entirely, but then his ground-anchored gaze flicked upward, just once, directly at Amanda. She saw the shadow of a leer on his pulpy lips.

"Come this way," Louise said. There was no time for explanation.

Amanda followed her glance to where Darvey was pressing forward, more quickly now, his trajectory having shifted directly toward them. A deathlike rigor seized Amanda's lovely features. She let out a terrified shriek.

Hand in hand, they squeezed through a dense knot of women in dark-colored, severe dresses. They might have moved faster through a vat of molasses, whereas Darvey had the advantage of his size and willingness to knock to the ground anyone who stood in his way.

Louise looked back over her shoulder. He was gaining on them.

She cast around frantically for the bobbies she'd seen earlier. But if they were still anywhere within this part of the park, she could no longer see them through the wall of bodies. As they left

Hyde Park by way of Cumberland Gate and burst into Oxford Street, Louise glanced around at the gated houses and shops with their CLOSED signs. They'd all locked down, in case things got out of hand and the ladies should suddenly take it into their heads to loot a butcher shop or hattery. She hastily calculated distances to safe havens. Neither Buckingham nor Kensington Palace were close enough to reach before Darvey fell upon them.

Amanda must have been thinking the same thing. She gasped, "My house. Run!"

They dropped hands and tore down Oxford Street, turning left then left again, into narrower uphill streets with smaller, less fashionable houses. Louise stopped paying attention to street names, trusting Amanda to lead them on the shortest route. She kept an eye open for anyone they might run to for help, but the police seemed nowhere around. Skirts lifted with one hand, hats secured with the other—they raced toward sanctuary.

Their shoes slapped and slid over rounded cobbles, skidding on spots slick with sewage and wash water. Wrenching her knee as she cornered yet again, Louise fought the pain and ran for her life. Ran until her lungs ached, pleading for air.

Dizziness threatened to send her reeling into a brick storefront. But the muscles in her legs, as if recalling childhood romps with Bertie and Arthur, miraculously carried her forward.

From behind her came the beastly shouts of the man pursuing them. Like an ogre from a childhood nightmare he shouted his awful threats, tormenting Amanda with disgusting promises of what he'd do to her when he caught her.

Lord, help us.

Ahead in the shadows of a narrowing street, Louise glimpsed a precarious stack of crates left behind after market day. Even from this distance she smelled the rotting fruit. Its sickly sweet, cloying odor fouled the warm air. Saved, no doubt, to be used as animal fodder.

Amanda was two long strides ahead of her. Louise saw her adjust her path to avoid the crates.

Louise gritted her teeth and angled her body toward the narrow space between the grocer's wall and the boxes. Lowering one shoulder she plunged ahead. Aimed for the third box from the top, chest high. Braced herself for impact.

Pain shot up through her shoulder, into her neck. "Ah!" she cried. But her strategy was effective. The entire stack tumbled over with a splintering crash.

Behind her Louise heard the grunt of their pursuer. The squelching sounds of trodden fruit. The thud of a body hitting paving stones. Enormously gratified with the results of her tactic, she lifted her skirts higher, lost her hat to the wind, but ran on after Amanda, who seemed unaware of the calamity they'd left in their wake.

Louise didn't dare slow down. She'd bought them only a little time.

Too soon, the pounding of iron-pegged boots returned, accompanied by snarls of vengeance. She snapped her head around to peer behind her, but in taking her attention from the uneven road felt her toe catch the front edge of a paver.

The street rushed up at her, a solid gritty brown, muck-puddled wave. *Don't fall. Can't fall!* He'd be on her in a second.

Still pitching forward, she jammed a foot down, regained her balance, and stumbled up the incline.

Louise recognized where they were now—the last few blocks before Amanda's house on Highgate Hill. There, at the street's pinnacle, loomed a stark, coal-blackened stone church with its single tower. And next to it—Park House, the women's shelter. The good Dr. Locock's brownstone waited just beyond.

Blessed safety.

Mere steps ahead of her, Amanda flew past the church, rounded a corner, and threw herself at the front door. She grasped Louise by the arm, as if afraid she wasn't moving fast enough, and dragged her inside before slamming the door behind them with a deafening bang.

Both women dove for the bolt and shoved it home.

Outside, a body crashed into the heavy wooden planks. A barrage of muffled curses assaulted them through the door.

"Is that Beelzebub himself chasing you girls home?" a cheery voice asked. "Or just one of your antisuffrage adversaries?"

Panting, clutching her sides as she tried to catch her breath, Louise turned to face the tall, elegantly mustached man who observed them from the kitchen doorway.

"Thank God you're here, Henry," Amanda cried, throwing herself into her startled husband's arms. "It's that terrible m—" Her words were cut off by another volley of curses from the far side of the door, followed by a thunderous pounding of fists. This time the words were clear, as if Darvey pressed his mouth to the door.

"Fuckin' bitch! Y'ain't gettin' away again."

Henry Locock froze, his expression grim. "Is that *the man*?"

"Go away, Darvey," Amanda shouted. "I'm no more yours to use."

"Nah, you's gonna pay, all right. Two more o' me girls ran off 'cause a you."

Louise knew Henry Locock had long ago learned of his wife's tragic past. He had made it plain to all that he didn't blame her for the desperate situation in which she'd found herself. If he ever got his hands on the man who'd so abused and debased her, he'd put aside his vow as a physician to "do no harm." But now that she'd actually witnessed Darvey's violence, Louise feared as much for her friend's husband as for Amanda herself.

To her horror, Henry took a step toward the door.

Before Louise could say anything, Amanda threw herself between the door and her husband. "No!" she screamed. "He'll *kill* you. You don't know what he's capable of. Please, Henry, for our children's sake, don't." Her eyes darted toward the back room where her son must have somehow slept through the commotion. "He'll go away."

Henry turned to Louise for confirmation.

She'd seen enough of Roger Darvey to convince her. She gave Henry a bleak look and shook her head.

"As I thought." Turning on his heel Henry disappeared into his examination room. Seconds later, he returned with his hunting rifle. "He won't come visiting again, if he knows what's good for him."

Brushing his wife aside, Henry unbolted the door, flung it wide, snapped the butt of the gun to his shoulder, and curled his finger around the trigger.

Surprised in the midst of his attack on the door, Darvey froze, fists raised above his head. Momentum carried him forward, propelling him into the gun's muzzle. It took him a moment to shift his murderous gaze from the face of the man in front of him to the weapon between them, its business end jammed below his ribs.

Darvey's expression switched in a flash from fury to shock. Then he was backpedaling as if on an invisible velocipede. He tripped off the curb and tumbled to the ground.

"You will never, *ever*, come to my house again," Henry shouted, advancing on him, thrusting his weapon's muzzle toward the man's face. "Neither will you approach or speak to my wife. Is that clear, sir?"

Darvey said nothing, but he cringed and let out a mongrel's whimper when Henry leveled the gun's barrel at the center of his forehead. He looked past the gun, past the doctor, toward the house, as if still contemplating a devious means of carrying out his revenge. But a second later, he was scrambling to his feet and off at a run.

"Good job, Henry." Louise patted him on the shoulder when he'd stepped back inside and shut the door. But his eyes were all for his wife.

Amanda threw herself into his arms, weeping.

Henry handed the rifle to Louise. He wrapped his long arms around his wife.

"I doubt the rogue will bother any of us again," he said, looking puffed up with pride at the reaction he'd got from Darvey.

"You were so brave. So very brave, my darling," Amanda sobbed. "Thank you."

"Even an educated gentleman, sometimes, can summon up a bit of the bully in him when necessary." He winked at Louise, over his wife's shoulder. "Now, now, dear girl. It's all right. The monster is gone for good. Enough tears."

Louise smiled nervously as she leaned the rifle against the wall beside the front door. Something in the way Darvey had glowered at them, his tail not quite between his legs, made her doubt they'd seen the last of him.

Now she wished she hadn't been so eager to avoid Stephen Byrne's attempts to protect her. Had the Raven been with them at the rally today, they would have been safe.

She wasn't sure why she knew this—that Byrne would stand between her and danger, no matter the cost to him. But she felt it in every fiber of her body. She had a protector—a knight, though not one in shining armor. A knight in a dirty brown duster and Stetson hat.

How very strange, she thought.

Twenty

He wasn't intentionally neglecting his duties. That's what Byrne kept telling himself. By nature he was neither lazy nor a coward. But since John Brown preferred to handle the royal family's security by himself—contrary to the queen's orders—Byrne felt justified in leaving the situation at the palace to the Scot while he continued hunting for the Fenian captain and Louise's misplaced lover. Headquarters might well object to his reasoning, but what they didn't know . . .

Byrne had strongly mixed feelings about the second of these tasks.

On the one hand, he wanted to please the princess, to be the man who brought her the truth about her first love. It seemed important to her, and he assumed she must have tried to find Donovan before this. Apparently earlier attempts had failed. He imagined her excitement, and the forms her *gratitude* might take, when he delivered proof of Donovan Heath's fate and whereabouts. Would she fling her arms around his neck and plant an impulsive kiss on his mouth? (God knew the woman must be starved for affection.) And if he then trapped her delicate figure in an embrace would she yield to her rumored passionate nature and press ever more seductively, eagerly against his—

Damn, don't go there, man. That's treacherous territory.

Treacherous in more ways than one because, instinct told him, what he'd eventually discover was a truth darker than black. One that well might bring Louise intolerable grief. The idea of hurting her even more deeply than she'd already been hurt, heaping more undeserved pain on the poor woman—this was what caused him to stall for time.

During his years fighting for the North in the War between the States, he'd been accused, sometimes rightly so, of being many things—a rogue, spy, seducer, pragmatist, arrogant, merciless, brutal . . . even of being the devil himself. But never had anyone called him a coward.

Perhaps now he'd become even that. A coward where Louise was concerned. Because he hadn't honestly put any real effort into finding Donovan Heath. And that was because he couldn't bear the thought of seeing her brought to her knees, crushed by a truth too awful to bear.

So he'd argued with himself. Was it wiser to pretend he'd searched for the elusive young artists' model and report he'd found nothing? Thereby saving Louise from the humiliation of learning she'd simply been dumped, or from the heartache of discovering the boy's early and very possibly violent death. Or did he owe her the absolute truth that his respect for her demanded?

There was something decidedly sinister about this whole business of the missing Donovan, though he couldn't yet put his finger on why. He didn't know Victoria all that well. But what he did know of the monarch convinced him she was capable of absolute ruthlessness if threatened. Perhaps the worst of all possible scenarios involving the missing Lothario was one that directly involved the queen. Above all, he didn't want to have to take news back to Louise that her mother had orchestrated the boy's disappearance.

Byrne finally made his decision. As soon as he had proof of the identity of the dynamiteers, and a better lead on their commanding officer, he would dedicate serious time to finding Mr. Heath. If he still existed.

And so Byrne met in London with an informer named Clifton Riley who offered news about the Fenians, for a price. At their second meeting at the Green Dragon in Bishopsgate, his snitch, who claimed to be a brother of one of the Fenian recruits, verified some of Byrne's suspicions.

"I heard two Americans came into the country." Riley's eyes glittered greedily. The more valuable the information, the higher his reward. "Rumor has it, they're the best Chicago has to offer. Prime black powder men."

"Who brought them here?" Byrne asked, looking around the pub, as if bored and ready to leave. "I need a name for their boss. I can get street gossip anywhere for free."

Riley stared into his empty mug, as if in deep thought. Byrne ordered him another ale.

Thus fortified, his man continued. "No one knows his real name. Just he's the Lieutenant."

"And the names of the foreigners?" Riley gave him a blank look. "Come, man, you have to earn your keep."

Riley flashed him a condescending glare. "Don't be ridiculous. *You*, keep *me*? I'm the son of a duke."

"The fourth son of a duke who has burned his way through his inheritance at the ripe old age of—twenty-five, is it? And you were in debt to half a dozen angry fellows at your club, who have delayed sending men to beat it out of you only because I gave you money to pay an installment on your gambling chits."

Riley took to whining. "But how can you expect me to tell you what I don't know? My brother only confides so much in me and hasn't gained enough of their trust to meet with those at the top. All he hears are rumors."

"What kinds of rumors?"

Riley hesitated. "Listen, I've told you enough for the price of a couple pints and some spare change. I don't want to get my brother killed."

"You're right," Byrne said, slamming his hands down on the table between them and standing up. "You'll both be safer if Scotland Yard takes the two of you in for questioning."

His snitch's eyes widened with panic then darted across the room as if in terror of others hearing. In rookeries like Bishopsgate, the Yard was the enemy. He wouldn't want anyone thinking he was either the police or aiding them. Most coppers wouldn't chase a criminal into these thieves' enclaves unless they had a veritable army battalion to back them up.

"No! You can't do that," Riley choked out. He reached over and pulled Byrne back down into his seat. "He'll know I've been talking about his private business, his politics. He's been promised a seat in Parliament and doesn't take to my running my mouth."

"Does he take to you accepting money from the police to settle your gambling debts?"

Riley blanched. "Please don't . . . don't tell him about that."

Byrne leaned back in his chair and observed the other man, letting him stew. The Green Dragon was busy tonight, which was all to the good. In the noise and bantering, no one was paying attention to them in their dim corner, but the crowd made Riley all the more jumpy.

Byrne hardened his eyes. "I gave you a lot more money than spare change. I haven't heard my investment's worth."

Riley hung his head, scratched at his sideburns, and winced stubbornly at the tabletop, but a few more swallows of ale and he perked up. "All right. I'll tell you all I've heard. But there isn't any more than this."

"Well?"

Riley leaned closer and lowered his voice. "Some days *mon frère* talks of them bombing another train station. Some days of an attempt to assassinate the queen's son-in-law on his way back to

Germany." *Fritz*, Byrne thought, *married to the Crown Princess, Vicky.* "The thing is, my brother thinks these are rumors to hide their real plot until the last minute, when orders will be given. They are playing their devious plans very close to the chest, if you ask me. Not so much as a believable whisper escapes to the foot soldiers."

Byrne pushed himself into the man's face. "You still owe me."

"I know nothing more!"

"Then find out more. Fast. You think owing your gambling buddies is dangerous? You'll find it a good deal less pleasant to be in my debt, sir." He pulled back the duster just enough to give the man a glimpse of the Colt.

Riley shoved himself away, his face red, voice shaking. "You wouldn't shoot a man for not delivering information he doesn't have."

"I've shot a dozen men for far less," Bryne snarled. It wasn't really a lie. There'd been a war on after all.

The duke's son closed his eyes then huffed out noisily through his trim mustaches. He might have gambling debts to pay off, but he hadn't missed a trip to his barber. "All right then. I'll find out what I can for you about their plot. Then I'll be free of your wretched blackmail." He stood up shakily and retrieved his gloves from the table.

Byrne smiled. "Make it soon." *Free?* The chances of that were slim to none. The fellow had a gambling addiction. He'd already run through all of his relations and friends. He had nowhere else to turn but to Byrne.

Having temporarily run into a dead end in his search for the Fenian commander, Byrne turned to Louise's mission. By now he expected she would be climbing Buckingham's walls, waiting for his return with news. With any luck he'd turn up just enough information to satisfy her. Then she would let go of the idea of reuniting with Donovan, if that was what she had in mind. Rekindling their affair might solve one problem for her, only to create a much more disastrous situation should their relationship become public.

His first stop was the National Art Training School in South Kensington. He interrupted a class taught by an elderly professor. After initially refusing to give Byrne any information about former students, the old man waved him reluctantly into an office across the hall from the classroom where he'd been teaching. He shut the door behind them.

"I wonder if I might ask you a few questions about the time when Princess Louise was studying with you," Byrne began.

"So you said when you interrupted my class," the old man huffed. "I repeat, sir, I do not provide personal information about students. And certainly not about the royal family."

"This isn't strictly about the princess; it's more about a missing boy. His name is Donovan Heath. I believe he not only took lessons here, but he also paid his tuition by modeling?"

The professor sat behind his desk and settled his folded hands over a rotund belly covered in a paint-smeared smock. "That is so. But he is no longer here. I haven't seen him in years. And I believe, now, you need to leave." He pointed his eyes toward the door, as if to provide directions for the way out.

Byrne tried again. "This is official business. A missing person's report has been filed." Technically. Louise's complaint to him.

"You are with Scotland Yard? You've offered no identification."

"It is not so much police business as it is the Crown's." He produced the simple card that served as his only identification as a member of the queen's Secret Service. There was no badge or uniform.

The old man stared at the paper rectangle for a moment without reaching out to take it, as if it might nip his fingertips. He looked back at Byrne with a puzzled expression. "I don't understand. By your accent I'd say you are an American."

Byrne gave a brusque nod. "That's beside the point."

"The queen wishes to locate this young man?" Byrne didn't correct him. He wanted to cloak Louise's connection to the search. The old man tilted his head to one side in contemplation. "I'd have thought Victoria would be glad he hasn't shown his face all these years or continued to pester her daughter."

"He accosted the princess?" A defensive anger roiled up in Byrne's chest.

The old man shifted in his seat, as if he sat on something with a sharp edge. "It is a sensitive matter. For a period of three months, the two young people—Princess Louise and Master Donovan—were inseparable. I tried to warn the girl off. Told her he was not the sort of boy she should be talking to, let alone going off with for the noon meal. But I suppose, while she was here at the school, she was experiencing the only freedom she'd ever known. It became a kind of drug to her."

"She was not chaperoned or escorted on her class days?" Despite what Louise had told him, this still seemed inconceivable to Byrne.

"She was, in the beginning. But after several weeks I noticed she was merely left at the door, on her own." He smiled as though at an affectionate memory. "You'd have to have known the princess in those days. She was headstrong, determined to do as she pleased. Somehow she arranged matters as she liked." He shrugged. "Hard to believe, I know."

"Not hard at all," Byrne murmured dryly. Some things never changed. "But weren't you personally responsible for her during the days when she was here?"

The old man coughed into his hand, looking suddenly flustered. His white-whiskered face paled. "I did my best to control the girl. But you must have heard the stories. When she was young the gossip columns called her 'the wild one.' Of all Victoria's children she was the little mischief maker." He seemed unable to keep from smiling at the memory. "Do you know she insisted upon sitting in the boys' sculpting class? No female had ever done so before. Not in this school or any other in London. The very idea was scandalous." His smile faded, and he retrieved a handkerchief from inside his smock to dab at his sweaty brow. "Yet she insisted upon sketching from a live model. That's how she met Donovan, you see. He was posing."

"Naked?" Byrne gasped out loud before he could stop himself. Somehow it hadn't occurred to him—the naked part. Society dictated that exposing a female to the sight of a male body risked sending her into apoplexy, hysteria, madness. He'd always rather doubted the theory, since none of the women he'd been with appeared infected by such negative aftereffects. Nonetheless it was a surprise that this had been a sheltered princess's introduction to sexuality.

The little devil. Byrne caught himself grinning.

"Yes, naked—but of course. She was right. How can any artist learn the human form through endless layers of clothing or by studying a wooden mannequin? In the end, I agreed with her."

"So, am I to assume that this friendship that grew between the two young people was a platonic one? Since both you and, I assume, the queen knew about it."

The professor's gaze dropped to his lap. He shook his head slowly, avoiding Byrne's steady observation. "Whether they did anything more than share lunch at the street stalls with the other students, I cannot say, sir. But I assume, from the way they behaved when they were together, the looks they gave each other, that special tenderness . . ." He took a deep breath then let it out with a sense of unrelieved weight. "Well, one would have to be blind to assume there was never intimacy between them."

Byrne felt a steady pressure building in his chest. The room seemed suddenly darker, the chemical-laced air drifting in from the studio across the hall oppressive. Young people were bound to find each other and experiment. Hadn't he managed to scout out willing girls on which to test his adolescent equipment? The natural curiosity of youth would not be denied. Particularly if the young woman, though properly raised, possessed Louise's spirit and passion. He'd already assumed there was more than friendship between the young Louise and her "friend."

Well, that was all well and good for a boy and girl of the lower classes, or even among the offspring of merchants' families. But a female royal who allowed a man to take liberties with her, a man who could never be her husband—such folly ruined her in society's eyes and brought her family disgrace that would likely never be forgiven. His mind leaped toward possibilities he'd only vaguely feared before now.

What, exactly, had happened five years ago? His thoughts spiraled down to the bleakest of possibilities.

If Victoria knew about Donovan, and somehow learned of her daughter's intimacies with him, she would have acted swiftly and decisively to prevent disaster. The only question was—how far had the queen gone to make *the problem* disappear?

"Supposing they did not simply walk and eat on the street with their classmates. Do you have any idea where they might have gone?" Byrne asked.

"At noon break?"

"Or other times."

The man rubbed the knuckles of his hand with increasing agitation. "No. Of course not. If I'd known—"

"But if you were to guess," Byrne prodded.

The professor shook his head, side to side, a great ox being led in a direction he didn't wish to go. "I suppose the most likely place for a tête-à-tête would have been in one of the artists' lofts where he was posing when he wasn't working here. While Louise was still studying with me, Donovan stopped coming to model, you see. She seemed upset by this. Terribly so in fact." The professor stood up abruptly but didn't move from behind his desk. He studied the fleur-de-lis pattern in the blue-and-gold carpet. "Perhaps she went off to find him. She would have gone to the places he was most likely to be working or that she had frequented with him while he still worked here. I doubt he ever could have afforded his own room anywhere in the city. One of the artists likely would have given him a corner to sleep in."

"Can you give me names? Anyone he might have worked for." This was the precious connection he'd been waiting for. The back of his neck tingled with anticipation. Louise had been holding back, he was sure of it. Giving him only as much information as she thought necessary for him to track down her lover. Not daring to reveal too much for fear of his guessing the extent of her relationship with Donovan.

The professor sighed. "I can think of no one in particular. It's been so long, you see." He paced away from the desk, back again then away, hands clasped behind his back, deep in thought. "The boy seemed drawn to a brotherhood of experimental artists who called themselves Pre-Raphaelites. It was because of their avoiding the more modern styles and suggesting a return to a purer art before the famous Raphael did his fine work. But to my thinking, they were a strange and dangerous bunch."

"In what way—dangerous?" Byrne stepped forward, wanting to shake the reluctant words out of the old man. He knew nothing of these artists, other than the general opinion that they had a reputation for loose living. He imagined a naïve, virginal princess becoming involved with such a group.

What had happened to her?

The professor said, "I believe there often has been trouble over their women. Affairs. Not that unusual, right? Made worse by the overindulgence of drink and certain drugs. The details, of course, I would have had no desire to learn. But I think the trouble among the artists in their group eventually split them up. I don't know if any or all of them are still in London."

"Can you give me a few names?" Byrne asked.

"Yes, there was John Everett Millais, William Holman Hunt, Dante Gabriel Rossetti, William Morris, and others. Rossetti, he was what you Americans call their ring leader. Of course Donovan might have been posing for and boarding with someone else entirely. Who am I to keep track of these young Turks? But I believe if Master Donovan were in London today, he would still be looking for work as a model or else turning to something other than painting to survive."

Byrne looked around the room, thinking: *maybe, or maybe not*. "You said he was an art student. What about selling his art? Was he any good?"

The old man gave a soft snort. "The boy had no talent. A pity really. I can't believe he'd ever become a true artist. He saw painting as a trick, a way to earn money he didn't need to work for. Donovan didn't have the heart of an artist. I could see that much even then."

Twenty-one

Byrne visited four other studios, looking for the artists the professor at the Kensington school had mentioned. All he learned was that painters were a notoriously slippery bunch. They seemed not to stay in any one location for long, moving after only a few months, often without paying their rent.

He finally found someone who knew Mr. William Morris. "He's visiting friends in the city. Back from his country house in Oxfordshire," an art dealer told him. Morris appeared to have found his calling and was raking in the rewards if he could afford a country estate.

"His paintings are selling well then?"

"Paintings?" The man laughed. "No, sir. Everyone knows he's made a wild success of his furniture and beautiful wallpapers. Very popular his designs are." Byrne hadn't known. Evidently the man's fame hadn't yet spread to America.

When the butler at the house where Morris was staying reluctantly agreed to summon the artist to the door, Byrne quickly explained his reason for calling.

"I knew Donovan, of course," Morris told him, planting himself in the threshold in lieu of inviting Byrne inside. "Many of us used him." He blushed, as if there were something shameful beyond the obvious advantage taken of a young man in desperate need of money. "As a model, of course. As I recall, yes, there was an incident with a young woman."

"Go on."

Morris rolled his eyes toward the smudgy sky. His lips tightened, gaze became guarded. "As this is between men of the world, might I be frank?"

"Of course," Byrne said.

Morris looked back over his shoulder into the house, as if contemplating continuing his story in the comfort of his host's drawing room. But after a disdainful second glance at Byrne's leather duster, all the dustier for his recent treks across London, Morris stood his ground in the doorway.

"Like most young artists, the fellow had his pants down around his knees more often than belted."

No surprise there. "Understood. But I'm most interested in his friendship with a specific young woman who was well connected." Until now Byrne had chosen to mention to Morris neither Louise nor her mother. To spread it around for whom he was working would inevitably generate gossip. He'd trusted her old teacher to want gossip even less than he.

"Yes . . . yes . . . quite so. Connected." Morris began inching the door closed, looking paler by the second. "But I really can't speak to that topic. You'd better go see Rossetti. It was at his studio, you see."

"What was at his studio?" Byrne braced the toe of his boot against the door to stop it from closing all the way. Something in the man's tone alerted him.

Morris's jowls flushed a deep red, making him resemble a turkey with its crimson wattles. He straightened and stepped back from the doorway, signaling the end of their conversation. A proper gentleman was expected to stand back from the door and return to the street with grace.

Byrne threw a shoulder into the disappearing space between door and jamb, making it impossible for the man to shut him out. "*What* happened there?" he repeated.

Morris shook his head violently and coughed into his hand. "Listen, my good man, it's just . . . I'm not at liberty to say."

"Why not?"

"I'd rather not become involved, you see. Go see Rossetti. He's gone back to the old place near St. Paul's. Anyone in the neighborhood can point out the house. Now, that is the end of it, sir." The man's eyes flared with indignation. "Remove yourself from the property, or I shall summon the police."

Byrne let him close the door this time. Short of throttling him, he'd get no more out of William Morris. Not that he was hesitant to use force on Louise's behalf, if pressed to it. But he hadn't yet run out of options.

It was now eleven o'clock in the morning, which he thought a perfectly decent hour to go calling on anyone, even a late-sleeping artist. He gave new directions to the driver of the hansom cab he'd requested to wait for him. But when he tapped on the door to the third-floor apartment in the building he'd been steered to by a young crossing sweeper, no one came to answer.

He fisted his hand and pounded louder. Covert noises issued from behind the door. It was clear whoever was inside had no intention of answering.

Byrne looked down at the knob, saw that it appeared to have been damaged, as if someone had forced the latch. When he laid his hand on the knob, it turned easily. He let himself in.

A large, black object flew at his head, missing by inches. And then only because he'd ducked.

He turned to see a cast-iron skillet crash into the wall beside him and land on the scarred wooden floor with a ringing thud.

"Oh, sorry there," came a voice from across the room. "Thought you were the landlord come for the rent."

"That sort of greeting would seem to encourage an invitation to vacate your rooms."

"Yes, well, in this part of the city one has to take a firm hand with these people." A portly dark-haired man with matching mustache and curling goatee looked around the edge of a canvas at him. He held a palette in one hand and picked up a brush in his skillet-heaving hand. Stepping back, he considered his project and spoke without looking back at his guest. "If I let him step in here anytime he wishes, he might take it for granted he can intrude upon my work at will. I've told him he must announce himself." He gave Byrne a look. "Appointments are appreciated."

"Putting a good lock on the door might help."

"Do you have any idea how much a lock and getting it installed properly costs these days? I don't even *own* the place. Making improvements isn't worth it."

Byrne looked around the room. Clearly improvements of any kind weren't the artist's priority. Partially finished paintings leaned against the walls, rested on easels, or hung from wires pegged with wooden clothespins. The sparsely furnished room was thick with fumes of various sorts, not all of which seemed connected with art. An undertone of cannabis sweetened the air, overlaid by whisky.

As he'd often done before, Byrne decided against identifying himself as an employee of the queen or a representative of any form of law enforcement. In his experience those living in risky circumstances, financially or otherwise, tended to lose their ability to speak when the police were mentioned.

"I'm looking for a young man who, I'm told, once worked for you. He did some modeling at the art school in Kensington before you hired him. Name of Donovan Heath."

Rossetti frowned at his painting, laid another dab of deep blue on it. "Can't be of much help to you, sorry. Haven't seen the little rascal for—let me think now—three . . . four years? Maybe a good deal more."

"Did he leave to work with someone else?"

"Probably, though he never told me. He'd have had to make a living somehow. There's precious little he was capable of. Standing naked—he managed that well enough. The boy could stand in one position for hours. Days." Rossetti winked at him. "I suspect his mind was of the sort that rarely sought challenges."

Byrne wondered what, exactly, about this very ordinary lad had so intrigued the beautiful and intellectually gifted Louise. But then, there was no figuring what made a woman fall for some men. Still, he was hopeful about coming upon the truth soon. At least the information he was gathering was consistent. By the end of the day, he might actually find Mr. Heath. Then, depending upon what the man looked like, and how he answered the questions put to him, Byrne would decide whether or not to tell Louise.

His growing compulsion to protect her kept whispering into the back of his mind. *Tell her . . . don't tell her . . . tell her . . . don't . . .*

However, there was always the possibility that something, or someone, had tempted Donovan away from London. In that case, he wouldn't find him today or, possibly, ever. Actually, he hoped Donovan had seen an opportunity far away and taken it. And he hoped he'd left on his own volition. Without Victoria's *help*.

"To your knowledge, did he have any particular girlfriends? Women he might have visited or gone away with to live? Might I find him with one of them?"

"Lady friends is it now? Then you don't even know what he looked like." The artist lifted a questioning brow at Byrne, who kept a straight face. "Guess not." Rossetti laughed. "Donovan was unabashedly, exquisitely beautiful. An Adonis. I've painted his face on the bodies of angels. He had no lack of female companionship, I'll tell you. Do you know, he actually seduced one of the royal princesses? Had the nerve to bring her up here to my apartment."

"Really." Byrne kept his reaction in check. Despite the acid leaching into his stomach that made him want to throw a fist into

Rossetti's leering mouth, he contrived an expression of disbelief.

So it seemed Louise had fallen for a common womanizer, a scoundrel, a juvenile Don Juan. Well, why not? She was an innocent, unaccustomed to anyone treating her badly. Donovan, with a handsome face and willing body, shared her interest in art. He was a free spirit who gave a curious young royal a glimpse of how the other half lived. He would have fascinated her.

"You don't believe me?" Rossetti said, misinterpreting Byrne's silence. "My friend and I walked in on them. Donny-boy had Her Royal Highness Princess Louise on that divan over there." He pointed. Byrne tried not to look at the tattered mud-colored upholstery but couldn't stop himself. "The girl was half naked, drunk as a dog on cheap wine. We managed to get her dressed, bundled her into her coach, paid off her driver to hold his tongue. And off she went."

Byrne swallowed his rage with increasing difficulty. After all, it wasn't Rossetti who'd seduced Louise. But until now he'd held out the hope that the two men had interrupted the young would-be lovers before things went too far. He still clung to one last possibility—that the inseparability her teacher had observed had been only a friendship after the embarrassment of being caught that one time.

"And that was the end of the affair?" he prompted.

Rossetti turned back to his painting, his gaze dissolving into the canvas. "Doubt it," he mumbled. "The girl was quite the little fool."

The man's callousness pricked at Byrne. He felt his control slip. He reached out, clamped a hand on Rossetti's shoulder, and wrenched the man around to face him. The brush flew out of the artist's hand.

"Don't you ever again speak of Her Royal Highness like that! Your queen's daughter deserves respect."

"I didn't mean anything by it." The man's eyes narrowed, locking with Byrne's, as if trying to gauge the likelihood his visitor might assault him further. "Who *are* you?"

"Nobody." Byrne released him, locking down his emotions again. He'd get nothing more out of the man by pummeling him, though he deeply longed to. "I just need information. Preferably, the truth. If you have any idea where Mr. Heath might be, you need to tell me. Now."

"Wait. I've heard of you. You're the American. The Raven they call you." Rossetti scrutinized his clothing. "I'd say closer to a vulture, feeding off of human carrion. Are you just curious? Or on an official mission for HRM?"

Byrne ignored the man's questions, annoyed that word of him had spread in London. "What happened after you found them together?"

Rossetti retrieved his brush from the floor and rinsed it in solvent before tenderly reshaping its point with his fingertips. "He didn't bring her here again, I'll tell you. He knew I'd toss the two of them out. I mean, was the chit insane? A member of the royal family! But I saw them together walking in the park more than once after that. Clearly they were enthralled with each other. I'm not trying to be rude or disrespectful when I say that girl couldn't have had any common sense whatsoever—taking up with a boy like that."

"She was how old?" Byrne said. "Seventeen . . . eighteen? How much sense do any of us have at that age?"

"Was she really that old then? Yes, I suppose she must have been. Acted and looked more like a child, if you ask me. I suppose she must have been very sheltered. Probably knew nothing of young men's desires or tricks of seduction."

"Undoubtedly," Byrne growled. "And the boy just disappeared? He told no one where he was off to?"

"Seems so. But I'll tell you what I have always thought happened." Rossetti pointed the tip of his brush at him, his eyes solemn. "I believe our good queen caught a whiff of the romance and arranged for that young man to be, shall we say, *discouraged*?" He quirked a heavy brow meaningfully.

"How, discouraged?" Byrne knew exactly what he meant—had thought it himself all along. But he was hungry for details now that he'd found a witness to Louise's affair.

Rossetti shrugged. "Unfortunate things sometimes happen to people who cross a king or queen. The Tower. Expulsion from the country. An unexplained accident. Beheading used to be very popular. Not much in vogue in this country, these days. But I hear she has men at her disposal, men who will do as she commands, whatever that might be." He looked away from Byrne, as if to pretend he wasn't talking about him personally.

Byrne's stomach twisted; another shot of acid burned. It was one thing to harbor his own fears. But hearing someone else voice similar suspicions, someone who actually knew Donovan and had watched his relationship with Louise develop—that sent him over the edge. "You're accusing the queen of—"

"If I were you," the artist interrupted, leaning toward him, as if someone else in the room might overhear, "I would have a man-to-man talk with Mr. John Brown about the convenient disappearance of Master Heath."

Byrne went rigid. "Why Brown?"

"Everyone in London knows Brown does the queen's bidding, even when it has nothing to do with her stables. It's said the Scot can be meaner than a she-bear with cubs when it comes to protecting HRM."

"You're saying John Brown might have done . . . what exactly?"

Rossetti returned to his painting. "Who can say? A skinny runt like Donovan confronted by a man like that? All it might have required was shouting 'boo' in his face. Or Brown might've chased him off into the country. Or across the channel to the Continent. The chit could be anywhere."

Bloody hell, Byrne thought.

"Or, the Scot might have just done the easy thing."

"Easy?"

Rossetti smiled. "I've heard it said a single blow from the Scot's fist could kill a man. Wouldn't it have been so much simpler if the loyal gillie was able to report to his queen that Donovan Heath, penniless commoner, would never again bother her daughter?"

"And if you're wrong? If he's still alive and somewhere in London?"

Rossetti shook his head. "I can't tell you where to look for him. He's not modeling, that's for certain. And I'd know if he were in the city. Maybe he found a rich woman. That would be a dream come true for someone like him. Fucking for a living. Ha!"

Byrne had heard enough. It was all he could manage to offer a civil thank-you to the artist and leave the studio without punching a hole through the wall.

He trod heavily down the steps at half the speed he'd taken them up, deep in thought. A story was emerging that he liked less and less. Worse yet, it wasn't one he could report to Louise. She'd be mortified if he told her what he'd discovered of the past she'd meant to keep hidden from him. And from the world.

Outside in the street he lit a cigar and breathed in the pungent-sweet smoke along with the coal-fire smog. His eyes burned, but somehow the air seemed cleaner outside the artist's garret than in it.

He climbed into a hansom cab and gave directions to the driver. Sitting back against the rough cushions, he closed his eyes and gathered his thoughts about what he'd just now learned. Donovan had used his employers' properties not only as a place to crash for the night but also to lure young women, regardless of their class. Byrne was fairly certain if Louise had known this about her lover she wouldn't have sent Byrne to find Donovan. She must still believe he loved her as much as she loved him. As worldly as she pretended to be, the princess at twenty-three still held on to her innocence in at least that one respect.

Ah, Louise.

If this were the case, maybe his fear that she hoped to reunite with her lost lover was true. The knot in his stomach tightened another notch. He pressed a fist into the center of the pain and closed his eyes as the hansom rolled and jounced on through London. He sucked down another lungful of cigar smoke. It didn't calm him in the least.

He thought: if Victoria had effectively chased away her daughter's lover once, and he, Byrne, brought the young man back to Louise, resulting in the couple getting together again—that would be the end of his career. Victoria's rage would know no limits. The first person she unleashed her bile upon would be him.

How had he gotten himself into this unholy mess anyway?

Despite his earnest attempts at investigation on behalf of the queen, things were becoming rather more than less complicated. A traitor lurked in the palace. Irish radicals were intent on blowing up or stealing a member of the royal family. Louise had dumped a mystery in his lap. And, most aggravating of all, he was struggling daily with unrequited *urges* because the object of his desire was a woman whose rank, not to mention marital status, meant he'd never have a chance to be with her.

He grew hard at the very thought of Louise. Her, *with* him. Touching him, kissing him, giving herself wholly to him. Indeed, God must have a perverse sense of humor to have created man's sexual organs with absolutely no regard to the practical matters of selecting a mate.

He'd best find a willing woman fast, before he did something he'd regret.

Twenty-two

Louise looked up from the sketch she'd been working on. It was from memory. Her father, Prince Albert.

Her heart swelled with remorse that he'd been taken so early in his life, and hers, from them. Poor Bea had still been a baby, really. Louise couldn't imagine she had much memory of him or of their happy family times together. Since his death, Victoria had clung in desperation to her mourning gloom, and expected all around her to join her.

Louise sighed. Thank heavens for her art. It was her respite from grief.

Today she was experimenting with a series of sketches of Albert, her very first preparations for beginning his statue. But getting the contours of his face and angle from which she viewed him just right—that was a challenge. Everything had to be perfect in the final sketch before she could even begin working on the small clay model that would enable her eventually to put chisel to stone.

She flipped a page and started again on a fresh sheet of paper, moving the tip of the willow charcoal wand across the textured white surface. Gently blowing away the excess black dust. Rubbing the long edge of the twig against the paper's grain to create

shadow beneath her father's jaw. Tenderly smoothing and redefin-
ing the lines with the tip of her middle finger or side of her pinkie.

All ten of her fingers and the heel of her right hand were black
with soot, her smock filthy, and she didn't care. It would have been
neater to draw with a soft-leaded pencil, but the effect wouldn't
have been as satisfying. Gradually now, the sense of light and shadow
softened, breathing life into the face before her. She loved the tac-
tile sensation of sketching with charcoal. She became one with her
art, with her subject. The separation blurred between paper and
human. Between past and present. Tears trembled on her lashes.

Dear strong, wonderful man. How she missed her father.

As she continued to work, a strong and commanding counte-
nance evolved beneath her moving hand—dark eyes, square chin
with just the hint of a cleft, Roman nose, a sense of the muscula-
ture that ran up from the chest to support a proud neck and head,
thick hair that was too long but somehow just right.

Lowering her hand Louise drew a sharp breath and stared in
shock at the face. "Oh!" she gasped aloud.

This wasn't Albert at all. This face belonged to another man.

"Is something wrong, my dear?"

Louise gave a start and snapped the sketchbook shut. She
turned toward the lounge chair a few feet away where Lorne sat,
reading in the sun. They hadn't spoken in hours; she'd actually
forgotten he was there.

"No. Nothing. It's . . . Father's statue. The sketches aren't working at all."

"Perhaps if I gave a look?" His blue eyes twinkled with humor,
as if admitting he'd be of no help. His hounds and horses were his
passion. To his credit, he'd given up both to keep her company
that day.

She ignored his outstretched hand. "No, it will come to me. I
just need to focus a bit harder." *And on the proper subject.*

"Ah, Mr. Byrne!" Her husband came to his feet.

Louise's heart stopped, then stuttered to life again. She turned around to find the Raven coming around the end of the hedgerow. Why did she never hear the man approaching? It was damned unnerving.

"Back from your investigatory duties, I see." Lorne shook Stephen Byrne's hand. "Any luck rousting out the hooligans?"

Louise watched the two men with an uncomfortable feeling. She glanced down at the sketchbook in her lap, wondering if she dared open it—to see if she'd truly captured the American. With a shake of her head, she quickly tucked her work away in the canvas bag at her feet and brushed what she could of the charcoal from her fingertips.

"Your Highness," Byrne said, letting a nod in her direction suffice as a bow. "I'm just on my way to see your mother."

His dark gaze sent a shiver through her. She wished she knew what the man was thinking when he looked at her like *that*, the meaning behind his eyes so nebulous. "Mr. Byrne." She hoped he had the good sense not to report his findings with regard to Donovan in front of Lorne.

In the months since their wedding, she and her husband had come to an understanding, of sorts. Louise actually found Lorne's companionship comforting at times. He was cheerful in a quiet way, polite, intelligent, docile, accepted her mercurial nature and insistence upon running her own life. If she wanted to be alone, he left her to herself. And if she felt lonely, he often made himself available for a game of cards, reading a bit of poetry to each other, or as an escort to the ballet or opera.

She never asked what he did with his nights away from her with his friends in Pall Mall. Some days he didn't appear until the afternoon, his eyes red-rimmed from drink and lack of sleep. He favored several gentlemen's clubs with questionable reputations—the Albemarle and Boodles, and worse yet, the Hundred Guineas Club. She knew this only from the gossip columns but didn't doubt their veracity. Louise decided she'd rather not learn any-thing more than was necessary about her husband's mysterious habits. He cooperated in the game by only casually asking about her activities.

Married life could have been far worse, she told herself.

She broke from her reverie to see Byrne turn, as if to leave. Louise stood up so abruptly she nearly knocked over the butler table, and with it the tea service. "Mr. Byrne," she called out, "may I have a word with you? It won't take a moment."

She was aware of Lorne watching her with a puzzled expression. His gaze shifted with open curiosity from her to the American.

"It's just a small matter my mother asked me to address with you," she lied with forced cheerfulness as she tried to draw him farther away from Lorne. "An escort for Bea to visit with a little friend of hers. I'll walk along to keep you from being late." She turned with a smile to her husband. "This won't take a moment, dear. Be right back."

As they walked, Stephen Byrne observed her from beneath the brim of his plainsman's hat, his expression as impenetrable as ever. She crooked a finger at him, as if he were a child being called off the park swings for naughty behavior. He obliged by bending down to better hear her.

"*Why* have you not reported to me, sir?" she hissed.

"When I have something of significance to convey to you, Prin-cess, I will." He looked down on her, unblinking, as convincing a show of innocence, she was sure, as any rogue could contrive.

"Do you mean to say that in all this time, you have found *noth-ing* whatsoever? Nothing that would indicate"—she glanced back over her shoulder at Lorne, far across the garden, who seemed engrossed in his reading—"where Donovan might have gone?"

"I've not yet located the man." Byrne's expression remained blank, his gaze fixed mildly on a marble bench placed beneath a hawthorn tree.

She could almost swear from the way he refused to meet her eyes that he knew *something*. Whatever it was, he appeared disinclined to share with her. "If it is terrible news, I still must know. Do you understand? I want to hear what you've discovered. Good news or bad, I've paid you for the truth."

Byrne's eyes slowly drifted from the bench to her. She felt their weight as if they were two hot black river-stones laid on her shoulders.

"I'm not sure that I do understand, Your Highness. Frankly, if your friend left you without explanation, he probably had a reason. Perhaps he didn't wish to hurt your feelings. Maybe there was someone else, and he took the coward's way out."

"No! That's impossible." Too late, she realized she'd shouted her objection. She lowered her voice again, not daring to look toward Lorne to see if he'd heard. "He loved . . . I mean to say, Donovan had a fondness for our conversations about art. And we had an . . . an understanding, a friendship that was very special."

Louise sighed, tears threatening. How pitiful she must sound. Byrne undoubtedly saw straight through her. To keep up this charade was senseless. But how could she admit to him, to anyone, *what she'd done*? She blinked away her tears, angry with herself for caving in to emotion.

"I don't care how insignificant whatever you found seems to you. Tell me. Now!"

Byrne grimaced, looking as resigned to his fate as a man before a firing squad. "I have contacted as many individuals as I could find who knew Donovan Heath from his days in Kensington." He looked at her and waited, as if expecting a reaction. She kept silent, but her heart tripped, then began to race. "I spoke with your old teacher there, and later with Gabriel Rossetti."

Louise's pulse shifted from racing to a dead stop. Her stomach clenched; her knees threatened to give out entirely. *No, no, no!*

This wasn't what she'd wanted at all. He was going about his search all wrong. This was supposed to be about Donovan's reason for disappearing and his current location. Not about *her*. Not about *her past*. Did the man have no sense of discretion?

She drew herself up and gave him her best imitation of Victoria's haughty glare. The one she used on her ministers when displeased with them. She must remind this Raven that he was "the help," whereas she was a royal princess who held the power in this relationship.

"Gabriel Rossetti," she said, "was most cold and cruel to my friend. He treated Donovan abysmally. You are not to go back to that man for any reason or take his word for anything but slander."

Byrne stared at her as if she'd ordered him to renounce walking in favor of flying. He stepped closer to her and lowered his voice to a frightening rumble that reminded her of how unpredictable he could be. "Listen, Princess. You asked me to track him down. How am I supposed to do that without questioning people, without trying to find those who knew him before he disappeared? People he might have told where he was going and why. Either you want me to do this, or not." He took yet another step closer. "Make up your mind, Louise."

She glared up at him, feeling the need to back away but refusing to let him intimidate her. "How dare you speak to me in that tone." She couldn't keep her voice from shaking even in her anger. Lorne was right. The man had no manners whatsoever. And calling her by her first name—such nerve.

"All right then." He let out a sound from deep in his throat, rather like a growl. "Here's what I've found so far. It appears that no one who knew Donovan Heath, either in London or the surrounding countryside, has any idea where the fellow has got to. He simply vanished. There are rumors, but I assume you want proof, not hearsay."

"Why don't you let me decide which they are." She opened her eyes wide and tilted her head in a suggestion of challenge. "Just give me the information you've gathered."

"Very well." He removed his hat, making him look only a little less a cowboy out of one of her brothers' penny dreadful novels. "The theories proposed by the people I've interviewed range from Donovan having found a rich woman to provide for him, to his falling drunk into the Thames and drowning. Some say he might have left England for Brussels, Paris, Venice, or Frankfurt in pursuit of his art. But the supposition that makes the most sense to me was voiced by Mr. Rossetti." He stopped and studied her, his hat rotating in his hands, as if he actually were capable of being nervous.

"Go on, go on," she said.

"Rossetti believes the boy might have either been frightened off or more forcibly encouraged to leave London, because of your association with him."

She let his words soak in, for a moment unable to speak.

She swallowed, threw him a look of desperation, then choked out the words, "But that's preposterous. Who would have done such a thing?" In her heart she knew what he was going to say. And it terrified her. "If you are about to accuse my *mother* of forcing my friend to leave the city, that's simply outrageous."

"Why do you say that?" he asked, his voice slipping into unexpected gentleness. His black eyes focused on her face.

"Because he disappeared before she even knew I was—" She swallowed back the damning words. "Before I told her we'd been special friends."

"You're telling me that Her Majesty has no way of discovering what is going on in her children's lives unless they *tell* her?" He kept a straight face, but somehow she knew he was laughing at her.

"I'm sure she has her methods of spying upon us when she's inclined. I'm just saying that, at the time Donovan disappeared, she had no reason whatsoever to be concerned."

Byrne leaned forward, making her feel even more uneasy at his proximity. She smelled the road on him, horse and leather, and a masculine tang that sent a strange thrill through her. He said, "Explain to me, Princess, what might concern the queen more than the danger of a commoner—in fact, not just any commoner but a boy barely out of the gutter—becoming *intimate* with her daughter?"

Louise caught her breath and raised a hand, overwhelmed by an impulse to slap him for his insult. Before she could make good her intent, he'd grabbed her wrist and pulled her closer still.

"Your mother must have known what was happening," he whispered in her ear. "Must have been beside herself with fear, realizing the boy would be your ruin."

"Stop it. Stop it this instant!" She choked back tears, wrenched her arm out of his grip, and pushed herself away from him. She pressed fingertips to her burning eyes. "You must not press this issue. Whatever happened between us is inconsequential. Totally beside the point." Her voice broke. "You must take my word that my friend had been missing for a month or more before my mother would have had reason for concern."

Byrne's eyes narrowed to dark slits, studying her as though trying to unravel a riddle she'd presented him. Did she secretly want him to know the truth? Was she feeding him just enough information to let him guess at what had happened—then falling back on her rank to deny him the answer? But that would be absurd.

Louise cleared her throat and looked up at him, surprised to find they still stood within inches of each other. She tried to make her feet step back, but they refused to cooperate.

"Now tell me," she said, in as firm a voice as she could muster, "what are your next steps toward finding Donovan Heath?"

Byrne rolled his eyes, shook his head. He jammed his hat down on his head and tugged the brim low over disturbingly stormy eyes. "There are a few leads I suppose I might still follow."

"And what leads are those, laddie?" a familiar voice thundered.

Louise felt her heart leap into her throat. How long had John Brown been lurking behind the hedge?

"You're not discussing your search for the Fenian captain with the princess, are you?"

"No," Byrne said. Whatever emotion he'd revealed to her a moment before now washed away from his features.

"It's a personal matter," she responded, giving the Scot a dark look. She felt Byrne tense beside her, as if he feared her revealing anything more.

Brown looked at her, then at Byrne. Animosity crackled in the air between the two men. "Personal," he repeated, tasting the word for hidden flavors. After a long moment, he gave a nod, as if he'd come to a decision. "I need to discuss a matter of security with Mr. Byrne. Might I borrow him from you for a moment, Princess?"

She hesitated, unsure she dared leave the two of them alone together, but gave him a nod of approval. "I still need to finish my conversation with Mr. Byrne, when you're done." *If anything's left of him*, she thought as she walked back the way she'd come, into the garden to where she'd left her drawing supplies, canvas carryall, and her elegant but hopelessly unavailable young husband.

Louise reached down for her sketch pad then hesitated, her fingertips tingling with suspicion. The binding was tucked low into the open mouth of the sack, half buried beneath a rag she'd used to wipe her hands. Had she stuck the pad down so deep? She stole a look at Lorne, who appeared not to have moved from his lawn chair in her absence. What if he'd seen the sketch of the American?

But perhaps it was just her imagination. The thing might have slipped of its own weight.

Loud voices disturbed her thoughts and the peace of the garden.

"Bloody hell. What's that all about?" Lorne grumbled. He rustled his paper, looked up for a moment. "Oh, it's just the Scot." He turned a page and disappeared inside his newsprint again.

Louise glanced worriedly toward the boxwood hedge blocking her view of the two men. She couldn't catch Byrne's exact words, but she had no trouble reading the irritation in the Scot's response.

"No! That's my answer, laddie, and the end of it. I'd nothin' to do with that nonsense."

Her breath caught. Was Byrne foolish enough to propose the same theory to Brown that he had to her? That her mother, perhaps even Brown himself, had frightened off her lover?

Her heart hammering, she wondered if, all those years back, she might have dismissed her mother's involvement too soon. Until this moment, she thought she knew the full extent of the queen's interference in her life. Was there really a chance that one of Victoria's henchmen had been dispatched to frighten or hurt the boy? Or worse.

Her heart sank. Unless she confessed to Byrne the rest of her story, she might never learn Donovan's fate. But this was the part she hadn't let herself think about in such a long time, for the pain was too sharp, too raw—and the consequences of what she'd done too utterly loathsome.

And yet, without knowing the whole story, as Byrne had so forcefully pointed out, he might be unable to find the truth. Louise weighed the dangers against the possible benefits of baring her soul to her mother's agent. Torn, she watched as John Brown snarled words at Byrne she could only imagine were a threat. He stalked off, leaving her mother's agent looking after him.

"Why do you bother with that uncouth foreigner?"

Louise jumped. She looked around to see that her husband had dropped the newspaper into his lap and was studying her face with a perplexed expression. "Clearly the man annoys you. I've never heard a civil word pass between the two of you."

"I told you what happened at the suffrage protest, about that horrid man who chased us."

"You shouldn't have gone is all. It's dangerous to be out on your own and—"

"I thought we had an agreement, you and I," she spat. "I will do as I please, Lorne, and you will do as you please."

"Yes, my dear, but this is your safety we're—"

She shot him a look that instantly silenced him.

"Do as you like," he said, holding up both hands in defeat. "I'll be heading to a hunting party with my friends this weekend. You won't be expected to accompany me."

"Fine." She turned in time to see Byrne walking away toward the nearest wing of the palace. "I'm going inside. Headache," she blurted to her husband before rushing off.

She caught up with Byrne before he'd left the garden. "I want to apologize," she said breathlessly. "I haven't been totally honest with you."

"Really?" Was that a twinkle in those bird-of-prey eyes?

She shook her head. "I know I've made your job all the harder."

"You seem to delight in making my days a challenge." He gave her a wry grimace. "Throwing yourself into the line of fire in the coach—"

"Yes, well, I explained that was an accident."

"Of course."

She raised a cautionary eyebrow. "Remember your place, sir."

"Always."

She hated when he slipped into male one-word-answer responses. She gathered up her courage. "I need your advice."

"Good. Rule Number One: forget about past loves."

She blinked and sucked in a breath. So he'd guessed. Was she that obvious where Donovan was concerned? "I beg your pardon?"

"I spoke with Rossetti."

"You told me that."

"He described surprising you and young Donovan in a compromising position. He said he expected it wasn't the only time the two of you—"

"Stop." She glared at him then glanced around them. No one appeared to be within hearing. "I have a different request that has nothing to do with your current task for me."

"Are you sure?" He looked at her hard.

"Yes. We will not speak of this . . . this relationship. Either you find Donovan without digging further into my personal affairs, or you don't. It will be however it turns out. For now, I need your advice on a matter involving my friend Amanda and her son."

He looked wary. "Go on."

"You may have heard that Amanda and I attended the suffrage rally."

"I did. Just now, from Mr. Brown. Most unwise that was."

"Possibly so, but if it's the only way to force reform . . ." She lifted her hands to let him fill in the rest of her thought. "Anyway, I told him the rally was exhilarating, which is true. But not for the reasons he assumes."

"Yes?"

"We were attacked."

He scowled, straightening up. "Why haven't you said anything about this to Brown or to me?"

"Because I was certain either one of you would have gone to my mother, and that would have accomplished nothing other than terrify her, resulting in yet another set of safety regulations for the family. Next thing we know we'll all be locked inside the palace, day and night."

"*Who* attacked you?"

She looked up at the sharpness of his voice; never had she seen him look more ferocious.

Louise took a deep breath before continuing. "His name is Roger Darvey. Amanda had an unfortunate few years after her

father's death. I won't go into details, but Darvey picked her up off
the street one day, fed her, got her bathed and dressed, then told
her she'd need to repay him by doing favors for him."

"For him or for other men?"

"Both. When she gave him the slip, he resented it. Lost income,
I suspect. But she managed to elude him and stay out of sight. She
hasn't seen or heard from him in years. He recognized her at the
demonstration, took after her, and chased the two of us clear back
to her house. Her husband scared him off with his gun."

"They do come in handy," he remarked.

"Husbands?"

"Guns." He grinned, lifted the edge of his duster to reveal the
rather impressive pistol at his hip.

She rolled her eyes. "What I need to know is how Amanda can
protect herself. She works at my shop, distributes broadsides she's
written for us, and has to be free to move around the city. Her
husband is a doctor and can't accompany her everywhere. Until
Darvey gives up on the notion of punishing her for her desertion,
I fear for her safety and that of her family."

He thought for a moment. "I could have a word with the man."
He said *word* in a way that made it sound physical.

"Would you do that for me?" Did she sound too urgently grateful? Before he could answer, she bit down on her lip and added,
"I'm just as worried about her son, you see. I think if Darvey can't
get to her, he might take it into his wicked head to harm the child.
And if . . . if anything happened to—" She surprised herself by
bursting into tears.

He reached out and took hold of her arm. "Are you all right?"

"Yes." She produced a silk handkerchief from her sleeve and
dabbed at her eyes. "It's just—he's my godson, you see, so very
precious to me."

He was frowning at her, clearly confused.

"I—I love children. Have always wanted . . . well, it seems I may not be able to—" She waved off the words, fearful of revealing more than she should of the desolation of her marriage. "Little Edward and I have been so very close since his birth, seeing that Amanda is almost like a sister to me. I can't stand the thought of him being harmed by that beast of a man."

"I'll keep an eye out for Darvey when I can, and encourage him to consider alternatives to hurting your friend and godson."

"Alternatives?"

He smiled. "Like staying alive."

She swallowed. "Oh, I see."

"But I'd still be careful and not go out alone, either of you, until he and I have a meeting of the minds. And that may take some time—as you and your mother have given me plenty to keep me busy."

She sniffled. "I suppose we are relying on you for a great deal."

Byrne looked past her for a moment then withdrew his hand, which had stayed wrapped warmly around her arm. "I need to leave now."

"Thank you," she said in parting.

When she spun away to return to her seat, she saw what Byrne must have seen before he released her. Lorne stood barely twenty feet away, just at the edge of the garden gate, watching her. She looked away, unsure why she should feel uneasy as he walked over to her.

Her husband cleared his throat and touched her on the arm exactly where Byrne's fingers had rested a moment earlier. "My dear, if you are seen carrying on with another man so soon after our nuptials, some people may not believe we're the happy newlyweds we pretend to be."

"Don't be ridiculous," she snapped. "He's my mother's man."

"Is he now?"

"Yes. I have no interest in him."

"But even if that is true, can we assume he has no interest in you?" There was an unfamiliar edge to his voice, and she wondered if his promise of guaranteeing her independence might not include every freedom. "Just remember our pact. Your freedom for my security. Don't do anything foolish like falling in love. You'll jeopardize both our lives."

Twenty-three

Louise's pride and joy, the Women's Work Society, provided a place where destitute girls and women might learn crafts—needlework, embroidery, and the repair of fine art items—which could then be sold at the Society's consignment shop in highly respectable Sloane Square. She hoped someday also to create a boarding school for girls that would be free to young women without family or a husband to support them. Meanwhile she was pleased that the London shop had already become a lifesaver for a dozen females of various ages, giving them a modest income for their handiwork. Barely enough to keep them off the dangerous streets, but still . . .

Amanda worked there forty or more hours each week, bringing her little boy with her, and they'd recently hired two other women as part-time clerks. Louise was hopeful of expanding soon.

As she stepped from the brougham then through the shop's door she tried to ignore the light headache that had plagued her for hours. Her anxiety had run high for days following the run-in with Darvey. Sometimes she feared she was being followed, watched. But that might as easily have been due to her clandestine body-guards. She suspected Byrne had assigned one or more of his men to follow her whenever he couldn't be with her. In fact, she rarely saw the man himself. He seemed reluctant to openly accompany her on her jaunts into the city, preferring to shadow her from a distance. Why this should be, she was at a loss to understand. Perhaps he thought a more discreet form of protection would draw less attention to her.

But when she realized she hadn't seen him around at all for days, a fresh form of worry came at her. The Fenians were desperate radicals, capable of ruthless violence. They would not hesitate to attack an agent of the queen if they saw him as a threat to their wicked plots. She feared for Byrne's safety as well as her own family's. And yet she, like Byrne, refused to stay shut inside Buckingham Palace. When fear of death became fear of living one's life, the Fenians would have won. And so she went about her routine, though she felt perpetually shadowed by evil.

She found Amanda at the shop, in a gray mood not unlike her own. Whereas days earlier her friend had inadvertently destroyed items out of sheer excitement over the suffrage rally, today Amanda was a bundle of nerves and incapable of picking up any object without immediately dropping it.

"I'm so sorry," her friend apologized after letting a second porcelain saucer slip from her fingers in less than twenty minutes. "I don't know what's wrong with me."

Louise watched her friend sweep up broken shards with trembling hands. "What's wrong? You're shaking from head to foot, dear girl."

"It's Darvey. I'm sure I've spotted him twice more, though he keeps his distance. I worry what he has in mind."

Louise closed her eyes and swallowed to calm herself. Either Byrne hadn't yet confronted the bawd or his threats had proved ineffective. "Come, let's just lock up for the night. I knew I wouldn't be long, so I asked my driver to wait for me. I'll deliver you and Eddie home where you'll be safe. One of my mother's men has been detailed to approach the scallywag and put the fear of God in him."

"Thank you. I'll feel ever so much safer in a carriage tonight."

Louise wrapped a comforting arm around her shoulders. "And where is my godson? I haven't seen him since I arrived."

"Sleeping in the back room." Amanda laughed. "He exhausted himself whacking away at crates and pots, pretending he was a drummer in the queen's guard on parade. You can go and wake him if you like."

"No, let him sleep a few more minutes while we tidy up and tally receipts. You can do the sums. Paper isn't fragile." She smiled affectionately at her friend. "I'll dust up the china while I wait for you."

A few minutes later, Amanda closed the account book and slipped the day's earnings into a small canvas bag. "Done. Let's wake the boy and be off before it gets dark."

Louise climbed down from the ladder she'd used to reach the top shelves where some of the more fragile objects were kept out of reach of small hands and ladies' bustles. "Are you still working with my tutor on your writing?" she asked.

Amanda beamed at her. "Yes, and that reminds me. I wanted to tell you what he said. He's encouraged me to submit one of my articles to the *Times*, as an editorial piece. He says it's quite good enough, better than many of the pieces by their own reporters."

"Oh, Amanda, I'm so very proud of you!" Louise went to her and clasped her hands. "Tell me what your article is about."

It was then—as Amanda started to explain the exposé she'd written about women of any age who, like her, had lost family property to a distant relative simply because he was a male—that Louise first heard the soft scuffling sounds. She turned toward the back room and smiled at Amanda, who stopped talking.

"What?" Amanda asked.

"I think Eddie's up and about. Maybe we should collect him and go." Louise glanced toward the shop's front window. "It looks like rain, and it will be dark early."

"Good idea." Amanda plucked her cloak from its peg and laid it across the countertop. "I'll go fetch him."

But as soon as she opened the door to the storeroom, clouds of oily, black smoke billowed into the salesroom.

"Oh, Lord!" Louise cried.

"Fire! Eddie!" Amanda shrieked. Frantic to reach her son, she dove into the smudgy clouds.

Unable to stop Amanda, Louise raced outside to summon her coachman and shout out the alarm. Her cries brought a handful of people into the street. Rain started to fall. A good wetting down of neighboring houses might contain the fire. The uniformed driver lumbered down from his perch, looking as if he'd been awakened from a nap. Where the hell was Byrne when she needed him?

From inside, she could hear Amanda calling out above the ever louder crackle of flames. "Louise, I have him. I—oh God, something's blocking—" Her voice broke off at a splintering crash from deep inside the building.

"I'm coming. We'll get you out." Louise turned to her driver. "Quick. Come with me."

She ran three steps but heard no one behind her. When she turned the man was backing into the street, away from the now visible flames and sparking cinders, a horrified look on his face.

"Stop!" she shouted. "We have to get them out of there."

Ominous creaking noises followed by another boom shook the building. A fierce burst of heat rushed out through the front door, stealing away Louise's breath.

The coachman's eyes widened. "I'll be off to roust up the fire squad, Your Highness."

"There isn't time. We have to—"

But he was off and away.

"Go then!" she screamed after him. *Coward.*

A shoeblack, whose stand she passed every day, shook his head woefully at her. "Them roofing timbers done burnt through and fallen. You'll not be gettin' past 'em, Your Highness."

"The hell I won't."

She held her sleeve across her nose and mouth and ran straight through the front room of the shop and into the glowing inferno of the storage area. The heat seared her flesh, unbearable, coming in blasts, each one sucking the breath from her lungs. Her clothing was no protection. She wondered how long before her skirts caught a cinder and ignited.

"Where are you?" she shouted. Every word released allowed burning air to singe her lungs. "Amanda!"

No answer came.

Dear Lord. Please don't let this happen. Please don't take them from me.

She sensed someone coming up behind her and felt a thin ribbon of relief that the coachman had a change of heart.

"Are you insane? Get out of here!" Byrne's voice.

"Amanda . . . Eddie, they're—" Her eyes burned and wept, and she choked on the acrid, scorching air. "Can't . . . can't leave them."

Byrne grabbed her arms and hauled her down to floor level. When their eyes met she saw a storm of emotions in his—fear among them, but something else that moved her.

"Stay down where the air is good," he shouted above the roar of the flames. He moved ahead of her but stopped at a single smoldering beam that had fallen at an angle and was now propped at one end on a soapstone sink in the far corner. Wrapping his hands within the sleeves of his leather coat to protect them, he bent low and braced one shoulder beneath the timber. He heaved upward with a grunt and threw the wood aside. A shower of sparks erupted through the blackness when it landed. In that moment of orange-gold brightness, Louise glimpsed two figures curled on the floor.

"There," she coughed out the word. "Behind the shelves."

Scrambling on hands and knees, she made her way to Amanda. Her friend had thrown herself over the little boy. Eddie was sobbing but his mother appeared unconscious. It looked to Louise as if a smaller timber had come down on her head just after she'd reached him.

"It's all right, Eddie. Come here to Auntie Lou-lou." She tucked him under one arm and drew her jacket over his head against the poisonous, broiling air.

Byrne hauled up Amanda and flopped her over his shoulder. "Go!" he shouted, his voice rough with inhaled smoke.

They crawled, staggered, and tumbled out into the street. A crowd had started to gather around the front of the shop. Three men with buckets sloshing with water raced past her; she had little hope they could do much good. Someone shouted that the fire squad had been summoned.

At a safe distance from the burning building Bryne deposited a soot-covered Amanda on a quilt supplied by one of the neighbor women. The glass display window exploded, spraying shards of glass across the street. Louise sat on the curb beside Amanda, rocking Eddie to quell his crying. Only when Amanda moaned and tried to sit up did Louise break down in tears of relief and hand the child to her.

They'd all made it out. It was a miracle. The shop would be in ruins, but the only thing that really mattered was—they were alive.

"Thank you," she gasped when Byrne returned, having organized a bucket brigade and informed the fire squad of the location of the blaze. "Thank you for saving them . . . us."

His coal black eyes looked more accusing than concerned now. "How did it start?"

"I don't know," Louise said. "The boy was sleeping in the back room. I suppose he must have knocked over a lantern." Her chest hurt. She had to stop and cough before going on. "We've no gaslights. Sometimes Amanda leaves a candle or small lamp lit to soothe the child to sleep. There are no windows to let in light."

She was sick with the realization of how close she'd come to losing them both.

"So you believe this was an accident?"

"What else could it be?"

He stared pointedly at her.

"Oh, no, it couldn't have been the Fenians. Why would they have targeted . . ." But perhaps it was possible.

Amanda gave her a look then buried her face in her little boy's scorched hair.

All around them, men rushed with hoses, buckets, and bowls—anything that might carry water. Others shouted encouragement and pushed a steam pumper into position. They doused not only the shop but also the neighboring buildings. If not contained, a fire like this could devastate entire blocks of the city.

Then the skies opened up and heaven released a deluge on them. Louise just sat there, soaking wet but grateful for the rain. Without it this might have been a far worse disaster.

Byrne said, "Let's move you, Amanda, and the boy to the carriage. I've had your driver take it down the street out of reach of the fire."

When they reached the barouche, her driver gave Louise a sheepish look as he helped Amanda and Eddie into the carriage. Louise supposed she couldn't blame him for his refusal to enter the burning building, as terrifying as the fire had been. Still, she would not use him in the future.

"We should get all of you to the hospital," Byrne said.

Amanda shook her head weakly. "No. Please, take us home. My husband will see to us."

Louise understood. With the mention of the Fenians they all naturally wanted to be in a safe place. Or was there another explanation?

"Darvey," Amanda whispered, turning to Byrne.

He scowled at her then shouted up at the driver, "Drive on, man!"

"The bawd. He might do something like this for revenge."

Byrne's jaw clenched. His neck muscles corded taut as ship's rigging. "Tell me exactly what you saw and heard just before the fire broke out."

"Nothing, actually."

"No threats shouted at you or the shop? No Irish radical slogans found lying about?"

She supposed she knew what he was getting at. Why bother to burn them out if they didn't take the opportunity to deliver their message and at least take credit?

"None," she said.

"And you heard no sounds of someone breaking in?"

"No," Amanda answered for her.

"Wait." Louise laid a hand on Byrne's arm and felt him tense at her touch. She left her fingers there for a moment, drawing strength from his presence, and he in turn seemed to relax. "I did hear soft sounds. They might have been someone moving about the room, just before we opened the door."

"We thought it was Eddie." Amanda drew the boy more tightly to her. He seemed cried out and had gone stone silent with shock, his face and hands smudged with soot, eyes glazed over. "But when I reached him, he was still asleep on the cot."

"But there's a door to the alley?" Byrne said.

Louise frowned. "Yes. How did you know?"

He ignored her question. "I agree with Amanda. This isn't Fenian work. You had a convenient glass display window in the front of the building." Which had exploded outward and into the street from the fire's heat, she realized, not from anything being thrown through it from the street. "Why would they sneak in the back way and risk getting caught? All they had to do was lob one of their bombs through the front window. That's much more dramatic. Makes a statement."

"Then it really was Darvey's doing?" she said, hardly feeling the jouncing of the carriage through her fury.

He nodded solemnly. "Most likely."

"You haven't had your 'chat' with him yet?" she said, not quite accusing him of slacking, but there it was.

If he heard that same tone of blame, he didn't let it show. "Our meeting is now overdue," he muttered darkly.

As if cued by the end of their conversation, the carriage stopped with a jolt. Louise watched Byrne duck out through the curbside door. She waited while he helped Amanda and Eddie out, observing him with a fresh eye.

He was, in many ways, quite normal in size for a man. More than a head shorter than John Brown. Broad of shoulders, but he didn't have Brown's horsey bones and bulk of body. If he had dressed in standard fashion—waistcoat, frock coat, and top hat—casting off that leather monstrosity and wide-brimmed hat that made him look like a ranch hand from the American West, he'd have blended well enough with any group of English gentlemen.

But Stephen Byrne, the Raven, wasn't the sort to bother blending. And he wasn't a gentleman, not by her or anyone else's definition. He went his own way, made his own rules—she could see that now.

He might pretend to take orders from his commander, her mother, or even from her. But he cut a wide swath through whatever instructions he'd been given. Why, she wondered, was he even in London when he could be back in his own country? No doubt making good money as a private bodyguard for men like J. P. Morgan or Mr. Rockefeller? Why come to England at all?

Whatever his reasons, she found she was glad he had come. To say she felt safe around him wasn't quite accurate. It was more that his presence made her worry less about *other* dangers because she was concentrating so hard on *him*. Because he was the most unpredictable of men. Because she was as intrigued by him as she was wary of what he might say or do next.

Twenty-four

Byrne had just walked out through Buckingham's gates into the street tangled with carriages when he heard the rapid thud of hobnail boots closing in on him from behind. He swung around, instinctively thrusting his right hand through the hip-high slit in the side seam of his leather duster, but didn't pull out the Colt.

It was John Brown. His stomach tightened. The Scot's eyes were bloodshot, as was often the case, but they fixed on him solidly rather than sliding away as when he was drunk. Reassuring. Brown appeared sober enough to not be a danger. Hopefully.

"Where you off to now, laddie?"

Byrne kept a neutral expression. "To do my job."

"Your job is here, protectin' the queen's children." Brown planted his big feet. Beneath the hem of his kilt, his legs looked like two knobby oak limbs. "I been savin' your skin long enough from Her Majesty's questions 'bout where you're at."

"Last I knew, the queen hadn't provided me with an office. The family's security relies on my confronting threats wherever they appear."

The Scot lifted his lip in a snarl. Byrne's hand closed tighter around the Colt's grip. "Riddles. You're full of riddles, aren't you, Yank? What devilment you up to now?"

Byrne considered his options then thought, *What the hell*. He told the Scot about the fire, hours earlier at Louise's shop, and watched the man's face grow darker, word by word.

"The princess is uninjured?" Byrne nodded. "And this Darvey scoundrel, he's still abroad?"

"He is."

"You want help?" Brown grinned as if anticipating a good fight.

"Not necessary. You're needed here. I can handle a lone pimp." The truth of the matter was, he didn't trust Brown. Byrne still felt as though putting his back to the man might end messily. "Besides, Victoria might disapprove of my . . . methods."

Brown shook his head. "Just to make things clear—you don't owe the villain sympathy."

"Not an ounce," Byrne agreed.

"Good luck then." Brown started to turn away.

Byrne let him take two steps before he decided the time was right to take a calculated risk. "Donovan Heath," he said.

Brown froze then slowly turned to face him. "There's that name from the past again. What about him?"

"You know him?"

"Aye, I did. What of it? Told you in the garden I had nothin' to do with whatever happened to the boy." Byrne didn't miss the choice of words. Not do, *did* know him. As one speaking of the dear, or not-so-dear, departed.

The Scot's eyes glowed with malice, whether toward the mentioned name or the mentioner, Byrne couldn't tell.

"Know where I can find him?"

"Best leave well enough alone, Raven."

Byrne stepped closer to be heard above the clatter of the street traffic and calls of costermongers shouting out their wares. "Louise wants to know what happened to the young man."

Brown sighed, and a great wind of boozy tobacco breath spewed from his lungs. His face contorted in anger. Byrne's fingers moved to wrap the Colt's grip again.

"What happened is the worthless little runt ditched Her Highness. That's the whole of it."

Byrne nodded. "Could be. But I don't think so."

"Don't matter what you think, laddie. Is what happened. Now leave it be." Whatever token goodwill the Scot had shown him moments earlier had vanished. He was being warned off well and good.

Bloody hell, Byrne thought. *In for a penny* . . . "Louise was in love with the boy, or thought she was."

"So?"

Byrne tipped his head and looked up into the other man's eyes for any sign of deception. "She thought *he* was in love with *her*."

"That's what women think when a man—" Brown pressed his lips together, apparently reconsidering his words. "No doubt he told her as much. She were a sweet little lass. Innocent. She'd a believed him." Brown almost managed to sound tender. Then he straightened up to his full, impressive height, eyes as dark as a cave. "Leave it be, Raven. Or I'll have to—"

"Did you get rid of him?"

The only answer he got was a look meant to make him piss his pants. A look that had probably worked on others.

"I don't take orders from you, Mr. Brown. The queen made that clear. She told me to look after her children. Louise's safety might well depend upon someone answering her questions about this matter. Would you rather she take off on her own in search of her lover? Because if I don't satisfy her, I'm convinced that is exactly what she'll do."

A sound emerged from Brown that was half growl, half moan. "She ain't never goin' to find him."

"Probably not. But she won't rest until someone can prove to her that Donovan is either dead or alive. And if alive, where he is. She needs to understand why he left her."

Brown let his great bearish head drop back. He glared up at the coal-fouled sky. "That pretty little bairn has never been anythin' but trouble for her mother."

Byrne narrowed his eyes and studied what he could make out, behind the beard, of the man's face. To what extent did this *trouble* reach? And what remedy had been taken to keep things quiet? Byrne felt an awful chill at the first possibility that came to mind.

"Did you, under orders of the queen, murder Louise's lover?"

The words hung in the air between them. Brown appeared not in the least shocked by the accusation.

He laughed but then seemed to seriously consider the question, as if there might be multiple interpretations of the word *murder*. "No. I didn't kill him."

"Or send someone else to do the job?"

Brown's features softened into what seemed a genuine smile. "You think I'm that low, Raven? A common assassin?"

"For queen and country." Byrne shrugged.

"Aye, well, if she'd asked me to, I guess I would've. I hated the little creep. But she didn't ask me." His eyes twinkled beneath bushy brows. "I'll admit to givin' the boy a little fatherly advice."

"Tell me what happened."

Brown looked back at the palace, the sentries and a cluster of dignitaries in frock coats and top hats, arriving to do business of one sort or another in the complex of offices within the sprawling palace. "Let's walk."

They turned to the right and started off along Stafford Road, which immediately led into Queen's Road, running parallel to the palace gardens and the royal stables. Brown seemed to need distance between himself and the grounds before he spoke further. Byrne kept pace in silence. The Scot crossed the street, turning left at Vauxhall Bridge Road, which would eventually lead to the river.

The River Thames, where bodies turned up daily, Byrne couldn't help thinking. So close and convenient to the castle, winding off through the city . . . to the sea, which had swept away the guilt and evidence of many a crime before this one.

At last Brown said, "You can't tell the princess but . . . her mother ordered me to send the boy packing."

"I see." If he could avoid passing this along to Louise, he would. The news might well cause an irreparable rift between mother and daughter, whose relationship was already strained.

Brown continued in a low undertone. "She was desperate, Victoria was. The lass got herself mixed up with these artsy-tartsy Bohemian types. They're famous for experimenting with absinthe, heroin, all manner of drink and behavior worrisome to her mum. Donovan, he was the last straw, you might say. She fretted the friendship was becoming too cozy."

This was what Byrne had suspected all along. If Louise had taken Donovan as her lover, she'd have lost her maidenhead—her ticket to a royal marriage like those her sisters Vicky and Alice enjoyed. She would have been considered "ruined," ineligible as a virgin bride. Worse yet, if the union with a commoner produced an illegitimate child, might it not be held up as an heir—destroying the unsullied lineage to the throne? He wasn't sure how all of that worked. Regardless, he couldn't imagine Victoria sitting idly by while Louise had an affair with the young art student.

"What did you do to chase off the boy, John?" Byrne asked, glad they were having this discussion in public. He might actually survive the interview. "How badly did you beat him? So bad he might have *accidentally* died after you left him bruised and bleeding?"

"I didna touch Master Donovan." Anger deepened the Scot's brogue.

"You expect me to believe that?"

"I do, as it's the truth, you bloody Yank." Brown stopped walking and turned to glare down at him. "I wanted to give him a thorough thrashin', I tell you. But I knew if I ever put my hands on him, I would kill him. All I did was give him the money Victoria told me to take to him. It was in an envelope, sealed. I don't even know how much she gave him, but she said it was enough for him to travel away from London and live off for a good long while."

"That's it?"

"Then I took him down to the docks and seen him onto a ship bound for Calais."

Byrne still wasn't sure he believed the man. "Was he distraught at leaving the princess?"

Brown roared with laughter. Passersby on the street turned and stared nervously. "Distraught? The lad was delirious with joy. Couldn't believe his good fortune. He was jabberin' on about gettin' himself a garret of his own in Paris. No more posin' for him. He'd be an important artist. I watched him break open the seal and peer into that envelope as if it were a bloody pot o' gold. His eyes lit up like twinkly diamonds, they did."

So Donovan had never been in love with Louise. Yet she still longed for him. It broke Byrne's heart. Twice she'd loved the wrong men and received nothing but heartache in return.

"Thank you, John," he said, meaning it. He stared down at his boots, wondering how much longer he could avoid telling the princess, if only to spare her heart.

"Then that satisfies you on Mr. Heath's account?"

"Yes." *No.* Byrne watched the other man's eyes for signs of deception. Even now, a nagging twinge in his stomach told him something was wrong with the story. Or maybe it was just that parts of it were still missing. Someone—Victoria, Brown, Louise (all of them?)—was keeping secrets from him. Why?

If he had any sense, he'd do as Brown said: leave it be. But he felt compelled to discover as much as he could about Louise. He'd become obsessed with the woman—damn her royal hide.

The key to getting to the bottom of this moral quagmire, he

thought, would be to find someone in the queen's or Louise's confidence. Someone in court or the family who might be willing to gossip about Louise's wild years. Ideally, someone who also might have an idea who had smuggled a clutch of rats into a heavily guarded castle.

Twenty-five

Rupert Clark looked up at Westminster Cathedral's soaring tower. He knew only enough about architecture to be surprised by the exotic mixture of light and dark brick work. It seemed more like something out of the Arabian Nights stories his ma used to read to him than in the middle of an English city. The cathedral was, of course, much larger than any church he'd attended as a boy. Meeting the Lieutenant here in the Chapel of the Martyrs seemed appropriate and reinforced his belief they were doing God's work.

Although . . . he wasn't 'specially keen to be a martyr himself.

Of course, Ma wouldn't have approved of his methods. But results were what counted. Hadn't she been firm in believing the South could only survive if it separated from the North? And wasn't it just as important to the Irish to have their own governance?

So maybe God hadn't been with them at Vicksburg after all. But He must have sorely regretted His neglect. The Fenians were giving God another chance.

Rupert led Will up the cathedral's steps. The interior was breathtaking with its soaring ceiling, mosaics, carvings, gilded statuary, and hundreds of varieties of marble. At first he felt disoriented by the magnitude of it all. They wandered along the nave and took several wrong turns into alcoves, each with its own altar, before they came upon the chapel where the Lieutenant had told them to meet him.

Will hadn't said a word since the runner delivered the note, calling them to a meeting. Now he followed along like a puppy dog—obedient but restless.

"Cat got your tongue?" Rupert asked. He breathed in a heady whiff of incense that had drifted from some unseen source. It reminded him of mass, back home, the priests dangling that smoking ornament that released a sweet scent.

Will frowned. "I's just wonderin' who this Lieutenant is."

"Don't," Rupert said. "These Irish lads don't want their names bandied about."

"I mean, in a general sorta way. Is he a priest? Is that why we're in a church?"

"Might be. Or he could just be clever. Safer this way, ain't it? Away from prying eyes."

"I guess."

Rupert stepped farther into the chapel. The atmosphere felt cleaner here, fresher than out in the street's stench. Here he smelled ancient wood, fresh wax, and odd aromas like the bear grease some gentlemen used to groom their mustaches or the rose water old ladies splashed on instead of taking a bath.

Fat, little crimson glass devotion candles burned in a rising bank, beckoning him toward them. He would light one before he went into the confessional. Might as well look the part.

"I don't need to go in there, do I?" Will slanted a sideways glance toward the chapel's altar. He'd once said churches spooked him.

"No. I'll do it. You take on a prayerful attitude. See that old lady there?" Rupert pointed to a woman whose head was bowed as she prayed from her knees. "Do like that. Down on the kneeler, eyes closed, and no looking around. You know how to pray, don't you?"

"Don't look hard," Will said.

Rupert paused to genuflect and cross himself at the altar. The gesture reassured him. One of their jobs had gone sour, although it wasn't his fault. Who could have predicted the queen's entourage would be diverted just two miles before the trap he'd laid on the road north of London? He'd expected the Lieutenant would give them another chance, and he had. Their next two jobs had been spectacular successes.

He was going to have to ask for more money soon; their living expenses had nearly run out. This wasn't like the army, where you got fed and paid regular. But it made sense for the Fenians to see to their troops' needs. If he and Will had to fend for themselves, get jobs or steal to feed and shelter themselves, they would become too visible—and that wasn't good for the cause.

"Be right back," Rupert said, spotting the dark wood confessionals the note had described, along the right side wall of the chapel. As he walked away he heard Will struggling with the kneeler. It clunked down on the marble floor with a dull echo. He should have shown him how it worked so he wouldn't be so clumsy with it. But there was only the one old woman in the chapel, so it probably didn't matter if the boy seemed a little nervous. Didn't lots of people get nervy before making their confessions? Facing your sins—your mortality.

He stepped into the penitents' side of the booth and closed the door behind him. It smelled musty inside—a good kind of odor, comforting. He imagined this was how tradition smelled. On the other side of the screen he saw a shadow move. For a moment, his heart leaped into his throat, and he worried there might be a real priest waiting to hear his confession.

Just to be sure he knelt down, folded his hands, and murmured the words he hadn't said in a very long time, "Bless me, Father, for I have sinned." He continued the familiar litany. The time that had passed since his last confession—more than six years, he guessed. And he was about to start listing his sins, but not all of them of course, when he remembered the agreed upon password. "Oh, and also, Father, I come from Appomattox."

A soft sound came to him, as if whoever was on the other side of the grille was also relieved. "Any trouble coming here unobserved?" a voice said.

"None, sir."

The invisible man said something in a low whisper Rupert didn't at first understand. "Sorry?"

"On your seat, the envelope."

"Oh." He shifted his hips and only then saw the small rectangular shape. When he picked it up it felt thick between his fingers.

"Open it."

He slid his thumb under the flap and tore upward, making a ragged paper mouth. Although he couldn't see in the darkness he could feel the leaves of banknotes inside.

"That should keep you comfortably for a while longer," the man said. His accent told Rupert he was definitely a Brit, and educated.

"Yes, sir. Thank you, sir."

"Now we get down to business," the man whispered, "before the priests return to wash away the weighty sins of old women and small boys."

Rupert smiled. Was the man making a joke? He decided it was safer not to laugh. "Yes, sir, to our task."

"I have a very important mission for you and your partner. We fear that our membership has been compromised by a spy in our midst. There is a job that must be done immediately. We cannot take the chance that those involved will be spotted and identified. You and your partner are new to the country, it's unlikely the queen's protectors know you."

"Yes, sir." Rupert could sense his value had just increased tenfold. He felt gratified.

"In that same envelope you've just received, you will find a photograph. Tonight when the opera lets out, the man in that picture will leave and, as is his habit, walk across the park to his club. If he is alone, you will kill him quickly and quietly before he has a chance to leave the park. If he is accompanied, you must kill whoever is with him as well."

"What if he has several companions?"

"That might be a problem. Perhaps you can isolate him. The important thing is that you cannot be caught, and if you are—nothing of our organization can be revealed."

"Understood."

"We count on your silence."

Did the man think he was inexperienced in warfare? Rupert shook off the sting of resentment. He was, after all, a soldier and knew what was expected of a soldier.

"Who is the target?"

"You will recognize him from the picture when you see it. The man's death will be a powerful and personal blow to the queen, as he is a favorite of hers. This will be the first part of a double strike against her. After you have carried out the mission, we will claim responsibility."

"How do I—"

"The method is up to you, but circumstances dictate stealth and speed. I would suggest a knife."

Rupert nodded. Hand-to-hand combat wasn't his specialty, bombs being a far less intimate weapon than a blade. But he'd been trained for such operations in the army. He made no objection.

"Tonight you said," Rupert murmured. "So soon?"

"It must be tonight. There will be no better chance."

"Then it will be done. Is that all?" He waited for a response or some signal that the meeting was over, but none came. "Sir?" he whispered.

After another few seconds he sensed that the priest's box was empty. He hadn't heard so much as the creak of a door.

Rupert walked out of the confessional, head bowed, fingers clasped, and knelt beside Will. "Did you see him?" Rupert asked.

"Who?"

Rupert sighed. "Never mind." He drew the envelope from his inside jacket pocket and peered inside. Will bent over to see what he was doing.

Rupert silently counted the banknotes. Many more than he'd expected. At least a month's worth of generous wages for the two of them. He smiled then felt the stiffer backing paper of a photograph. When he pulled it out, he saw that it wasn't a simple daguerreotype. It was an elaborate calling card with the gentleman's full standing image in an elegant pose on the front, his signature superimposed over the picture, his address on the reverse.

"Who's that?" Will whispered.

"Our target."

His partner scowled. "Dapper fellow. Can't read the signature though."

Rupert smiled at the importance of their job. "This is Mr. Benjamin Disraeli."

Twenty-six

Louise stood in the front room of her little consignment shop and looked around at the nearly empty shelves. Nothing could have made her happier.

She had proposed a Saturday Fire Sale. Amanda wrote the announcements, posted the broadsides, and ran an advertisement in the *Times*. The publicity brought in new customers and resulted in twice as many sales as on any previous day of business. Starting early in the morning, customers crowded into the little shop looking for bargains. They'd bought nearly everything she'd put out.

Now that she and her staff had scrubbed down the walls of the display room, the stench of charred wood was tolerable. After a good bleaching, most of the doilies, antimacassars, linens, and delicate handwork had been restored nearly to their original color. Well, close enough anyway. Pristine whites became cream, butter creams became ecru, ecru became chocolate brown. No one the wiser. Nevertheless some articles were more obviously smoke damaged and could only be sold at much reduced prices.

Now that the shop was closed for the night—Amanda having

left to make dinner for her husband and little boy, her shopgirls exhausted and dismissed—Louise stayed on after dark to finish her inventory.

It seemed a miracle that the fire brigade had been able to save the building. But they had, with the help of the rain. And the day after the fire her merchant neighbors gathered round to lend a hand in making repairs. They brought with them a carpenter and crew who replaced weakened or fallen timbers to make certain the building was safe. A glazier replaced the front window for the cost of the precious glass. Others volunteered to help clean and put out at the curb anything Louise deemed too damaged to sell in the shop. No sooner was an item set out than it disappeared. Londoners were great re-users. Even the humblest of items would bring a small profit to someone on the street.

Now it was dark outside, the gaslights dimly glowing, passersby dwindling. Louise set the CLOSED sign in her new window, framed by lovely gingham curtains donated by Belle & Co, down the street, then she finished moving a half dozen large wooden picture frames to the street. Even damaged, she'd thought they might sell. Now she decided that was unlikely. If nothing else, they'd make firewood to warm someone.

When Louise returned to the shop for her reticule and shawl, she heard footsteps approach close to the front of the shop then hesitate before moving on. She turned just in time to see a shadow pass in front of the display window then stop again. A face, features obscured in the dark, peered in through the glass. She held her breath, trying to remember if she'd locked the door after stepping back inside.

A terrible thought struck her: Darvey had not yet been caught. There was no guarantee he wouldn't return.

Before she could dive for the latch, the door swung open and a figure stepped through.

She fell back with a gasp, hand to her throat.

Stephen Byrne took off his hat and moved into the light of the only lamp still burning.

"Dear Lord, you terrified me!"

He gave her an unconcerned look then took in the rest of the room. "I saw the light on and assumed, at this late hour, someone had broken in."

"Late? Is it?" She supposed it was. But when she worked as hard as she'd done this day, time flew.

"Where is your carriage?" he asked.

"I sent it away long ago. There was too much to do here to have a driver sitting outside waiting for me."

"And you intended to return to the palace how?"

"That's what hansom cabs are for, I believe." She was in no mood for a scolding.

He shook his head at her, smoothed the brim of his hat with the backs of his strong fingers.

"You find taking a hired cab so unusual?" she said. "People do it all the time."

"Not the queen's daughter. Have you no regard at all for your safety? Spending daylight hours here with others to keep you company is one thing. But it's nearly eleven o'clock. No one at the palace knew where you were."

So he'd come intentionally looking for her, maybe was even sent by her mother.

She turned away from him, pretending to straighten a much diminished stack of aprons, handmade by a clever little seamstress whose products sold almost as soon as they hit her shelves. "I care about my safety almost as much as I care about my freedom. I refuse to surrender my ability to move about the city."

She felt him step up closer behind her. "The rest of this can wait for another day," he said. "You look exhausted. You can't have had much sleep since the fire. I'll deliver you home."

She stiffened, a frisson of irritation creeping up her spine. "You'll *deliver* me? Like a parcel?"

His voice dropped an octave lower, a shade softer. "Like a woman who needs a bath and food."

Louise plucked a hothouse rose from the arrangement sent to her by her neighboring merchants, sniffed its fragrance, and turned to narrow her eyes at him. If he thought she'd allow him to boss her around, he was mistaken. She thrust her chin forward and stepped toward him. "And you'll no doubt instruct my maid to escort me straight off to bed?"

"It wouldn't be a bad idea." His eyes had focused on her face, on her mouth to be precise, in a most disturbing way.

Something came over her—an inexplicable urge to tease or put him in his place or even to shock him.

"You worry more than my old nurse." She slipped the rose into the buttonhole in his coat's lapel and stretched up on the tips of her toes, intending to plant a mollifying kiss on his roguish whisker-stubbled cheek.

At the last moment, he turned his head just enough to meet her lips with his. The kiss was no more than a brush of their mouths, but she laughed, delighted with herself for flirting a bit and even more so for the look of surprise on his face.

Before she could draw away, the scent of his skin came to her. The tiny follicles of ebony hair in his sideburns swam in front of her eyes, and her fingertips itched to reach up and stroke the spot just there in front of his ear. Her breath caught, and she prudently backed away.

How long had it been since she'd felt such a thrill at being close to a man? Delicious.

Half a second later, she glimpsed the warning flare in his eyes.

"No," she breathed, instinctively raising her hands between them.

One step forward was all he needed to wrap an arm around her waist and pull her up hard against his chest. Her eyes flew wide. She whimpered as his mouth came down over hers. Unlike the other, this kiss was hard and hot and shockingly intimate.

When he released her mouth, she felt dizzy, bewildered. Perhaps her teasing had backfired?

"Don't play games with me, Princess," Byrne warned, his voice abrasive with emotion she couldn't identify. "You won't like my rules."

He released her as abruptly as he'd seized her. She staggered away, out of breath, supporting herself against the new pine shelving. "Why did you . . . do *that*?"

"If you're going to throw yourself at a man, you might as well do it right."

"Throw? Throw myself at—" She gulped down a bubble of indignation. "That wasn't my intent."

"Really."

"It was more a kiss to—well, to gently chide you. A sisterly kiss." Did even she believe that?

He glowered at her, black eyes fierce, glittering in the brilliant flame in the lamp. "I'm not your brother."

She was totally confused now. "You sound angry. How can *you* be offended when *you're* the one who has behaved in such an abominable manner?"

For a heartbeat, it appeared he was vacillating between diving for the door and wringing her neck. Just in case, she stepped behind the sales counter. He tossed his hat on it and vaulted over.

She screamed when he came up just short of plowing into her and knocking her over. Byrne gripped her shoulders between his two wide hands.

"When you look at a man that way, Louise, you can't expect him to control himself forever. What is it you really want? Tell me."

"Want?" She shook her head, trying to come up with something acceptable, but all she could think was that she'd really like for him to kiss her again. Maybe even harder. Longer. On other places than her mouth. *Oh, Lord!*

Lorne had kissed her no more intimately than a tidy peck on the cheek, and only in front of others, for effect. She had enjoyed no real affection from any man since Donovan disappeared—unless you counted the occasional, brief physical contact necessary while dancing at a ball.

But wasn't this sort of scenario what she'd imagined when Byrne appeared in her nighttime fantasies? A romantic interlude. A stolen kiss. A forbidden touch then regretful parting. And sometimes . . . sometimes she opened herself to far more intimate possibilities.

"I want you to"—she blinked up at him, stalling for time and sensible words—"to go outside and summon a hansom for us, while I finish up here."

The tension in his features dissolved into something that was almost a smile, even though he didn't release his grip on her. He slowly shook his head. "Liar."

What to say to convince him? She simply couldn't allow the man to think . . . to *know* that she had lustful thoughts whenever he came near her.

"Princess?" He gave her a little shake. "I asked what you want from me."

How could she think at all when he was touching her and standing so close she could feel the warmth of his body all down her front? She cleared her throat and said, "I want you to . . . to tell me this instant what you've found out about Donovan."

The amusement in his eyes faded. The flesh around his mouth tightened. "Your friend is in Paris. Or, at least, that was his intention."

"In Paris? But this is good news. Wonderful news." Surprisingly, she had to work at sounding excited. "It was my mother, wasn't it? She made him leave."

Byrne released her shoulders and stepped back to rub the knuckles of one hand across his eyes. A moment earlier he'd seemed so very animated. But now, for the first time, she realized how tired he looked. "There is that chance," he said.

"She sent him away, didn't she? Oh, Mother, you've taken so much from me—but this is . . . is . . . But she didn't hurt him. I mean, send someone to beat him or—"

"Whatever might have transpired, it appears he's survived. You can be happy about that."

"Yes, I suppose I can." But the question remained, if he was alive why had he not at least tried to get word to her? If he longed for her as she longed for him . . .

At least she had always thought she longed for Donovan. Being kissed by Byrne was affecting her strangely. She had trouble remembering what it felt like when the young artist had made love to her. Whereas she still felt the demanding pressure of Byrne's lips on hers. She shook her head to drive away the unsettling sensations.

"Thank you for finding him. Did you see him?"

"No. A man owes me a small favor. He lives in Paris and was good enough to spend some time asking around about your Donovan."

My Donovan? Was he still hers? Had he ever been?

"And he's there, in Paris . . . in good health and painting still?"

"So my source tells me."

"Good," she murmured. "Yes, very good work, Mr. Byrne." This was all so confusing. Perhaps changing the topic was best. "And you've confronted Mr. Darvey about the fire?"

"Next on my list."

She gave a firm nod. "Excellent." Louise took a deep breath, stepped out from behind the counter, and looked away from Stephen Byrne, not wanting to see his reaction to what she had to say next. "And once Darvey's been dealt with, I suspect there will be very little reason for you and I to see each other."

"I suppose not," he said after a moment.

She'd handled that well. She was letting him know she wasn't interested in having a lover. This was a proper and much more satisfying way of managing the incident of the accidental kiss.

Future awkwardness averted.

And yet . . . she still hadn't answered his question. What *did* she want?

Twenty-seven

Head down, Byrne wove through the maze of halls, corridors, and back ways of the palace. He must have taken a wrong turn or two because when he looked up he found himself in an unfamiliar wing of the castle. Lost again—this time due to his bleak mood.

Bleak because of the princess's cool dismissal of him as a man who might ever be capable of arousing passion in her. And because she'd put him in his place as nothing more than a servant.

He stopped walking, looked around, and cursed the damn architects for not including directional signs.

"You look like a big old vulture, hunched over like that," a youthful voice said.

He turned toward the room to his right, its door open and Princess Beatrice standing in it. She studied him with unabashed interest.

He managed a smile for her. "It's the coat. Flaps about like horrific wings, don't you think?" He demonstrated by waving his arms.

Beatrice giggled. "Mother calls you her Raven. Is that why?"

"Part of it," he said. An idea struck him. He'd been so distracted by his unsuccessful search for Darvey, and even more so by Louise's kiss and subsequent rejection, he hadn't followed up on his plan to locate a gossipy palace insider. And here, before him, stood a likely candidate—a young, bored princess.

"May I ask your help, Your Highness?"

Beatrice's eyes sparkled all the brighter. She tossed her blond curls and playfully curtsied, as if he were the royal and she the subject. "Of course, Mr. Raven sir."

"My sense of direction always deserts me when I'm in this part of the palace. Would you be so kind as to point me toward the courtyard?"

She turned to peer over her shoulder, back into the room she'd just left. "My governess is napping," she whispered. "I'll walk with you, to make sure you don't get turned around again."

"Is that allowed?"

She laughed, and he heard a little of Louise in her. "Walking with a gentleman?"

"Without your governess or one of your sisters as chaperone."

She sniffed. "If Louise can run all over London unattended, I can walk from one side of our home to the other with my mother's agent." Beatrice batted feathery blond lashes at him.

He stopped himself from laughing, unsure whether she was seriously flirting or just playing with him, as young as she was, not yet fifteen. Louise must have, at one time, been this innocent, this unaware of her own power as a woman, and her own vulnerability.

He observed the girl out of the corner of his eye as they walked. Beatrice must have been eight or nine years old at the time of the disappearance of Louise's lover. How much information would she have been privy to at that time? And how much might she remember?

There was only one way to find out, but he needed to maneuver cautiously toward those questions. "I was with your sister just last night," he began then lowered his voice as if speaking in confidence. "She has asked me to look up an old friend of hers."

Beatrice stopped walking, turned to him, and lifted her nose, as if sniffing a secret about to unfold. "What kind of a friend?"

"Can you guess?"

"Amanda is her best friend, but Louise knows where she is, of course. They see each other all the time."

"She must have made many friends while she was studying at the art school."

Beatrice frowned. "I don't think so. Not special ones, though she's kept in touch with some of the girls. Mary Reinhart is one, I think. She was very cozy with—" She broke off and blinked up at Byrne. "But I'm not supposed to talk about *him*."

"Oh." He laughed. "A boy. Yes, I suppose some people might not understand. Was it . . . let me see—Donovan Heath?"

Beatrice grinned. "Yes-s-s." She covered her mouth with one hand before launching with enthusiasm into the forbidden topic. "You guessed. So I didn't tell you, did I?" He shook his head. Beatrice laughed. "Louise told me all about him. We shared a bedroom back then with one of my other sisters. Donovan was all Louise ever talked about." She rolled her eyes. "Louise used to sneak off during her lunch break at the school and walk with him in the park."

"Well, that's not so awful," he said as they continued on their way, moving through an entire wing devoted to government offices. "Just a stroll in the park."

She tugged on a golden strand of hair and pouted. "That's just what I said too. But she was still afraid Mama might find out."

"Would you tell your mother if you had a beau?"

"Probably not now. But I was such a baby then."

"And now you're much more mature and have your own thoughts on life . . . and love?" he prompted.

The youngest princess glowed at his compliment. "I do have a theory," she whispered, "about Louise and that boy."

"And it is?"

Beatrice stopped walking and leaned against a tapestry-covered wall, hands tucked behind her back, eyes wide. "I always felt so confused in those days. Such strange things happened."

He tilted his head to encourage an explanation.

"Like the way Louise was acting. She stopped talking to me, you see. Stopped telling me about the school and most particularly about Donovan. She got very angry when I asked about either of them."

"Angry," he said.

"Yes. I thought Louise and Donovan must have had a fight and she was sad about it. Then Mama took her out of the school, and that put Louise in an even worse mood. Louise and Mama shouted at each other all the time. When Louise wasn't acting angry, she was crying, but she refused to tell me why she was upset."

"Did her art mean as much to her then as it does now?"

"I don't know. I suppose it did. So you're thinking maybe she was furious with Mama for withdrawing her?"

He nodded.

She shrugged and started walking again. "I guess it's possible. But I don't think that's all of it." She hesitated. "I think that boy broke her heart. He ran away or maybe another girl took him away from Louise. She refused to talk about him at all. You should have seen her. She was miserable. She cried for days and days."

"Losing your first love is very traumatic," he said, following her lead as they turned another corner.

Beatrice smiled dreamily. "Just having a first love at all, I think, would be grand." She gave a quick look over her shoulder, back the way they'd come, as if worried someone might be following them. "I just remembered something."

"Yes?"

"Louise would probably kill me if I told you this. She'd say it was too personal to discuss with a man. With anyone, really, not in the family."

"Oh?"

"But I don't care." She beamed at him. "You're rather nice."

"Thank you. I like you too," he said, meaning it.

She glowed all the brighter.

He wondered if he ought to back off now and not put her into the awkward position of going against her sister's—not to mention her mother's—wishes. Before he could say anything more, the little princess was rushing into her story.

"You see, my mother's women's doctor was summoned to the palace one day. They say he used to come and go all the time—Mama was always having babies while Papa was alive. But then after Papa died there was little reason unless she felt a pain or fell ill. We didn't even know he was here that day until one of my mother's ladies of the bedchamber came to summon Louise to see him. Which seemed to me very, very strange indeed, since he never came for any of *us*. I mean, why would he?"

"Why indeed?"

"Anyway, Louise seemed very upset but she went with the woman to see the doctor. When she came back she was sobbing and wouldn't explain why."

"Did you ask her what was wrong, whether she was ill?"

"Yes, of course. I was worried for her. I thought she was dying or something. But she wouldn't tell me anything. Then, maybe three or four months later, Louise started getting fat and wouldn't undress when anyone else was in the room."

Byrne mentally shuddered. He didn't like where this was going. Not at all. "What about her maid?" he asked.

Beatrice shook her head. "Louise just said she wasn't pretty anymore, and so why should she want anyone to see her all fat. Mama hated us to get fat, you see. It was fine for Mama, but not for us. Anyway, before I could tell Louise that it didn't matter, I'd love her even if she was immense as an elephant, she was gone."

"Gone?" he asked.

"Yes. One day Louise told her maid to pack a trunk of clothes for her and all of her art supplies, and off she went to Osborne House." *On the Isle of Wight,* he thought. This was the strange retreat from the family he'd already heard about. "And she stayed there for three months, and we weren't allowed to go with her."

"That sounds odd."

"Very," she agreed. "Mama told us she was studying French with a special tutor, and we were to allow her this time alone to better concentrate on that and on her art."

"But you don't believe this was the real reason?"

"No." The little princess pursed her lips in thought. "When Louise came back to London, she was thin again, weepy, and refused to attend any court functions with Mama. She wouldn't smile at anyone or play with me. It was as if she'd changed into another person. A sad, cold, ghosty thing."

"And now?"

Beatrice pointed to a door, which he pushed open and into the courtyard. They both stepped outside. "Now she's better, kinder, sweeter to me . . . but not the same as she was. I still don't think she's happy."

Byrne felt touched by the loss that shadowed the young princess's eyes. Within the royal family, Louise and Beatrice were closer in age than many of the other girls. Beatrice was the last of the five princesses, the youngest of all of the nine children.

"There are different kinds of happiness," he said. "And Louise was then, what? Eighteen or nineteen?"

"About that, I guess." Beatrice looked up at an open window on the second floor. From inside the room, maids chattered and laughed at their work. "I've always wondered . . ."

"About?"

"You won't repeat this to anyone—especially not to Louise?" Her pretty eyes pleaded.

"Of course not."

"Well then—" She leaned in closer to him. "I've always wondered if Louise had a baby."

He looked at her solemnly. Hadn't the same possibility come to his mind more than once? "Donovan's baby?"

"Yes. I've thought about that a lot, Mr. Raven. Maybe that's why Mama sent her away. So that no one would know when she had it. No one would ever see it." Her eyes filled with tears.

"Did you ask Louise about this?"

She observed him with something close to horror. "No! How could I? I didn't want to make her sadder."

Something occurred to him. "Do you know the name of your mother's physician?"

"I did once, I think. But I've forgot now. Mama dismissed him soon after all this stuff happened." She sighed. "Do you think Donovan was sad too—that Louise didn't have her baby? And maybe that's why he went away?"

"I don't know, Your Highness." It was all he could do to answer her, his throat was so tight, his gut a mass of knots.

What did they do to you, Louise? What did they *do*?

If Byrne had been in a black mood before, by the time Beatrice left him in the courtyard, he was nearly blind with fury. Wicked possibilities swirled through his mind. Victoria, who had married her daughter off to a man who couldn't possibly make her happy, had meddled in Louise's life before. What had happened between mother and daughter that had so disturbed Louise she'd refused to participate in court functions for months after her return from Osborne House? And why—when the family, often accompanied by the entire court, traveled together—was the fourth princess banished alone to the Isle of Wight?

He could think of only one possibility.

An abortion. Performed late in the princess's pregnancy—if

Beatrice was right about her sister showing her condition. It would have been performed by the queen's personal physician, in a location away from the London gossips. An illegitimate child, killed before it was born or, if Louise was allowed to carry to term, soon after the baby took its first breath. The thought sickened him.

He supposed that such desperate means were not so very rare in a culture where, historically, royals had a habit of murdering each other for the right to wear the crown. Victoria wouldn't have tolerated a wrinkle in the family ancestry, if there was any way she could help it. Although she had produced legitimate male claimants to the throne of England, bastard babies muddied the waters, sometimes laying claim to what they felt was theirs. If not the crown, then a title and royal stipend for life.

Regardless of the motive, he felt shocked and disgusted at the thought of what might have happened to Louise's baby. *If* Beatrice was right. *If* it ever existed.

Byrne took off in long strides across the courtyard. He was nearly to the palace gate when he saw Victoria's carriage stop at the porte cochere. A footman climbed down and opened the carriage door. Victoria appeared from inside the palace, attended by her son Leo and Brown. John Brown lifted the queen in his arms up and into the brougham, then climbed in after Leo. Byrne stepped back into the shadows and waited until the carriage had moved away down the drive toward the gate.

Byrne turned and rushed through the palace doors the queen had just left. Less than a hundred yards down the hall he reached the first of the royal offices. One of the queen's secretaries sat at his desk, just outside her private inner-office.

Byrne stopped and smiled at the man. "I hope I haven't kept Her Royal Majesty waiting." He smiled apologetically at the man.

The secretary squinted at him, looking confused. "Oh dear."

"I beg your pardon?"

"You've just missed her, Mr. Byrne. She only now left here for her carriage. Brown is riding with her though, so you needn't worry."

Byrne shook his head in mock consternation. "She told me she needed my report by this morning, as early as possible." He did his best to sound panicky. "You don't suppose you could flag her down before they get out the gate, do you?"

The secretary was already up and out of his seat. "It must have slipped her mind to tell me you'd be here. I don't even have it on her calendar. She's doing that more and more often these days. Forgetting things, not keeping me informed. I'm so sorry." He rushed out the door, his words trailing after him. "Wait right there, sir."

Not bloody likely.

Byrne spun toward the closed door leading to the queen's private office. He tried the knob. It turned; not locked.

Byrne let himself in.

He crossed the room that had become familiar to him over the months he'd been detailed to the palace as a member of the queen's Secret Service. Although he'd seen a range of file cabinets across one wall of the outer office, he suspected that anything as delicate as the queen's personal medical records would be kept by her alone, away from the prying eyes of clerical help.

He bypassed the double desks facing each other in the middle of the room. Neither had collected a speck of dust although one hadn't been used in all of the years since Prince Albert's death. Victoria insisted on her husband's blotter, inkwell, writing instruments, and framed portrait of her remaining on his desk, just as they'd been while he was alive and they'd worked here together.

Sure he'd noticed a file cabinet somewhere in the room, Byrne looked around. And there it was. Between the two tall windows, a small three-drawer mahogany chest. He squatted in front of it and pulled at the top drawer. It was locked, as were the two beneath it.

Byrne drew a slim leather wallet from his inside coat pocket. It held assorted fine-tipped metal picks. He selected one. Thirty seconds later, he was into the first drawer, flipping through neatly labeled file folders *A-G*. He moved to the second drawer on the theory that *M* for *Medical* should be there. It was.

Shouts wafted up from the courtyard. The secretary, calling out to the sergeant at arms to stop the carriage. How many minutes before the secretary, or an angry queen, appeared at the door?

He grabbed for the folder marked *Medical*. His eyes skimmed dates at the top of pages, moving back through the years—1870, '69, '68, '67. He slowed down. Nothing in any of them about Louise or any of the other children. In fact, there wasn't a word on any of the pages about anyone in the family but Victoria. Frustrated, he knew the most he now could hope for was the name of the doctor who had delivered the queen's children. Did a gynecologist do that? He didn't know.

Beatrice was the last of the babies in the royal family, and she was now fourteen. He looked in the appropriate year, found Victoria giving birth on 14 April 1857, at Buckingham Palace.

And there it was. The baby was delivered by a Dr. Charles Locock.

Locock. The name hit him with the impact of John Brown's fist. He didn't even have to stop to think about why it sounded familiar.

Was it mere coincidence that Louise's friend Amanda had married a Henry Locock?

He fumbled the pages back into order. Closed the file. Shoved it into its place. Shut and locked the drawer.

The sound of a door opening in the outer office sent him rocketing from a crouch to his feet. Footsteps approached. Hesitated. "Mis-ter Byrne?" came the secretary's voice, sounding irritated.

Byrne dove for one of the guests' chairs, kicked one boot up to rest across his knee, and leaned back in a posture of relaxed waiting.

The door swung open the rest of the way. "Mr. Byrne." Displeasure tugged at the secretary's narrow, white face.

"I hope you were in time," Byrne said with a note of concern, flicking a crust of mud from his boot and onto the pristine carpet.

"You shouldn't be in here when—"

"No luck, huh? Too bad." He stood up and moved toward the door. "Best schedule me at Her Majesty's pleasure but preferably soon. She'll want my report before the prime minister's speech on Thursday."

Twenty-eight

Louise sat with her family in the queen's opera box. Victoria loved Gilbert and Sullivan's operettas, and although Louise was somewhat less fond of the performers' silly antics she adored music of all kinds. And the songs in *The Pirates of Penzance* were delicious.

Lorne sat on her right, every now and then leaning over to whisper a comment in her ear. He reached for her hand and drew it over to rest on his thigh. A tender gesture that meant nothing, she'd learned. No doubt for the benefit of others in the box, and for the second and third grand tiers, whose occupants employed opera glasses to spy upon their fellow audience members. Gossip would start afresh the next day based on the pairings of the night, the jewels worn, the indecency of a neckline, a straying hand or stolen kiss.

Louise sighed and played along with their marital charade while the actors rushed about onstage. But her mind flew off to another place and time, and a face other than the actors' or her husband's. *The Raven*. His dark aspect continued to haunt her.

With ruthless resolve she banished Stephen Byrne from her thoughts and concentrated on the news he'd brought her.

Donovan was alive and in Paris. What might that mean to her now or in her future?

The action below on the stage seemed to dissolve into mist before her eyes. She tried to remember what her first (and only) lover had looked like on the last day she'd seen him. What would he have said or done if he'd known of her secret suspicions. At the time of his disappearance, she'd already begun to notice the changes in her body, but she hadn't yet told him of her fears. Would he have stayed in London if she had told him she was carrying his child? *Stayed with her?*

Louise felt herself flush as she recalled the delicious, intimate things they'd done whenever they'd had the chance. In artists' garrets during the day. In the park under cover of darkness. And, most dangerously, in the cozy attic of the art school. A flow of warmth worked its way down through her belly. She let her head drop back, felt the beginnings of a long-absent release, and . . .

Horrified, she withdrew her hand from Lorne's and clasped her fingers in her lap. Breathing deeply, she tried to calm herself.

"Are you all right, my dear?" Lorne asked, studying her face. "You look feverish."

"I'm fine," she whispered, but even those two words sounded, to her ears, intense with lust.

Lorne frowned at her.

"It's just . . . the music, it's so very moving," she said quickly.

"Hush," her mother said from her other side. Victoria turned to whisper to Alice, seated behind her, "They can hardly contain themselves, so in love they've lost their manners."

As soon as the lights came on for intermission, Louise rose to her feet, feeling desperate to escape the closeness of the royal box and prying eyes. Most of all, she needed to get away from Lorne. They would never be lovers. Never be husband and wife in the most intimate sense. But he already understood her too well, read too much in her reactions. If he suspected she might try to see Donovan, he'd likely feel threatened and tell her mother.

She couldn't let that happen.

"I need to walk," she said, moving toward the draped entry to their box. She knew her mother wouldn't follow. Victoria never left her box to mix with the crowd in the chandeliered foyer.

But the queen's hand reached out for her. "Sit, dear. It's far too crowded out there. Our gentlemen will bring refreshments."

"No, truly," Louise said. "I need fresh air. It's stifling in here with the perfumes and flowers and hot lights—"

"I'll accompany you," Lorne offered, standing up from his seat.

She closed her eyes and wished him away, but there was nothing she could do to make him let her go alone.

"You've always been so restless, Louise," Victoria scolded. "I don't understand what's wrong with you. Stay here where you're safest."

Louise glanced at John Brown to see if she could use him as an ally. But he merely shook his head, cautioning her against leaving, or perhaps just against challenging her mother.

All of her life she'd been a prisoner. Cushioned in luxury, yes, but a prisoner nonetheless. She refused to remain so any longer.

Besides, was this plush velvet-lined box, which tonight suddenly reminded her of a casket, safer than any other place outside of the palace? Wasn't the American president assassinated in a theater?

Well, one couldn't live in constant fear. Risks had to be taken to enjoy life.

"I won't be long," she promised, shooting Lorne a look that begged him to stay behind. She slipped between the curtains, past the uniformed guardsmen standing watch.

Lorne caught up with her before she'd gone a dozen steps. He clasped her hand and drew her arm through his. When she looked up at him, his smile was closer to a pained grimace. "You shouldn't push her so." His blue eyes flashed with urgency.

"Why should I give in to my mother's every whim? She gets more impossible every day." Her throat and cheeks felt unbearably hot. She had half a mind to claim illness and call for the carriage.

"Certainly you can let her have her way in little things," Lorne suggested. Now that they were out among the glittering crowd in the lobby, he let go of her hand to light his pipe. "Like how to spend intermission."

"You don't understand." She turned away then swung back at him, tugging her heavy skirts around in an awkward pirouette. "I'm a married woman now. Our arrangement was supposed to give me more freedom, not less. If I don't assert myself she will destroy me."

He laughed, his eyes suddenly brighter, less concerned. "Destroy? Isn't that a trifle melodramatic, my dear?"

"You have no idea. None at all," she huffed. She started to move away from him before he could ask her to explain, but a cluster of men sipping cognac at the bar stood in her path.

"Louise, my dear." A tall, elegantly turned out gentleman stepped out from the group.

Lorne said, "Disraeli." He dipped his head in acknowledgment to the politician and writer.

The former prime minister pursed his lips and slanted a sly look at her husband. "Marquess. And how does married life suit you?" Did she imagine an amused twist to his lips?

"How could a man not be deliriously happy, married to the most beautiful woman in all of London?" Lorne proclaimed, a little too loudly.

"How indeed?" Benjamin Disraeli's intelligent gaze skimmed Louise from beneath half-lowered lids. Her mother thought the man handsome and virile, as did many women both in London and abroad. Louise was not in the least attracted to him. He was too full of himself. "And you, my dear, I see color in your cheeks. Can I hope that the cause is connubial bliss?"

"You may," Louise lied.

"It is lovely as well as lucky that I should run into you tonight, Your Highness."

"Really, why lucky?" she said.

Disraeli's gaze slid almost imperceptibly toward Lorne, as if to let her know he preferred to speak to her without her husband present. "Why, for the pure pleasure of your company."

"Lorne dear," she said, "would you mind hunting up a glass of Champagne for me? The servers are so slow reaching this end of the lobby."

He drew another puff from his pipe and smiled agreeably. "Of course, my dear."

Louise watched him go then turned back to Disraeli. "The queen will be deeply hurt if you don't stop at her box to pay your respects."

"And I certainly shall. I was just introducing my friend, visiting from Paris, to a few MPs." He glanced back at the group he had just left. "But I'm glad we have a chance to chat."

"About what?"

"I have been desperately worried about your mother."

She frowned. Did he, a close confidant of Victoria's, know something she didn't? "Why worried?"

He laughed and shook his head. "How can I not worry? There have been more than one attempt on her life in recent months. The Balmoral trip, a case in point."

"A lone student, most likely drunk."

"Not that. The other incident. The aborted bombing."

"And where did you hear about that, since it has been kept from the newspapers?" Louise squinted at him. Victoria's advisers had agreed that the failed Fenian plot should be kept from the public so as not to cause panic. No longer prime minister, Disraeli had not been briefed. "Did my mother tell you? Brown advised her not to."

He shrugged, as if to say, *Well, so what if she did tell me?* "It's no secret that the Fenians are determined to force the Crown's hand. They believe if the queen gives in to their demands, Parliament will follow. If she's frightened enough, she might give up Ireland. And if she were dead, the Prince of Wales would succeed her, and fearing the loss of more family members, he might be moved to release his troublesome Irish subjects."

"And are they right?" she asked. "Do you think it would work in their favor—an assassination?"

Disraeli tipped his head to one side in thought. "Who knows. But it might be one of the partisans' more effective moves." He lowered his voice and leaned in. "I've also heard you have faced a setback in one of your personal ventures."

It took her a moment to untangle his meaning. "The fire," she said. "Yes, the shop had only just started to be successful and draw regular clients. Thankfully, we only had to close down for a few days to repair and clean up."

"I admire your efforts, dear lady. Although I must admit your political views are far more liberal than mine. A woman's days should be spent in the home, not in business. Even your mother upholds that very sensible rule." He held up a hand when Louise opened her mouth to object. "Nonetheless, I would like to make a small donation." He slipped his hand inside his evening coat and brought out an envelope. "As I've said, I had hoped I'd see you here tonight, and I came prepared."

She took it from him. "This is very generous, sir. Thank you."

"It won't build you a new shop, but it might at least cover a good deal of the repairs."

She smiled, forgiving, for the moment, his all too commonly held views of a woman's role in society. At least he was willing to help this once. "Would that other gentlemen felt as moved to aid our cause and reduce the number of women forced to the street."

"I shall do my best to pass the word," he said. "Perhaps there is some middle ground. Compassion shouldn't be limited to either Tories or Whigs."

The lights in the lobby flickered, signaling the end of intermission. Louise tucked away the envelope in her reticule.

Lorne returned with her Champagne. "Too late, I fear," he said.

"Not at all. I'll just bring it along with me." She took his arm. "Delicious to sip through the second act."

As the crowd moved toward their seats, Louise looked around, half expecting to see Byrne somewhere among them. After all, wasn't he supposed to be watching over her and her siblings?

But then John Brown was here, along with her mother's guard. And she'd sent Byrne off to deal with the awful Mr. Darvey. She should he happy that he was following her orders. For once.

"What did that sly devil want?" Lorne asked as they took their seats.

"Disraeli? He donated money to the Women's Work Society. A rather generous amount, I'd guess, from the plump envelope he just gave me."

"Really."

"Yes." She was amused by the irritated look Lorne cast across the concert hall toward Disraeli's balcony. Apparently masculine pride leaped barriers of sexual preference. "I'll let you know how much he contributed to our cause, dear." She patted his cheek with her white-gloved hand. "Perhaps you'd like to match his donation?" She grinned up at him.

He looked startled but recovered quickly, straightened his lapels, and dipped his head at the idea. "Why not? Maybe I'll even double it."

This might turn into a better night than she'd expected. She celebrated the moment, mentally prioritizing the additional improvements she'd now be able to afford.

Twenty-nine

The pupils of his partner's eyes had dilated, giving him a wild, frenzied look in the gaslight outside the Royal Opera House.

Rupert Clark laid his hand on the younger man's shoulder. "What's wrong, Will? Not like you to get nervy."

"Don't like knives," Will grumbled. "You only gets one chance. Takes nothin' for a man to turn the tables on you."

"It'll be fine. Two of us to the one of him."

"I s'pose. Still wish we could do him with a pinch of black beauty."

"And how's that gonna work in a crowd like this?" Already the opera house doors were opening, a bejeweled audience spilling out into Bow Street. "Lieutenant wants 'em to know it's Disraeli who's the target. We lob a bomb in the middle of that crowd, newspapers'll get it all wrong."

"How do we know he won't take one of them carriages lined up yonder?" A sea of top hats and plumed heads, even now, flowed toward the long line of waiting curricles, phaetons, and cabriolets.

"Connections. In the palace. Told you afore. Now," Rupert warned, "pay attention. We don't want to miss him." He found it hard to track individual faces in the crowd beneath the vaporous gaslights. The flames turned everything a sickly yellow-green in the night. The ladies' features were further obscured by veils and dipping hat brims, the men's eyes shadowed by top hats, their expressions masked by beards. But Disraeli, in the photograph, was clean-shaven, lean, and tall. He'd stand above most of the crowd.

"There," came a hoarse bark from Will after they'd watched for a few minutes.

"Where?" Rupert squinted into the haze. The boy's eyes were sharper than his.

"See those two? One on the right has no beard."

"You get a look at his face?"

Will grinned. "He's a dead ringer for the swell in that picture."

Rupert hesitated, needing to make sure. He watched the pair cross the street into the park then take the same path the Lieutenant had described in his note. They'd walked it earlier in the day, checked out every one of the surrounding horse trails and wooded lanes. He'd picked out three spots, any one of which would be good for waylaying and dispatching their man.

Rupert looked back toward the opera house. The crowd was thinning. Only a few couples heading into the park by different paths, cuddling, clutching each other amorously. None of the other men resembled Disraeli. The remaining operagoers were splitting up into the last of the remaining carriages. If he and Will didn't follow the two men soon, they'd lose them entirely.

Rupert wiped the sweat from his brow and concentrated on the two frock coats already disappearing into the darkness. "Let's go."

He and Will split up as planned. Rupert's route wound to the north and came out on a rise thirty feet above Disraeli. Through the trees Rupert could hear the two men below him, talking about the opera and a woman one of them was interested in.

As soon as the pair below turned the next bend, Rupert silently slipped down through the trees behind them. Will would come at them from the other direction.

Up ahead, Rupert caught a sudden blur of motion in the dark, and his heart nearly stopped. Will had lunged at his victim without waiting for his signal. Now there was nothing he could do but make his move.

One of the men shouted, "Watch out!"

Rupert ran up behind Disraeli, who seemed so stunned by the attack on his companion he was unable to move. Rupert whipped his arm up and around the taller man's throat, knife in his other hand. He slashed once. The diplomat sagged to the ground, gurgling blood.

"Help. Murderers! Assassins!" Screams echoed in the dark from a ways off. Will's man was escaping.

"Fuck!" Rupert swore and took off at a run to silence the man before his cries brought the coppers down on them. How had Will let him get away?

Just over the next rise, Rupert spotted his partner. Down on top of a figure. Stabbing repeatedly into the waistcoat with his knife. *Make it look vicious*, the Lieutenant had said—the better to horrify the queen and her subjects. Will was doing his job with enthusiasm. No doubt the man was already done for—he wasn't moving at all. And as for Disraeli, he'd have bled out by now.

"Enough." Rupert grasped Will by the back of his collar and pulled him off the body.

Thirty

On the arm of her handsome blue-eyed husband, Louise stepped into the splendor of the grand ballroom of Stafford House. Near St. James's Palace, this was the exquisite home of the Duchess of Sutherland during the Season. Even after the duke's death, his widow entertained on a lavish scale. A patron of the opera, she had opened her home to the elite of London after that night's performance.

Victoria declined to attend, instead sending Louise and Lorne to represent her. She'd claimed fatigue and the need to conserve her energy for her Accession Day celebrations in just two weeks.

Bertie had convinced the queen that she must make a public appearance for that occasion, if for none other during the year. The queen's subjects were growing impatient with her self-imposed isolation and obsession with mourning. And so there would be a formal procession by carriage, accompanied by the horse guard from Buckingham to Westminster Abbey, where the service would be held celebrating Victoria's taking up the crown worn by her uncle, King William IV.

Once she began planning the day, though, the queen grew more enthusiastic. Louise felt greatly relieved that her mother had agreed to follow her ministers' and Bertie's advice. Louise, far more than anyone else in her family, understood the common people and their need to believe their country still had strong leadership.

As soon as Louise and Lorne were announced, the orchestra launched into Strauss's "Artist's Life" waltz, in honor of the princess and her love of art. Dancers whirled across the floor, ball gowns shimmering, medals glinting from lapels. Smiles were the expression of the evening. Fear of Fenians, wars in Europe, or uprisings on the Dark Continent—all that was serious seemed distant and inconsequential. But Louise could not cast off a premonition that something evil lurked close by, ready to steal away what little happiness she might grasp for herself.

After the Viennese, she danced a cotillion with Lorne then a polka with the new Duke of Wellington who had so recently lost his beloved father, the hero of Waterloo. The duke was gracious even in his mourning, and a fine dancer. She looked around for Stephen Byrne, but he was nowhere to be seen. Either he wasn't here or he was making himself invisible, as he so irritatingly managed to do whenever he chose. She had counted on him being here tonight, with good news about Darvey.

Another waltz began. Lorne reappeared at her side, his blond curls and flashing sapphire eyes the focus of every female in the immense room. And not a little admired—she noticed—by several of the men. "Shall we?" Lorne said, holding out his hand to her. "The orchestra seems particularly fine tonight."

She managed a smile for him, or rather for the hundreds of watching eyes. Lorne escorted her onto the dance floor. She rested her fingertips lightly on his sleeve, lifted the hem of her gown with her free hand, and off they flew. Louise caught an approving gaze from her brother Leo as they swept past him and his little clutch of friends.

"You ought to have been an actress," Lorne murmured in her ear. "Everyone is commenting on our love match."

"Oh, please," she said.

"But I must admit to a small amount of distress on one count."

They negotiated the end of the room with a graceful heel turn and floated on down the length of polished parquet floor.

"About what?" she asked.

"I have heard that you are making inquiries of a . . . sensitive nature. Is that true?"

Louise tensed even as the music swelled to a glorious crescendo. Had Byrne told her husband about her interest in finding Donovan? "I am, although it is nothing to concern you."

His voice sounded less casual now. "It is most definitely my concern if those investigations put at risk my credibility as your husband."

Did she hear threat in his tone? "We have a bargain. I will keep it."

"All I ask is that you keep me out of Newgate, my dear. Your freedom for mine. *Oui?*"

"Yes." She had to admit he was keeping up his end of the deal. He hadn't once questioned her right to travel alone, to run the Women's shop, to spend hours with her painting or in Amanda's company. "I keep my promises."

His gaze softened. "There are discreet ways in which you might satisfy your needs."

She looked up into his dazzling eyes, now piqued with sensual intrigue. "It is more complicated for me," she said.

"Is it? I might easily find you a willing lover."

She should have been shocked. It was a scandalous suggestion. But all she could do was laugh at the absurdity of her situation.

She shook her head at him. "Oh, Lorne. You really wouldn't be in the least jealous?"

"How could I be?" He studied her face, his eyes tracing her lips, throat, bare shoulders. "And yet, you're right, my dear. There's still my pride to consider. I cannot bed you, but part of me is reluctant to see you in the arms of another man. Foolish, is it not?"

"Foolish indeed," she agreed. But there was a sweetness about the marquess that she knew would never let her stay angry with him for long. She tenderly stroked his cheek with a gloved hand. The music slowed. She swayed in his arms, and she imagined to anyone watching they must have made a pretty picture. "Lorne, what are we to do? Is this how I am supposed to live out my life? Forever without affection? Without children?" It was a repeat of their wedding night conversation. But something she still couldn't let go of.

"I will be as affectionate and caring as many husbands, my dear. I promise you every consideration, but the one."

The lump in her throat swelled, threatening to choke her. She drew a shaky breath as tears teased her eyes. "I wish . . . I wish . . ."

"Yes?" he asked.

She blinked away the droplets. "Never mind." It was hopeless.

The music had ended. They stood in the middle of the vast, glittering ballroom beneath a triple-tiered chandelier of hundreds of Murano glass prisms as couples slowly drifted back to their seats or exchanged partners. Louise felt unable to move. He was a kind man. She really should be happy.

"Come," Lorne said, reaching for her again, "this is a gentler waltz. I will show you off to London tonight, and soon to all of Europe. They will see what a beautiful woman I've married and say, 'Ah, what a perfect couple they make.' We will trick the world, my dear. Be brave."

She blinked away the last of her tears, rested her right hand in his, her left reaching up to lightly touch his elegant shoulder. Louise let him guide her through the intricate, swirling one-two-three steps of the opening strains of Carl Maria von Weber's gorgeous "Invitation to the Dance." Her pearl gray gown swept the floor, rustling at her ankles, her heart lifting with the soaring strains of the violins.

It might never be possible for her to be truly happy, but the joy of the dance lifted her spirits.

They had completed only one circuit of the ballroom when, during the subtle break before the faster *Allegro vivace* movement, a voice from behind Lorne said, "May I take the princess for a turn?"

When Lorne stepped aside with an expression of irritation to address the intruder, she saw that it was Stephen Byrne.

Her breath hissed inward with delight as she took in his costume, so unlike anything she'd seen him wear before. It was an officer's military dress uniform, one she recognized from photographs of the American Civil War. Dark blue jacket, with polished brass buttons, fringed epaulettes, and a fitted waist that showed off his wide shoulders. She was stunned at his change in appearance. Without the great flapping leather duster and Stetson he looked every bit the gallant young nobleman.

Although Byrne was nearly a head shorter than the lofty Lorne, she sensed her husband felt intimidated. After a moment's hesitation, he stepped back and waved a hand in her direction.

"So long as the lady does not object, she is yours," Lorne said with a chill smile. "For the moment."

"Thank you, Marquess." Byrne held out his hand to Louise as the music swelled exuberantly, sweeping other dancers past them in a frenzied vortex of silk, satin, and jewels. "Your Highness?"

Unsure why he had stolen her away from her husband, mid-dance no less, she observed him with caution. Did the American officer even know how to dance?

He did, she discovered. Magnificently.

They joined the throng, circling counterclockwise around the ballroom. But as soon as they reached the side farthest from the royal dais where the Prince of Wales and her brother Leo sat, Byrne whirled her out of the maelstrom of dancers. He lifted the latch on the balcony doors, dropped an arm around her waist, and scooped her outside into the night.

Thirty-one

It happened so fast, Louise didn't have a chance to protest. She was still preoccupied with catching her breath when she realized he was wrapping a leather strap he'd pulled from his pocket around the two exterior door handles, effectively locking the doors with the two of them outside.

She touched wary fingertips to the pearls at her throat. "What is *that* for?"

"So we won't be disturbed. You wanted a report?"

"Yes. Darvey." She breathed a little easier. "Have you dealt with that cruel man? Are Amanda and her family safe now?"

Byrne walked over to the ornate stone balustrade that edged the balcony, his boots striking the paving stones forcefully, his expression unreadable. "The pimp has gone missing."

Louise frowned. "Maybe we should consider that good news? He's been frightened off, knowing the police will arrest him for arson."

"I doubt it. The police, at least some among them, are likely to have been paid to protect Darvey's business. And that might extend to his other shenanigans."

She huffed. "I hardly call burning down a building with people inside it 'shenanigans.' As if he were a schoolboy prankster."

"Despite our differences in word choice," he said, fixing her with a dark stare, "the man's lying low. I'll catch up with him eventually. In the meantime, I've visited the Lococks and let them know to stay close to home. Henry promised to meet with as many of his patients as possible in his examination room, rather than making calls. That way, he'll be better able to keep an eye on his wife and child."

Louise was trying to pay attention to what he was saying. But even as he spoke, Byrne was observing her with an intensity she found worrisome, almost predatory.

"Then I suppose," she said, "there's nothing more you can do for the time being."

"There is the other matter. Donovan. Your young lover."

"Yes, what have you—" She cut herself off, realizing he'd tricked her. "Don't be crude," she snapped. "I never said we were anything but friends."

"No, you didn't," he said and stepped closer to her. "But you *were* more than friends. You were lovers."

Louise was certain she'd stopped breathing entirely now. She opened her mouth to speak but found she could not. Not a word. Not a whisper.

"Louise, it's insane what you're doing. You're hiding things from me. You expect me to help you, but you refuse to give me what I need to do my job."

"But I—"

"You can't go on protecting secrets that need to be brought out into the open, at least between us."

Emotion surged through her, cramping her chest, sending a lightning bolt of pain from one side of her forehead to the other. She balled her fists in rage. "How *dare* you presume to require personal information from me. You have been commissioned to do two jobs for the royal family. One for the queen, officially, and one for me, unofficially. That is all you need to know." Was there ever a more infuriating man? "I stand under no obligation to feed your curiosity by . . . by spilling out the events of my personal life for your entertainment."

He seemed not to have even heard her reprimand. "It's not Amanda's safety that's so very important to you, is it?" His voice had become as still as a pond. His eyes so dark she lost herself in them. They were no less fascinating than the distant black spaces between the stars overhead. He stepped toward her. "Is it?" he repeated.

"Of course Amanda's welfare is important." How had they come to be standing so close? She could hardly draw a breath without the bodice of her gown brushing his lapels. "She's my dearest friend."

"But there is, or was, someone even more precious to you than Amanda Locock."

She felt confused, then terrified. *No. No, he can't have found out!* She fell back into the safety net of her practiced story. "Donovan was a fellow artist and friend whose—"

"Donovan be damned!" Byrne roared, making her jump. He took a breath, calmed himself again with obvious effort, but his expression remained pained when he at last spoke again. "There was a child. That's the secret you're trying to protect. What happened to it?"

Before she could answer, a loud pounding set the terrace doors shivering. "Your Highness, are you there? Are you all right?"

In desperation, she glanced back the way she'd come, toward the ballroom. "It's our guardsmen," she whispered. "Someone must have seen us come this way."

"Answer," Byrne said. "Tell them you're safe."

Was she? One scream from her, and the Hussars would break through and escort her back to her brothers, and take Byrne away.

"I'm fine," she called out shakily. "Please, I just need a little fresh air."

Louise heard muffled conversation then retreating footsteps but was pretty sure they'd have left a man close to the door in case she should need him. The orchestra began to play another dance. She squeezed her eyes shut and fought a fresh surge of panic. He couldn't force her to tell him. She could run . . . just dash for the door and call out to the guard—

Byrne seized her arm as if he knew escape was on her mind. "Not this time. You're staying here until I hear the whole story. No more lies, Louise."

She tried to shake him off, but he held all the tighter, pulling her closer still, lowering his face to capture her frantically wandering eyes with his. The muscles along his jaw tightened, as rigid as carriage springs. His gaze turned brittle with determination.

"Louise, please, tell me. What really happened between you and the queen and your mother's physician Charles Locock? Did you give birth to a baby out of wedlock?"

She gave her head a violent shake. *Lost. Everything is lost now,* she thought miserably.

Stephen Byrne had discovered her shame. And now he would force her to return to that fateful night.

Had anyone else found out, she might have borne it. But this was a man she'd come to respect, if only for his dedication to her family and stubborn insistence on the truth.

She closed her eyes on a wave of vertigo that nearly sent her plummeting to the stone terrace at his feet. "It's the past," she whispered, clutching his lapels to keep from falling. "For god's sake, leave it be. Please, don't make me revisit—"

"Listen to me," he said between gritted teeth. "If you are ever to find happiness, woman, you must confront the truth. Don't let it defeat you."

Why had she let this man into her world? What insanity had gripped her to make her believe she could trust him?

She rallied the little pride still left to her and looked him in the eyes. "Sir, I order you to release me. I absolve you of all commitments to me." She struggled to pull out of his grip, but he held firm. "I insist you allow me to return to—"

"You *killed* it, didn't you?" Any warmth his voice had held a moment earlier dispersed like vapors into the night.

Her eyes widened. She thought she might swoon, except he was holding her up by both arms now, fixing those mesmerizing black eyes on hers, demanding she confess all. Torturing her by ordering her to relive the worst days of her life.

"Louise." He gave her a shake.

Her throat burned with the salt of unshed tears. "I—didn't—kill—anyone," she whimpered. Her tongue felt so heavy in her mouth she could barely form the words.

He released a strained breath. "If you can't say it, I will."

Her eyes widened with dread. "Please. No! Don't."

He ignored her and continued in a low voice. "This is how I believe it happened, Princess. A few months after you started a love affair with the young artist Donovan Heath, your mother suspected you were sleeping with him. She decided she must find out for certain if she'd guessed right and put an end to the affair. She ordered her gynecologist, Doctor Charles Locock, to examine you. He not only found you were no longer a virgin, a blow to Victoria, who had hoped for a royal match such as she'd already arranged for your older sisters, but you were pregnant. This news may have been as much a shock to you as it was to your mother."

Byrne watched her face, waiting for a response. Louise could only stare at him, feeling the world slipping away beneath her feet. Her body went mercifully numb.

He continued. "The queen must have been desperate. She had to work fast to avoid scandal. She commanded Locock to get rid of the illegitimate fetus. Is that much right?"

Before she could stop herself, she'd given him a tiny nod.

"Right," Byrne growled. "The rest is conjecture on my part, but let's see how close I can come." She shrank from his condemning glare. "You begged your mother to spare your baby. Whether you wished to give it up for adoption or keep it, I don't know. But neither option would have satisfied Victoria. So long as you refused the procedure to end the pregnancy, the scandal threatened to tear holes in the royal family. To the queen's way of seeing things, permanently disposing of the problem was still the only solution."

His voice gentled at seeing the agony reflected in her eyes. "Louise, I'm not saying you *wanted* your baby to die. Victoria is a powerful, determined woman. She probably talked you into going off to the family home on the Isle of Wight for your confinement, letting you think it would be only to deliver the baby away from prying eyes."

Louise wept openly now, no more able to stop her tears than she could have willed away a monsoon. Her breast heaved, wracking her entire body. "How can you be so cruel? I hate you, *you monster*!" She sobbed. "To speak of such things—"

Inconceivably, Stephen Byrne pulled her into his arms. He cradled her head against his deep chest, the coolness of his military medals soothing her flaming cheek. "I'm sorry. Truly I am, Louise. But you need to face what happened and leave the guilt behind."

"Oh Lord!" she cried.

He was ruthless. Why wouldn't he just shut up? But she let him hold her, feeling so much safer in his arms than standing apart from him on the balcony, in the chill wind.

He kept on talking, more to himself than to her now. Fitting pieces of the puzzle together in his mind, a man obsessed with the desire to understand. "You gave birth to your baby. Sir Charles Locock, father to Amanda's husband, attended. You probably weren't even allowed to see the child. Maybe Locock told you it was stillborn. Maybe you didn't believe him. Therefore your resentiment of your mother and the closeness you've developed with your best friend's child. Ironically, Edward Locock, the doctor's grandson, has become a surrogate son to you."

Louise tearfully shook her head, rejecting his words. What she had done had been wrong. Loving Donovan. Deceiving her family. Keeping her pregnancy from the world. But she couldn't let Stephen Byrne think her sins were as black as he painted them.

She sucked down a deep, shuddering breath and seized fragile control of her thoughts. *The truth. There was nowhere to go now but to the truth.*

"It—wasn't—like—that." She gulped down air between convulsing sobs.

"No? Then tell me how it was," he murmured into her hair.

Louise closed her eyes, pressing her feverish cheek against Byrne's chest. She listened to his heart, strong and steady and reassuring against her ear. She breathed in the scent of him, and he wrapped his arms even tighter around her. Only in his embrace did she find the strength to remember how it had been, and say the words out loud.

"You're right," she whispered, drifting back in time, "but only about some of it."

And then she was in that horrid room again. The old doctor and his wife standing over her bed. The crashing sounds of the ocean pounding the rocks outside her window, and the unbearable pain tearing apart her body as she struggled to bring her baby into the world.

She remembered every detail as if it were yesterday . . .

Thirty-two

Osborne House, Isle of Wight, 1866

Louise threw her head back against the sweat-soaked pillows and screamed as the contraction climaxed. The pain pressed up through her belly, hardening the muscle in a wave that rounded into her lower back. When she opened her eyes as the discomfort lessened, she saw the doctor, holding a cloth in one hand and an amber bottle of ether in the other.

"No!" she gasped. "Take it away." She pushed herself halfway up from where she lay on the mattress, bracing herself on her elbows.

"But, Princess," his wife coaxed, "it will ease the pain."

"Your mother ordered it for you," Dr. Charles Locock said. "She asked for ether when her last two children were born. She swears by it."

"No. You'll make me lose consciousness."

"Would that be so bad?" cooed the woman. "When you wake up, it will all be over. Just like a bad dream." The doctor took a step forward; the ether cloth came at her again.

Louise kicked with both feet, sending the couple stumbling back out of range. "Stay away from me!" she cried. "Stay away from my baby."

The doctor and his wife exchanged looks. She knew what they were thinking, knew what they intended to do.

"We just want to help you," Locock said. "You can't give birth on your own like a squaw."

"After the baby is born, if it is healthy . . . if it survives the birth, it's better if you don't see it," his wife said, her voice softly coaxing. "You know you can't possibly keep it. I will carry it to a couple in the village who are waiting for it. It will have a loving family to care for it."

"Liars!" Louise screamed on the rise of another contraction. She panted to catch her breath, portioning out words between inhalations. "I saw . . . the letter . . . she sent. My mother wants . . . to kill my baby."

The doctor's wife reached out as if to brush a hand over Louise's sweat-damp hair, but stopped short of touching her. "Oh, no, dear. What a terrible thing to say. The queen is so worried about you. She wants what's best for you, and the babe will be—"

While the pain eased, Louise spilled out her proof. "She said in the letter, 'Do what you must.' That's what she said. She didn't say to find my baby a home. She didn't say to— *Oh, God!*" She felt herself tearing then the hardness of the baby's head pushing between her thighs, and she fell back against the tangled linens, unable to gather enough strength to hold herself up any longer.

They were right. She needed help. She couldn't do this on her own.

She felt the doctor's hands guiding the baby out of her as his wife encouraged her to push. The woman stood beside her, holding her hand, smoothing a cool hand over her forehead, whispering, "It will be all right, Your Highness. It's all going to be just fine.

You'll see. Now the worst is over. The babe's out. Rest now. We'll take care of everything."

Despite refusing the ether, Louise suddenly felt so very tired, so sleepy, she could hardly keep her eyes open. "My baby," she whispered. "Please, give him to me." They hadn't told her it was a boy, but somehow she knew.

"Now dear—"

Tears pooled in Louise's eyes, blurring the room around her. "Please, *please* don't take him from me."

She could hear them talking in hushed voices on the far side of the room. Water was being poured, she imagined to clean away the birth blood. A lusty cry broke the silence as the babe took his first breath. Her heart sang. Her son was alive.

But before she could reach for him, there came a sudden splashing sound, and the cry stopped.

"No!" Louise shrieked.

"What are you doing?" The doctor's voice. "Not here, woman. Get it out of the room!"

And then she knew for certain, there was no village couple.

"Stop!" Louise pushed herself up on one arm despite the searing pain the slightest movement caused. To her relief, the woman had stepped back from the tub of water with the writhing, wet infant in her hands. "If you harm that baby . . . if you take one step out of this room with him," Louise vowed, "I shall tell the world you have murdered the grandchild of Queen Victoria."

The doctor and his wife exchanged worried glances.

Locock took a step toward her. "Princess. Please, let us take care of this complication for you. The scandal would kill your poor mother."

Nothing on God's green earth has the power to kill that woman, she thought. *Nothing. She'll die when she's good and ready.*

"Give me the baby," Louise commanded.

Neither of them moved. But the wrinkled pink newborn, lying like a pagan offering, still unswaddled in the woman's open hands, suddenly began flailing and wailing furiously. He was probably just cold. Louise knew that. But to her ears, there had never been a more beautiful sound. Her son was calling to her.

"Go! For godsakes get out of here!" the doctor shouted. "She's bluffing."

The doctor's wife looked down at the baby in her hands then at Louise. There was a flash of pity in the older woman's eyes.

"If you kill my child," Louise warned, her voice crackling with white-hot rage, "I swear to you, I will go to the police, but first I will tell every newspaper in London what you have done. You will both be charged with murder and found guilty, because my mother will deny knowledge of your wicked deed. She will protect the Crown, while all of England calls you monsters and applauds your execution."

As if launched by a spring, the doctor's wife rushed toward the bed and nearly tossed the squalling infant at its mother. Louise tenderly rested the babe across her belly and pulled the blood-stained linens up over them both for a bit of warmth.

"In the morning, you will see things differently," Locock said, his eyes grim, lips tucked in tight. "You will realize you have no choice but to—"

"There are always choices," Louise said, giving in to her exhaustion and closing her eyes as she cradled the baby to her body. "Go. Leave us."

That night, as tired as Louise was, she forced herself to stay awake. A few hours later, the doctor's wife slipped into the room. Before Louise could warn her off, the woman pressed a finger over her lips. "Hush, Your Highness, I won't hurt you or the child. I've brought clean sheets and blankets for you. Let me wash you and check to make sure you're not hemorrhaging."

The woman was efficient and gentle, but so silent in her ministrations that Louise knew she had come without her husband's knowledge.

"Thank you," Louise whispered.

"I have a son too," the woman said, her eyes kind. "A fine grown son. You fought for your babe's life tonight. I would have done the same."

Thirty-three

Louise shifted away from Byrne's chest just enough to look up into his face, needing him to see her eyes and know that every word she'd confessed to him was the absolute truth.

"When Locock came into my room the next morning, he tried once more to convince me I was being foolish. I assured him if he killed my baby, he'd have to kill *me* to keep me quiet."

Byrne was staring at her with an expression of such wonder that she knew he hadn't guessed this part. She thought she saw a subtle brightening in his gaze, and relief.

"Aren't you going to ask where the child is now?"

"I'm pretty sure I know."

She smiled. Yes, she supposed he did. "By morning I'd come up with a plan."

"And that plan involved a young woman who scrubbed floors at the art school where you'd met Donovan?"

"Yes. I sent a carriage for Amanda. Then I told Locock to summon his son. Henry was a medical student, soon to complete his studies. I'd met him at parties with my artist friends and liked him. He seemed generous of spirit, gentle, wise beyond his years.

When they both arrived I introduced them to each other and made them a proposition. I offered a generous portion of my dowry to set them up in a nice house in a respectable part of the city—if they would marry and take my baby as their own. Amanda would never have to scrub another stoop, and Henry could open his practice years earlier than if he were struggling on his own or dependent upon his penny-pincher of a father. All they needed to do was provide a safe and loving home for my little Edward. And allow me to spend time with him whenever I could."

Byrne closed his eyes and breathed in deeply, as though to cleanse away the wickedness of his accusations. "I'm sorry I thought for even a moment that you might have—" He shook his head. "This is a much happier tale than I'd imagined. You were terribly brave." He touched her cheek with rough fingertips. "You stood up to your mother and—"

"And acted just as she would have done." Louise didn't try to hide her bitterness. "I ordered people around, forcing them to alter their lives to suit me."

"No. You saved an innocent life and brought two people together who seem very happy with the marriage you arranged for them."

Louise had to agree with that at least. Although she'd often felt guilty for bullying Amanda and Henry into a marriage every bit as contrived as her own to Lorne, she had watched them fall in love during the years they were raising her son as their own. "I've just learned that Amanda is expecting a child of her own. Henry is as proud as a man can be."

"So there," Byrne whispered. "Fate put you in an impossible situation, but you did the very best anyone could. Your son is a healthy, happy boy, due to your courage."

"But he'll never know I'm his real mother." That alone broke her heart.

"There may come a time when you can reveal the truth to him."

She looked up at Byrne, seeing something new and unexpected in the man. Beneath the facade of a rogue was an intelligent and sincere man. A man of moral strength.

"Why did you put me through this ordeal?" she said, pressing her palms to his chest to move a little away but not quite out of his embrace.

"Because you needed to heal. I told you that."

"No, I mean, why do you care? You, personally. About me."

He tipped his head to one side and smiled. "Because I just do." She watched as he lowered his head, knowing what he was about to do. He kissed her on the lips, long and thoroughly.

Already weak from her emotional outpouring, Louise dissolved at the soft pressure of his mouth over hers. She lingered, enjoying the moment, then sighed. "No one in my family cared enough to face the truth. No one," she said. "It's a forbidden topic. My fall from grace."

The tenderness in his gaze shifted almost imperceptibly to something with more sizzle.

"Mr. Byrne?"

"My Christian name is Stephen," he reminded her.

This would take some getting used to. "Stephen. I understand you're a compassionate man. Comforting me and being my confidant is one thing, but . . . I need to know what you're thinking. Why are you looking at me like that?"

"Oh, well—" He lowered his lips to her throat and kissed her once, twice, thrice in a descending pattern to the top edge of her bodice. "I'm just trying to convince myself not to throw you down on this stone floor and make love to you."

She reached up and placed her palms on either side of his face to make him look up from her breasts and into her eyes. "That would be a very ungentlemanly thing to do."

"I suppose so. But then—"

"—you're not a gentleman."

"Right." He cleared his throat and released her, as if the simple action of opening his arms required as much strength as lifting a smoldering timber off of Amanda. "But if you stay out here another five minutes with me, your reputation will be shot to hell."

She smiled. "I suppose so."

He took her by the hand. "Back to the ball, Princess."

Thirty-four

In the days following Louise's encounter with Stephen Byrne at Stafford House, Louise found it a challenge to think of anything but him. His strong arms holding her. The scents of leather and earth that seemed always to cling to him even when he was indoors. His eyes, as black as the onyx stone in the signet ring her father had left to her. In her dreams, he kissed her again, and again. Each time demanding more from her.

Louise's only defense for shutting out these fantasies, and others far too vivid and intimate to even think about, was by keeping very, very busy. She decided the necessary distractions should come in the form of helping the American investigate the rat incident. While he was in pursuit of Darvey, she would lessen his load by doing a little sleuthing at Buckingham.

The first step, she decided, was to confer with her mother, a task she looked forward to with even less enthusiasm than usual, so soon after revisiting the most traumatic days of her young life.

Byrne had forced her to acknowledge her feelings of guilt, deserved or not, for giving up her son, and for hating (or at least deeply distrusting) her mother. That emotional catharsis was no doubt long overdue—though she failed to see why Stephen felt it his particular duty to bully her into confession. The problem now was—she feared this awakening of emotions might renew the tension of her daily encounters with her mother. Until this moment, their relationship, though strained, had survived. They had come to an uneasy truce. By unspoken agreement, neither spoke of the past. Her mother even seemed capable of pretending, while around Amanda and Eddie, that she wasn't the boy's grandmother. Incredible.

When she arrived at her mother's office, she found the door shut. Her personal Cerberus looked up from his desk. "Your Royal Highness, I hope you're well."

"I am. Quite." In fact, she felt positively renewed. As if she saw the world through fresh eyes, unclouded by self-doubt. "I need a few words with my mother."

The secretary blinked at her apologetically. "I'm afraid she is in conference with Mr. Disraeli. I don't know how long they'll be."

Louise sighed. "It's quite urgent that I see her soon. I don't suppose—"

The door swung open, and the magnetic gaze of Benjamin Disraeli peered around the doorframe's dark wood. "I thought I heard your voice, Princess. Please, if you'd like to join us?"

She smiled. "I would indeed. Thank you, sir."

An elaborate tea service for two had been arranged on a butler's table.

"Ring for another cup if you like, dear," Victoria said when Louise walked in.

Louise waved off the invitation. "It's not necessary. I don't want to interrupt, but I do need to discuss something of importance with you."

"If it is of a personal nature," Disraeli said, "I'll be happy to take my leave."

"Oh, Dizzy, no. Please don't, you've only just got here," her mother cooed.

"Only if you wish for me to stay, my Faerie dear."

Louise rolled her eyes. It wasn't the first time she'd heard the two of them exchanging pet names. This was a side of her mother she didn't understand, or much enjoy. The woman could be a harsh taskmaster to her children, ruthless to politicians and clergy who stood in her way, as tough as a general when crossed by the court. But she always kept around two or three pet males whom she pampered and flirted with outrageously. The suave Disraeli was a current favorite. A choice she made obvious and which, Louise suspected, annoyed John Brown to no end. Not to mention Disraeli's adversary, the present prime minister, Mr. Gladstone.

Brown was all physical masculinity, the gillie from Balmoral that Victoria had made into a personal bodyguard and attendant. The commoner from Scotland wasn't much liked in court, whereas Disraeli's charm and elegance won him the admiration of many women in and outside of the English court. Predictably, neither man seemed particularly fond of the other.

"What is it you wish to speak to me about?" Victoria asked, setting her cup down on its saucer in her ample lap.

Louise arranged her skirts around her feet as she settled into the chair Disraeli pulled up for her.

"I wish your honest opinion and observations, Mama."

"I would never give any but honest ones, my dear." Victoria tossed Disraeli a coy smile.

Louise wished she'd caught her mother in a more serious mood, but saying so would only set her mother against her. There was nothing to do but begin. "Neither Mr. Brown, nor your agent Mr. Byrne, have discovered who released the rats into the nursery. Is that so?"

"It is," her mother said then glanced at Disraeli with sudden anxiety. "Oh, Dizzy, it was such a terrible scene. So disturbing. And with a threatening note to my dear children. Horrifying!"

"I was here that day. Remember, dear lady?"

"Oh, yes, of course you were. As was Mr. Gladstone."

Now this is something, Louise mused. She had worried that someone among their staff might not be trusted. But she hadn't considered visiting dignitaries. Including men of such stature as the current and past PM among the suspects, well, that seemed illogical.

But was it really?

She tried to remember if she'd seen either man, with or without accompanying secretaries, wandering the castle's hallways or anywhere near the nursery wing. But she couldn't say that she had. Then again, so much had happened since then to cloud her memory of that day.

"I know that thinking about that day is unsettling to you, Mama. But here's my question: if you were to consider someone in our midst who might turn on us from within, could you offer up any candidates?"

Her mother's jowls trembled and tiny porcine eyes sparked with displeasure. "God help us, Louise, how can you even suggest such a thing? Of course no one in our service, or in the court, wishes us ill."

"I would like to think so as well," Louise said carefully. "But the fact remains, someone did smuggle those rats into the castle. And, according to Mr. Byrne, the spy, intruder, or whatever you wish to call this person, also seems to be feeding information to the Fenians about our daily routine and travel schedules, making it easier for them to plot further assaults."

"He's said as much to me." Victoria pursed her lips in displeasure.

"Dear lady, if you will allow me." Disraeli spoke to his queen but flashed a conspiratorial gaze toward Louise. "Princess Louise is right, as is your agent. Concern for your security outweighs your loyalty to those around you. No one should stand above suspicion."

Victoria shook her head in denial but didn't interrupt.

Disraeli continued. "I myself have many enemies."

"I cannot believe anyone would harm you, Dizzy."

Louise rolled her eyes. *Oh, Mama.*

"Of course they would, for a purpose. One must be ever vigilant." Disraeli sighed. "Thus your report from Mr. Byrne makes perfect sense."

"Report? What report?" Louise said.

Disraeli reached over and patted her hand. "Violence between men is nothing new, Your Royal Highness. We have merely refined our weapons over the years." He turned back to Victoria. "I'm grateful to Mr. Byrne for his acute eye and for warning me to take precautions." He pointed to a copy of the *Times* that lay on the table beneath the tea service, then slid it out from under the heavy silver tray and handed it to Louise.

The page to which it was opened showed photographs of two men. They looked as if they'd been taken for government identification. The headline read: BOTH MURDER VICTIMS MINOR SECRETARIES TO THE MINISTRY OF FINANCE.

Louise stared at the faces of the two men. Only after a moment did she look up at the former PM with understanding. "You and this one gentleman are not unlike in certain respects."

"Yes," Disraeli said, "that's what Mr. Byrne has pointed out. He believes it was my life the attackers intended to take—and these poor men were innocents. He also told your mother that my death would have served the Fenians well. The man has a way with words." He shook his head. "Ice water runs through his veins, I'm sure."

Louise covered her mouth with one hand, hiding her smile. *Not always.*

"Enough of this talk of assassins." Victoria waved a hand in dismissal. "They're hooligans, all of them—out to cause mayhem to no purpose. Louise, you said you came to discuss our rats? I can think of no less delightful topic."

"Yes, I did." Louise ignored her mother's chiding glare. *This had better be worth my time*, the queen's eyes warned. "I've been thinking. Mr. Brown and your guardsmen assure us that no deliveries were made the morning the rats appeared. And all visitors were accounted for—those, at the time, being Mr. Disraeli, Mr. Gladstone, and their secretaries. And the rats could not have been in Bea's room for long without being discovered."

"Sounds reasonable," Disraeli agreed. "Have the staff as well as gentlemen and ladies of the court been questioned?"

"They have. To no good result." Louise paused. "I believe, therefore, that the person to blame is someone not presently among us. Some person or persons who at one time deserved our trust but now harbors a violent grudge, and has become allied with the Fenians for the purpose of revenge."

Her mother blanched to nearly the whiteness of her lace collar but said nothing.

"You know someone who fits that description. Don't you, Mama?"

Victoria's eyes met hers and slowly widened. Louise watched her mother's fear transform into revulsion. "The baron," she whispered.

Louise shuddered at the mention of the man. There were, of course, many who owned that title, throughout England and the Continent. But she had no doubt who her mother meant.

"Baron Stockmar," Louise said to Disraeli's questioning look. She turned back to her mother. "He's dead, though, isn't he?"

The queen broke into a smile and actually cackled her pleasure. "He hates me so much, maybe he's come back from the grave to haunt us."

Louise chewed her bottom lip. Yes, she thought, if such a thing were possible, she had no doubt Stockmar would do it. The question remained—how?

Thirty-five

Rupert stood on the splintery dock inches above the fetid flow of slime called the Thames River. He listened to what the Lieutenant was saying, but used the time to get a better look at him. The man's cap brim hid the upper half of his features. A thin slash of lips interrupted a beardless jaw. His chin jutted forward in a way that made him look as if he was always leaning forward, on the verge of striding out, even when he was standing still. He spoke with the slightest of accents—an Irish lilt mixed with something else. Northern European? Napoleon III had just lost the Franco-Prussian War. Maybe he was a defeated soldier like them?

It didn't really matter. Rupert was used to taking orders as long as there was a strong man at the helm. He didn't even blame the Lieutenant for speaking harshly to him and Will after it became clear they'd killed the wrong men in the park. Will had worried the Fenians would send him and Rupert packing without so much as a penny for a pie. Or worse, shoot them and dump their bodies in the river, no one the wiser.

But he also knew that one good black powder man was worth a battalion of foot soldiers. So he wasn't surprised when the Lieutenant kept them on despite their mistake.

"Arrangements have been made for the two boats you requested," the man was saying. "A skiff and a steamer." He glanced down at Rupert's right hand. "You say you can manage both vessels between the two of you?"

Rupert stuffed his injured hand in his pocket and nodded. "Yes, sir."

The first vessel, a sturdy, flat-bottomed rowing boat, would be loaded with powder and primer and, after he and Will worked their magic, become their bomb. The larger steam-powered ship was a retired ferry, just twenty feet long and a rusty junker, but with a solid working engine. Like the other boat, it would blend in with the commercial craft clogging the river. Neither boat would attract attention from the queen's security detail.

"Yes, sir. Will here, he ran a steamboat afore the war, on the Missouri."

"Excellent. Let's be clear, gentlemen. I need that center span destroyed and the queen's coach isolated from the forward escort, so that my men can move in and make the snatch."

Rupert imagined the violent clash of the two forces on Vauxhall Bridge above them. The queen's Hussars would fight to the death to protect her. "Our boys'll have to come in from the rear and overcome the following guard," he pointed out.

A smile creased the officer's cheeks. "All we need is the advantage of surprise and half the queen's men out of action. John Brown out of commission, or dead, would be the best possible outcome."

It was a daring plot, and Rupert knew they'd lose brave comrades. But taking Victoria herself would, sure as the sun rises in the east, bring worldwide attention to the Irish cause. It was a grand and glorious statement of the will of a small nation. David victorious over Goliath.

Rupert felt a surge of exhilaration unlike any he'd felt since his last mission for the proud South. "We'll do our part, sir."

He'd spent the last eighteen hours designing the most effective blast. He and Will would hand-light the fuses, rather than trust a flint and timer. Neither could they rely on charges planted directly on the bridge with a pressure trigger for a carriage wheel to strike. He'd tried to think what he'd do, if he were in charge of the queen's safety. First, order all roadways and bridges along the parade route searched. And he'd send a hundred men to crawl through every inch of Westminster Abbey, where the ceremony was to be held, then secure it until half an hour before the ceremony. He'd send an outrider or wagon ahead of the first carriage to make sure there were no trigger plates or trip wires.

That left only one way to blow this damn bridge—from the water.

"You'll of course move far enough away," the Lieutenant was saying, "to protect yourself from the blast. But then I want you to hold up as close as possible for five minutes or so after the explosion and keep an eye on the water."

Rupert understood. For survivors. "For our fellas?"

The Lieutenant shook his head. "If all goes well, our boys won't be the ones in the water." He turned to observe the bridge. "You'll be our insurance. In case one of the royal family takes a plunge."

Rupert nodded his agreement. But he figured the chances of them hauling a live body out of the water were pretty damn slim. If the blast or the fall didn't kill 'em, a dunk in this poisonous old river likely would.

Thirty-six

A noxious fog, thick as his mother's New England fish chowder, obscured Byrne's view of the street. He didn't see the boy coming until the lad thrust a scabby head through the open window of the moving carriage in which Byrne and Princess Beatrice rode, on their way to her favorite bookshop.

Byrne had set half a dozen young crossing sweepers to watch for Darvey and report to him when the pimp turned up. Now the lad, hanging on like a monkey to the outside of the jouncing carriage, whispered into Byrne's ear.

"Hey, you boy, get off from there!" the footman shouted down from his perch at the back of the carriage.

Byrne slipped a coin into the boy's hand before the urchin dropped down from the side of the vehicle and darted away between rumbling omnibuses, costermongers' barrows, and pedestrians.

"What a filthy little boy," Beatrice said, wrinkling her nose. "What did he want?"

Byrne scowled at his hands. "Nothing important, Your Highness." Before she could ask another question he said, "Will you be long in the shop?"

"No more than two hours," she said. "I shall read for a while, before deciding if I will buy anything. Will you hate having to wait for me?" Her smile had just a hint of girlish infatuation in it.

"Not at all. In fact, I have some business to attend to. I'll leave you in the care of your coachman and guard. If I'm not back by the time you're ready to leave, they'll take you home." He'd replaced the usual footman with one of the queen's guards. The man was armed and trained to protect the family. Beatrice would be in good hands.

"You needn't hurry," Beatrice said. "I can spend hours and hours in a bookshop. Mrs. Shrewsberry doesn't mind, and she always has jam cakes for me when I come."

"Good," said Byrne, thinking what a relief it must be for the youngest princess to be free of her mother for even a few hours. Victoria treated Beatrice more like a personal maid than her child. As a result, he'd noticed, the girl had little time to herself and no friends at all her own age. Byrne's heart went out to her.

After securing the bookshop, which closed its doors to other customers while the princess visited, Byrne waved down a hansom cab and directed it to Henry Locock's home and dispensary. His crossing sweeper had spotted someone who looked like Darvey in the Lococks' neighborhood.

Byrne ordered the driver to leave him a block away, paid him, and strode off down the alley behind the physician's house. He'd arrived almost too late.

Darvey stood on a crate, at eye level to a rear window of the Locock home. He was shoving a crowbar beneath the lip of a windowpane. From his end of the alley, Byrne heard the creak as the wooden frame weakened. It gave way with a dull crack.

Byrne broke into a run, loping toward the pimp.

Darvey turned to observe him with a welcoming expression that struck Byrne as inappropriate to being caught in the act.

"Took you long enough, boy-o," Darvey called out. "Another two shakes of a lamb's tail, I'd been on me girl, helpin' her remember her trade." He chuckled.

Byrne stopped just feet away from him. "You're coming with me."

"Is I? Where to?" Darvey looked more amused than worried.

"I'm taking you to Scotland Yard to be held for arson and attempted murder."

Still looking pleased with himself, Darvey shifted the crowbar from right to left hand, and pulled a knife from inside the cuff of his pant leg. "So come ahead, Yank."

Byrne brought out the Colt. He could shoot the man dead on the spot, or take him wounded to prison. It didn't much matter to him which.

Darvey tilted his head to one side and eyed the weapon with the air of a connoisseur. "Nice piece. So, you're in this for queen and another man's country? Don't seem reason enough for a fella to die."

"I ain't the one dying today, Darvey," Byrne said.

"Oh no?" The voice came from behind Byrne at the precise moment something that felt like a lamppost came down on his head.

He felt the gun leave his hand, heard it skitter across the gravely ground. The sound of metal ringing against metal came to him from the far side of the alley. He staggered to find his balance.

When his eyes focused a second later, he turned and saw two men blocking the alley's mouth. The Colt was nowhere in sight, but Byrne suspected the iron-barred sewage grate had swallowed it up.

"Come on, Yank," Darvey taunted. "Let's you and me have a bit of fun before my mates join the party."

Byrne cursed himself for assuming the man fool enough not

to have brought backup. Darvey had expected this confrontation. Was it possible this entire scene had been staged for his benefit? The casing of the house from the street observed by the crossing sweeper? The daylight break-in? All of this to ambush him.

But if he hadn't responded to the challenge, what would have happened to the Lococks? He didn't like to think of it.

The fight started out badly.

Byrne figured that taking out one of the thugs would at least even up the odds a little. With two against one, he had a chance. He spun and rushed the bigger of the two men, a head taller and thirty pounds heavier than him. His sudden aggressive attack surprised his opponent and landed him on his back with Byrne's head buried in his gut. The man's skull banged back against the rock-hard ground of the alley; he went out like a snuffed candle. But the second thug was on him the second Byrne scrambled to his feet. He grabbed Byrne from behind.

Darvey had waited his chance. Now he swung the crowbar at Byrne's kneecap and connected with a sickening crunch. Byrne managed to stay on his feet just long enough for Darvey to drive a fist into the side of his face. He went down, the pain in his knee agonizing but only a shade less than the ringing in his head.

Lying on the ground, he fended off their kicks to his ribs and face as best he could. Byrne tried to regain his feet, but they kept knocking him to the ground. His face swelled up, his vision blurred, keeping him from getting a fix on Darvey in the hope he could wrench the iron bar out of his hands.

But what he saw next took his breath away, and with it went all hope.

Out of the shadows of the surrounding buildings loomed yet another figure, this one bigger than either of the others. The man seemed to fill the entire alley. His body blocked out even the narrow strip of sunlight that managed to slant between the brick walls around them.

Oh God. It's all over now.

He might fight off two, if he could just get hold of something to use as a weapon. But not this monster as well.

"Told you I be keepin' an eye on ye, lad." The voice had a wonderfully familiar ring.

Byrne looked up in time to see a distorted image of John Brown clubbing Darvey's remaining conscious partner on the head with his bare fist. Byrne got the impression the man's feet must have been driven inches into solid ground with the impact of the blow. The thug's eyes rolled once, his knees buckled, he dropped to his knees as if in prayer for just a moment before keeling over, face-first.

Darvey looked around him, as if unsure of his next move. Now he was alone against one man standing, another man down. He scowled at Brown then, apparently having made up his mind, came at him in a run. Darvey swung the crowbar hard at Brown's knees, just as he'd done to Byrne. It didn't work this time. Because the targeted knee was a foot higher than the pimp's accustomed angle of attack, his swing of the metal bar seemed to throw him off balance. Brown reached out, grasped the bar, and whipped it out of the man's hand. He tossed it aside as if it were a toothpick.

"There now, son, you won't be needin' that. You sit yourself down over there and cool your heels before you hurt yourself." Turning to Byrne, Brown grasped him by the shoulders of his leather duster and hauled him to his feet.

"No," said Darvey. "NO!" He pulled a pistol from inside his jacket.

Byrne didn't wait to see what Brown had in mind as a response. He put all of his weight on his good leg and launched himself low at Darvey. A shot went off. Byrne plummeted to the ground but took the pimp down with him.

He willed himself to turn and see if Brown had been hit, or whether Darvey was aiming now for him. But every time he tried to get his legs beneath him, his vision grayed with the pain. He felt dizzy then nauseated then surreally light-headed.

With effort, he brought his head up. His vision returned, and he saw Darvey throw his pistol at Brown's face. Had he emptied all the chambers? Byrne wondered if he'd blacked out; he hadn't heard a thing.

In two strides, the Scot was face-to-face with the pimp. He pulled back his arm and unleashed his fist straight from the shoulder, stepping into the punch, and drove it into the bridge of Darvey's nose. The knuckles seemed to plow straight through skin, cartilage, bone, and brain.

Darvey's body didn't so much as fall over as cave in. Dead before he hit the earth.

Thirty-seven

At first Louise wasn't certain of the source of the noises. The uproar that invaded the tranquil garden where she sat reading with Lorne sounded like a cross between braying donkeys, caterwauling felines, and some otherworldly beast. She had to listen for a bit before she began to pick out two distinct human voices—one a full octave deeper than the other. As they came nearer, she finally made out actual words of an old Scottish drinking song:

> *Towerin' in gallant frame,*
> *Scotland my mountain hame,*
> *High may your proud standards glor-i-ously wave,*
> *Land o' my high endeavor,*
> *Land o' the shining ri-ver, Land o' my heart forever,*
> *Scotland the brave!*

Then she knew.

Although it was still early in the afternoon, this could only be the drunken carousing of men. Two in particular. *Not again*, she thought.

Lorne shot to his feet and stood at the ready, as if to protect her from armed invaders.

"It's all right." She touched his arm as she set her book aside and rose from the stone bench. "I have a feeling I know who it is."

John Brown and Stephen Byrne lurched around the hedgerow, arm in arm, bleating out another verse she suspected they'd made up themselves. Something about bloody battles fought and foes vanquished in Londontown.

Lorne stared with incredulity at the American. "How any of the ladies of the court can find *that man* appealing . . . ," he muttered.

It was all she could do to keep from laughing. At Lorne's comment, as well as at the incongruity of what appeared to be a burgeoning friendship. The antagonism between Byrne and the Scot had been so constant and extreme, she'd never imagined them in such a companionable, albeit filthy and disheveled state.

If her mother saw them like this . . . She stepped forward, blocking their progress toward the main wing of the palace. "Gentlemen?"

"Oh," Byrne said, staggering to a halt with a sheepish grin. "It's a . . . a princess."

"That it is, my bonnie lad. A royal personage of great beauty. Your Highness." Brown bowed tipsily, but his sloppy smile faded as he took in a solemn Lorne. "And her sweet little . . . whatever."

"Sh-sh-sh," Byrne said, finger to his lips. "Is a secret."

"Not much of one!" Brown bellowed, laughing so hard he pressed a hand to his belly as if it hurt.

"You are both disgustingly drunk," Louise accused them. "Don't pay any attention to them, Lorne. Goodness. In the middle of the day and in the queen's garden of all places. What's wrong with the two of you?"

Byrne removed his companion's arm from his shoulders and stood to attention, favoring one leg. "Right you are, ma'am. We are sloshed."

"In-inebriated," said Brown.

"Seven or eight sheets to the very wind." Byrne spiraled a hand skyward.

"Good lord." Louise looked at her husband, who seemed no less perplexed than she. It wasn't unusual for Brown to carry an alcoholic aura on his person through the day. But she'd only ever seen him truly drunk on a few occasions, and then just late at night after her mother was off to her bed. The only time she'd seen any evidence of Byrne's drinking at all was in Scotland, the morning after his brawl in the pub with Brown. "What has happened? Why this ridiculous display?"

"Cele-brating," Byrne stated. He swiped his Stetson, much the worse for wear, from his head and smiled at it crookedly.

"Defeated the emenn-emy," the Scot said.

She bent down to better look up into Byrne's eyes and waited for them to focus on her. "What enemy?"

"Dirty Darvey," he said. "Dead. Long story. Need to sit down now." His knees began to fold under him and, if Lorne and Brown hadn't held him up, he would have collapsed to the ground.

Louise spoke to the only sober male in the group. "Lorne, we'd best get them both inside and cleaned up before my mother sees them. She'll have a fit."

"As well she should," he grumbled. "Who is this Darvey, and have they really killed the man?"

"Later," she said.

Lorne went ahead to chase the servants out of the lower kitchen. Once she and Lorne had maneuvered the pair inside where there was access to water and soap, Louise got to work cleaning up Stephen Byrne, while Lorne stood by with towels as Brown gave his hands and face a scrubbing and told the story of their battle with the bawd's gang.

She wasn't sure how much of the tale might be true, and how much a product of the Scot's love of drama. But one thing was clear to her—Stephen Byrne had risked his life to protect Amanda's family. Indeed, he'd saved the life of *her son*, the only child Louise could ever expect to have.

With bruised and scraped hands and faces clean, the extent of the pair's injuries seemed less life threatening than they'd at first appeared. "Now off with your shirts," she said.

Byrne smiled at her. "Thoughtyou'dneverask," he slurred, and reached for her.

"Stop that." She smacked away his hands and caught Lorne's curious gaze hesitating over her then shifting to Byrne. Whatever he was thinking, she hadn't the time to find out. She frowned at the gash in Byrne's left trouser leg, which appeared to be crusted with dried blood. "What's this now?"

He shrugged. "Crowbar. Hurts"—he hiccupped—"like hell."

She tried to roll up the pant leg. When that didn't work she peered inside the slashed fabric but could see nothing. "Drop the pants."

Byrne grinned.

She cast Lorne a desperate look. "He's hopeless." When she turned back again, her mother's agent had collapsed against a cabinet, eyes closed, his beard-stubbled face pale as porcelain. While he was passed out and harmless, she ripped off the pant leg at the tear. "Oh my, that is bad."

"Don't think it's broke," Brown mumbled, resting his head in his hands. "He was walkin' on it. To the pub and back here."

"Was he now?" She examined the purpling flesh and jagged wound. Best if it were seen by a physician, but perhaps it would heal on its own. She did all she could to clean up the rest of him, trying to ignore the little spurts of heat through her fingertips as they grazed his lovely muscled abdomen and chest.

It occurred to her, as she heard more of the story from Brown, that Stephen Byrne might have died in that alley had the Scot not come along when he did. The thought sickened her. Moreover, *she* would have been the cause of his death. Had she known Darvey wasn't just a bully capable of picking on the weak, that he was truly a dangerous killer, she'd never have asked Byrne to confront the man.

Louise cleaned him up as best she could then ordered Brown and Lorne to carry him to one of the empty servants' rooms in the attic, to sleep off the drink. She followed along, thinking it was probably a good thing he was drunk. The alcohol numbed the pain, for the time being.

When the other two men left the room, Louise lingered behind. She tenderly pulled the sheet up over Stephen Byrne, smoothed her fingertips through the black wing of hair fallen over his forehead. "Sorry," she whispered. "I'm so very sorry." Then she sat down to watch over him while he slept.

Thirty-eight

Byrne woke with a start. He flung a defensive arm wide and bolted upright—disoriented, lungs rasping. No one came at him with knife or cudgel, but needles of pain jabbed his knee.

On a bed. He was on a bed, alone in a room . . . somewhere. He fell back down into the linens with a groan, lay still, waited for the wretched knee and dregs of the nightmare to subside. But now his ribs ached from the sudden movement. And his head throbbed like a military drum. He squinted down at his body. Someone had undressed him, but for breeches, and taped his knee and ribs. His face felt stiff with bruising. Every muscle in his body called out to him.

He had imagined himself back in the alley, set upon by a dozen pipe-wielding thugs. Then he recalled that Darvey was dead. And, unless he was still mixing dreams with reality, there had been a bizarre interval of camaraderie with the Scot that must have resulted in his current hungover state.

Slowly events reeled back through his mind. He recalled Brown retrieving his Colt from the grate, hauling him to his feet.

Byrne looked around the dim, silent room, trying to place himself. The space was not much larger than a closet, the bed narrow, single window darkened with a heavy muslin curtain. The walls were plastered and clean but bare, except for a plain wooden crucifix over the door, as if left by a previous occupant or put there as a suggestion of piety to a future resident. A monk's cell? More likely servant's quarters.

But of course. Brown, or whoever had helped him out of his clothes, and into bandages and bed, wouldn't have snugged him up in Buckingham's family wing. They'd hidden him away, hoping Victoria wouldn't discover he'd been fighting again. And yet he wasn't concerned. It was fighting Brown that had gotten him into trouble before. Not fighting alongside the Scot, for the protection of the queen's daughter and grandson. Although, he was sure, Victoria would never publicly recognize Edward Locock.

Slowly, muscle by tender muscle, Byrne eased himself into a semitolerable sitting position and shifted his legs off the side of the bed. He let his body adjust to this new angle, then looked down and saw a sodden bundle of toweling. *Ice*, he thought. Someone had taken care to apply cold compresses to his injured knee while he slept. That was probably why the swelling was no worse than it was now.

He tried to stand and felt elated when he was able to put weight on the leg. A minor miracle.

Someone had cleaned and hung on a peg his clothing—minus pants, which must have been ruined. They'd been replaced by another pair with a drawstring at the waist that looked like something a gardener might wear. He relieved himself in the chamber pot then dressed, cuffing the too-long trousers. It took him a good twenty minutes to make himself moderately presentable.

He heard someone on the stairs outside his door and tensed. A moment later a soft knock sounded at the door.

He hobbled over and opened it.

Louise stood there, her face aglow, her lovely golden brown hair brushed loose and shining down her back. She looked even younger than her years. She smiled. "You're standing."

"I am. Damn proud of that."

She held up a tray arranged with what appeared to be a fortune in silver-domed dishes. "I thought you might be hungry."

"Starving, but you didn't need—"

"I did need to. What little I would have paid you to watch out for the Lococks wasn't sufficient for risking your life as you did."

"I doubt it was that serious."

Louise gave him an "oh, please" look and brushed past him and into the room. She looked around, seemed startled to see no table to set it upon. It occurred to Byrne how heavy the blessed thing must be and he kicked himself for not having taken the tray from her right away. He pulled the one straight-back chair over near the bed then took the tray from her and set it on the chair's seat—an improvised table.

She said, "I heard enough of Mr. Brown's recital of the fight to come to the conclusion you very nearly died in the line of duty, Mr. Byrne." She met his eyes. "Stephen," she amended.

"I am, I admit, in debt to the Scot. But it's possible I'd have survived."

"Well, that's an optimistic view." Her laugh, to his ears, held a near hysterical edge. Her eyes glittered with unshed tears as she turned away from opening the curtains to let in the sunlight.

Byrne sat on the bed and smiled when he noticed two cups on the tray. He patted the mattress. Louise sat demurely on its very edge, a good two feet away from him.

He poured tea, lifted the lid of one of the servers, and found thick rashers of bacon and fat sausages.

"There are hard-cooked eggs under the other cover," she said then lifted a cloth napkin to reveal slabs of toasted bread under pools of butter.

"A meal fit for a king," he murmured over his split lip. It would hurt to eat, but he was famished.

"I seriously am most grateful," she said. "If that dreadful man had got into their house, had put his hands on Amanda ever again . . ." She shuddered visibly and blinked at him. "You cannot know what she went through before she and I met."

"I think I have an idea," he said.

"And the child."

"Your son."

"Yes, *mine*." She blew out a little breath. Of relief, or merely acknowledging the truth? "My . . . son. Though we shall never speak of him as such in the presence of others."

"Understood. But he will learn someday."

"Will he?" She frowned. "Amanda thinks we should tell him when he's older. I believe such knowledge would only cause him pain, and much trouble. Better that he believes he's the son of a fine London physician than the bastard of a reckless princess."

He smiled at her. She was so beautiful, so young. Yet she'd been through so much. And all because she refused to confine herself to the role her family dictated for her.

He had heard the way ladies and gentlemen of the court, and the queen's subjects, spoke of Louise. The "wild princess." The young royal who fought her parents' authority at every turn. She demanded the right to study art with commoners and—even more shocking—to sit in the same classes with men and learn what they learned. The princess who caroused in pubs and smoking dens with her Bohemian friends. Until something happened to cause her to settle down.

Gossip said Louise finally grew into adulthood and accepted her royal role. How could she not, with Victoria's thumb on her? And now that she was married, they expected her husband would take over the reins and control her. He'd give her children to further anchor her to a respectable life. Like a ship caught up in a gale, if you took down her sails and threw out enough anchors, she'd eventually weather the storm. That's what they thought.

Little do they know.

Byrne watched her sip her tea, select one of the smaller strips of bacon, and nibble it. She gave the appearance of being utterly at peace. But beneath the outward calm he sensed extraordinary effort. Against what forces was Louise fighting now?

He ate without speaking, forcing himself not to gulp down the food all at once. It tasted so good. He felt so good!

That was the best part of a fight. After it was over, you felt more alive than ever, because you had feared, and nearly known, the alternative. Because you'd straddled the line between life and death.

"The Fenians," she said, out of the blue.

"Yes?" He lifted his eyes to fix on hers and felt as if he was tumbling into them.

"You are still on their trail? Still concerned that they will strike again?"

"I am, on both counts."

She finished her bacon in one bite then stared out the window for a long while, as if in contemplation of the future. "Why are you doing this?"

Wasn't it obvious? "It's my job."

"No, I mean, this isn't your fight, Stephen. You are an American, not a subject of the Queen of England. You are putting your life on the line daily for us. These are dangerous men, desperate men. They will stop at nothing." Her voice quavered with emotion. "Whether or not their cause is valid, what they *do* is not right. They kill innocent women and children who happen to be in the path of their bombs. They won't hesitate to murder a man who has vowed to stop them."

"True." He studied her profile. It was so finely shaped, she might have been etched in glass or carved from pearly onyx. It seemed right that the sculptress should herself be perfect.

"I am going to ask the queen to dismiss you," she said.

"What?" He stared at her. Of all the things she might have said to him, nothing could have shocked him more.

"I will tell her you fought again with Brown. Convince her that you are a dangerous influence on her Scot. She will have no choice but to send you home."

He threw back his head and laughed.

She seemed startled by his reaction and pulled away to stare at him in confusion.

"You would *lie* to your mother to have me fired? Why?" Then it struck him. She thought she was protecting him. "You can't believe that I would live my life any differently back in America than I am doing here."

He saw the fear fill her eyes again. "I can't watch you . . . watch you *die* for us!"

"But you can send me packing and never see me again? Is that what you want?"

She stood up abruptly, made it halfway to the door before he caught her around the waist. Byrne pulled her into his arms. He knotted his fingers through her hair, tugged her head back to turn her face up to meet his. He kissed her fiercely and long, and he didn't release her delicious mouth from beneath his until he felt her body go limp in his embrace and she was fighting for air.

"Oh no!" she cried, staring at him, then kissed him back with equal urgency.

Within seconds, his soldier's mind took over. *Might we be discovered?* Unlikely in this rarely used wing of the castle. *Will anyone miss her?* Yes, possibly, but why look here? *Who knows I am here?* Brown at least, maybe a servant. Then he remembered Lorne. The marquess had been here too, at least he thought so. A vague memory was coming back to him. Not good. *Alternative locations for bedding the lady?* None. *Solution: barricade.*

Byrne spun her around, gripped her shoulders, and without a word, sat her on the bed. He shifted the tea tray from chair seat to floor then wedged the chair back under the latch to prevent it from releasing or the door from swinging inward.

Satisfied, he turned to face Louise, half expecting her to have de-materialized. But she was still there, just as he'd left her. Even better, no questions clouded her beautiful eyes.

"I think Lorne knows," she whispered.

His already racing heart leapt. His gut clenched, which made his ribs ache. "About us?"

"About me, at least. That my nature is too passionate to stay faithful to my vows."

"He took vows too. If he cannot keep his—"

"Then why should I? It's not that simple."

The pain in her gaze broke his heart. How could any man not throw himself at her feet and beg for the honor of making love to her?

He hesitated, stepped closer to her. "Do you want to talk about it?"

"No," she said, opening her lovely arms to him. "No talk. Not now."

He went to her, fell down onto his one good knee, a supplicant. His arms closed around her waist. He laid his head in her lap—all memory of other women and other times gone.

"I have wanted you from the moment I first saw you," he whispered into the blue satin ocean of her skirt.

"And I you," she said, her voice husky with emotion.

She'd said no talk, but he couldn't stop himself. This was too important to be done carelessly or without letting her know his concerns. "I am not your Donovan."

She laughed. "No. Indeed you are not."

"I won't be his substitute."

"Do stop talking and—" She brought his face up from her lap with her hands and leaned forward to kiss him softly, nibbling his lips again and again until he was driven to press his mouth hungrily over hers. Tasting her. Glorying in the flavors of her breath, the scent of her body. *Rose petals and lavender*, he thought.

He pressed her down onto the narrow mattress and disheveled linens, stretching his body over hers, holding his weight above her for fear of crushing her. But she would allow not even air to separate them. Reaching up, she wrapped her arms around his chest and brought him down hard on top of her. He winced at the twinge through his ribs.

"I want to feel you. *All* of you. I am not a fragile woman."

She was, in point of fact, the strongest woman he'd ever known. In spirit, in heart, in soul. And even through her clothing he felt her softly defined feminine muscle.

He forgot all restraint. He ravished her body, and she seemed to delight in every touch of his fingers and mouth as he uncovered and explored each tender, yielding inch of her flesh. And when he plunged within her warmth he held himself at agonizing abeyance for as long as a man is capable, for he needed to make this moment last for her. For both of them. Because he couldn't believe it would ever happen again.

Thirty-nine

Louise lay in Stephen Byrne's strong arms, drowsy with the delicious warmth and floating sensations of a well-loved woman. Her desert landscape of an existence had been restored with the life-giving rain of this man's loving her. Impossibly, she had bloomed again.

What her legal husband had been unable to offer, this strange and wonderful man had given her. She refused to think of the consequences of what they'd done. Refused to consider what obligations her rank might demand of her in the next hour, or day, or year. *Please, let me linger in this moment for as long as possible.*

In truth, she dared not move in Byrne's arms, for fear of breaking the spell. They lay entirely, delectably naked, her arm draped across his chest, her head pillowed on the muscle of his shoulder. She listened with the attentiveness of a musician to the even rhythm of his heartbeat, soothed by the rise and fall of his chest. Her fingers played with the crisp curling hairs that ranged down from his chest to his stomach and beyond. When she reached up to stroke his face, her fingertips grazed the dark stubble, and even that seemed titillating, a pleasure to be savored and inviting more kisses.

He read her interest in having more of him. "You have spent me, woman."

She smiled, turned her head to touch her lips to his flat, muscled belly. "I will be patient. Until you are ready for more of me."

"You demand too much of a man, Your Highness."

She giggled, feeling drunk with her own power. When was the last time she had laughed like this? Girlishly. No, *wantonly*.

"Will you be missed?" he said.

She ran her fingers down his thigh, marveling at its hardness. "Not for a good while. But I must join my mother and sisters later, for tea."

"Ah." Then he was quiet for a while before clearing his throat and beginning again. "I need to ask you something."

"Yes?" A thousand possibilities rushed through her mind. What if he asked her to leave Lorne? She didn't know what to say if he did. In her heart, she'd already taken the emotional leap away from her husband, giving herself over to Stephen Byrne. But if he asked her to leave her family, leave all she was and everything she could be to run off with him—as she'd imagined doing in her young, foolish days with Donovan—how should she answer?

His next words she hadn't expected.

"Baron Stockmar," he said.

"What about him?" she asked. Already the luscious floating sensations were leaving her.

"While I was sleeping, I think I heard you talking to yourself. Either that or I was dreaming. You said that name. Baron Stockmar."

She sighed. Well, this was a cruel way, indeed, to be yanked back into the bleak reality of her life. "I did. The baron was in charge of virtually our entire household while my father was alive. In particular he oversaw our education—mine and my brothers' and sisters'."

"But he's no longer around?"

"Right." She edged up onto one elbow to better see his face

while she explained. "When I asked my mother if she could think of anyone who hated us enough to want to hurt us, she mentioned his name. The baron was a terrible man. I believe he loved power more than anything else in the world—certainly more than people. But Albert, my father, admired him deeply. The baron had been his personal adviser back in Germany, before my mother and father married. He actually coached my father to encourage the possibility of Mama falling in love with him when they met, if you can believe that."

"In other words, he gambled that she'd accept him over other suitors?"

"Yes, and his gamble paid off." She smiled. "Later, when Papa came here to wed Mama, he brought the baron with him. My father intended for Stockmar to bring a kind of masculine order to our lives."

Byrne laughed. "Organizing nine children? That seems near impossible."

"Nevertheless, the baron threw himself into the task even before most of us were born. He believed children should be educated on a strict schedule. He fought constantly with my mother's beloved former governess, Baroness Lehzen, over our education. After my parents' wedding, Mama had given the baroness over to care for us children as we came into the world and became old enough to be taught. Mama trusted her, I think, more than any other person. They were devoted to each other. The baroness tried to protect us, tried to reason with Stockmar, telling him we were only children and needed time to play. The baron believed play a waste of time."

Stephen Byrne's fingers seemed incapable of remaining still. As she spoke he stroked up and down her back. She tried not to think too hard about the little shivers his touch produced. If she did she'd be unable to speak for the pleasure of it.

"Eventually," she continued with no little effort, "Stockmar pressured my father to dismiss the baroness. Lehzen was sent back to her home in Germany. My mother was furious and wept for weeks at the loss of her dear friend, but the men refused to listen to her. From then on, the baron had full control over us and our tutors. He traveled everywhere with us—to Balmoral, Windsor, Osborne, and lived here with us at Buckingham. He had my father's ear in all matters."

"But the man's no longer around. What caused his fall from grace?" Byrne said.

Louise remembered so vividly those sad, tempestuous days. "It was my father's death. When Papa contracted typhoid and died very suddenly, the shock nearly killed my mother. She was beside herself with grief. I half expected her to reach out to the baron for strength. Instead, she did the opposite."

He smiled and hugged her. "Good old Victoria canned him."

"Like lightning. She banished the man to Germany, just as he had done to her dear friend the baroness. He lost everything. His grand suites in our castles. His royal pension. The invitations to state banquets. All gone."

Byrne toyed with a lock of her hair, kissed the tip of her nose. "I shouldn't wonder he'd be bitter, even though he'd brought it on himself." He thought for a moment. "When you said his name out loud while I slept, were you thinking he had more than enough motive for vengeance? Could the baron be in league with the Fenians?"

"No. I was just recalling my mother's words. She thought his ghost might have returned to haunt us. He died in 1863, destitute."

"He's dead?" Byrne looked disappointed, as well he might be. She suspected he'd hoped this was the missing link between their household and the Fenians. It wouldn't have surprised her to find Stockmar had planted a spy in the palace. If he'd still been alive.

"So, you see," she continued, "he can't possibly be involved. That's a dead end."

"What about his family? Did he have a wife, brothers, sisters, children who might wish to avenge him?"

"His wife passed away years before him. They had a son, Christian. I know him. He's a good man, successful in his own right, not the sort to hold a grudge on behalf of his father, or to use violence. In fact, I don't believe he got along well with his father at all. I can't believe he'd have a hand in any of this madness."

Byrne frowned. "If it's not Stockmar, then it's someone else equally determined to aid the Fenians. We must identify them before they do worse damage." He gently moved her aside and started to rise from the bed.

Louise reached out to stop him, placing her hand on his arm. He sat on the edge of the bed and looked at her. She let her fingers slide down his arm, to his hand resting on his bare thigh, and then to the place on his body she most wished to influence—and enjoyed the intriguing effect her touch had on him. He seemed to have recovered.

"As you have no fresh leads to follow," she said, "I don't suppose a delay of an hour or so more would matter?"

He grinned down at her. "Guess not."

"Excellent," she said.

Forty

Victoria released her grip on the heavy claret-velvet drapery, one of a set of five that reached from floor to ceiling above, covering the elegant bow window of Buckingham's Music Room. She looked out through the glass from John Nash's elegantly designed garden front of the palace. Above her a domed ceiling of diamond-shaped gold medallions arched, held aloft by black onyx Corinthian columns.

A lustrous ebony Steinway grand piano stood to her right. She'd left off playing a Chopin piece moments earlier when Lorne interrupted. Even now as she stepped back from the window, the young Scotish noble continued his wearisome petition, unaware she had ceased listening to his list of "needs" for the suite he and Louise temporarily occupied.

Few rooms in any of her properties were so sumptuous as this Music Room, overlooking the long swell of lush greenery across the palace gardens to the pretty pond with its resident swans. But now, gazing out through the tall window, she shuddered. What she had just witnessed beyond the crystal-clear panes proved her worst suspicions.

Moments earlier, she had watched Louise leave the wing of the palace beyond the ballroom, a location reserved for housing servants and providing extra work areas for staff. Her daughter had no reason to be there. None at all. Five minutes later, she saw her American agent step from the shadow of the same doorway.

Of her six daughters, Louise had always been the most determined, self-assured, and maddeningly independent. From early childhood, she seemed to fear nothing—from vaulting stone walls on her pony to venturing on foot into the filthy streets of London. Although Vicky, the Crown Princess, was groomed to be an empress, her first child didn't possess Louise's natural inner strength. She'd had to be molded into regal shape by Albert. Neither, thank God, did Vicky have Louise's rebellious nature, which had jeopardized the girl's welfare more than once. Victoria had hoped—*no, prayed*—that marriage would settle the girl. Now, she feared history was repeating itself.

She drew a deep breath. It didn't help calm her nerves or the increasing pain in her bothersome foot.

The Raven. Such a romantic figure he cut in his outrageous leather overcoat and black felt hat that made him look quite dangerous; she had to admit he possessed a certain allure. Louise's attraction to the man was understandable. But intolerable. It had to end. Fortunately, she'd anticipated such a situation arising.

Victoria turned to face Lorne and broke in on what now had become a plea for a new suite entirely, either in Kensington or St. James's Palace. "And how are the two of you getting along?" Victoria asked.

Lorne fell silent.

She watched confusion cloud his eyes. "Louise and I? We get along brilliantly. I love her dearly, of course." He laughed, but it sounded forced.

Victoria tilted her head back and stared down the length of her nose at him. It was an attitude of imperial displeasure she'd cultivated and used sparingly, most frequently these days on stubborn MPs. Those who knew her well understood it as a warning.

Lorne cleared his throat. "We've become closer with each day, ma'am. I'm a very lucky man."

"Then, as you two are such a good match, I expect before long you shall give me a grandchild to add to my collection." She hadn't much liked her own babies, not as infants. She found newborns ugly and scary. But grandchildren could be brought to her a bit fleshed out. And once they developed personalities she doted on them.

Lorne shrank under her gaze at the mention of children. *Just as I thought,* she mused. *He's hopeless in that way too.*

"Such things take t-time," he stammered.

"Time, yes," she said, returning from the window to the piano bench. She'd carried a file with her, in case she had an opportunity to speak with the young couple about their future. Apparently the Raven was doing her son-in-law's job for him. The time for a chat had come.

"We are"—Lorne coughed to clear his throat—"we are most happy, ma'am. And grateful for your support of our marriage."

"I'm sure." She brought her right foot up to rest on the bench's cushion, under her skirt and out of sight. A return of the horrid gout, she feared. She'd have to summon her physician and demand a more aggressive treatment.

"Lorne," she began afresh, "one of the qualities I most admire in you is your dedication to public service. Having married my daughter, you know you need never work at anything. Yet as a member of the House of Lords, you have a fine reputation for working hard in Parliament and serving our people."

"Thank you, ma'am." He actually blushed.

"I would like to reward your dedication," she said. "I was thinking of an ambassadorship or some other position of importance in the government."

His face lit up, just as she'd imagined it might. Those famous blue eyes flashed. His mane of blond hair, so admired by the ladies of her court, made him look even younger. Maybe, she thought, he saw this offer as an excuse to spend more time away from his wife, to travel the Continent alone and in style, to impress other men who shared his peculiar preferences.

"I would be most grateful for any appointment that would enable me to serve the Empire."

Now, here was where she killed two little pigeons with one boulder. "My dear marquess, I expect that, should it become necessary for you to leave London, you will take your lovely wife with you."

She might have imagined the slightest of hesitations. But he responded quickly enough. "Of course, Your Majesty."

"Even if Louise is inclined to remain in London, out of dedication to her charitable works, she recognizes the importance of a wife standing at her husband's side, as do you, no doubt." She could tell he didn't yet understand her intentions, but she had decided it wiser not to come right out and tell the fool he was being cuckolded by a commoner even lower in society than himself, and a foreigner at that.

"Yes, she is dedicated to the Women's Work Society, and to her friends, of course." Lorne contrived to look saddened. "I suppose she might choose to stay in London. I truly wouldn't object if she—"

"But you *would* object, Lorne. You must," Victoria said firmly.

"I must?"

"Absolutely. You have no concept of how tongues would wag. Imagine—a royal couple, living separately, hundreds if not thousands of miles between them."

"I suppose you're right. Scandals have built upon less." He shuffled his feet, as if standing on too-hot sand.

"And I would worry about Louise, on her own, lonely, without your care and vigilance. She does take risks, you know, mixes with inappropriate society." His frown deepened as she spoke. "Isn't it quite natural for a man to want his wife to be nearby? To bear his children. To make a home for her family." She arched a brow at him.

"Of course," he agreed. "We will travel together wherever you wish to send me."

They had never openly spoken of his differences from other men. The thought of such a conversation was repugnant to her. But she had to let him know he must put aside his follies long enough to consummate his marriage and do his duty by bringing children into the world. She would come back to that task later. For now, she was satisfied with putting Louise at a safe distance from temptation.

"Good," she said. "I have an opportunity for you." She opened the file and took from it a copy of the letter of resignation she'd received a few weeks earlier, which now required her to send a replacement for the position. The post was one that promised to be difficult to fill, as experienced diplomats were likely to turn it down in favor of a more glamorous location. She handed Lorne the paper.

He blinked as he read it. His face went a shade whiter.

"I have decided to make you my new governor of the British Commonwealth of Canada."

Despite the impropriety of sitting down before the queen gave permission, Lorne dropped suddenly and hard into the Louis Quatorze chair nearest the piano. She imagined him picturing the vast stretch of untamed, barely populated land that ranged from the Atlantic Ocean to the Pacific. A northern land so immense it dwarfed little England, yet remained under British influence.

He finally found his voice. "I am of course honored that you'd—"

"Then you will accept?"

"I, yes. Well, how can I deny Your Royal Majesty anything?" He looked dazed.

She smiled. "Then you may pass along the good news of your promotion to your wife. You'll both begin making arrangements to travel to your new home, as quickly as possible."

Forty-one

Less than three hours after Byrne and Louise had departed from the little room where they'd made love, he was walking his horse into the courtyard from the stables when he saw the enamel-black landau parked at the side of the drive. The small, open carriage frequently conveyed guests to the palace from the train station. When he came up alongside, a yellow-gloved hand extended gracefully from inside and beckoned. He hid a smile as he stepped up to the door.

Louise leaned forward from the tufted velvet cushions to speak to him. She wore a perky little hat with a seductive veil over her sparkling eyes and pearls at her throat. He envisioned kissing his way around each and every one of the little white orbs.

"Get in," she said.

"I'm off to find Christian Stockmar." Not that he wouldn't give anything to spend more time with her.

"I guessed as much. We're going together."

He lounged against the side of the carriage, aware that the driver was within hearing, though the man pretended invisibility and a deaf ear, as any good servant would. "I wasn't aware of that arrangement."

Louise gave him a smug smile. "That's because I just thought of it."

Byrne lowered his voice. "I don't think it's a good idea—your interviewing Stockmar. He could be dangerous."

"Well, I think it's an excellent idea."

Byrne thought: *This is the problem with having a princess for a mistress.* Louise would likely never take no for an answer. He tried again. "The baron's son might be reluctant to speak openly about his personal life in front of a woman."

"He will be more reluctant to speak to a total stranger. I know him. You don't. Get in, Stephen, and stop trying to boss me around. It won't work." Her eyes lit up in the most delightful way.

Byrne grinned. "Yes, ma'am." He gave up his horse to an equerry, who would take it off to the royal mews, and joined her.

It was a cozy little carriage but not designed with privacy in mind. Open to prying eyes from the street, and to the weather when the top was folded down, it was meant to display the wealth of its occupants' clothing and jewelry. But Byrne suspected Louise enjoyed it because she could feel unencumbered by walls, stone or otherwise. He'd learned how much she loved feeling close to the people of the streets.

Louise gave him room to sit beside her then slid closer. When he turned to speak just after they'd driven out through the palace gates, she kissed him boldly on the lips.

"A ride with benefits. How can a man object?" he said, making her laugh.

Byrne felt the happiest he'd been in years. Perhaps happier even than before the war. Before he'd witnessed the destruction of so many lives, the repulsive brutality of man against man. He found it difficult to explain why, feeling as he did about bloodshed, that he'd chosen to enter a profession likely to not only attract violence toward him but also to demand it from him. However, saving a single life, now and then, dimmed his memory of the thousands of bodies he'd witnessed strewn across battlefields. He hadn't been able to save his president's life. But maybe he could buy back his self-esteem by protecting a queen's family.

Louise pressed warmly against his side. He thought better of curling his arm around her, bringing her to his chest. One never knew where gossip columnists lurked; the royals were prime targets.

"Does the driver know where we're going?" he asked.

"I've told him." She peeked up at him. "You thought I might have forgotten to instruct him?"

"It occurred to me you might be kidnapping me. Whisking me off to your secret lair to have your wicked way with me." He touched the tip of her nose with one finger. God, how he loved her little nose. And her eyes. And her . . . oh, Lord . . . everything.

He looked around quickly and seeing no one watching from the street, kissed her quickly again. It was all he could do not to drag her down onto the soft cushions; he was nearly out of his mind with wanting her. Again.

As if she'd had the same thought, Louise drew back and looked into his eyes. She shook her head. "We have to stop, don't we?"

He ran his finger along her kiss-moistened bottom lip. "For the moment."

She blinked at him, looked suddenly flustered. "This morning, in the room. It wasn't just . . . well, something that happened, was it?"

He grinned at her. "No."

"But it might"—she blushed—"happen again?"

"I sincerely hope so," he said. "I am, Princess, forever at your service. Whenever. Wherever."

She released a contented little sigh, closed her eyes, and leaned her head back against his shoulder as they drove on. "Good. I think I may require your services rather frequently."

He laughed out loud, gave her a quick hug. His need to be near her nearly knocked him senseless. But he understood something she might not, yet. His devotion to her would likely lead to impossible complications in both of their lives. Although his sacrifice, for a woman like Louise, would be worth it, he wondered if she would feel the same when the time of reckoning came. She had so much more to lose than he. Now, however, wasn't the time to talk about it.

Louise told him she'd sent word ahead of her arrival. Short notice, but he supposed if a member of the royal family came calling, you didn't object.

"Here it is." She indicated a modest but pleasant-looking brick town house when the carriage stopped. Byrne noted that neither its construction nor its location were expensive. Had Albert still lived and the old baron remained in favor, no doubt the son's situation would have been far grander. Despite Louise's defense of the man, he felt they should reserve judgment of Christian Stockmar's innocence. Money was a powerful motivator. And money stolen, in the eyes of the loser, was as good an excuse as any for revenge.

The footman climbed down from the carriage and went up to knock on the front door of the house. Byrne and Louise waited in the carriage while the man spoke to someone inside, then returned to the carriage.

"Baron Stockmar is awaiting you in the salon, Your Highness." He opened the carriage door and lowered the metal steps.

The name momentarily startled Byrne, until he remembered that the son would have inherited his father's title.

Byrne climbed from the carriage first, helped Louise down the steps, then hesitated, unsure how she would want to be seen with him. Certainly not on his arm, as that might convey too much about their relationship. Ordinarily, he'd precede her into a room to inspect its security or at least follow close behind, keeping a sharp eye for trouble. But Louise seemed to have no inclination to keep him "in his place."

She reached for his arm and smiled up at him, as if to say, *This is how it will be from now on.*

He was at first surprised, then realized she was taking a page from her mother's book. Victoria often accepted John Brown's arm for a tour around the castle gardens, or when entering a room where she was entertaining. It was a familiarity most of her children—Bertie in particular—objected to. But their complaints did little to dissuade her.

Perhaps Louise's siblings would also take offense at her familiarity with him. Her husband certainly should. But Byrne didn't much care at the moment. Whatever made this woman happy would make him happy.

The room into which the butler led them was more of a library than the typical salon reserved for greeting guests. Shelves of books ranged from floor to ceiling in two tiers, with a balcony running around three walls to access the upper level of shelves. A large Germanic Biedermeier-style desk sat in the middle of the room, its top covered with paperwork and ledgers, as if the young baron planned to return to them as soon as his uninvited guests went away. Two no-nonsense, straight-back chairs had been arranged in front of the desk. No tea service or cordial tray was in evidence to prolong conversation.

A pale-complexioned man with straw-colored hair, full mustache, and beard stood up from behind the desk to greet them. He moved around the desk to kiss Louise's hand before gesturing them to the chairs and returning to his own. "I understand this has something to do with my father?" His tone was solemn, his eyes unhappy. "Since he is the subject, and I have little to offer in the way of information, I expect this, regrettably, will be a short visit." He paused, as if having second thoughts about his brusqueness. "But if you'd like refreshment—"

"No, please don't bother," Louise said quickly. "I shall come straight to the point of our call. It's been years since your father was involved with our household."

"Yes," Christian said.

"And I realize there were hard feelings at the time of his . . . departure."

"My father was a difficult man. Many found it a challenge to live up to his view of perfection. Your family was not to blame."

"That's very generous of you." Louise sent him a gracious smile. "But I have good memories too, about the times you visited with us, Christian. I remember your entertaining us with stories of your childhood in Germany. Your mother raised you there, did she not?"

"Yes. But as to the stories, more likely I bored you to death." He gave a dry laugh. "Life at the queen's court was so much more interesting to me. I wished my father had brought me there more often." He turned to Byrne. "My father liked to keep his family and professional lives separate, or so he claimed."

"You must have missed him," Louise said in sympathy.

Christian winced, picked up a pen, and turned it end over end three times before placing it back on the desk blotter. "I'm not sure that is an accurate description of my feelings toward the man. I suppose I resented his being away, but I also felt relieved not to have him always hovering over us. He was, as you well know, Your Highness, quite the tyrant."

Byrne said, "So your relationship with your father was strained?"

"That would be a mild descriptive."

"And," Byrne added, "I assume that means any perceived wrongs done to the baron would be of little concern to you?"

"Wrongs?" Christian asked, looking from Byrne to Louise and back again.

"His dismissal by my mother," she said, her voice gentle.

The laughter that burst from Christian's lips made Louise jump. "Oh, my . . . that is amusing. I've always thought it amazing he got as far as he did, using Albert's family as his personal entrée to English society. You see," he said, turning to Byrne, "my father had unlimited power in the English court because of his relationship with the Prince Consort. It's my understanding Albert let him get away with just about anything, and gave him the money to do it with. No wonder Victoria hated the man. Didn't she, Louise?"

Louise tipped her head in diplomatic acquiescence. "Mama pleaded with my father to send him away. As I've told Mr. Byrne, he was the cause of her losing her dear governess. Mama never forgave the baron for that."

Christian shook his head. "But he lost everything when the prince died."

Byrne looked around him. The furnishings in the room were of high quality. Several fine oil paintings decorated the rich wood paneling on the one wall not covered in book shelves. This was not the home of an impoverished man. "He died destitute, Louise tells me."

"Yes."

"Yet you seem to have been left with a more than modest income."

Christian raised a brow. "If you mean these books and paintings, yes. They are all that my father was able to keep of his possessions. The rest of his belongings, including nearly all of his personal art collection, he was forced to sell. I inherited his estate, such as it was. But as to the house and anything else I own, I've earned it."

Louise must have also heard the defensiveness in his tone. "Oh, Christian," she murmured, shaking her head. "I'm so sorry if we've insulted you."

"Don't be. My education, as distasteful as it was to me at the time, stood me in good stead. I don't often use my inherited title. To be called 'baron' means nothing to me, as there is no land and no money attached to it. I earn an adequate salary tutoring the children of several wealthy families. And I supplement that by writing books, several of which have done quite well. I don't live off a royal pension, as my father did, and I'm happy not to. Within two months I will marry the daughter of a successful and very wealthy merchant. My fiancée's dowry will add considerably to my comfort, and she is thrilled to become a baroness. Titles, it seems, are worth *something*." He widened his eyes at Louise, who smiled back at him.

Byrne respected the man. Christian seemed practical and not unkind. He also didn't seem the type to set rats loose to terrify young princesses or pass along information to radicals.

"Thank you for meeting with us," Byrne said, "and for being so forthright." He was about to stand and leave when Louise stretched out a hand to touch his sleeve.

"I do not wish to be indelicate," she began, her eyes resting on Christian with compassion, "but I wonder if you know of anyone else who might have resented the queen's dismissal of your father."

Christian's eyes flared for a moment then settled back into calm, brown ponds. "I assume by that you mean a mistress?"

"Your father was away from Germany so much of the time. It seems not unlikely."

The young baron sighed. "I am sure there were many women of various sorts with whom he kept company."

Louise looked deflated, as if she too suddenly realized they were destined to come away empty-handed. "No one special?"

Christian looked down at his blotter then back up to her. "Every family has its, shall we say, black sheep?"

"True." Louise exchanged a hopeful look with Byrne, and he wondered if she considered herself the black sheep of her family.

"After my father died," Christian continued, "I had to go through his papers, pay off enormous debts, inform correspondents of his death." He swallowed and looked away in pain, as if the words he was attempting to force past his lips had razor edges. "He had a bastard child."

"I see," Louise said.

"I suppose he would be about my age today. It seems Father gave the child's mother support and arranged for the boy's education. Before Father died, he used what influence he could to find my half brother a respectable position."

"And you discovered all of this through his papers?" Byrne asked. Christian nodded. "Do you know his name?"

"If he's kept the one I saw in the documents, yes."

"Did you ever meet your half brother?" Louise asked.

"No." Christian's eyes widened in shock. "Nor do I ever wish to," he nearly shouted, and seemed stunned at the sudden silence when he stopped speaking. "I'm sorry. This is unpleasant and embarrassing family history. I should have said nothing."

"If you never met him," Louise said gently, "I don't suppose you know how he might have felt about the baron's fall from power."

Christian considered this as if it were an entirely new thought to him. "I suppose his view of our father might have been very different from mine. He certainly saw our father more often than I did."

And, Byrne thought, *this other son might have been grateful for the education and other benefits he and his mother received over the years.*

"Will you tell us his name?" Louise asked.

"Philip Andrew. His mother was Irish, her family from County Cork, from what I've been able to learn. I assume he took his mother's name, since my father never publicly acknowledged him. Prince Albert, you see, knew my mother and considered Father morally irreproachable. He wouldn't have tolerated the scandal." Christian drew a breath, let it out, picked out a spot on the wall and seemed intent on studying it.

"And the mother's name?" Byrne pressed. His hopes rising, he could hear his own pulse thumping encouragement in his ears.

"The documents and letters I found mentioned a Mary Rhodes."

Byrne frowned. Where had he heard that name before? It

clanked in his head, begging for him to remember. Rhodes . . . Rhodes . . . Rhodes.

When he glanced at Louise, he saw her face had gone as white as the pearls at her throat. She blinked at him, warning him to silence.

"Thank you, Christian," she said. "We will bother you no longer."

Forty-two

Louise felt as though the air in the room suddenly had turned to porridge. It was far too thick to breathe. Her head spun. She stood up from her chair and reached blindly for Byrne's arm. Somewhere in the distance she heard Stephen thanking Christian Stockmar for his time. She barely felt him guide her outside and into the carriage.

"To the palace," Byrne called up to the driver then turned to her, looking worried. "Are you all right?"

She waved off his concern and concentrated on taking as deep breaths as her horrid corset stays allowed.

"Rhodes," Byrne said. "He's one of your mother's staff?"

"No." She shook her head violently. "Philip Rhodes is the prime minister's secretary. He has access to all of our residences, either while accompanying Mr. Gladstone or when transporting documents to and from my mother."

"The day of the rats, was he—"

"Yes, both Gladstone and Disraeli were there that afternoon. Gladstone had his secretary with him to take notes of their meeting with my mother." Her mention of the former prime minister's name set off another suspicion. "Oh lord, the murder of the two clerks—one resembled Disraeli."

"But Rhodes would have nothing against the former PM," Byrne said.

"True, but his employer does. They are bitter political opponents. Do you suppose Mr. Gladstone himself might have ordered Rhodes to kill Disraeli? That he also might have wished to terrify my mother and all of us by delivering the rats?"

Byrne was shaking his head before she finished talking. "Gladstone seems to me a cold, calculating, and ruthless man, politically. But I can't see him sending anyone to knock off his Tory foes. Aside from that, there's no love lost between Gladstone and the Irish rebels. He'd never do anything to aid the radicals' cause. And remember, they claimed responsibility for the murders."

She reached for his hand as the carriage rattled away down the street. "Then Rhodes is acting independently?"

"It would seem." He gripped her fingers so tightly she knew he was unaware that he was hurting her. She loosened his strong fingers before they crushed hers.

He leaned back in the carriage, propped one foot on his other knee, closing his eyes in thought. Absently, he stroked the back of her hand. "Let us assume Philip Rhodes had an innate hatred for your mother, passed to him from his father. The baron likely complained to the boy about the queen and their battle for control over the royal household. When Albert passed away and Victoria dismissed the baron, Rhodes would have been . . . how old?" He opened his eyes and looked at her.

"Perhaps eighteen, nineteen," she supplied.

"He would have felt the shame of his father's being tossed out of England. Most likely any financial support he had been receiving from the baron was reduced or cut off entirely."

"Oh, dear," she said.

Byrne continued with his theory. "So we can assume the young man felt the sting of his father's banishment to Germany in more ways than one. For his father's sake, and for his mother's as well as for himself, as they were now suddenly very poor."

Louise felt an urgency to be back with her family. To warn them. Protect them in whatever way she could. As familiar streets swept past she counted the minutes.

They were nearly to Buckingham when Byrne's eyes flashed open and he snapped out of his silent contemplation to speak again. "The real question is, how deeply is Rhodes connected with the Fenians?"

She gasped. "You really think it's not just a personal grudge? You believe he is in league with them?"

"It makes sense he would align himself with others who have a reason to hate the queen and wish to do her harm. And he *is* Irish on his mother's side. The Secret Service suspects the Fenians have infiltrated the government and placed some of their officers in high positions. It would be to their advantage to have direct access to the prime minister."

Louise shuddered. How she wished she could remember everything that had happened on *The Day of the Rats*. Where had Rhodes been? With Gladstone the entire time? Might he have left the PM long enough to wend his way through the palace to the old nursery wing and drop off his filthy cargo? And how would he have carried live beasts, undetected?

A vision of the man swam before her eyes. Germanic features, but with unlikely dark hair (black Irish, they called that coloring), and not tall like his father. He often carried a briefcase the size of a small trunk—easily large enough to accommodate a ream of paper.

Or perhaps three drugged rats?

Forty-three

Louise fairly flew through the long hallway, her mind gathering up and trying to make sense of scattered facts she and Byrne had discussed in the carriage less than an hour before. It was the logistics of the day that Byrne couldn't verify. Where had Rhodes been in the palace, if not always with Gladstone? Or were they jumping to unsupportable conclusions? It was still possible someone else was to blame for the rats and the information leaks. After all, they had no proof Rhodes was the culprit.

While Byrne was off trying to locate and talk to Philip Rhodes, they'd agreed Louise might find out if anyone in the palace remembered seeing the secretary in or near the nursery that memorable day. She interviewed several of the queen's guardsmen. One remembered guiding a "lost" secretary back out of the wing of private suites.

She was on her way to her own room when she rounded a corner and ran straight into Lorne. He braced her shoulders between two hands. "Ah there, darling, where are you racing to? I've been looking all over for you."

"Have you?" Her head hummed with her news. She needed to tell Byrne what she'd learned. But how to reach him? She could send a messenger to intercept him at Gladstone's address, since she was fairly certain that would be one of his stops.

"Yes, I have," Lorne said. "Come have tea with me."

"I'm sorry, I can't now," she said breathlessly.

"What's wrong?"

"Nothing." *Everything!*

She suddenly thought it unwise to reveal all she and Byrne had recently discovered. They had found one culprit, one man who well might be in league with the Fenians. But that wasn't to say there might not be others in their midst. They'd agreed to tell no one, not even her mother, until they had evidence to support their accusations.

It seemed disloyal to not be totally honest with her own husband, but when it came right down to it, hadn't she already been unfaithful to him in other ways?

His deep blue eyes delved into hers. "It's rather important that we talk, dear girl. I don't think it can wait." It wasn't like him to be this insistent. Had he somehow found out she'd slept with Stephen Byrne?

"All right," she said. "Where shall we sit?"

"The Breakfast Room, I should think."

She glanced sideways at him as they walked, puzzling over the reason for this emergency conversation. When he offered his arm, she took it with reluctance. Their charade of intimacy no longer felt even vaguely right.

"Your hair isn't done today, again," he said. She thought she heard censure in his tone.

"I prefer it loose."

He smiled. "So you've said before. But you look like a young girl, rather wild and free."

"Is that so bad?" She lifted a brow at him.

"Your mother was remarking she wished you would let your maid crimp and arrange it for you."

Louise grimaced. She would wear her hair as she pleased, just as she would live her life as she pleased. She hoped Lorne wouldn't take up her mother's harangue about her choice of clothing and hair fashion.

"Is this what was so important—how I wear my hair?" She couldn't hide her annoyance.

"No." He laughed. "Oh, no, good God, it's far more significant than that." He waved a hand at her light-colored day dress, another departure from the more formal styles and dark hues of the times. "That's quite pretty, my dear."

Why, she wondered, the weak attempt at conciliatory flattery? If that was what it was.

When they reached the Breakfast Room, she saw that a pot of tea and plate of biscuits had already been laid out on one of the small, square tables draped in white damask. The Chinese decor of the room had been transplanted from Brighton Pavilion, when the property had been sold off nearly twenty-five years earlier to pay for the renovations at Buckingham requested by her parents. Priceless Oriental vases, tapestries, and Persian carpeting complemented the borrowed Brighton fixtures. Although the room itself was the size of Amanda's entire house, it was an intimate retreat when compared to the vast formal salons of Buckingham, and she loved it.

So, Lorne had actually staged this meeting. Louise slanted him a suspicious look, which he didn't acknowledge.

She took up the task of pouring for them, to cover for her nerves. He settled into the gilt, upholstered chair across from her. When they each had their tea, he took a breath and smiled at her.

"I have exciting news, darling," he said.

"Yes?" She sipped and found the Darjeeling just the right temperature.

"The queen, your mother that is, has offered me an excellent position within the government."

She smiled at him, relieved. If that was all this was about . . . "I'm so glad. It's what you wanted, isn't it?"

"Yes," he said, looking away. "I want to be useful, to have a career beyond just sitting in the House of Lords."

"Do I sense reservation in your tone?" She sipped again then put down her cup and saucer.

"Not at all. I believe it's an ideal situation for us."

Suddenly suspicious, she turned her full attention on him. "Us?"

"Well, yes, of course." He picked up his cup and saucer but returned them to the table without drinking. "I believe you will enjoy the adventure."

"We aren't leaving London, are we?"

The corners of his lips tweaked up but never reached a smile. "I'm to be posted to Canada, as the new governor of the common-wealth."

Louise felt her stomach drop. A weight pressed down on her chest, not unlike the crushing sensations during her last two months of pregnancy carrying Eddie. "Canada? But that's so far from—" She closed her eyes and swallowed. *So far from Stephen.* She'd only just found him. Only just now understood how much she loved him. "How long before we must leave?" After all, it might be months, and plans change. She might persuade her mother that Lorne wasn't the man for the position.

"Three weeks, maybe less." He said it so quietly she barely heard. He seemed unable to meet her eyes.

Louise shot to her feet, fists clenched at her sides so tightly they hurt. "Why, Lorne? Why does she not put you in charge of one of our estates, or let you manage game and fisheries for the family. You'd like that—wouldn't you?"

He stared down at his clasped hands. "She didn't give me her reasons."

Her skin itched with her fury. Only the tightness in her throat kept her from screaming. This whole scheme smelled of her mother's manipulation. Why? Why send her away now?

Then it struck her. Of course. Victoria had somehow caught wind of her affair with Stephen Byrne. Or else she'd merely assumed they were lovers, or soon to be.

"She has no right to do this to me," she spat, fighting back tears of rage. "No right!"

Lorne launched himself out of his chair and knelt beside her, taking her hands in his. "My dear, I'm so sorry. I had no idea the news would be other than pleasing to you."

He did appear sincere. But she pushed him away, freeing herself to pace the carpet.

"Listen, darling, this will mean adjustments for me as well." He stood and brushed off the knees of his trousers. "I shall have to bid farewell to many dear friends in London. But I'm sure we will each find new companions to our liking."

"Don't you understand?" She turned on him and stomped her foot for emphasis. "This is punishment, not a reward. She's getting rid of the troublemakers in her life. Us!"

"Oh, now that's a bit overly harsh, don't you th—"

"It's the truth, Lorne. She might have had her suspicions about your habits before we wed, but now she is convinced, and she'll do anything to avoid scandal. Anything. That's the one thing she fears. She dodged it once before, when my indiscretions—"

"Yes, the art school boy, wasn't it?" He laughed. "That's not such a horrid thing, dear girl. An innocent fling. More young ladies than their mothers can imagine wander before they're wed."

"But they don't all have babies!" she shouted at him.

He stared at her. The room fell silent. "A child? You bore a child? What happened to it? No, don't tell me. I don't want to know." His face turned a sickly moss green. "Oh dear. So it's true. She wants you away from London and the gossip."

"And you. I suppose she thinks that the company you'll keep

in Canada, if done discreetly, will likely stay on that side of the Atlantic."

He smiled sadly. "Well, at least it isn't Newgate."

Louise bit down on her bottom lip and tried to rally her courage. But it was no use. Lost. She felt abysmally lost. She'd enjoyed a fragile glimpse of happiness. But fate had swept it away as quickly as it had come. *Oh, Stephen.*

She looked at her young husband. He stood, shoulders bowed, eyes filling with tears—the image of utter desolation. He was dependent upon her for his very life. If he refused the post her mother offered him and stayed in London, living as he was doing, he might well be arrested, might never survive whatever sentence he was given as punishment for loving in a way society didn't understand.

And wasn't she in love with a man other than her husband, and breaking the laws of morality in her own way? *What a pair we are.*

"I'll go with you," she whispered. "Don't worry." She stepped up to Lorne and combed his long blond hair out of his beautiful blue eyes with her fingertips, as if he were her little brother. "It will be all right, Lorne."

He lifted his gaze to meet hers. "My dear," he said, "I don't know what to say. Thank you."

There was no other way. Her mother had won. Again.

Lorne sniffled, pulling himself erect, then shyly looped his long arms around her and held her. He was not Stephen Byrne. Could never be Stephen. But there was some measure of comfort in his embrace.

"I promise. I'll make this up to you. Somehow, I do most solemnly promise."

Foolish, foolish man, she thought.

Forty-four

If William Gladstone's butler had willingly allowed Byrne through the front door at 10 Downing Street, he wouldn't have had to force his way inside and interrupt the PM's meeting.

"Sir!" a red-faced Gladstone bellowed. "What is the meaning of this intrusion?"

The butler made a token snatch for Byrne's arm while the other half dozen men in the room wrenched about in their seats to stare at them. A warning glare from Byrne's black-as-sin eyes froze the PM's man where he stood.

"I need to speak with you immediately, Prime Minister," Byrne said. "It is a matter of your nation's security."

Gladstone returned his attention to the sheaf of papers before him on the table. "Winters, summon the police." The servant evaporated through the doorway.

Byrne swore, not quite under his breath. "I *am* the bloody police, sir." Not technically true, but that caught the prime minister's attention. Byrne extracted a card from his pocket and held it out. "Her majesty's Secret Service."

Gladstone allowed him a stiff nod. "I remember you now. The American." He said it as if he were naming a lower species.

"I need fifteen minutes of your time, in private please." When he got no reaction he added, "The queen's life is at stake."

A disturbed murmur rose around the table.

Gladstone scowled at Byrne but spoke to his ministers. "Gentlemen, allow me to humor the man. If you will adjourn to the parlor. Winters, please see to refreshments . . . where did the man go?"

"To summon the police," Byrne said helpfully.

"Right." Gladstone cleared his throat. "Gentlemen, thank you for your cooperation."

The ministers filed out of the room, casting Byrne annoyed and doubtful looks. When the door closed behind them, Byrne turned back to face the prime minister and noticed a pistol had appeared on the desktop. It rested inches from Gladstone's right hand.

"That won't be necessary," he said, meeting the PM's steely gaze.

"I'll be the judge of that."

Byrne motioned to the chair nearest the prime minister. "May I?"

Gladstone nodded. "Be quick. I have business to attend to. The queen's life is, of course, important but I'm not yet convinced that what you have to say has anything to do with me."

To Byrne's mind there were two equally critical issues at hand. He began with the one he knew the least about. "Your secretary, I see, isn't attending this meeting. I assume he normally would be here to take notes?"

"That's right. And I can tell you I'm most disappointed with Mr. Rhodes at the moment."

"Then his absence isn't excused?"

"It is not." Gladstone turned his famous glower on Byrne. "Have you come to inform me of the man's death?"

"Why would you think he's dead?"

"You've identified yourself as law enforcement. Has there been foul play? An accident? Another bombing?"

"So far as I know, Mr. Rhodes is not a victim of any crime. Quite the opposite."

Gladstone's frown deepened. "Out with it, man."

"It appears that your secretary may have delivered a threatening note and three rats into the palace on a day when he accompanied you there in March." Seconds before Byrne had stepped from his carriage, one of his sweepers delivered a message from Louise, telling him of the secretary's sneaking into the family quarters.

"I won't be insulted." Gladstone shoved himself to his feet. The halo of white hair that circled his head stood out as if electrically charged. "This is an outrageous accusation. To say I had anything to do with—"

"You couldn't have known, sir. The rats were probably doped to keep them quiet. Rhodes would have carried them in his valise. Can you recall if he gave an excuse to leave the queen's office for any reason?"

"I do recall." Gladstone sat down again. "He needed to return to the carriage for papers he'd left there."

"One of the queen's guards found him wandering the hall outside the private suites, claiming he'd become confused and lost."

"Might that not be possible?"

"Yes, if it were not for other factors." Byrne paused just long enough to make sure he had the man's attention. "Are you aware of Mr. Rhodes's heritage?"

"No particulars. Just that he was raised by his mother as his father died when he was very young. An uncle, I believe he told me, saw to his education."

Lies blended with snippets of truth. "Rhodes is the bastard son of the late Baron Stockmar."

Gladstone stared at him, his eyes narrowing to slits. "You are certain of this?"

"Yes. He was born in Ireland, came to England to be educated at the expense of his father, at Oxford. Lost his accent, made valuable connections within this country. We believe his sympathies for his country of birth led him to become involved with the Fenians. It's possible also that his loyalty to you encouraged him to plot against Mr. Disraeli, who was the intended target of the recent opera murders."

Gladstone stared at him. "You accuse *me* of—"

"—of conspiring to murder your political adversary? No, sir. I have every faith you would have turned your secretary over to Scotland Yard had you any idea what he was up to."

Gladstone huffed out a breath. He returned his pistol to the top drawer of his desk. "It's difficult for me to imagine such a quiet and obedient man could be involved in plots against the government. Are you quite sure?"

"As sure as I can be without actually catching him in the act."

"Dear Lord, this is most distressing. To think I've harbored such a devil in my own home and delivered to him information—" He broke off and stared at Byrne. "But you said the queen was in danger."

"Yes, her entire family in fact."

"What may I do to help? Is there another plot brewing?" He sighed. "I expect you wouldn't be here if the rat prank were the only threat."

"True. I believe it's possible that Rhodes is a Fenian officer who has been orchestrating recent bombings and may have plans to kidnap one of the royal family, as a means for pressing Ireland's case for separation from England."

"I see."

"I need Mr. Rhodes's home address. It's urgent that we find him.

If we can capture and question him, we may be able to avoid a terrible tragedy. At the very least, if I'm right about his involvement, we will have removed one of the most active Fenian officers from the conflict and get the names of others from him."

Gladstone was on his feet and rushing to an outer office where a small secretary's desk, bare except for blotter and inkwell, stood beside the door. Byrne followed and watched as he drew out a notebook—addresses—and flipped through it.

"No, not here." Gladstone gave him a frustrated look.

"He wouldn't need to keep track of his own address."

"Yes, of course." The PM raced back to his own office and unlocked another file drawer, from which he pulled a thin folder. "Interviews for the position of my secretary. Here it is." He copied the address quickly on a clean sheet of paper. "I needed an address to get back to the man if I decided to hire him. Would that I had chosen more wisely. It's more than a year old, but maybe it will help, even if it's not current."

"Thank you, sir." Byrne took it from him.

"Please know, and reassure the queen and Mr. Disraeli, that I had nothing to do with this man's schemes."

"I will tell her." Byrne turned to leave.

"Sir," Gladstone called out, "do you know his next move?"

"No, sadly."

Gladstone thought for a moment. "The queen's Accession Day parade and ceremony, June twentieth. If the Fenians wish to make a grand statement against the monarchy—that will be the time."

Byrne mentally whacked himself upside the head. Had he been more familiar with the country and its customs, it would have occurred to him immediately. Here they were, just days away from the ceremony. "The usual precautions are being taken for security along the parade route and at the church," he said.

"I'm sure they are. But are they enough?"

"If we have the men, I'd like to see the church thoroughly

searched, top to bottom, the day before the ceremony then kept clear. All those attending can be screened as they enter."

"I'll see that you have as many men as you need," Gladstone said. "We'll bring in constables from the countryside if necessary. Meanwhile, I hope you'll find Rhodes at that address."

Byrne nodded. He held out little hope. If Philip Rhodes was the mind behind recent deadly attacks, he would have gone underground by now. But what Byrne did hope for was evidence and, if he was very lucky, a clue to where and how the next attack would be staged.

Forty-five

John Brown took the note from the runner. Having made his delivery, the crossing sweeper, who couldn't have been more than eight years old, held out his grimy little hand in a bold manner. Brown grunted his irritation and pressed a shilling into the lad's palm.

"Off with you now," he grumbled, stepping back inside the palace gate where he'd been summoned by the sentry.

There was no envelope, just a torn quarter sheet dirty as barnyard muck from the boy's grip, but he recognized Byrne's spiky hand. He stopped walking as soon as the meaning of the two brief but chilling sentences grasped him:

> *Accession Day plot by Fenians. Tell Her she must postpone*
> *ceremony.*

Her. Victoria, of course.

Brown thrust a hand through the wiry tufts of hair at his crown and curled his lip. He had vowed to protect Victoria Regina with his life, and by God he'd do it. But Byrne must think him a miracle worker if he believed him capable of convincing the woman to not venture out on the anniversary of her taking up the crown. He went off anyway, to try.

John Brown found the queen not in her office but with Beatrice,

Louise, and Arthur in the palace's Blue Salon. "I would speak with you in private, woman," he said.

Arthur slanted him his usual disapproving look. Beatrice pretended she was too engrossed in sorting her playing cards to notice him at all. Louise looked up at him mildly and smiled.

Victoria raised her brows and tilted her head toward him in question. He knew he sounded like a man giving his wife an order, a tone the queen tolerated from no one but him. Sometimes she even seemed to enjoy when he spoke so intimately to her. In front of others, though, he usually took care to address her with formal deference.

"She is not a woman," Arthur said. "She is Your Royal Majesty to you, sir."

Victoria waved her youngest son to silence. "Can't you see we are engaged in a game of whist? Let it wait awhile, John."

He looked down at the note, considering just handing it to her. Lately she seemed to place more trust in Byrne's advice than in his, at least when it came to matters of security. At first, he'd resented the Yank's influence over her, as he would any man's. But if Byrne's efforts made her safer, he was for it.

He held the scrap out to her.

"And what's this?" Without laying down her cards to take the note from him she let her eyes drift over the smudged words. "What sort of nonsense is this? A plot? On my anniversary?"

"They wouldn't dare," Arthur scoffed.

"I expect they would," Louise said, and Brown thanked God there was one level head in the family.

Victoria started to set down her cards then seemed to change her mind. She played one card, watched as Arthur, Beatrice, then Louise played in turn. She took the trick with a satisfied smile.

He tried again. "Mr. Byrne and I strongly advise canceling, or at least postponing the ceremony."

The queen huffed at her remaining cards. "I can't do that. There have been so many complaints about my seclusion since dear Albert's death. Bertie says I really must appear in my coronation coach in our parade to the church. I have been too long a recluse. The nation must see their queen."

"Mama," Louise said, "please listen to Mr. Brown. If Mr. Byrne has uncovered another plot, remaining here in Buckingham or removing to Osborne House might be far wiser."

"And do you believe we are secure here?" Victoria snapped, glaring at her daughter. "Have you so soon forgot the rats? For weeks you've all tried to convince me that we have enemies within. I tell you, I feel safer among the street people these days."

"Please be reasonable, ma'am," Brown pleaded.

"Am I to be a prisoner in my own home?" Victoria shouted. She slapped her cards down on the table. "No. I cannot disappoint my subjects any longer. They complain bitterly of my absence, so I shall show myself. A monarch must set an example, so says Mr. Gladstone. She must be strong. Accession Day will come as planned."

Louise shook her head and gave Brown a sympathetic look. He noticed the princess didn't look half as cheerful as last time he'd seen her. All the light seemed to have drained from her bonnie eyes. Another spat with her mother? Or was something else behind her melancholy?

"Mama," Louise said, "at least eliminate the parade. Let your guardsmen convey you to the church in a less visible way."

"She's right. It's the ceremony that counts," Bea added, barely above a meek whisper.

Victoria laughed. "Have you not heard what I've just said, all of you? My subjects wish to *see* their queen. They have a right." Her eyes shrank to dangerous pinpoints as she glared up at Brown, and then he knew the cause was lost. "As we haven't room for all of London in the damn church, John, I must show myself along the way there and back."

"This is ridiculous," Arthur said, groaning. He shook his fistful of cards at Brown, who wished he could knock them out of the boy's hand and give him a good thrashing. "Have we not sufficient guardsmen to protect the royal entourage? Order up a hundred Beefeaters if necessary. A thousand! Add as many from the army as you require. A handful of anarchists won't stand in the way of the will of the British Empire." Anarchists . . . Irish, the boy didn't seem to know the difference.

"It's my bloody job to see your mother's safe," Brown bellowed. *You pompous little ass.*

"Children, Mr. Brown . . . please, you are giving me a headache." Victoria touched both her hands to her temples, as if to demonstrate. "Louise, do you agree with Mr. Brown? Must I surrender to these ruffians and give up my day of celebration?"

Brown looked hopefully to the princess, who had settled down so well after her troubled youth. Perhaps he could count on her as an ally?

"Mother," Louise said, her voice a cheerless shadow of its usual spirit, "we all wish you safe, of course."

Victoria leaned across the card table toward her daughter, forcing their eyes to meet. "And you, my girl, what would *you* do in my place, if *you* were queen? Would you let criminals frighten you into hiding? Would you let your own men, who claim to care for your security, worry you to death with their warnings and bully you into staying away from your subjects?"

Brown got a sinking feeling in his gut. Something was going on between these two—mother and daughter—and there was no way he was going to insert himself.

"What *I* would do," Louise began, her eyes flashing with anger, body rigid in her seat, "and what *you* should do are two different—"

"Are they?" Victoria cut her off. "Are *we* really that different, Louise Caroline Alberta? You who brazenly refused to listen to your parents, your governesses, or anyone else who stood in the way of your pursuit of whatever whim struck you. You who still ignore your duties as a princess to pursue your *private passions*?"

A hidden message passed through the air, one Brown could not hope to interpret. Arthur and Beatrice exchanged glances, looking no less confused than he was.

Victoria continued. "Tell me, Louise, were you in my position—would you take orders from these men?"

Louise hesitated, glancing at Brown with an apologetic look. "No," she whispered. "I suppose not."

"Speak up, girl."

"No!" Louise shouted, grit in her voice that made him think of ground glass. "No, Mama, I would not. I would go out to my people and let them see I was not afraid."

There was an eruption of objections from Arthur and, remarkably, from meek little Beatrice. But Brown knew the damage had been done. He shook his head at Louise, but rather than turn away she rose to stand in front of him.

"The note's from Mr. Byrne, isn't it?" she said. "He's found out something more."

"Aye, and you should be ashamed of yourself, encouraging her like that."

"Should I?" She looked toward her mother, busy fending off objections from her other two children. She was a small woman, plump in her later years. But what Brown saw now was a woman whose course had always been set, whose will was iron and destiny had never been determined by any of the men in her life. Not even by him.

"I think she's already made up her mind, Mr. Brown," Louise said. "Nothing you or I can say will change it. You know that as well as I."

He closed his eyes. "Then God help us come Accession Day."

Forty-six

Byrne whistled up another hansom cab and rode directly to the address Prime Minister Gladstone had given him. He could have taken one of Buckingham's carriages when he'd set out earlier, but he didn't want to mark himself as coming from the palace.

Philip Rhodes lived in Bloomsbury, a respectable area of professional families. The town house appeared to have been divided into three ample flats. He knocked at the door and an aged man promptly answered. A quick conversation established that he was the landlord/owner who let out the two upper floors while he lived on the ground level.

"Is Mr. Rhodes in?" Byrne asked.

"He is expecting you, sir?"

"Actually, I'd rather hoped to surprise him." Byrne showed off his most winsome smile and hoped for the best.

"Well, you can knock if you like. He's right above me. But I've neither seen nor heard from him in three days, which is odd I have to say. He is a man of impeccable routine, he is, Mr. Rhodes. In and out of the house like clockwork." He chuckled. "Private secretary to his honor the PM. Did you know that?"

"So I've heard. I'll give it a go then, just in case," Byrne said pleasantly.

He climbed to the next floor. Instead of knocking, he pressed an ear to the door and listened. Nothing. The rooms had the feel of a vacuum. No living sound from within, not even the buzz of a fly.

"You may have to knock rather louder," the landlord shouted up the stairs. "He sometimes gets involved in his little hobbies and takes no note of the outside world."

"Thank you," Byrne called back to him. "But I think I hear someone stirring inside." Although he did not.

He snapped open the blade of his knife and ran it along the crack between door panel and jamb. Its tip stopped at what felt like a latch. He manipulated the blade cautiously. Heard it give. But he did not swing the door open. Ever so gently, Byrne eased the door less than half an inch. Although the light in the hallway was limited by the single window at its end, he could just make out a slender wire as delicate as a spider's web.

Clark's handiwork, no doubt, on behalf of his boss.

He remembered seeing such an arrangement once before. That time his sergeant had beat him to the door. Before Byrne could warn him, the older man shouldered his way into the booby-trapped shed. The explosion had killed him instantly.

Now Byrne gently angled the knife blade and then two fingers through the crack and slowly sawed at the wire, supporting it with his fingers to avoid putting pressure on whatever it was attached to. He held his breath. Sweat dribbled beneath his shirt, pooling at the base of his spine, chilling the flesh in a spot the size of a silver dollar.

At first he worried the knife might only be sliding over the wire, doing no real work. But at last the strand divided. Standing back in the hallway, as far away from the door as possible, Byrne lifted one boot and eased open the door with his toe.

The hinge creaked but made no louder complaint. He breathed again.

When he walked in he left the door ajar behind him. The single window in the combined sitting and bedroom was closed but unlatched—Clark's means of escape after setting the booby trap.

The room was not what he'd expected of a highly organized man. No clothing remained in the freestanding cupboard, but two flannel shirts and several pairs of socks in need of darning lay on the floor. The mattress had been slit open and sagged in a deflated lump off the bed frame. A mirror that had hung on the wall, as evidenced by the less faded rectangle of wallpaper, rested with its reverse side to the room, its brown paper backing torn off and hanging in shreds. Books were stacked against one wall on the floor and on top of the dresser. It was as if all that had been deemed important in the room had been hastily removed and all else abandoned.

The landlord would not be pleased.

Byrne went first to the mirror. The paper backing appeared newer than the mirror itself, which had undoubtedly come with the room's furnishings. In fact, as he squatted over it he could see that it already had a much sturdier cardboard backing, probably the original. So Rhodes had hidden something of value here. Something thin. Letters or money? Maps? Or plans of some sort. Maybe blueprints of a targeted building. Whatever it was, it was gone now.

His stomach churned. Why remove something you'd hidden in a presumably safe place . . . unless you are ready to use it?

He turned to the disheveled bed. More than half of the straw stuffing was gone from the mattress. Not just pulled out, totally gone. Something had been stored in its place, stuffed up inside the mattress casing.

Byrne squatted down to study the canvas sack. He thrust his hand inside, felt around. Just straw. He ran his hand along the bed frame. He stretched out flat on his belly and slid head first beneath the oak frame.

"Hey, what you doing there, mister?" The landlord, at the door. Byrne paid him no mind.

"You're destroying private property. Won't have none of that, will we now? I'm fetching the bobby down the corner, I am. Mr. Rhodes he'll be furious when he sees . . ." The voice faded down the stairwell. An outside door banged shut.

Byrne rolled to his side, letting in more light from the window, through the frame's slats and past his shoulder. There. There *it* was, as he'd suspected. He licked his finger and touched it to the floorboards midway across the width of the bed. When he scooted out from beneath the frame and lifted his finger to the light, fine blue-black flecks speckled his fingertip.

Charcoal, saltpeter, and sulfur. Black powder.

Rhodes had stored it here. A terrifyingly powerful supply, he estimated from the portion of the mattress that had been left empty. And now it was gone.

Which meant the Fenians were about to use it. For all he knew, the bomb might already be in place.

The question was—where?

Forty-seven

Louise peered out through the window at the top of the grand staircase overlooking the courtyard. Preparation for the Accession Day celebration had proceeded with all the energy of a military campaign. Servants had prepared elegant suites in the palace for distinguished guests. A steady stream of vendors delivered meats, fish, produce, grains, vegetables in abundance to the kitchens, hour after hour, day and night. Tonight the gala dinner would place immense pressure on the staff. Extra help had been hired, trained, liveried. Two footmen would attend each guest. The concert following the banquet included performances by scores of musicians and two famous composers.

Every person allowed entry into Buckingham Palace to work there was interviewed by the queen's security detail. No guest would be allowed inside without identification.

But it was the procession by carriage to the church the following day that most concerned Louise, despite her support for her mother's journey across London.

"I'm sure all will go smoothly," Amanda said to Louise's fretting.

Louise turned to her friend with a smile. "You're probably right. Are you sure you and Henry and Eddie won't join the parade? He'd love it, and I can arrange for a carriage."

Amanda grimaced and pressed a hand to her immense stomach. Louise couldn't believe only one child grew in there. "A bouncy carriage ride then sitting on a hard bench in church is not my idea of a pleasant day."

Louise remembered her own baby's ponderous weight and mysterious little kicks. His movements within her told her he was healthy, full of life, but also brought heartache every time she remembered he would not be allowed to stay with her. She looked down at little Edward now, entwined in Amanda's skirts. He was small for his age. With his brown hair and eyes so much like her own, it was a wonder to her no one had guessed the truth. Even his mouth had the same gentle bow as hers.

Yet Victoria, well aware that he was her grandson, seemed immune to Eddie's charms. Louise wondered if her mother actually had convinced herself the baby was Amanda's, since she'd never seen Louise holding him as an infant. Her mother had a gift for pushing to the back of her mind anything she found unable to deal with on her own terms. Whereas Louise never seemed to stop worrying about every little detail. Only while she'd been with Stephen Byrne in the tiny servant's room had all her worries flown away, like so many doves released in a carefree burst of flight, up and into the air. Such bliss.

She sighed, aloud apparently, for Amanda turned to her with a frown. "Something wrong?"

"No, my dear friend. I'm only concerned for you. Most women I know, with less than a month before their babies are due, take to their beds. Henry still encourages you to stay up and travel about?"

"As active as I feel able, he says. It's the new way of dealing medically with pregnancy, he says. As long as I'm healthy and have the energy, he claims I'm less likely to suffer complications and will have an easier labor. We shall see if he's right." Amanda's eyes sparkled with anticipation of the blessed event.

"I still think that working at the shop is far too great a strain on you," Louise said.

"Well, you had better take advantage of my time now. After the baby is born, I will likely need all of my strength to nurse this brute." She smiled, stroking her bulging belly.

Louise wasn't sure she believed Henry's rather revolutionary medical theories, but today Amanda seemed convincing proof. She glowed with inner health and joy.

"But you *will* come join us for the banquet and performance this evening?" Louise asked.

Amanda hugged her, as best she could in her current rotund form. "I wouldn't miss it. The performance will take my mind off this child's fierce kicks. Oh!" Amanda yipped, her face puckering with momentary pain.

"That must have been a hard one. Are you sure that baby won't come earlier than Henry predicts?"

Amanda whispered, "As it's my first, he says it's more likely to arrive late rather than early."

Louise nodded. Sometimes, for just a moment, she forgot the little boy with them had indeed once been hers. She closed her eyes to forestall a wash of tears.

"Let me see. Let me see!" Eddie shouted.

Louise bent down to the child's level and peered over the windowsill to see what had caught his interest. He was only able to peer outside by clinging to the sill and jumping up and down on his toes. He ran to his mother and tugged on her dress, lifting his arms to her.

"Come to me, Eddie," Louise said. "Your mother can't pick you up these days, fat as she is."

"Oh, I like that!" Amanda cried, laughing, and swatted her with her fan. The day was warm. Even within the cool stone walls of the castle, Louise felt the rising heat. So unusual for June. *Rain,* she thought, *let it rain tonight to cool things off.*

Eddie spotted another carriage rolling into the courtyard. He pointed frantically at the horse pulling it. He loved horses and delighted in naming them, as if they came from his personal stable.

"Oh yes," Louise crooned, "that's a lovely gray, isn't it?"

"Smoky," the little boy crowed. "I name him Smoky."

"Whose carriage is that?" Amanda asked.

Louise looked more closely. It wasn't one of theirs, with the royal crest on the door. A tall man with a graying beard stepped out; he carried a black leather bag. "Dr. Lister," she said, surprised.

The famous surgeon had been summoned before to the palace by her mother's personal physician, Dr. Edwards, a gentle soul with considerable ability. However he sometimes became nervous at being the sole physician responsible for the aging queen. When it had become necessary to cut and drain a painful abscess on the queen's arm, he'd called in Lister to perform the operation.

Amanda whistled. "A surgeon—and Joseph Lister no less! Oh, dear, this does sound serious."

"My mother has been complaining of not sleeping well nights, from discomfort in her foot."

"You don't suppose it's a return of the terrible gout she had years ago?"

"I don't know." Louise set Eddie down. He continued trying to scramble up the wall to better see out the window. "I had better go and check on her."

"You must. And we'll be off. It's time for Eddie's nap, and his mother could use a rest as well. I'll see you tonight at the banquet, my dear." Amanda kissed her on the cheek. "We'll walk ourselves out. Eddie has to play horsy along the way and annoy the servants."

Louise rested a hand on the little boy's head, and her heart swelled with affection. She'd come to terms with giving him up, hard as it had been. Amanda was a wonderful mother. Giving him over to her was the best thing she could have done for him, under the circumstances. How many other desperate mothers had sacrificed their babies—unable to afford to feed them or to face society's scorn at their bringing a child into the world without a proper husband? The very thought made her feel ill.

Louise ran into her mother's maid of honor on her way through the palace. "What's happening? I saw Dr. Lister arrive."

The woman shook her head, frowning. "Her Majesty's foot is causing her excruciating pain. She's been so very brave, not speaking of it for days. She's worried he won't let her leave her bed. She could barely walk on it this morning."

"Oh dear," Louise said. "Where is she now? With Lister, I assume."

"In her privy chamber, Your Highness. She hasn't left it all morning."

Not a good sign, Louise thought. Her mother usually was a whirlwind of activity, tackling one task after another so long as her health held. But when she was in pain she might spend an entire day, or as long as a week, shut off in her room.

Louise arrived at her mother's chamber, breathless. Her brother Alfred was already there, standing outside the closed door, pacing.

"What's Lister saying, Affie?" she asked.

"Not a word yet."

"She will be so disappointed if she can't go to the church tomorrow."

He nodded. "I think her own doctor has already advised her not to go." He chuckled and brushed a hand over his dark beard. "At least I expect that was the reason for the outburst a moment ago. I heard her shout something quite rude at the man." He gave her a bemused smile. "If she's able to rally that much energy I can't believe she's as helpless as these physicians think."

Louise couldn't have agreed more.

Finally the door opened. Edwards and Lister stepped into the hallway, consulting in hushed voices, their faces drawn. Louise stepped forward to be seen, and the two men stopped and bowed.

"Your Royal Highness," Joseph Lister said, "you, at least, look in good health."

"I am, sir. And you? You are involved in experimental treatments I've heard."

"Yes indeed, important studies of aseptic treatment of wounds, and I'm anxious to return to the work immediately. I must excuse myself. Dr. Edwards will fill you in on your mother's condition and my recommendations." He bowed again and took his leave.

Louise turned to her mother's physician. "Is it the gout again?" She was aware of another figure joining them and glanced around to see the Prince of Wales step up beside her. Although still early in the day, Bertie was already decked out in full military uniform with epaulets, gold braid, and enough medals to sink a small ship.

"The gout," Edwards repeated, "yes, as I feared it would be. The good news, according to Lister, is that it will be temporary and subside if she keeps off the foot."

"Good luck with that," Louise said.

Affie stepped forward. "But the Accession Day celebration, tomorrow?"

The doctor rolled his eyes. "Yes, we've both suggested a postponement might be in order. But I'm afraid your mother is having none of it. She will go to the church despite the cost in pain."

Louise nearly smiled. So predictable her mother was. "What about treatment?"

"I've bandaged her foot, dosed her mildly with morphine for the pain, which is all she would allow. I've prescribed laudanum, and she can take that at any time. Whether or not she will take it, I cannot say. Her diet will be changed—less meat and rich foods, more vegetables. I'm on my way to her head chef to give my instructions." He looked gravely at Louise. "Perhaps you can encourage her to make, at least, a few simple changes in the arrangements for the rest of today and tomorrow?"

"Anything. Just tell me what I'm to do." She hadn't forgotten the impossible situation her mother had put her in. Marrying her off to Lorne had been bad enough. Shipping them to the Canadian wilderness was a devious trick, and Louise would confront her mother and tell her so when the time was right. Eventually she'd need to decide whether or not she could ever forgive the woman for manipulating her life so. But Louise found no joy in seeing her mother suffer.

"Her Majesty's spirits are low," the doctor was saying. "She needs to be distracted from dwelling on the pain. If you can, get her out of that oppressive dark room when she wakes from the medicine. Wheel her around outside in her garden chair."

"Of course."

Bertie said, "And I? What can I be doing, doctor?"

Edwards thought for a moment. "Just spending time with her will be encouraging but—"

"Yes?"

"Tell me, do you know her actual arrangements for traveling to the church tomorrow?"

"She'll use her coronation coach, of course. It's partially open, allowing her to be seen by her subjects and wave to them as we pass. There will be six in her coach. Rather a tight fit if you ask me, but that's her plan."

"I see." Edwards nodded and touched the knuckles of one hand to his lips in thought. "The thing is, she'll be better off with the foot elevated. The garden chair can be adjusted to allow for that here. But she'll need to be carried into the church. She won't like it, but I've told her it's the only way, as she's to put no pressure at all on the foot. The other problem is the open carriage. With so many of you in it, she won't be able to keep the foot supported without it being seen from the street. To make the trip easier on her, I suggest you arrange for a smaller, partially closed carriage. Let her take one other person with her for company. She can keep the foot elevated without feeling self-conscious."

"I'll go now and see the stable master about that," Bertie said. He turned to Louise. "Perhaps that ornate lacquered sedan chair, the gift of the Mikado, might be employed to convey her in grand fashion from the carriage into the church? She might fight that less than being carried."

"Perfect," Louise agreed. "I'll arrange for it to be brought up from the carriage house." She gave her brother a cautionary look. "She won't like any of this, you know."

He laughed. "Oh, how well I know!"

Forty-eight

Louise had just ordered the wheeled garden chair brought to her mother's room, and was on her way there herself, when one of their servants approached her from the opposite end of the hall. He stopped just ahead of her, bowed, and held out a silver salver on which rested a folded sheet of paper.

"Thank you, Henson. Is a response expected?"

"The young"—he coughed delicately into his hand before finding a gentle enough word to express his disdain—"*person* who delivered it did not wait for one, Your Highness."

She nodded. Then this was from Byrne, by way of one of his urchin runners. She hoped he was all right. The last she'd seen of Stephen, he was moving with less obvious discomfort from his ribs and knee but still limping slightly. Again she thought she'd never have forgiven herself if he'd been killed that day when he'd fought Darvey's gang. He was such a maddeningly reckless man. Reckless and oh, so wonderful.

The smile that came to her lips so easily on thinking of him faded as she read the words in his note. She refolded it, tucked it into her sleeve, and marched on toward her mother. *This* was something the queen needed to know, whether the woman wanted to hear it or not.

Lorne, it seemed, had been spending time at one of his favorite, and least reputable, clubs—and not being very discreet about it. Men of nobility, although expected to have mistresses from time to time to supplement their wives' affections, generally kept their dalliances secret and their naughty behavior in the bawdy clubs behind closed doors. But one particular club had become notorious of late and, worse yet, involved in a police investigation. Leaks to the newspapers were inevitable.

The jackals of the press would step up their attempts to follow Lorne. If Louise didn't inform her mother of the details, the queen would learn them from the newspapers, too late to do anything about the maelstrom of horrid publicity at the expense of the entire family.

Her mother was sitting in a chair alongside her bed, her dresser having somehow got her into her clothes for the day. Tomorrow would be even more difficult, with the donning of the weighty, ornate black silk gown now hanging in front of her cheval glass mirror. Louise could only hope that, within the next twenty-four hours, the angry foot might have improved.

"Mama, I'm so sorry to hear that you've been suffering. I had hoped by now you'd be sleeping and more comfortable."

The queen looked up at her. "Sleeplessness has become routine. It is the pain I find intolerable. And these drugs are worthless."

"Can you not take the laudanum Dr. Edwards left for you?"

"The dreadful stuff puts me straight out and gives me hallucinations. I won't have it. There is too much to be done to prepare for tomorrow." Victoria dropped her head into her hands and held it there for a moment.

It wasn't that Louise felt no sympathy for her mother. She just found it near impossible to separate her mother's real medical issues from the collection of imagined ailments the queen employed to avoid work, making unpleasant decisions, or attending to social responsibilities she found distasteful.

Louise knelt beside her and used her gentlest voice. "Mama, I know this is a bad time, but there is something you must know."

"There is never a good time for bad news." She looked up at Louise then squinted in suspicion. "I can see from your expression, which is always plain to me who knows you so well, my dear, that this will be truly annoying news."

Louise hesitated. This was not going to be easy. "I expect the newspapers may soon carry a vicious rumor involving my husband."

Victoria rolled her eyes. "The marquess promised me he would be good." Her voice came out as a whine.

Louise took a breath for patience. In many ways, her mother remained naïve to the ways of the world, particularly when it involved sex. Victoria didn't seem to understand that Lorne's preference for the company of other men wasn't something he could turn off like a water spigot.

Apparently Lorne was becoming bolder in his evening activities, thinking he was safe from the law, now that he had married a princess and been accepted into the royal family. Louise took from her sleeve the note she'd received from Stephen.

"This information just came to me. Scotland Yard has been carrying on an investigation of certain gentlemen's clubs in a provocative part of the city and—"

"Oh, give me that!" Victoria snapped. "I don't see why you can't just come out and say what the trouble is."

Because, Louise thought, *you can't tolerate the truth.*

"It can't be so very bad," Victoria muttered. Her tiny glittering eyes darted across the page. She looked up at Louise with a frown then glanced down to reread the note while Louise waited, her heart racing.

"But this is preposterous. Impossible! Who wrote this letter to you?"

"Stephen Byrne."

"My Secret Service American?"

Louise hesitated. *Hers?* As if he were a pet poodle or a mahogany chiffonier. "Yes."

"But he is to report directly to me. By what right does he write to you?"

This was touchy ground indeed. "I believe he is concerned for your feelings. He had thought I might more tenderly couch the news about Lorne than if you'd discovered his activities from the newspapers."

"Tenderly couch?" Victoria roared, her cheeks flushing with rage. "These are *lies*!"

"Mama—"

"It says here that Lorne has been diddling rent boys at this awful establishment."

"Yes, it does."

"Has he not accepted his marital responsibilities? Is he not content with your bed?" Her voice was accusatory, her eyes brittle. Louise felt as if they were slicing through her flesh.

"Lorne's proclivities are different than I had believed when I married him. But you knew, Mama. *You* knew he was—"

Victoria held up an imperious hand. "I knew he was different and perhaps had experimented. That's what men do—they experiment. Until the right woman draws them to the straight and narrow." The queen's voice shook with emotion. "You are not trying hard enough with him, Louise. If you had satisfied the man in bed he would not be—"

"Mama!" Louise shot to her feet. "How dare you turn this into my fault. His character is his own doing, or God's doing . . . I don't know or care which. But you cannot blame me for the man's actions."

Victoria waved the note at her. "It's no matter. I don't believe this for a minute. When I see that Raven, I'll—"

As if the mention of his name conjured him out of the atmosphere, Stephen Byrne appeared in the doorway. Louise turned to him with a desperate look, hoping against hope he could calm her mother and help her see reason.

"Your Royal Majesty," Byrne said, removing his hat. He inclined his head toward Louise. "Princess."

"I was just now relating your information to my mother," Louise said, her words clipped with exasperation.

"I can see that." Byrne focused on the note in the queen's hand. "I thought it important that you learned of this investigation before it became public knowledge, ma'am."

"It's rubbish, Mr. Byrne. This is a trick of my enemies in Parliament. They are trying to make trouble for my family." She arranged her mouth in a grim smile. "My children are quite happy in their wedded state." She looked at Louise as if daring her to say otherwise.

Louise shook her head at Byrne, in resignation as much as denial.

It was a nearly unnoticeable gesture, but unwise. The queen's eyes narrowed.

"I am not at all pleased, sir, with your pursuit of private matters in my family's life. They are of no concern to you. Your job is to provide for us security. Lorne is not a threat to us. Do you agree?"

"I do, ma'am."

"Then you have severely overstepped your mandate, sir. I shall have to ask for your resignation."

Louise gasped, overcome with shock. She felt dizzy, unable to breathe. She took a shaky step forward. "Mama, please. Mr. Byrne has been nothing but sincere and diligent in his protection of our family."

"I see it differently." Victoria's lips compressed into a thin line. She looked from one to the other of them. "I will tolerate no secrets. Do you understand? Neither will I tolerate vicious gossip about members of my family."

"But Lorne has been *seen*!" Louise burst out. "It's past rumors and gossip now." She stepped closer to Stephen, the better to support his argument. "If Scotland Yard is investigating a sex ring, this business of the rent boys being brought into the clubs, it's only a matter of time before the newspapers catch on, if they haven't already. Then it will be all over London. All over the country, Mama."

"Don't you shout at me," Victoria warned.

Louise threw up her hands in defeat. "I'm not shouting. I'm trying to reason with you. Lorne will always be Lorne. We can caution him, but he will not change. And you shouldn't blame the messenger"—she waved a hand at Byrne—"for bringing bad news. He's just doing his job."

"I will do as I please. Until my death I am queen, my girl. On the day the Prince of Wales takes the throne, you may petition him as you wish. Until then—" She whisked her hand through the air, leaving the rest of her thought unsaid. There was to be no further argument. "Good-bye, Mr. Byrne. Your services are no longer needed. You may return to your own country."

Louise's mouth fell open. Her heart plummeted to her feet. She peered up from beneath eyelashes already damp with rising tears at her Raven. Not her mother's Raven. *Hers.* This was the man who had captured her heart. Who would too soon leave her. Would she never again see him?

She closed her eyes, unable to watch him go.

When Louise heard no retreating footsteps, she slowly opened her eyes and looked out through her misery. Miraculously, Stephen Byrne still stood there, straight and strong, his black eyes clear and solemn. He didn't look as if he were aware he'd just been canned, sacked, dismissed . . . given the royal boot.

When he spoke, his voice sounded to her as calm as a country brook. "Ma'am, there is another issue. It is my duty to report this to you before I leave my post, as it pertains to your personal safety."

"Then you may deliver your report to Mr. Brown or the captain of my guard." Victoria leaned back in her chair, folded her plump hands across her lap, and fixed a stony gaze on him.

Byrne still didn't move toward the door, but his dark regard shifted momentarily to Louise before returning to her mother. "Under your orders, ma'am, I have continued my investigation of the Fenian threat."

"I say, leave me now, sir!"

"And it appears danger is imminent. The opera murders were a mistake. The intended victim was Mr. Disraeli, and the aim to cause you distress, as he is one of your favorites and you his supporter."

Victoria's eyes flashed her fury. "You've told me all of this before." She shifted in her chair, and a shadow of pain crossed her face as she readjusted her foot on its cushion.

"Yes, but we've now discovered the identity of the man responsible for ordering Disraeli's murder, as well as for bringing the rats into the palace and leaving the threatening letter. He is Mr. Philip Rhodes, your prime minister's secretary—and secretly an officer in the Fenian army."

Louise reached out with the intention of grasping Byrne's arm, but her mother's sharp eyes stopped her hand midair. "Has Mr. Rhodes been arrested?"

"He has disappeared."

"Good riddance then." Victoria smiled, as if that solved everything.

"But not forever, I fear. I searched his room and found he'd vacated it but left behind evidence that a large quantity of black powder had been stored there. Since it has been moved from its hiding place, and with the Accession Day celebrations just one day away, I worry this means an attack is imminent."

"And you, too, would have me change my mind about the parade and ceremony?"

"I would, ma'am."

Louise saw a flicker of fear in her mother's eyes, but then her features screwed into their customary mask of obstinacy. "Mr. Brown has been informed of these theories of yours?"

"He has, ma'am."

"And your commander in my Secret Service has also been informed?"

"Yes, and we have alerted Scotland Yard. Reinforcements from the army have been sent to search the parade route, Westminster Abbey as well. But we cannot guarantee your safety. I respectfully beg you to stay where you are safe—here at Buckingham."

Louise held her breath, hopeful that Byrne's argument for caution would have more effect on her mother than her own pleas. She counted her heartbeats in the ensuing silence: one, two, three . . .

The queen blinked up at Byrne. "On the contrary. I'd say all is in good hands now, with so many precautions taken." Her lips turned up in a satisfied smile. "My men will keep me perfectly safe."

Louise let her eyes drift shut in resignation. They were at the mercy of bomb-wielding lunatics. And Victoria, with her twisted iron will, seemed intent on making their nefarious work all the easier for them. Brown had already informed her of the route.

Rather than proceed the short distance directly from the palace to Westminster Abbey, no more than a ten-minute carriage ride, she had insisted on a wider loop through the city. They would drive along Vauxhall Street, across the bridge, then circling round to recross the Thames River on Westminster Bridge, thereby taking in a variety of elite and poor sections of the city, to see and be seen by more of her subjects.

A moment later, Louise became conscious that Byrne was speaking again.

"I request one favor before I leave England," he said in that deep, tranquil voice that resonated with her soul.

Victoria merely looked at him, offering no encouragement for him to continue.

Byrne said, "I would like to remain long enough to see to your family's safety this one last time. Please allow me to accompany you tomorrow on the way to the church."

Louise got the sense that he wanted to turn and look at her, that he was trying to say something personal to her. But he refrained from making eye contact.

"We thank you for your service," Victoria said. "We wish to not see you again, Mr. Byrne. Have a safe voyage home."

And that, thought Louise with a sinking heart, is that.

Forty-nine

"Stop, Louise. Stop!"

Louise knew it was Stephen, but she couldn't bear to face him. Her mother had humiliated the man, tossed him out of the palace and her daughter's life. Furthermore, she'd acknowledged their affair—if not in so many words, at least by her dismissal of Byrne and elevation of Lorne to provincial governor. Victoria had more than enough spies within her court and staff to have had people watching Louise. Did her mother even know about their night in the servants' quarters?

Why hadn't she been more careful?

Because, Louise thought, *I'm in love.* And when you were in love you were blind to all else but that one person who meant everything to you.

Now nothing mattered.

Stephen would return to America. They wouldn't even share a few precious weeks together before she and Lorne left for Canada. There was no possibility of Stephen remaining in London, disgraced as he was, unable to work at his profession. The Secret Service couldn't keep him on after the queen's dismissal. Scotland Yard certainly wouldn't hire him and risk her displeasure. No member of Parliament, or even the minor nobility, would think of using him for private security for fear of turning Victoria against them.

Her heart broken, Louise ignored Stephen's shouts and ran the length of the Queen's Gallery, until her breath caught and ached inside her chest, like a bone lodged halfway down her throat. What must the man think of her? What could she possibly say to him now that her mother had mortified him and ruined his career?

By the time Byrne caught up with her, he nearly had to tackle her to bring her to a halt. She felt his hands come down and clamp both of her shoulders. He dragged her to a stop and pulled her in to his chest.

Gasping and spent, she sagged against him.

"What are you doing?" he said, sounding far less winded than she, though his knee must have slowed him down.

"I-I *h-hate* her," she choked out. She refused to cry although her eyes burned. Damn, damn, damn her horrid family!

He laughed. "Does that mean you hate me as well?"

She turned in his arms. "How can you act as if this were a joke? As if I could have been with you the way we were, but feel nothing for you less than twenty-four hours later?"

"I know. I'm an insensitive cad."

She smacked him in the chest with her fist, taking care to avoid injured ribs. "There you go again, making light of . . . of what we have." *Had.*

"I'm not doing any such thing." He rocked her in his arms and kissed the top of her head. "Do you think that woman has the power to make me stop loving you?"

She savored this new word. *Love.* "You love me?"

"How could you not know that?"

"I-I suppose because . . ." Because she had given up hope until he'd said the word with that honest openness of his. "Oh, Stephen, what are we to do? I am trapped, as I've always been, by my destiny."

"You won your freedom to be an artist, to venture into the world of commoners on your own."

"But this marriage—"

"It is an impediment, agreed."

"The scandal would destroy my family. If just one of those horrid journalists catches us, or even suspects, they'll all begin following me around and digging into my past. Amanda's family will suffer. Little Eddie will be labeled a bastard. And I have no doubt poor Lorne will land in prison. I can't do that to him, though he is foolish to take the risks he does."

"Hush," he said and stepped to one side, drawing her into an alcove and behind an immense sculpture just as footsteps approached.

They waited for two servants to pass. Then he kissed her long and deeply until her head spun and little ripples of happiness rose up through her like Champagne bubbles, and she felt consumed by him. For a moment she actually forgot about all of the obstacles that stood in their way.

Louise tenderly touched his cheek with her fingertips. "You are leaving England as she commanded?"

"Yes."

"You have no more choice than I do then."

He shook his head at her, smiling. "Because I'm temporarily returning to America doesn't mean I need to stay there."

"I don't understand. You can't turn around and come back here."

"I enjoy traveling and working on-assignment in different countries. I took this job on little more than a whim. The queen's Secret Service contacted their American counterparts at headquarters in New York; they said they needed a man with my skills. I thought—England, why not?" He paused and let his eyes roam her face, an almost smile on his lips. "I might, on a similar whim, accept a post with the Royal Canadian Mounted Police."

Her eyes widened as she began to understand. "It appears you've heard Lorne and I will be living in Ontario for a time."

His eyes actually twinkled, in a dark sort of way. "Small world."

"You would follow me?"

"Sounds sickeningly romantic, doesn't it?" He laughed when she pouted. "Seriously. For as long as you'll have me, Princess, I'll come to you."

Her heart soared. "You will?"

"I promise. Wherever you might be, I'll find you."

"Oh, Stephen." Tears of happiness filled her eyes despite every effort on her part to stop them. Louise clung to him. "There's Lorne to deal with. He won't be happy if we are less than discreet. And, in his illogical way, I think he's rather jealous of you."

Byrne's expression tightened. "The man has made his choices and will have to live by them." He kissed the tip of her nose. "I have made mine."

She closed her eyes and savored his words for a moment before asking the question that hung over them like a storm cloud. "When will you leave for America?"

All traces of pleasure left his face. "The sooner the better to satisfy your mother. Your life will be easier if she sees I've gone."

"And tomorrow? You won't be with us for the anniversary celebration?"

He thought for a moment. "I'll talk to the Scot. If I can't be there, he'll need as much information as possible."

Although she'd have done anything to keep him with her, Louise knew the limits of her mother's patience. If they ignored her command that Stephen leave England, Victoria might imagine a conspiracy of some sort, and accuse him of treason. If found guilty he'd face prison, or worse. Men had died for lesser indiscretions.

More precious to her than Stephen Byrne's presence in her world was to know he was safe. For now, that meant being anywhere but in England.

Fifty

"Ditch the bloody duster," John Brown shouted. The Scot tramped to the rear of the line of carriages in his Highland tartans. He scowled up at Byrne on the big roan Arabian he'd ordered up on the sly for the American from the queen's stable. "HRM peeks out her carriage window and sees that thing, she'll be havin' both our hides."

Byrne laughed but suspected Brown was right. He'd stand out like a cabbage in a rose garden in the leather coat that had become his trademark all about London. Around him, on horseback or foot, ranged the queen's guard in their brilliant crimson jackets and high-topped fur helmets. As the June sun was unusually strong that day, promising even more heat by the time the procession circled through London to Westminster Abbey, he was already sweating. Relieving himself of a layer would be a pleasure. Aside from that, it would make the Colt more easily accessible.

Byrne dismounted, removed his coat, rolled it into a neat cylinder, and strapped it down at the back of his saddle like a bedroll. His white cotton shirt, damp and blowsy now, would dry out in the warm air soon enough. He'd still be conspicuous among the panoply of vivid uniforms and glinting military decorations, but at least he wasn't a marked man as far as the queen was concerned. With reluctance, he removed the Stetson and tucked it in with the coat. Another tip-off out of the way.

Brown stood beside the roan, its bridle in one hand, his other splayed across the horse's strong neck. He waited while Byrne mounted up again, studying the line of carriages, all the way to the very front of the procession and the modest ebony brougham that would carry the queen in as much comfort as possible. Everyone was in place, in carriage or on horseback, except for Victoria, who hadn't yet emerged from the palace.

Byrne looked down from his saddle at the bearded, weather-worn face of the big Scot with something strangely close to fondness. "You've done all you can, John. Scotland Yard, the army, Victoria's own Hussars, the constables brought in from the countryside—it should be enough. The parade route has been searched, the church is secured."

"And we've found nothing," Brown grumbled.

"True."

"That's what worries me, laddie. You say they stored a cart load of powder. Where the bloody hell did it all go?"

Byrne shrugged. "It's possible the Fenians have determined to wait, seeing the level of protection for the anniversary. They wouldn't want to chance wasting their cache on the one day when the government is best prepared for them to strike."

"I got me a mighty nervous gut tellin' me you're wrong."

"All we can do is keep a wary eye." But Byrne had that same feeling. As if Big Ben in Mr. Pugin's famous clock tower was ticking down the minutes before catastrophe. And there was not a damn thing he could do to stop time.

Just yesterday he'd looked up through binoculars at that same tower, wondering if a marksman might use it to snipe at the royal party as they passed beneath it. What he remembered seeing through the magnifying lenses still sent a chill through his body. It wasn't a man or a weapon perched high above the street. It was the gilt Latin letters engraved beneath the huge opal-glass clock face:

DOMINE SALVAM FAC REGINAM NOSTRAM VICTORIAM PRIMAM. O Lord, *keep safe our Queen Victoria the First.*

Could he? Could Brown, or anyone, keep her safe?

"You're riding with her then, as planned, in the forward carriage?" Byrne said.

"Doc's orders, and I'm glad for it." Brown brushed a fleck of cinder from his kilt. "I'll be right beside her, some idiot tries anythin'."

Byrne nodded. It was good the little queen had such a stalwart champion. Byrne held no grudge against Victoria. She believed she was doing what was best for her people, her family, even for Louise—though to his mind she'd gone about it in all the wrong ways.

"There she is," Brown said.

Byrne looked up to see the queen, dressed in her customary mourning black, appear from the porte cochere in her wheeled garden chair. A flash of red from a ruby brooch on her left shoulder and starched white lace collar brightened the somber effect. Brown took off at a run. He'd lift her out of the chair and into the brougham, and do the same for her at the church, where the Mikado's sedan chair waited.

Byrne drew a deep breath then let it out, wishing to God he knew what the day would bring. He looked toward the gold-encrusted coronation coach. Anyone watching the procession would assume Victoria was in it. She'd of course acknowledge the crowds of onlookers lining the streets from her smaller carriage, if she felt well enough to do so. But any plans the Fenians already had in mind should be concentrated on the far more elaborate conveyance displaying the obvious Royal Coat of Arms. Only members of the royal family and the guardsmen knew of the last-minute switch.

But this still left Louise and others of her family riding in the coronation coach, and that worried him.

Byrne rode down the line of carriages. The immense coach, encrusted with gold, was third in line from the front, right where Byrne had thought the queen should be for maximum protection. Unfortunately Victoria had pressed her own wishes on the captain of the guard.

"If I'm to ride in what might as well be a pony cart, I'll at least be up front."

And so her carriage led the way, just behind the forward contingent of mounted guard, followed by the carriage transporting the Prince of Wales, his wife Princess Alix, and their two sons. Third came the coronation coach, carrying Louise and Lorne, princesses Beatrice and Alice, and Alice's husband—Louis IV, Grand Duke of Hesse-Darmstadt. Other members of the royal family followed behind in lesser but still elegant conveyances. Disraeli and Gladstone each had been invited to ride in the procession but had declined, choosing instead to be seated in the church to await the queen's arrival.

He made one last ride, quickly, up and down the line, looking for anything out of the ordinary, any clue that a carriage or harness had been tampered with. If an axle snapped or wheel came off in the middle of the procession, the parade would come to a halt. He figured a stalled carriage made a far easier target than a moving one. As it was, on Brown's orders they would drive at a faster clip than normal parade pace, even if this meant less comfort for those in the carriages. Faster was safer.

They'd reduced the risks considerably, but would it be enough? Byrne didn't know.

When he passed the coronation coach, he slowed the Arabian

to a walk and glanced inside. Louise was seated at the far window, resting her head back against the cushioned seat, eyes closed. She looked pale and unhappy . . . and breathtakingly beautiful in her white silk gown with peach blossoms tracing the low neckline. Lorne sat beside her, leaning in and talking to her, or rather *at* her, since she seemed intent on ignoring him and wishing herself elsewhere. The others in the carriage—Princess Alice and her husband, Princess Beatrice—sat with formal stiffness, waiting for the procession to move forward.

He wished he could somehow signal Louise that he was still here, looking after her and her sisters, without risking Lorne seeing him. He didn't trust the man not to inform the queen he was still around.

Byrne scanned the faces in the crowd outside the palace's black wrought iron fence, jostling one another to get as close as possible to the main gate through which the carriages would soon emerge. Everyone seemed in a festive mood. Some carried flowers to toss at the queen's coach. Some had brought baskets of food and jugs of ale to tide them over during the long wait.

He looked for Rhodes among the mob. He didn't see him. As clever as the man had been at concealing his connection to the Fenians, Byrne hadn't really expected him to put in an appearance. Not here at the palace. Maybe at a critical position to observe the result of the Fenian assault, if there actually was one. On the other hand, Rhodes might be on the run, suspecting he'd been found out. The police were busy at all ports, checking departing ships for America, Europe, and elsewhere.

Byrne brought his mount up behind the queen's modest black carriage and surveyed it from an angle that wouldn't put him in Victoria's line of sight. The family's coat of arms was neatly stenciled in gold over the glossy black lacquered doors.

Byrne thought for a moment then rode back a ways to shout at one of the pages stationed at attention along the parade line. "Boy, go tell the carriage master I need a tub of good black axle grease, nice and thick. Fast now!"

The lad gave him a suspicious once-over.

Byrne leaned down from his saddle and tweaked the boy's ear. "Now, son, orders of the queen's agent." Something in Byrne's dark gaze encouraged motion. The page took off at a run. The Scot would be furious if he saw what he was about to do. And he didn't dare imagine Victoria's reaction. But to his mind, that damned crest, though far less obvious than the elaborate carved carbuncle on the gilded coach, still attracted too much attention. Hopefully the carriage master would assume Byrne was trying to correct a sticky wheel.

The captain of the Hussars gave the order to move out. Byrne looked around anxiously for the page. Another few seconds and they'd be out the gates, among the populace, and it would be too late. Someone was bound to see him and raise a ruckus, thinking he was defacing the carriage.

Suddenly the boy appeared, carrying a tin bucket. "Sir?"

"Good lad," Byrne said. "Now back to your post."

Byrne sidled his horse up to the left rear wheel of the queen's carriage. He scooped up a handful of the thick, evil-looking black goo. He leaned down from his saddle and smeared the coat of arms with grease then repeated his cloaking treatment on the other door. The coverage wasn't complete, but it was good enough to obscure the crowned English lion and Scottish unicorn guarding the royal shield.

He left the pail by the side of the drive and wiped his hand on a post, getting off most of the grease. "Sorry there, fella," he apologized and completed the job by scrubbing his hand over his mount's rump. "You'll get an extra good brushing and oats for your trouble, after this is over."

The gates opened, and the carriages began to move forward.

Fifty-one

Louise felt the carriage jolt. She opened her eyes and looked out at the cheering crowd lining the street as the carriages left Buckingham's gates. She loved London, loved its people. It broke her heart to think of leaving this city. But what she most missed, already, was her Raven.

She had said nothing about this to anyone, of course, but somehow her husband must have read her thoughts.

"I'm truly sorry you're unhappy, my dear." Lorne kept his voice well below the camouflaging roar of the cheering crowd. "But it's all for the best, you know."

"What's for the best?" she said dully, staring at the lump under her glove made by her engagement and wedding rings. A glint of diamonds peeked through the lace. Gold, diamonds—what could they mean to a woman when they failed to signify love?

"The American's dismissal. He wasn't your type. I was wondering how long it would take you to realize that. You do understand that now, don't you?"

She glowered at him then shot a look at her sisters on the facing seat. Both were so engrossed in waving to the ecstatic crowd they showed no interest in anything she or Lorne might say. Even Alice's duke seemed overwhelmed by the sheer volume of the celebratory mob.

"My type, sir," Louise hissed, "is not for you to decide." It came out rather more vehemently than she'd intended. But her patience with the marquess was fast running out. She hadn't slept a wink since she'd last seen Byrne the day before. It seemed so unfair that, at last, when she'd found a man who not only excited her but truly moved her, she couldn't have him. He was everything a lover should be—strong, ruggedly handsome, a born protector, and sensitive to her physical as well as emotional needs. How could she not fall in love with such a man?

"I'm sorry," Lorne whispered. "Truly I am. But there's nothing to be done about it. He's dismissed and ordered out of the country. I'll do what I can to help you . . . you know, find someone appropriate, once we're established in Ottawa."

She'd told Lorne about her assignation with Stephen. To keep secrets would do neither of them any good. But why couldn't he understand? It wasn't just any lover she wanted. It was Stephen. Or no one. *Ever.*

Her head pounded with fatigue, her body ached with restlessness. But she reminded herself of the one thing she could cling to—Stephen's promise. They might need to wait for a while, but he'd come to her. They would find times to be together. She would live for those golden moments.

Lorne patted her hand, as if to say, *Poor, poor girl. How naïve you are.*

But she wasn't. Not anymore.

She knew all about love—that beautiful, exquisitely painful but precious journey. Donovan had come and gone. She no longer mourned his loss, no longer cared where he might be or why he'd left her. It was enough to know he was safe and living his life as he chose somewhere in the world. And as to Lorne and her hopes for their marriage? In truth, she didn't now and never had felt married to the marquess. It was all for show. A relationship that would never be consummated, despite their vows. This was not love.

She pulled herself erect, determined not to stew through the entire day. Stephen Byrne had pledged himself to her. She trusted his word. She'd focus on future stolen moments they'd share. They would create a marriage of the spirit—although they could never appear in public as a couple. To the world she would be the Marchioness of Lorne, and after Lorne's father passed on, the Duchess of Argyll. But in her heart, she was the Raven's bride.

She tested her smile for her mother's subjects. They lined the street, four and five deep, waving flags and bowers of flowers, shouting, "Long live the queen!" It occurred to her that many of them still thought Victoria was in the coronation coach with her. She covered her mouth with one gloved hand to hide a wicked smile. If her mother realized she was being overlooked, she would be furious.

"We're going too fast," Beatrice complained. "We always parade at walking pace. The people want to *see* us."

"It's all right, Bea," Louise comforted her. "We must be behind schedule. The guardsmen need to get us to the church in time for the ceremony. I'm sure we'll travel at a more leisurely speed on our way home."

Beatrice pouted, playing with the lace ruffles of her gown. It was an exquisite dress, in three colors, which had recently become all the rage in Paris. An underskirt of blue faille with gathered flounces, an apricot overdress trimmed with pale green silk ruches, and a discreet bodice designed to hide any suggestion of a bust— which no doubt pleased the queen, who still was intent on keeping Baby an innocent.

"By then everyone will have gone back to their homes, I'm sure," Beatrice fretted.

"You'll have plenty of chances to show off your pretty new dress when we arrive at the church, my sweet. Journalists from all of the newspapers will be waiting outside Westminster Abbey, writing down everything about your gown and how lovely and grown-up you look."

Alice rolled her eyes but said nothing to Louise's obvious flattery of their youngest sister. Beatrice seemed mollified and took to leaning out the side window to better extend her arm and wave. By the time they'd passed half a mile down Vauxhall Bridge Road toward the river, Bea had collected a lapful of posies, nosegays, and woven crowns of wildflowers thrust into her hands by well-wishers.

Flowers, Louise thought.

They reminded her of that day when Byrne had first kissed her in her shop, where she always kept a bouquet. Or rather, she had kissed him, little knowing where *that* would lead. She knew he must have taken himself out of London by now. She wondered where he was. Already on a dock waiting for a ship to America? Or maybe it would take him a while to arrange for transport.

Strangely, she felt his presence even now. As if in his absence he still watched over her, letting her know that he loved her, that he cared for her safety.

It was silly, of course. She knew that. He wasn't here. She hadn't caught so much as a glimpse of him. He would have been easy to spot in the courtyard while they were boarding the carriages and waiting for her mother to appear. She sighed but did her best to turn a cheerful face toward the window and greet the people of London. The people she'd come to feel so much closer to than any of her brothers or sisters possibly could.

She felt a moment of pride. She alone had ventured beyond royal walls, sat with commoners in parks and pubs, invited them into her shop, worked alongside them, painted them into her art. She loved these people, from the grimiest street urchin to the eldest gin-guzzling granny, from the corner flower sellers to Fleet Street's paperboys and the penny-desperate little crossing sweepers. From the costermongers wheeling their barrows of produce up and down cobbled lanes to the bootblacks and market stall hawkers, draymen, performing mountebanks, and even the disgusting but necessary rat catchers. They were her people. Being among them, and helping as she could, had brought her immense satisfaction and friends far richer than she might have cultivated within the closed circle of her mother's court.

She had earned for herself a truly rich life, and she was more hopeful than ever for the future of women, and not just those in London. She would do what good she could in Canada and, God willing, elsewhere in the world to bring women into their own.

Louise tossed a kiss to a little girl in the crowd as the carriage climbed toward the middle of Vauxhall Bridge. It was then that the explosion shattered her world.

Beatrice cried out at the deafening noise.

"Oh Lord, what's happening?" Alice shrieked, reaching for her husband's arm. The duke frowned out the window.

Their coach lurched drunkenly. Louise gripped the inside armrest on the door. She looked out her window, now slanted toward the pavers, and peered forward along the parade route, trying to locate the source of the explosion. Her mother's little brougham and the Prince of Wales's larger carriage had both stopped on the bridge ahead of them.

It took her several seconds longer to comprehend the impossible—that the bridge simply *ended* twenty feet beyond the coronation coach. A gaping maw of missing stonework separated the two lead carriages from the one in which Louise and her sisters rode. The entire center span of the bridge had been blown away in front of them.

Everything that happened after that moment seemed to occur in slow motion, enabling Louise to fix each detail of the disaster indelibly in her mind. As she watched, transfixed by the horrific scene, the space between the two halves of bridge widened, more and more stones tumbling down and splashing into the river below. Then the entire slope of the roadway beneath their coach shifted, making her gasp at their precariousness. The road slanted downward, then settled momentarily, as if trying to decide whether it too would give up and drop away beneath the royal cavalcade.

All was mayhem in the coach—Bea and Alice sobbing, the duke trying to calm them, Lorne looking confused.

"We're safer here than out there on the road," the duke said when he saw Louise try to leverage herself out of her tilted seat and reach for the door.

She thought he might be right. Onlookers who had lined the bridge to watch the parade pass were running toward the shore, knocking one another down in their panic.

But then she felt the immense carriage, weighed down by its ornamental carvings and gilded embellishments, continue to grind forward despite the driver's and footmen's attempts to brake. It pushed the terrified, screeching horses ahead of it, ever closer to the brink.

A man wearing a white shirt rode up to their coach on horseback, shouting, "Jump. Jump now!"

Startled, Louise looked up at his face. *Stephen!*

He was here, with her, watching over them.

It took her less than a heartbeat to understand what Stephen meant, and why. As he slashed the traces with a knife, freeing the team of horses from the coach, letting them run back as they'd come, it became clear to her. He was afraid if the horses went over the edge and into the water, they would drag the coach over with them. Everyone still inside would drown. If they survived the plunge.

"Get out. We have to get out now!" she shouted.

Alice looked horrified. "How? The coach is tipping over. What if it falls on us?"

Lorne flashed Louise a look that told her he understood. He tried to open the lower of the two doors, but it was jammed.

The duke said, "It has to be up and out the other way. Ladies, follow me." Standing on one of the seats he shoved against the door, now almost directly overhead. He'd barely broken the door open when something in the coach's structure gave way with a loud snap.

"Go!" Lorne shouted.

The duke clambered through the door then reached down for his wife and pulled Alice, squealing in fright, petticoats and skirts billowing like a pink cloud, up and out. Louise felt the carriage still skidding forward, wood and metal screeching against stone. How far to the broken end of the bridge's roadway? Did even ten feet remain?

Lorne grabbed Louise's hand.

She fought his grip. "No! Beatrice. Take her next." She shoved her little sister into his arms. Realizing from his hesitation he was about to argue with her, she screamed, "Go, Lorne! For god's sake, go." She shoved them both up and out the door even as the front wheel of the coach grated over the last crumbling stones.

The last one out, Louise poked her head up and through the door just in time to see Lorne and Bea tumble to safety. The fat body of the coach teetered, creaking on the stone lip. Beside the carriage, the white-shirted rider hastily dismounted. "Stephen!" she cried.

He ran to the edge of the broken bridge, reached for her, but she was too far away. She climbed halfway out on the broken carriage frame. He appeared ready to fling himself aboard even as she scrambled for a grip to pull herself the rest of the way out. But two guardsmen seized him by the arms and held him back.

And then she felt the coach beneath her go suddenly weightless as the blast-weakened stones supporting it finally gave way. Louise and coach plummeted down, down, down into the river.

Fifty-two

"No!" Byrne screamed, as if by the sheer force of his voice he could stop the inevitable. From atop the ruins of the bridge he heard a sharp crack, the sickening sound of splintering of wood as the coach slammed into the bridge's stone abutment, breaking apart the monstrous thing before it hit the water.

He stood in shock, unable to breathe, his gut a ball of fire. Never had he felt more helpless. More lost. The two men holding him back dropped his arms, called off by their sergeant. Faced with more pressing problems than protecting the queen's agent they raced off to fight their attackers.

All about Byrne was madness. Gunfire echoed from the direction of the shore behind; the guardsmen who had been bringing up the rear were fighting off a heavily armed force. He should join them to protect the two princesses and other civilians trapped in the melee. But he couldn't move. Couldn't stop staring down into the putrid, gray flow beneath him. At the bobbing wreckage of the royal coach.

Where was she? He stepped to the edge, prepared to jump in at the slightest sign of life. At least from here, above, he had a better chance of spotting her. There might still be a chance of getting her out, of her surviving. *Oh, God, there has to be!*

At first he could make out nothing but debris in the wretched, reeking confluence. Then a billow of white blossomed at the water's surface, reminding him of a graceful, pulsing jellyfish in the dark water. As he squinted, trying to make out what the thing was, a long white-gloved arm appeared.

"Louise!"

"Bloody fool." A hand clamped down on his shoulder before he could step over the edge. "You'll do her no good dead. Come, there's a better way."

Byrne hung back, trying to extricate himself from Lorne's grasp. He looked across the open space where the middle span of the bridge used to be. The queen's carriage had made it across to the other side before the blast ripped a hole through stone and mortar. Hussars now surrounded the boxy little brougham. Brown had taken one of their horses and was standing in the stirrups, trying to see what was happening on the other side.

"Take her on!" Byrne shouted above the sounds of battle, waving him off. His throat closed, blocking further words. If the Scot left now, the queen and heir to the throne would be safe with the bulk of her guard as escort. The Fenians seemed not to have yet realized that Victoria wasn't in the coronation coach.

Lorne hadn't given up tugging on his sleeve. "Move your bloody ass!" the marquess ordered, and this time Byrne snapped to action, drawing the Colt out from the hip holster where it had stayed to leave his hands free to reach for Louise.

They broke into a run, past the princesses and Alice's duke, now surrounded and sheltered by the queen's guard. Perhaps because of his love of the hunt, Lorne instinctively found the one hole in the fighting and made for it. Byrne followed on his heels.

An instant before they reached the foot of the bridge, Byrne caught a glimpse of a thin man in a dark cape, aiming a pistol at the running Lorne. He recognized Gladstone's secretary, the Fenian officer.

Philip Rhodes's first shot missed. Byrne's shot didn't. Rhodes staggered two steps, firing a second volley too wide and high to hit anyone, as a crimson stain spread across his chest. He fell to the ground; Byrne didn't stop but felt satisfied the wound was fatal.

As soon as they were clear of the bridge, Lorne turned down the steep incline and raced, mud flying from beneath his boot heels, down the embankment toward a nearby boatyard. A covey of fishing skiffs, a barge, and a tugboat were docked there.

Believing he knew what the marquess had in mind, Byrne shouted, "We'll never reach her in time, rowing." Even putting up a sail would take precious minutes. And there was barely a breeze, this rare hot day, to fill the canvas.

Lorne pointed. "If that steamer tug is stoked up—"

Byrne's hopes soared at the sight of gray smoke starting to billow from the tugboat's stack.

But Louise still might have been killed in the fall. Crushed beneath all that heavy wood and cursed metal hardware. Drowned as her gown sucked up water and dragged her down by its weight. Knocked unconscious by falling rubble as more and more stone blocks tumbled into the river. He agonized over the myriad ways she might have met her end. After all, he'd seen a dress and an arm, nothing more. He hadn't seen her face or been able to tell from the height of the ruined bridge if she was even breathing.

His heart felt as if it would detonate like an Irish bomb. He stared out over the water, scanning the filthy froth surrounding the rubble and shattered, half-submerged coach. Now, as he ran, he could see nothing at all that looked human in the water.

When they were just feet from the tug, Byrne heard the grinding throb of its engine. It was a relatively new model, he guessed—no paddle wheels, so there would be a propeller beneath the water to move her forward. Lorne exchanged a hopeful look with him, the pallor of his face less deathly. A bearded man in a waterman's smock and cloth cap was coiling heavy lengths of hemp rope while a younger fellow, stripped to his waist, shoveled coal into the boiler, stopping only to consult the steam gauges.

The captain saw them coming. "You from the queen's party up yonder?" he bellowed over the noises of the engine and the fighting above them.

"Yes," Byrne shouted. "Can you get us out there, to where the coach fell in?"

"Just what we'd in mind, sir. How many in her when she went over?"

"One. Princess Louise."

"Lordamighty," the captain said.

"Shit," added the boy, "she's good as dead, she is."

The captain silenced him with a look. "Engine's near ready. Lucky we were already heading out for a job when it happened. Hop aboard. It'll take a few minutes to get us out there."

"Can't you shove off *now*?" Lorne wailed, his blue eyes electric with panic. He grabbed binoculars laying nearby on a crate and scanned the water.

"Pressure's gotta build. Almost there," the captain assured him. "We started her up soon's we saw that boat blow."

"Boat?" Byrne scowled at the captain.

"Dory or some such, covered over with tarp. Tied to that middle strut there. I thought they were bridge repair boys. Musta been filled to the gills with powder." The boy slammed the iron boiler door closed and nodded at his captain. "We're off, boys."

The tug swung away from the dock and picked up speed.

"Let me see those." Byrne took the binoculars from Lorne and rushed to the bow to better see the water directly ahead of them.

If there was any chance of Louise swimming to shore he didn't want them running her down.

Lorne came up behind him. "She loves you, you know," he said.

Byrne's heart stopped. He said nothing.

"If she's alive . . . if you save her"—the marquess choked on his words—"I won't stand in your way."

Byrne shot him a quick look. Their eyes met in a moment of understanding. Then Lorne looked away, his tear-filled eyes narrowing on the water. "There!" he shouted.

"Where?" Byrne's heart leapt with hope.

"Two o'clock. Another rescue boat." Lorne pointed.

Not her. Not her, damn it.

"With another boat helping we'll have a better chance of finding her," Lorne yelled in his ear over the engine's growl.

Immediately following the explosion, the river had cleared. Merchant ships, ferries, fishing trawlers—all made quickly away from the area, no doubt fearing their boats would be damaged by more blasts. But this lone boat had now reversed direction and was moving toward the catastrophic scene.

Byrne had always wondered whether he'd know his old enemy Rupert Clark, if they ever met face-to-face. He'd only ever seen a photograph of him during the war. And then there were the statements of a few witnesses, filling in physical details.

Now, as he peered through the binoculars at the two men aboard the rusty old ferry steaming across the water, Byrne felt his sixth sense kick in. One man stoked the boiler. But it was the other who drew his eye. He was tying a large open loop in the end of a length of rope, using his teeth to hold the rope secure while manipulating the strands into a knot. Even from this distance, Byrne could tell that something was wrong with the man's right hand.

Fingers missing. The badge of a black powder man.

The rope man's face was back to him. But he knew Rupert

Clark by his shock of red hair and war injury. His work with the rope done, the former rebel soldier's attention fixed on something in the water beneath the bridge. Something he intended to haul aboard with his lasso?

Byrne shifted the binoculars by sixty degrees to follow the general direction of Rupert's gaze. At first he saw nothing but floating rubble. He swung the binoculars to the right, and stopped. There.

He'd have recognized those smooth white shoulders anywhere.

Fifty-three

Louise felt cold, dreadfully cold, head to foot. From her waist down, she was submerged in the Thames River's slime—dark as tea, the consistency of congealed gravy. The upper part of her body stretched across a shattered door of the coach but was no less wet. She'd swallowed mouthfuls of the filthy water before kicking off her shoes and hauling herself up onto the only part of the broken coach within her reach that seemed not to be sinking.

She was fairly certain a bone in her shoulder or collarbone had snapped during her fall. Her ribs ached, and the pain whenever she took a breath was unbearable. The stench coming off of the water filled her mouth and nose. She concentrated on drawing only shallow puffs of air into her lungs between coughing fits.

Swimming was impossible without the use of both arms, even if she had been able to free herself of the wretched, water-soaked gown. She prayed a boat would come along and rescue her before she lost the last of her strength and slipped off her makeshift raft into the river to drown.

She might have lain there for two minutes or two hours, for she lost all sense of time. A guttural throbbing sound roused her from her semiconscious state. Clinging with her good arm to the door, she turned her head, trying not to move her shoulder or shift her torso and thereby anger her ribs.

A boat. Oh, Lord, yes—a boat.

It was moving swiftly toward her, propelled by twin paddle wheels, one on either side of the wide hull. She hoped the captain saw her because there was no way she could move out of his way. She was reassured when she saw a figure standing at the bow, waving to her. Never in her life had she seen a happier sight. She blinked, hoping she wasn't hallucinating.

The captain brought the steam-powered boat chugging up to meet her as gently as if he'd been docking the queen's yacht. Her heart swelled with gratitude.

Down came a rope and a shout from above. "Hold on a moment longer there, miss. We've got you. Never fear."

Although Louise couldn't see her rescuer from water level, she heard his shouted instructions over the thump-thump-thump of the engine and understood he was telling her to slip the open loop around her body. The least pressure on her shoulder and chest caused her increased pain, but she struggled to obey, thinking only of resting safe and warm upon a dry deck. She gritted her teeth, eased her left arm and injured shoulder through the loop, then leaned over to guide the rope around her back and thrust in her good arm.

The man must have been watching closely. As soon as the rope was secure, he began pulling her up.

Louise swallowed a shriek of agony as the rope cinched tighter around her chest. Her weight, so much more due to the sodden gown, added to the pressure of the rope tightening around her. She fought to stay conscious. Now that her rescue was guaranteed, all she could think of was her family. She had ejected her sisters from the coach, along with Lorne and the duke. But had they survived the onslaught of attackers? From a distance she still heard shots being fired, the ring of bayonets on sabers, shouts of men, and terrified cries of horses.

But her thoughts were cut short when, with a final effort, two men in dark suits leaned down over the gunwales of their boat, grabbed her by the arms, and pulled her up and over the wooden rail then down with a careless thud onto the deck.

"Oh, please, gently!" she cried. "Sirs, I'm broken."

Their rough hands released her. She looked up into the faces of two strangers.

One was older than the other, his coarse red hair whipped up by the wind, as he wore no cap. He observed her with dull-eyed marsupial interest, devoid of emotion. "Open her up, boy," he growled at his companion. "Let's get out of here."

"Yessir." The younger one beamed at her then bolted away toward the drive house. His exuberance reminded her of a beagle on the scent.

Red hair turned back to her, his eyes fixing on her, flitting away then back again, as if in deep calculation. "Went fishin' and caught us a princess. That right, dearie?"

She was in too much pain to react to his rudeness. "You don't look like watermen," she murmured. In fact, they didn't sound like it either. Their accents were wrong. *American?* She tried to at least straighten up to a more dignified sitting position from her sprawl on the teak planks. "But I thank you with all my heart. You've saved my life."

The man leaned down and peered at her gown then still closer at her face. "Which one is you?"

If he was American, maybe he knew Byrne? She felt an immediate surge of hope at the thought of her lover. If Stephen had been down here instead of up on the bridge, he'd have swept her up in his arms, laid her on a cushion, and covered her shivering body with a toasty quilt.

"Do you suppose you might find me a blanket. Anything for warmth. I'm so terribly c—"

The stranger reached down and grabbed her hair by the roots. He wrenched her head back, forcing her to make eye contact with him. "I said, what's your name?"

To as much as touch a princess, if you were not her husband or a family member, was unimaginably rude, a breach of etiquette as well as the law. She was so shocked she could only stare at him and answer.

"I am Princess Louise, the marchioness of Lorne." Since she didn't know whether it would help or hurt her cause to lie, it didn't seem worth pretending she was someone she was not.

He released her hair and stood up, hands on hips. His satisfied smile turned her stomach. She should have lied.

Louise held her injured shoulder with her opposite hand to keep the bones from shifting against each other. Held immobile, it hurt a little less.

"That's grand," the man said. He stood above her another moment then lifted one foot and nudged her shoulder.

"Ah!" she cried. "Please don't. It may be broken." Or dislocated. Just as bad.

"No need to tie you down then, is there? You won't be going anywhere." He turned and trudged away from her toward the other man at the wheel.

"Please. Take me to the nearest dock," she shouted after him. "I need to get back to my family." She had to let them know she wasn't dead. Had to find out what had happened to them and to Stephen, and how many men they'd lost in the explosion and fighting. "I'll pay you anything you like. Anything!" she screamed at the red-haired man's back.

He didn't respond, although she was certain he'd heard her. The younger one turned and glanced once at her then gave a whoop and did a little jig at the wheel.

So . . . they considered her a prize.

What did they want her for? If these were Fenian raiders, they might easily have killed her by now. Did they intend to leave her body for the police to find—like those two unfortunate civil servants in the park? Or would they hold her for ransom? Both Parliament and her mother had pledged noncompliance with Fenian demands. Then again, what if they simply spirited her away as their prisoner of war, intending to keep her indefinitely, saying they would only release Her Royal Highness when Ireland ruled herself. Which would be never, if her mother had any say in the matter.

Either the foul water she'd swallowed, or the realization her life might well end within the next few minutes, sent a spurt of sour bile up into her throat. Louise closed her eyes and fought back her fear.

Fifty-four

Byrne lowered the binoculars. "She didn't drown. They've got her."

"Thank God," Lorne said, grinning.

Only then did it occur to him that Lorne didn't know who had pulled his wife out of the drink or what Rupert Clark was capable of. He made short work of an explanation, watching Lorne's face transform from joy to utter despair.

"But what will they *do* with her?"

"I don't know. Doesn't matter. We have to catch up with them and take her back before they reach land." Byrne tossed the binoculars back to the marquess and raced from the bow to the cockpit of the tug, with Lorne close behind.

"Why before? Wouldn't it be easier at a dock, on dry land?"

"No. They'll have arranged to meet their mates. We don't know how many of them will be waiting, and there's no way to alert the police." Byrne glanced at the old man and his son, trying to gauge how much they'd be willing to risk for the life of a princess. "See that steamer up ahead, Cap?"

"The one just hauled that lady outta the drink?" The old man chuckled his approval. "He done a good job gettin' her out alive, I'd say."

"Those two men are the ones who blew up the bridge," Byrne

said. The captain's brow rose as one piece above milky eyes. "And the woman he just beat us to is Princess Louise."

"Gor'," said the boy.

" 'Tis a dark day on the river," the captain said, shaking his head.

"It will be darker if we don't stop that boat. Can you catch up with them?"

"Don't know." The captain frowned. "Them's pretty sprightly boats them old ferries. Tugs're built more for pushing and pulling than speed."

"But your engine is powerful. You have a screw propeller, no paddle wheels—more thrust, right? Maybe up to more stress than theirs. If you had to run her hard, could you overtake them?"

Byrne saw decision flash in the old man's eyes. "Mebbe." He turned to the boy. "Johnny, get busy with that boiler. Give me all she's got." He looked back at Byrne. "I'll bring you close to the bastard as I can. How you get aboard, I've no idea."

Neither do I, Byrne thought, but that's exactly what he'd have to do. Or Louise would be lost to him.

Fifty-five

Louise propped herself up on the wide, wooden planks of the deck and worried her bottom lip between her teeth. She breathed carefully, supporting herself with her uninjured arm as she looked around, unwilling to give up yet.

A dingy canvas canopy, shelter against sun or rain, rose above her head. The men who'd taken her were fifteen feet away, tending to the boiler and wheel. She was ten or fewer feet from the rail. If she got to her feet, or even crawled to the side of the boat before they noticed, she could throw herself overboard. But jumping back into the river, in her damaged condition, she'd likely drown before anyone else came along. Her captors likely knew this. Even if the boat had been running much closer to shore she wasn't capable of swimming with just one good arm.

That left the only other possibility she could imagine. She must find a weapon with which to defend herself. If she made it difficult enough for these two to do whatever they had in mind, she might buy enough time for someone on shore or from among the royal party to realize she was in trouble and send help. Though, from the ominous clatter and gunfire still coming from the direction of the bridge, she guessed the queen's guard had their hands full.

It might be a while before they took a head count to see who was missing.

She scanned the deck, hopeful of finding something sharp, heavy, or pointed. Anything at all she could jab, throw, or swing in self-defense.

The only possibility she saw was a long-handled boat hook with a metal prong on one end. They'd used it to help haul her onboard. But the red-haired man had taken it with him and leaned it against the wooden housing beside him, as if to have it handy for his own use . . . or because he'd foreseen her desperation and wanted it out of her reach.

There was nothing else. Nothing at all she could put her hands on.

Heartsick, she watched the younger man take up his shovel again and stoke the boiler with four more shovelfuls of shiny black anthracite coal from an iron tinderbox. The frame on the container was sloped lower on the side facing him, making it easier for him to thrust the blade of the shovel into the mound of coal and come out in one continuous swinging motion to toss his load into the roaring flames.

Steam engines. She dragged from her brain every last little thing she had learned about the new inventions. It wasn't much. Their fuel was coal. Without the coal the pressure would drop and the engine would stop.

But how long would that take? She had no idea.

However, she did know one thing. She didn't want to put any more distance between her and the scene of the explosion. The farther away they took her, the less likely she'd be found.

She slid a little closer to the tinderbox. It was made of heavy, sooty black iron, almost indistinguishable in color from the coal itself except for rusty patches. On the back side of the box, facing her, was a door about a foot wide and equally high. The latch, if lifted, would allow the little panel to swing open. She guessed it was for the purpose of cleaning out the box when the coal dust at the bottom became too thick and might create a fire hazard. The engineer could either sweep it out or flush it with a hose. In fact, she could see a darkened patch on the wood boards running between the door and the side of the boat where the dust had been swept or drained over the side.

How much coal, she wondered, *could she toss overboard before her captors realized what she was doing?*

The constant rumble of the engine and whoosh of the paddle wheels cloaked her awkward, crablike scramble to the back of the box. She half expected coal to come clattering out through the door, instantly alerting the men to her pitiful plan, but when she lifted the latch and, holding her breath, slowly opened the clean-out door, nothing at all happened.

Her heart sank.

Just inside the door, the chunks of coal were jammed together, the weight of the load above holding them in place. She sat for an instant, staring in disgust at the stuck rocks then shook her head. *In for a penny*.

Using both hands, Louise clawed out chunks of coal and started throwing them as far out into the water as she could. She worked blindly, keeping her eyes on the backs of the two men. To her amazement neither the sound of her scuffling hands nor the soft plunk-plunk of coal hitting the water, drew their attention . . . until the pieces she'd already ditched in the water left enough space at the bottom of the box that the whole load shifted and, with a loud clatter, more than half of what remained shot out through the door and scooted across the deck with a choking puff of black dust.

The red-haired man spun around with a startled expression. She didn't hesitate. Ignoring the pain in her shoulder and chest, she flung herself down on the deck. Using both arms she swept as much of the coal as possible off the side of the boat and into the river.

"Bitch!" he roared and came at her, arm raised.

He struck her once on the side of the head, ringing her ears. Louise squeezed her eyes shut, gasping at the sting of his hand against her jaw and cheek. She kicked her wet skirt around and managed to send another shovelful of coal over the side. He came at her again, cursing, this time aiming a kick at her shoulder.

"Rupert. No, hey, no!" The younger man rushed to him, holding him back from striking her again. "She ain't no good to us dead. The Lieutenant, he'll want her in good shape. The better to bargain with."

Louise lay still, pressing her face to the coal-blackened boards, one arm over her head as her only protection. She barely had the strength to breathe. She hurt everywhere. Maybe, after all, she should have thrown herself in instead of the coal.

"Fuck!" She recognized the younger man's voice.

"What?"

"Looky there."

Louise had no idea what had caught their attention. She was just grateful something had distracted them from beating her. She peered up around her arm.

"He's following us. Coming up fast," the one called Rupert said. He exploded in a fit of cursing. "Must've seen us pick her up."

To Louise it seemed as if a lifetime had passed since they'd dragged her out of the river, but now she realized it had probably been only minutes.

The two men totally ignored her. They started throwing as much coal as they could retrieve from the deck, and the little left in the tinderbox, into the boiler. The boat had been traveling at a modest pace but suddenly, with the added fuel, it lurched forward at the younger man's prompt from the throttle.

Louise pushed herself up, sitting with her back pressed against the boat's low gunwales for support. Her dress clung to her thighs and calves—a muddy, snarled mess. She grasped handfuls of ruined satin faille and crepe de chine at her waist, tearing away layer after layer of fabric as she focused on the following boat. It looked like a workboat of sorts with its high, padded prow. Although it was gaining on them, she feared the boat she was on might reach a dock before they could catch up.

At first the following boat had been too far away for her to make out who might be on it. But now she saw two heads at the helm, and two more figures on the bow.

One wore a white shirt, blousing in the wind. The man's black hair streamed back from his face as the boat sped toward her. Tears came to her eyes.

Stephen.

He'd braced his feet wide to keep himself from being thrown to the deck as the boat jounced and banged into the tidal waves. He was looking directly toward her. Stephen was coming for her. Tears filled her eyes.

Behind her, she could hear the two Fenians arguing. She looked over her shoulder. There was almost no coal left on the deck.

"Open her up, Will. Open the god-damn throttle!"

"No." The younger man pushed his partner away from the boiler and jabbed a finger at the gauges. "You see that? Pressure's too high. Safety gauge has shut her down."

Rupert grabbed the younger man by the front of his shirt and yelled in his face. "You let that engine stop, and I'll *kill* you, boy."

As Louise held her breath and watched, Will looked at the fire, then at his partner. "All right. Dump the last of the coal in. I'll override the safety." He removed the kerchief from around his throat and used it to tie down a lever on the face of the engine so that it couldn't move. "Old racing trick," he mumbled, looking nervous.

Louise glanced back at Byrne's boat. It was lagging behind while the boat she was on thrust forward ever more powerfully. The hope she'd felt moments earlier died.

And then she heard a loud hissing noise.

She remembered Lorne telling her about a steam engine disaster on the Manchester train line. Trains and ships had the same problems with faulty pressure gauges, or with engineers who ignored them. When the pressure built too high, the engine could explode.

Louise heard someone shouting at her and looked up to see Stephen hanging off the bow of the trailing boat, waving and shouting at her. "Jump! Jump!"

She looked back at the two men. Rupert was reaching for the boat hook even as she pulled herself to standing at the cost of wrenching pain in her shoulder. Eyeing her with murderous intent, he lurched toward her. She hobbled to a spot as far behind the churning paddle wheels as she could, and threw herself over the side and into the river.

Byrne saw Louise go in . . . and under. She looked as weak as a baby bird spilling from its nest. He signaled the captain to cut his engines. Tying a line to his waist, he dove into the murky water, aiming for the place he'd seen her go down. Did she even know how to swim?

When he surfaced he bobbed in one place, treading water, looking around him for the slightest disturbance in the water's surface. But it was so full of floating garbage he despaired of finding her. Then he heard a sharp, high-pitched cry. He turned.

Louise was not twenty feet behind him, coughing and wheezing for air. He swam to her—pushing aside half of a balsa crate, a green glass bottle. His arms closed around her. She clung to him but didn't struggle as the drowning often did. She laid her head against his shoulder and opened her eyes wider at the sudden percussion of an explosion less than a hundred yards downriver.

"It's over," he whispered in her ear. "I'm here. You're safe, my love."

Epilogue

Louise laid down the gold Montblanc fountain pen. There. She'd written all through the night to finish her story.

She turned to observe the shockingly high pile of vellum pages that had grown beneath her pen. Well, she could have told Eddie more. But it was all that a boy, now a grown man, needed to know of his two mothers and how he'd come into the world. She hadn't told him of her life in Canada. Neither had she shared news of her long visits in Bermuda, or the months at spas on the Continent, where she retreated with her lover whenever she could. Those were the happiest times of her life—more romantic, in many ways, than a traditional marriage. Stephen was true to his word. He always found her. And when they were together their love filled whatever room they shared. The rest of the world simply dissolved into inconsequential mist.

When Stephen was away from her he wrote her long letters describing his adventures, his assignments with the RCMP and, later, with his new employer, the American Secret Service. She read each letter exactly three times then burned it. What they shared was far too precious to expose to historians, gossip columnists, or even her son. Edward Locock would have become the next Duke of Argyll had she been able to acknowledge him publicly, for she and Lorne never did consummate their marriage, and therefore never had a child of their own.

She hoped her son was content with his life as it stood. He had taken up his adoptive father's profession and was now a fine surgeon. Amanda's talent for writing had rubbed off on him too. He wrote articles that were published in highly acclaimed medical journals.

No mother could have been prouder.

Louise sealed the thick envelope, using the same perfumed wax she affixed to each of Stephen Byrne's letters, stamping it with the Duchess of Argyll's seal. It somehow seemed right that her mother's life had ended here at Osborne House, where little Eddie's life began, despite the queen's plans.

She sighed, holding that thought for a moment before a soft knock sounded on her door. Lady Car peeked around the edge. "Princess, you have a caller." Her lady-in-waiting's impish smile told her she'd be pleased. Bertie had arrived last night, along with Alix and the children. The Prince of Wales was now officially King George IV, and his princess had become Queen Alexandra. But Louise suspected her guest was neither of them.

She nodded for Car to allow her visitor to enter. "How did you get here so quickly?" she said when Stephen Byrne walked in and took her hands in his. She observed the subtle changes in his face, hair, clothing since they'd last been together. He seemed stronger and more handsome with each year, and here they were into the fifth decade of their lives, yet still lovers, still crossing oceans to be with each other for whatever time fate allowed.

"Beatrice telegraphed that your mother was likely not to last the month. I booked passage the next day." Byrne took her in his arms and kissed the top of her hair, her forehead, her lips, then looked into her tear-filled eyes. "I wanted to be with you. I'm sorry I was too late."

"It doesn't matter. You wouldn't have been allowed into her room at the end. Bertie stood guard over her. But how did you know we'd be here on the Isle of Wight and not in London?"

He shook his head and smiled. "I told you I'd always find you, didn't I?"

"You did. And you have kept your promise, my love."

He glanced down at her escritoire, the open inkwell, the sealed envelope fat with pages, then back to her. "You've told Edward then. All of it?"

"As much as he needs to know, yes." She nodded. "I hope he will not think me evil . . . for my deceptions."

"He'll realize how much you've sacrificed for him. He'll love his godmother all the more, knowing her as the woman who gave birth to him."

He wrapped her in his arms and held her close as Victoria's mourners continued to arrive by carriage, coach, and horseback. A new refrain echoed through Osborne House, and indeed, throughout the Empire: "God save the king."

Afterword

The Incident at Vauxhall Bridge, as it came to be known at Scotland Yard, was hushed up by orders of the prime minister to minimize any positive press for the Fenians. All the public ever learned was that radicals managed to blow up a bridge and by doing so delayed the queen's arrival at the church. The two dynamiteers responsible, reported the London *Times*, were so inept that they managed to blow themselves up in the boat they'd used to plant the bomb. Happily, the press noted, other members of the queen's family who had planned to travel along the parade route had been ill and, unable to attend the ceremony, were out of harm's way.

Missing from the story in the newspapers around the world was the fact that Victoria's magnificent coronation coach was destroyed in the attack and had to be rebuilt from scratch. It was later used by Victoria's great-granddaughter, the young Queen Elizabeth II, for her coronation. Very few people knew it wasn't the original.

In 2003, the grandson of a Dr. Edward Locock attempted to prove he was a direct descendant of Queen Victoria, with rights to the throne, claiming that his grandfather was the illegitimate child of one of the royal princesses. But the good doctor had requested his body be burned at his death along with his private papers, the ashes strewn over the rose garden at Osborne House. Therefore nothing could be proved and the case was dropped from the court dockets. Why Locock chose this odd location for his remains to be returned to the earth, requiring special permission from the British Parks Service, no one seems to know. Except, it was said, the doctor cherished a love of roses.

To My Readers

What's real and what's make-believe? Here are a few hints. . . .

Yes, the royal family depicted in this story did exist. Queen Victoria ruled the longest of any British monarch to this date—sixty-three years. She and her husband, Prince Albert of Saxe-Coberg and Gotha, a first cousin, had nine children—four princes and five princesses. All of the children eventually married, and their offspring, in turn, produced rulers and enriched the noble bloodlines of many European countries. (See "Queen Victoria and Prince Albert's Children and Grandchildren" on page viii.)

Much controversy surrounds Princess Louise (later also, the Duchess of Argyll) and her marriage. She was a beloved and respected royal both in her own country and in Canada, where she accompanied her husband, Lorne, on his appointment as governor general of the Dominion of Canada. Gossip, but never proof, surfaced regarding the marquess's sexual preferences, but, in fact, he and Louise never had children. Another rumor whispered that Louise was unable to have children as a result of a botched abortion during her teenage years. But again, there is no proof. She was affectionately known in the queen's court, and among the queen's subjects, as the "wild child" of the royal brood. Her studies (at her own insistence) at the National Art Training School in Kensington (renamed the Royal College of Art) helped her become one of the few recognized female artists of her day.

Stephen Byrne is the fictional hero this author believes Louise deserved. Although various romantic liaisons were suspected during her lifetime, I know of no historian who has successfully confirmed that she indulged in romantic affairs. However, we do know that Louise spent a good deal of time away from Lorne, encouraged by him "for her health," visiting various spas in Europe; she often traveled great distances on her own. Louise particularly loved Bermuda. The exquisite Hamilton Princess hotel on the island was named after her and opened in 1885. It would be difficult to believe that this fourth and high-spirited princess never experienced passionate love. Thus I gave her the dashing American Civil War hero Stephen Byrne.

The Fenians were a particularly militant group of Irish radical separatists, and they did blow up part of Parliament and various other buildings in London to make their point. Many attempts were made to assassinate Queen Victoria by different political factions. More than one theory exists of a plot to murder HRM on the occasion of her Golden Jubilee in 1887. In *Fenian Fire*, author Christy Campbell presents evidence that high-placed members of the British government actually planned to assassinate Victoria and blame it on the Fenians.

If you wish to learn more about Princess Louise's real life, try checking out these books:

Princess Louise—Queen Victoria's Unconventional Daughter,
    by Jehanne Wake (London: Collins, 1988)
Victoria's Daughters, by Jerrold M. Packard (New York: St.
    Martin's Press, 1998)
Darling Loosy—Letters to Princess Louise 1856–1939, ed.
    Elizabeth Longford (London: Weidenfeld & Nicolson,
    1991)

The Life Story of HRH Princess Louise, Duchess of Argyll, by
   David Duff (Bath: Cedric Chivers, 1971)
Royal Rebels—Princess Louise and the Marquis of Lorne, by
   Robert M. Stamp (Toronto: Dundurn Press, 1988)

Still not sure what's history and what's Mary Hart Perry's whimsical way of looking at the past? Ask her. You can reach the author at Mary@MaryHartPerry.com. She loves to hear from her readers and will answer your questions. You can also "like" her Facebook page: Mary Hart Perry, or follow her on Twitter @Mary_Hart_Perry.

For more royal intrigue and Victorian romance, look for Princess Louise and Stephen Byrne when they return for guest roles in *Seducing the Princess*, by Mary Hart Perry, the next novel in the Novels of Queen Victoria's Daughters series. Youngest of all of Victoria's children, Beatrice is destined to remain forever her mother's companion in her declining years, and if the queen gets her way, Bea will remain "pure" and never marry. But attending a royal wedding on the Continent exposes shy Beatrice to temptation in the form of not one but two charming suitors—Prince Henry of Battenberg (one of four famously handsome brothers) and a charismatic Highlander who resembles the recently deceased John Brown, favorite of the queen. Will Beatrice remain meekly loyal to her mother, or fall in love and into a political trap meant to draw England into war?

Jean Korten Moser

MARY HART PERRY lives in Maryland with her two cats and her husband. She teaches at the Writer's Center in Washington, D.C., and is an inspiring speaker for international and regional groups interested in the joys of writing and history and the promotion of teen and adult literacy. You can reach her at Mary@MaryHartPerry .com. For news about her appearances and upcoming books, feel free to like her Facebook page, or follow her on Twitter @ Mary_Hart_Perry.

www.MaryHartPerry.com

Mary Hart Perry